C H O S E N

Chosen

A NOVEL

Chandra Hoffman

HARPER

An Imprint of HarperCollins*Publishers*
www.harpercollins.com

HarperCollins books may be purchased for educational, business, or sales promotional use. For information, please write: Special Markets Department, HarperCollins Publishers, 10 East 53rd Street, New York, NY 10022.

FIRST EDITION

Designed by Eric Butler

Library of Congress Cataloging-in-Publication Data

Hoffman, Chandra.
   Chosen : a novel / Chandra Hoffman. — 1st ed.
     p.   cm.
   ISBN 978-0-06-197429-8
   1. Social workers—Fiction. 2. Adoption—Fiction. 3. Adopted children—Fiction. 4. Adoptive parents—Fiction. I. Title.
   PS3608.O4776C56   2010
   813'.6—dc22   2010004913

10 11 12 13 14   OV/RRD   10 9 8 7 6 5 4 3 2 1

FOR CHERRY, WHO BELIEVED

C H O S E N

Prologue

Chloe Pinter is trying to develop a taste for coffee. It's Saturday morning, and sunshine pours through her dormered office windows, shines on her carefully organized desk, a stack of pink phone message slips and a mountain of empty sugar and cream packets. She sips, adds another sugar. Outside her window, a warm breeze is rustling the rich emerald evergreens. The summer sunshine is creating geometric patterns of light on passing cars and beyond them, sparkling on the Columbia River. Perfect weather in Portland, an oxymoron only to those not lucky enough to live here, Chloe thinks.

She slips from its crinkled bag the small keepsake album she bought while browsing Powell's bookstore earlier this morning with her boyfriend. The album has the word BABY stitched on the front, as though the letters are the jet stream left behind by the dizzy diapered bumblebee grinning in the upper right corner of the pale blue cover.

There are photos in her filing cabinet, babies and their new parents, waiting to fill this album. She slides the metal drawer open and pulls the folder labeled COMPLETED ADOPTIONS. She pictures the next photo, due any day now: Chloe, in her "signing paperwork" charcoal suit, paired with the blissful Paul and Eva Nova cradling and beaming over Amber's newborn daughter, set against a fluorescent-lit delivery room backdrop. A photogenic happy ending worthy of the first page of her album, something to put out on the coffee table here in her office when she meets with prospective parents. She can't wait.

Chloe smiles, remembering Dan's adorably stricken face when the clerk at Powell's this morning thought the album was for them; that they were expecting.

"Bless your heart   what a lovely thing you do, bringing babies to barren couples," the Powell's clerk had exclaimed when Chloe told her about her job, director of the Chosen Child's domestic adoption program. The woman had nodded, eying Dan the way women always do—that endearing smile, those ruddy cheeks—putting his glossy windsurfing magazine in a separate bag.

"It's an honor," Chloe had continued, meaning it as she always does, "to be part of such an important moment in people's lives."

A CAR HONKS IN the parking lot below—Dan. She'd promised she would be quick, just pick up her files. Chloe grabs the stack of pink phone message slips, calls she should return. She folds them neatly in half and puts them in the pocket of her cutoffs. She waves to Dan from her window—*coming!* Next stop on their mutual day off: the Hatchery in Hood River, where Dan will spend the afternoon on a windsurfing board carving the cresting dark river water. Chloe will drink up the summer sun from a blanket on the hillside, returning phone calls for work with her cell phone, slipping photos in the new album, sipping sweet, creamy coffee. Afterward, unless she gets paged by one of her birthmothers in labor, she and Dan plan to eat dinner at the Hood River Brewery, followed by a rare uninterrupted evening at home.

Juggling her small purse, baby album, files, and half-full coffee cup, Chloe locks the office behind her and jogs across the parking lot toward her boyfriend and the perfect day stretching ahead of them. She thinks, *I am living the dream.*

Red Flag

CHLOE

They're in there. Chloe Pinter bangs on the metal door of the apartment, lights on inside, as freezing rain pelts down around her. The grocery bag sags off her arm, Thanksgiving turkey still warm against her thigh.

"Penny! Jason!" she calls out as she hammers with her free hand. She knows her clients are inside; she can see movement through the broken section in the slatted blinds.

At last the door is opened a crack; the loose brass flashing screams as it scrapes along the threshold. Penny's eight-month-pregnant belly fills the doorway, and her shorn head pokes out, her first expression scowling, suspicious.

"Yeah? Oh, it's you." She doesn't step back to let Chloe in. Behind her, in the apartment, Chloe hears voices.

"Hi. Happy Thanksgiving!" Chloe says, forcing brightness. "I brought you guys some dinner. A turkey, the works."

Penny sticks out her hand to take it. Chloe grips the plastic handles, waiting.

"Is Jason home? Can I come in for a minute?"

Penny looks over her shoulder, yells, "It's the social worker!"

From inside, "What's she want?"

"She brang us dinner!" Penny calls back. She smiles apologetically at Chloe, exposing the dark space along the right side of her mouth where there should be teeth.

The rain comes in earnest, hard-pelting, swollen drops that make audible pops as they hit the puddles in the muddy courtyard. As always, Chloe is wearing the wrong clothes, nothing but a jean jacket. The cardboard poster cylinder she has under her arm is getting wet, and she makes a show of pulling together the top of the food bag.

"Your dinner's going to be soggy." She smiles at Penny, waiting.

Then Jason appears, a head taller than Penny, and yanks the apartment door open.

"Jesus, Pen, you leave her out in the rain?" He jerks Penny out of the way so Chloe can duck inside. The apartment reeks of cigarette smoke and mold, dark spores collecting in the corner of the popcorn ceiling overhead.

A couple sits at the folding table in the kitchenette. She looks sixteen, crack-skinny, yellowish, pimpled complexion, the marks of meth around her mouth, and when she turns to Chloe her eyes don't focus. The man—he's older—takes the cigarette out of her hand, taps the dangling burn of ash into a Pepsi can, and takes a drag. He has dark hair pulled in a low ponytail, and he gives Chloe the long up-down, his black-hole eyes unblinking.

"That's my brother Lisle," Jason says smoothly. He does not introduce the girl. Jason is so tall he has to duck under the crooked brass light fixture in the entry, two bulbs burned out. "This is a friend of ours, brought us some dinner."

"Thought Penny said she was a social worker." Jason's brother hasn't broken his stare, just moved it to the bag of food in Chloe's hands. He draws on the cigarette, blows smoke in his girl's face. She blinks, slowly.

Jason doesn't answer, and Chloe doesn't either. *Confidentiality*, she thinks. She moves to the table, clears a space among coupon flyers, chipped saucer ashtrays, ketchup packets, and empty soda cans, and puts the Fred Meyer bag down.

"You might need to reheat the side dishes," she says, and then notices there's no microwave. "I sat in traffic forever. You wouldn't think, on a holiday . . ."

And then Chloe sees it. It's right there in the corner of the living room, and she feels their eyes on her as she looks at it. A bassinet; the kind that comes from Kmart, with scratchy white eyelet fabric cut cheaply and stretched awkwardly over a plastic frame. In the bassinet there's a stuffed green bunny rabbit, its painted eyes fixed stupidly on the ceiling.

"What's that?" Jason gestures at the cardboard tube still jammed under her arm.

"Oh, it's nothing. I just remember the other day you guys said that this place didn't feel like home, so I brought you some posters."

They are old posters, ones that didn't fit with Chloe's scheme for her house when she decorated—she now has nothing but black-and-white photography, mostly Dan's but some Helmut Newton, a few attempts of her own, the framed U2 *Joshua Tree* poster that has moved everywhere with her since high school. Chloe had decided that in Portland, she and Dan would paint the rooms bright colors but let the art mimic the weather: stark contrasts of black, white, and gray.

"I mean, you don't have to put them up. I just thought anything is better than bare walls."

Jason takes the tube, pops the end off. Inside there are two posters: a reprint of Goya's *Gatos Riñendo*, something she bought at the Prado's gift shop when she was in Madrid three years earlier. The other is a dizzying photograph of the Palio, the horse race around the Piazza del Campo in Siena, where the townspeople line the walls of the city center with their mattresses to protect horses and riders in the brutal dash to the finish. Since they left Spain two years ago, Chloe has wanted to go back, visit their old friends in Tarifa, and travel north to Siena for the Palio, but there have been babies due, adoptions to arrange, and summer is Dan's busy biking season anyway.

While Jason unfurls the posters on the orange shag carpet, Chloe takes a moment to inventory the apartment. Just the bassinet, and over by the edge of the sofa, next to a carton of Kools and a jumbo bag of sour cream and onion potato chips, there is a case of store-brand diapers, size N for newborn.

There is an exchange; Penny says something to Jason Chloe can't hear.

"Let me handle it!" Jason hisses.

"Pardon?" Chloe asks; she should know now, if it's all falling apart.

"I said, you better get on home. Roads are always dangerous on holidays."

At the table, Lisle snickers. "Is that your idea of a threat, Tonto?"

Jason walks to the door and opens it for her. Chloe pulls the edges of her jacket close, gives a wave to the room.

"Happy Thanksgiving," she says with cheer she doesn't feel. Penny waves back—she is picking turkey right off the carcass with her fingers, a piece of brown skin dangling between them.

CROSSING THE LITTERED COURTYARD, Chloe glances across to the apartment where another birth mother, Heather, and her toddler son live. Chloe has six birth mothers right now, and eighteen sets of adoptive families in her pool. She can't bring them all dinner, has to be choosy about the ones she needs to woo. Still, it would have been nice to stop by and surprise Heather with the turkey and sides. The lights are off; they are probably having a proper Thanksgiving dinner with Heather's grandmother. Heather's adoption plan is rock solid, the adoptive parents perfect, all the important meetings completed and checked off on the dry-erase board in Chloe's office. Heather doesn't need Chloe's turkey or drop-ins; everyone is simply waiting for the baby now.

In the parking lot, she hears footsteps behind her, disturbing the rotting leaves that have collected by the Dumpster. Chloe reaches in her pocket, wishing she had put the pepper spray on her key chain instead of clipping it to her gym bag. She fingers her keys, adrenaline flooding as the steps speed up behind her, along with the jingling, a sound like loose change in the pockets of whoever is following her.

At the side of her Jeep Cherokee, Chloe unlocks the door, hands shaking.

"Hey!"

She glances at the empty parking lot in front of her, spins around— it is Jason, his face barely visible, harshly shadowed in the epileptic flickering of the lone fluorescent light by the Dumpster. Rain is falling on his shaved head, his scalp skin a sickly green.

"Scared ya, huh?" He laughs. He has the cardboard tube in his hand, tosses it from one to the other. "Didn't know it was me, huh? Gotta be careful out here in Felony Flats, Chloe Pinter."

He takes a step closer to Chloe, so that she has to tip her head back slightly to see his two-tone eyes. Down by her side, Chloe sticks her ignition key out between the knuckles of her second and third fingers, the way she learned in her college Rape/Aggression/Defense class.

"About the crib and shit. My brother don't know about the baby, that we're giving it up."

Making an adoption plan for, or *choosing a family for*, Chloe should correct him, but she doesn't. Pretending she is shifting her weight, she puts another four inches between them.

"Okay," she says evenly.

"He and Brandi are staying with us awhile."

If Judith, the director of the agency, knew this, she would insist on reducing their rental assistance. Chloe won't mention it to her boss.

"Oh, and these?" Jason holds up the poster tube, inches from her jaw. "The walls aren't really the problem here."

"This is the best I can do. You've been incarcerated before; you know how hard it is to get a place with that on the application."

"This place is a shit hole, full of dealers and shit. It's no good for a baby."

Chloe's stomach lurches—great, another one going sour. She takes a stab—"But the baby's not going to be living here, right?"

She swears Jason flushes. He shuffles from one heavy black motor-cycle boot to the other.

"It's no good for Penny." He juts his chin out.

"It's the best I can do."

"Anyway," he says, chucking the poster tube into the Dumpster behind her car, "we don't need your *art*."

"Okay." Chloe opens the door. She would have kept the posters; he didn't have to throw them out. She gets in the car, one hand hovering discreetly over the automatic lock on the door panel.

"Sometimes," Jason says as he turns to go back in, hunching his black leather jacket onto his shoulders against the rain, "something isn't better than nothing."

2

Thanksgiving

PAUL

Paul Nova checks his reflection in the leaded floor-to-ceiling windows across the well-laid Thanksgiving table of their hosts' formal dining room and takes stock of his life. Thirty-one years old, moderately attractive, full head of hair, reasonably fit—not as regular to the gym as he'd like to be, but the physical demands of Paul's line of work keep him in decent shape. He is the owner of an inherited, steadily growing electrical contracting business, transitioning somewhat smoothly from the middle to the upper middle class. He recently purchased a carriage house, albeit a fixer-upper, in one of Portland's most prestigious zip codes. Fortunately, Paul is adept, ticking his way through the honey-do list of projects for their home. "Handy guy to have around," his wife always says.

He is happily married to the woman sitting beside him, her head level with his in the reflection, though this is mostly because she has a long torso. (Paul stopped growing at a respectable five foot nine inches, but in bare feet he still has an inch on his wife, and that's including that hair of hers.) He meets her eyes in the glass, and she gives a quirky, half-cocked smile.

Eva is the blond, bohemian college sweetheart who plucked Paul, working-class guy at a state school trying to get his business degree to help the old man out, from the boredom and irrelevance of Anthro

101, inserting herself permanently into his life twelve years ago. Now they are perched on the precipice of parenthood, expecting for the thirteenth time, Lucky Number Thirteen, they call him, their first child, due in two weeks.

So why, Paul wonders to his reflection, is he not the captain of this ship, carving his own turkey in his own cozy, if slightly dated, last-on-the-list-to-be-remodeled dining room three blocks away? Why is he stuck, like a gawky preteen at the kids' table, at an obligatory holiday dinner listening to conversations bounce around him without a shred of interest?

You owe me so huge, he wants to hiss to his wife, who accepted this invitation without asking him. They are in The Zone, the home-stretch! Eva's thirty-eight weeks pregnant, could go at any time! This meal could be their Last Uninterrupted Supper, and they are sharing it with John and Francie McAdoo, mere acquaintances. Their only common threads: that they both live in Portland Heights (though the difference in square footage between the McAdoos' house and the Novas' could be the answer to a long-division problem) and that once, when they had suffered a dozen miscarriages, Paul and Eva were briefly clients of the Chosen Child, the same adoption agency where John and Francie connected with their current birth mother.

But though Paul wants to tell his wife how miserable he is, he doesn't. He already pissed her off and got a tight-lipped look by snarking about their hosts on the short drive over.

"Don't the McAdoos just *look* like infertile people?"

"What is that supposed to mean?" Her bristly answer should have stopped him, but Paul sometimes doesn't know when to quit.

"John's old enough to have had his balls shot off storming the beaches at Normandy, and Francie just looks . . . dried out." He'd had the good sense not to tell his wife about the one accidental sex dream he had had about Francie McAdoo after they first met, not an inconceivable thing until you got to know her; a decent body, if you go for that type, average face, but in the dream, when he had tried to put it in her, she was so dry he got paper cuts.

Now, stuck at the McAdoos' dining room table, because he is not always so challenged in knowing how to say the right thing, Paul leans over into Eva's mass of spring-loaded blond hair and whispers, "Next year, our house. Just you, me, and Junior."

Eva methodically spears a piece of turkey, a rolling cranberry, and a fluff of stuffing, swipes her fork through gravy, and turns to their hostess. She chews her perfect bite, nodding as Francie McAdoo yammers on about back-ordered Pottery Barn furniture, but Paul knows she heard him. With her right hand, she reaches under the table and strokes Paul's knee like it's the head of an obedient golden retriever.

"So, Paul, you're still with Nike?" John McAdoo asks him. It is the first he's spoken since they all loaded up their plates at the cherry sideboard after a stiff half hour of cocktails, salty Costco hors d'oeuvres, and strangled small talk.

"Mm"—Paul wipes his mouth—"I'm actually not." He does not add, "I have my own company," though he does. His father would have taken this opportunity to dig in his pocket for a business card, "SuperNova Electric—a super company with service you can trust!" But Paul is not his father, in so many ways. "Maybe you're thinking of someone else from the agency. What was their name, honey, the Nike people?"

Eva, whom he has seen successfully attend three conversations at once, doesn't miss a nod for Francie but says, "The Severins, Nate and Gina, both with Nike."

Francie veers erratically off topic; she abandons distressed wood nightstands and jumps into the husbands' conversation. "They're getting a baby soon too—January, I think. I heard they got the most wonderful birth mother, really desirable, your absolute dream—Heather W. She's white, blue eyes, bright, a college student, I think, or maybe she wanted to go to college, remember I told you about her, from the message boards, John? They say she has that adorable little boy?"

John swirls the ice cubes in his drink, and there is silence. Paul wonders if John also resents these all-consuming adoption and infertility message boards. At first Paul had humored Eva's obsession, even enjoyed coming home to the sagas of her online world, rolled his eyes when she had to get a wrist brace because of carpal tunnel syndrome from hours at the keyboard. These days, it was taking her ninety minutes twice a day just to keep up with her posting.

"John," Francie repeats, "remember me telling you about that perfect birth mother, Heather W.?"

To Paul's relief, John finally raises his eyes to his wife's piercing pigeon glare and nods. Though they have known each other casually for two years, Paul is sure he wouldn't be able to pick John McAdoo out from one of a dozen puffy, rich, Scotch-ruddy, fifty-something executives sagging around a boardroom table. The guy made his money in the Silicon Valley dot-com world and is now semiretired, doing some hobby brewery, the Soaring Scotsman. His beer, offered to Paul before dinner, sits full, bitter and undrinkable.

"Oh, that's nice. Good for the Severins." Eva comes to the rescue, still constructing the same perfect bites; turkey, berry, stuffing, swipe.

In the quiet that follows, the clinking of silverware against plates, Paul puts his fork down and looks around the dining room. Hanging over the table is a chandelier that he recently saw in a trade magazine for $2,600, wholesale. It has feldspar finish with three loopy tiers, amber shell shades, and clear crystal trim. If a client asked his opinion, and more often now they do, Paul would never recommend it for an authentic period Tudor dining room like this.

By accident, Paul meets John's eyes in one of those awkward, mid-chew, looking-around moments that he hates at dinner parties when the conversation doesn't come easily.

"So——" John swallows his bite, though not quite all the way; Paul can still hear the mashed potatoes in his throat when he garbles, "Did you two ever get a baby?"

"John!" Francie's neck flares red. "Eva is due at the same time as our birth mother."

John puts down his napkin, swallows harder, and addresses her in low tones, though there are only four of them in the room—everyone can hear. "I can see that. I meant, before they got one the natural, old-fashioned way, did they—"

"How a child joins your family is irrelevant, and I hope you won't say anything about natural or old-fashioned with all your implications when our son arrives." Francie never raises her voice, but her hand has a tremble to it as she reaches for her water glass.

"I thought I remember you saying, last year, they got picked . . ." John falters on, genuinely confused, and Paul feels for him. These can be tricky waters.

"We don't. We didn't," Paul jumps in. "I mean, this will be our first." He reaches over to palm Eva's round, warm belly, coated under one of his thick cabled wool sweaters, and is rewarded by her own squeeze to his knee, *Thank you.*

"It didn't work out," Eva says breezily, as though Amber's baby was a weekend trip they were going to take that had been canceled. Paul remembers the reality, like living underwater: dark, rain-soaked days, chronic crying, Eva's endless baths. It wasn't the first baby they had lost, and tragically, it would not be the last, but when Amber's adoption fell through, Eva took it on the chin. Not that it didn't hurt Paul too. Sometimes he pictures their lost offspring like a heartbreakingly pathetic, underdog baseball team striking out, twelve little batters in a row. But now, late in the game, his hand still on her belly, he feels the roll of lucky number thirteen, their hopeful home run.

"You were picked very quickly," Francie says. "You and Paul had just joined the agency, after they hired Chloe Pinter. You never had to deal with the case manager before her. Remember her, John? She was awful! She let our portfolio sit, languish, for a year before telling us we weren't getting good feedback from birth mothers. They thought we looked old!"

"Terrible," Eva murmurs.

"Oh, well, all's well that ends well," Paul says, glancing surreptitiously at his watch just as the phone rings. John jumps up, a marionette jerked to life.

"I'll get it."

"Chloe Pinter has been a godsend, though." Francie starts fresh, smoothing the red napkin in her narrow lap. "John always says someone had their thinking cap on when they hired that girl. I don't know where the domestic program would be without her. This calendar year alone they have done fourteen U.S. adoptions. It's unprecedented."

"Well, and good news for you too," Eva says from where she is piling more cranberry sauce on her plate at the sideboard. "We can be mommy friends."

Francie sniffs, and Paul is horrified to see she's almost crying. "You know"—she sniffs again and makes two little circles of emphasis with the thumb and forefinger of both hands, sharp points, as though she is shaking out a wet T-shirt by the shoulders—"this has been the *hardest* thing in my entire life. I have wanted this more than I have wanted anything, and to have it be so difficult to attain—"

John comes back into the dining room and doesn't sit down. He clears his throat like he is about to make an announcement, then changes his mind, and sits. He picks up his orange napkin, shakes it out, crumbs flying. Francie has dropped her hands and, to Paul's relief, stopped emoting.

"Well?" she pounces.

"That was Chloe, Chloe Pinter. From the agency."

"Ah, the famous Chloe Pinter," Paul says, full of warm expectation.

"Is it time?" Francie's words tumble out on top of one another. "But the baby's not due for two weeks! What? John, is it good news? Is it time?"

"It's not news." John's words march out, scrubbed clean, careful. "Penny is not in labor. Chloe just wanted to let us know that, tonight, when she went to take Thanksgiving dinner to them, at the apartment, there were some baby items."

"Wh-what do you mean? What kind of baby items? Did she say?"

"She wasn't very specific, but she did mention a crib."

As much as he dislikes the McAdoos, Paul feels in his gut where this news hits them.

"She did say," John continues dully, "that they had an explanation, but—"

"What?" Francie's head snaps up. "What did they say?"

"They said Jason, the birth father," John explains, "that Jason's brother and his girlfriend have moved into the apartment as well, and that they aren't aware of the adoption plan."

"Oh my god," Francie whispers. "Oh my god."

"It could be nothing, Francie." Eva lays her hand on Francie's forearm, thin as a cashmere-wrapped golf club. "It could be exactly what she says."

"It's a classic red flag. I should never have gotten my hopes up."

From the kitchen behind him, Paul can hear one of the McAdoos' two whisper-quiet Whirlpool dishwashers change cycle.

Seven excruciating minutes later, the evening has limped to a close and Paul is warming up the car as Francie and Eva stand in the doorway of the McAdoos' looming Tudor. Eva leans in to hug Francie, her enormous belly an intrusion between them. She walks slowly, backlit by the golden glow of the replica 1800s gas lamp in their breezeway. She settles beside him in the brand-new Volvo Cross Country, a splurge for the safety of the baby, and snuffles as she strains to buckle her seat belt.

"Well, let's put *that* on our calendar for next year," Paul says.

"Oh my god, it was brutal. Poor Francie."

"Yeah." Paul drives out between the stone pillars with more replica gas lamps. They are made of copper, oversize. He could probably get them for $1,200 each, wholesale. Retail, they'd run about two grand, and the McAdoos have four of them sprinkled on the pillars, all the way down here by the street, like it's nothing.

"And you! Honey, you could have made more of an effort with John."

"What?" Paul has just remembered that they abandoned Eva's fabulous pumpkin cheesecake, the one potential bright spot in this miserable evening, in the McAdoos' Sub-Zero.

"Come on, honey."

They drive the few blocks in silence, winding through Portland Heights. Against his better judgment, Paul lets the thoughts in his head tumble out into the charged air of the car, unfiltered.

"I can't wait for this to be over."

"Pardon?"

"Nothing."

"No, I'm sorry, *you* can't wait? I weigh ten pounds more than you, I can't breathe, I look like an elephant, I'm never comfortable, I have to pee every five freaking minutes, I am about to have hemorrhoids hanging out of my ass, and *you* can't wait?"

"I meant, I can't wait for us to have our baby, cross the finish line, and be out of this psychotic parallel universe."

Eva is silent, the car filled with the sound of her breathing. She yawns open her mouth and wiggles her lower jaw back and forth like an anxious mare, and while Paul knows she is so congested she is trying to clear her ears, he feels a deep stab of annoyance. He keeps going.

"I'm just so sick of talking about birth mothers and agencies and caseworkers and babies and birth and placentas—"

"Nobody said 'placenta' tonight."

He pulls into their driveway and they sit in the running car, neither one making a move to get out.

"I just remember that night when we were in Costa Rica at your brother's and we went outside, and the sky was thick with stars. Remember? Everything seemed so clear, so simple. I felt like you and

I were all that mattered in the universe, and I wonder, sometimes, how we went from that to this."

Eva doesn't respond. She takes her index finger, slightly greasy from turkey skin, and traces her signature swirls and paisley doodles on the condensation of the passenger-side window. Months later, after the unthinkable has happened, before the police impound her car, Paul will sit in this same seat, in his own driveway, nowhere to go but desperate to unzip out of his skin, his life, and the morning dew will make the pattern reappear. He will wonder how he ever thought things were anything but perfect on this Thanksgiving night.

But now Eva breaks the silence and says, "Rock paper scissors for who gets to give Henry his shot."

They both throw rock, three times in a row, and then simultaneously, five pairs of scissors.

"Great minds . . ." Eva giggles.

"I'll stab the cat." Paul sighs, and she tips her head onto his shoulder, and they laugh, friends again, one of a hundred, a thousand, little repairs they do to the fabric of their relationship.

Earlier that month, Eva had told him she was doing an evening prenatal yoga class at their gym, when out of the corner of her eye she saw a man reflected in the studio mirror, coming in from the parking lot through the gym's glass doors.

"And I got this incredible rush of, of *attraction* just from this partial glance, and it was so strong, so visceral."

"Uh-huh," Paul had said, shoving his hands in his pockets in an attempt to be casual but thinking, Why are you telling me this?

"I was almost embarrassed to look, but the feeling was so intense that I couldn't *not* look, so I turned all the way around, and it was you."

PAUL UNLOCKS THEIR FRONT door, his hand on her elbow as she goes over the threshold in the dark. They are greeted by the tangy stench of cat piss—Henry, the diabetic cat, is ruining their hardwood floors, one dark stain at a time. Paul tells her to go to bed, he'll handle it, but then he can't find either the tabby or the puddle.

Upstairs, Eva is sitting up in bed trying to hold her nostrils open with her fingers. Paul suggests a Breathe Right strip, and she nods. He brings her one, and she tilts her face up to him like a little girl, asks him to put it on while she holds her nose in the right position. Afterward, he kisses her forehead.

"Okay?" he asks.

"No, I'm miserable!" She starts to cry.

Paul opens his hand, lets the heavy boots he is carrying crash to the floor from hip height. He undresses slowly, debating if he should ask what's wrong. He does, thinking, Ticket for one on the Hormone Coaster, please.

"It's Amber. And the baby. I wonder about them."

The baby that had almost been their daughter, a year earlier. Amber, a pudgy thirteen-year-old birth mother, her own mother only twenty-eight, had chosen the Novas as the adoptive parents for her baby. Chloe Pinter had arranged their first meeting at a Red Lobster, an obese pair of slow-blinking, loud-chewing women. Paul's tongue-tied comment, "You could be sisters," had offended them equally. They had strung the agency along for six months, huge expensive meals, dragging Chloe through the grocery store for hours. Chloe told Eva and Paul that Amber and her mother had each pushed a cart filled with Doritos, jumbo boxes of Froot Loops, doughnuts, crumb cakes.

"Doesn't the agency do nutritional counseling, or anything?" Eva had asked, and Chloe had sighed, said it was a really delicate situation.

"I won't lie to you guys," she had told them one chilly October evening as they sat on Chloe's overstuffed floral couch, rain pounding on the dormered windows of her cozy Troutdale office. "This one is not rock solid. Let's just wait and see. They say they are still on for our meeting at Pizza Hut next Thursday, and we're supposed to work on the birth plan. Who's in the delivery room, who cuts the cord, who holds the baby first, all that jazz."

And then a week before her due date, Amber's mother had called Chloe to say they were keeping the baby, would raise it themselves, thanks for the food and everything.

"Yes." Paul doesn't say more now, peeling back the covers. It had surprised him how quickly he had gotten on board with the concept of adoption. Selfishly, he relished the idea of bringing a baby home like a puppy—no, that's not fair, something more difficult and precious, a baby monkey, maybe—and adjusting only to one new variable without having to factor in Eva's recovery, the waves of hormones, and her changed body (how he loved her old flat stomach with the soft, fine blond hair around her perfect oval belly button!). But when adoption was presented in the specific, in the form of the gum-smacking Amber, Paul can admit to himself that he was shaken. He had felt such relief when it was over, no longer worried about their half-wit, sleepy-eyed Baby Huey of a daughter who would be knocked up at age twelve herself, nature's triumph over nurture.

Paul gets into bed, wraps around his wife's back, rubbing the bumpy landscape of their baby, their son, growing in her belly. "Shhh . . ." is all he says. Somewhere downstairs, Henry the cat lets out a plaintive meow. "Shh," Paul whispers.

3

The Famous Chloe Pinter

CHLOE

The Cherokee's engine whines as Chloe drives uphill toward home, a run-down former fraternity annex house she and Dan rent in Portland Heights. Beside her on the seat is the second cooling Fred Meyer bag with mashed potatoes, gravy, stuffing, and green bean casserole. She flips her cell phone open, no messages, her stomach queasy from her trip to the apartment complex. Her boss will hit the ceiling if Jason and Penny fall through, after all the money the agency has spent on them. Chloe puts the phone back in her purse but leaves it turned on. It may be Thanksgiving, but as the Chosen Child's only domestic case manager, she's still on call.

Chloe looks at her hands on the steering wheel, the loose ring with its fake diamond slipping around her left ring finger. They stopped shaking when she crossed the Burnside Bridge, her heart rate evened out once she turned south on Vista. They have no car—what's Jason Xolan going to do, follow her by bus? Despite the assault charges on his record, she's not afraid of him. Yet. He is simply a man cornered by circumstances, dependent on a woman, and that can be a dangerous sort of animal. This is familiar territory to Chloe; there is one of these waiting for her inside at home.

Inside the dark living room, Dan is sulking in front of ESPN, bundled in a DaKine sweatshirt and thick fleece socks. Last week he put clear packing tape along their old windowpanes, complaining of the draft, but he still walks around hunched over like he is bracing against an icy draft as he scales Everest.

"Hi, babe." She takes off her coat and drapes it over the arm of the couch he is curled on.

"It's fucking freezing in here, and I've got the thermostat turned all the way up." Dan doesn't have a car, has to ride his bike home from the bus line, almost four miles uphill, every night.

"You should have called me—I could have picked you up tonight."

"I thought you said you had to do a dinner thing with someone."

"I did. I'm done." Chloe squints at the thermostat, walks over, and holds her hand over the register. "It's blowing cold; did you check the pilot?"

"Yes," he snaps.

"Well, did you call the landlord?"

He doesn't answer.

In the breakfast nook she sets a table, tries to pry him away from the TV. "Honey. Dinner."

"No turkey?" He walks in and leans against the doorframe, purposefully lifts his sweatshirt in a stretch to expose his delicious rows of sinewy abdominals.

"I got this on the agency credit card when I was getting a dinner for some birth parents—thought Beverly would question more than one turkey."

"We can't have Thanksgiving without turkey!"

Chloe's face burns. She didn't think he cared, thought he liked being frugal more than traditional. Whenever she makes an effort to cook, he has already eaten, or isn't hungry. He's lost twenty pounds since they left Tarifa. "I have a chicken in the freezer." Chloe gets it out, and it thunks on the counter like a brick. "I can thaw it out, I think."

"Forget it," Dan says gently, taking her plate to heat in the micro-wave. "This is fine." He picks up the freezer-burned chicken. "Good to know we have this. I could use it if we need to prop a door open, maybe, or if it gets windy, it'd be great to hold some papers down." He smiles when she laughs at his joke, kissing her head before sliding into the seat across from her. Her stomach unfurls for the first time since seeing the bassinet at the apartment. The candlelight dances its reflection on the rain-smattered window by the breakfast nook, and their plates of side dishes send up steam. His feet brush against hers under the table.

"Poor McAdoos. I was just at their birth mother's, remember Penny and Jason?"

"The ex-cons?"

"Yes, who I finally got set up in the apartment complex in Southeast. I went to take them Thanksgiving dinner—"

"So they have our turkey?"

"Or we have half their sides, however you want to think of it. When I got there, Jason's brother and girlfriend had moved in, and they had filled the place with baby stuff."

"Oh. Uh-oh."

"Yeah. The birth father said they just hadn't told the brother about the adoption yet, but it seems like—"

"A red flag?" Dan offers, serving himself more stuffing. It tickles her when he uses adoption lingo. She rubs the arch of her foot over the top of his fleecy sock.

"Mm-hmm."

"Who're the adoptive parents?" Dan does this sometimes, acts like he is listening, then carelessly reveals he wasn't.

"The McAdoos."

"Ah, Francie Much Ado About Nothing. Serves her right, calling here twenty times a day."

Dan is exaggerating; Francie calls several times a week, Chloe's mistake for giving her their home number. In the boss's eyes, though, keeping the McAdoos happy is critical. Francie is a Boarder, a client who frequents the adoption message boards and has the capacity to make or break the agency reputation with a handful of posts. Francie's entries have been more positive than negative since they got a placement, bringing in a dozen new referrals, over twenty thousand dollars in nonrefundable application fees. It is a wonderful thing, except that Chloe is solely responsible for getting and then keeping the birth mothers for all these high-profile, edgy Boarders. Sometimes it is all Chloe can do to stop herself from approaching young pregnant women on the street, business card in hand. Her most recent stroke of genius was to put flyers up in Portland Heights, at the swanky grocery store and the gym—not for potential birth mothers, but to hook adoptive parents who want to believe that there are birth mothers up here in the Heights, nice college-bound white girls who "got in trouble."

Her boss Judith had actually kissed her forehead when Chloe told her what she was doing. "Brilliant! And then once we get them in here, we'll direct them toward China, something more stable. Nonrefundable application fees! Put some flyers up in Lake Oswego too—see if we can get them into Starbucks!"

"How was your day?" Chloe asks Dan as she carries their dishes to the sink. He is behind her, putting the leftovers in the fridge. Their elbows and shoulders bump comfortably in the narrow galley kitchen.

"Shitty. I need a new job. I need a car."

Chloe nods; this is an old conversation. In the four years they have been together, two in Tarifa, two here in Portland, Dan has never had his own car. "What kind of job were you thinking, for the winter?"

"One of the guys does mountain bikes in the summer, then teaches snowboarding up at Mount Hood."

"But it's practically winter now. Don't you think those jobs are snatched up early on?"

"God, why are you always so negative?"

They never argued in Spain; here it seems like every week.

❧

CHLOE HAD STUMBLED ON Dan in a wind-whipped town in southern Spain at the end of her backpacking tour around Europe after college graduation. Sipping sangria at an adjacent table in the Intercontinental Café, in sun-bleached Birdwells and a hulking Bull jacket made of windsurfing sails, he was the most edible thing she'd ever seen. When he opened his beautiful mouth and spoke casual, perfect, California-grown English, she leaned over and kissed it, so tired of mangled, deeply accented pickup lines over the past three months.

He was a bit of a pothead, she thought, but so were they all, back then. He was older, twenty-five, and had lived in Tarifa for several years, teaching windsurfing, working part-time at the Bull sail shop, banging everything from cute tourists to skinny-legged local goatherd girls. He fell hard for Chloe too.

Her friends left, bored with Dan's surf buddies, longing for serious relationships, convenience, fast food back home, but Chloe stayed on, renting an efficiency at El Beaterio, a former thirteenth-century convent. Dan joined her, moving out of the grungy grotto of rooms down by the fish factory where he lived with Kurt and Paolo from the shop, hanging his damp surf shorts over the towel bar by her curiously small square bathtub.

Chloe took a job training horses for a beach riding operation by the hotels. She never got used to the rats that ran underfoot like cats or the rudeness of the German girls who led the tours and treated her like a stable mucker instead of a trainer.

A year passed. During the windy season, even her eyebrows were being blown into disarray by the *poniente* wind. Chloe went to the Internet café more and more, browsing social work jobs back in the U.S. She attended the Escuela Hispalense on the edge of town and learned enough Andalusian dialect to give tours at the stable. The German girls laughed nastily as she lisped her way through the monologues about the wind farms, Guzman El Bueno, pointed out the coastline of Morocco across the straits.

That February, the wind changed direction for a week. Just as the verb conjugations in her second semester were getting complicated and she thought the way the relentless *levante* wind blew her hair against her cheeks might make her crazy, Chloe bought a *tarjeta telefónica* and called her father from the pay phone at the edge of the cobbled town square.

"I've applied online for a position at a small adoption agency outside of Portland," she told him, and as she spoke, she loved the way the English language tumbled out of her mouth, tasting like a home-cooked meal, like mashed potatoes and roasted chicken.

"Might be good to put your degree to use," Dr. Pinter agreed, his toddler twins from his new marriage screaming in the background.

"That's what I was thinking," she said, smiling, and she wanted to tell him more, how she would be the director of the entire domestic program, but he excused himself to help put the twins to bed.

Two weeks later, she was in an Extended Stay America outside Portland, loving American shopping ("J.Crew has stores now!"), Starbucks coffee, and, more than anything, her brand-new job at the Chosen Child. A month after that, Chloe had found her dream house, and Dan sent her an e-mail with his attached flight itinerary from Madrid to Portland and four words: *I'm nothing without you.*

A LOT CAN CHANGE in two years, Chloe thinks, washing the leftovers off their plates. She figures if they are fighting tonight, they might as well fight about something that matters to her. She follows Dan into the living room.

"I'm only asking because I want to know what our plans are, if we're going to get married, and how that fits, timewise, with—"

"So now we're going to fight about setting a wedding date again? Woo-hoo! I can't wait!" He turns on the TV, a period of punctuation; they're done.

Chloe hates how they go at it in sound bites, thinks they could solve more if they just had it all out, but they are both haters of conflict.

As usual, they will go to bed in silence, Chloe first, pretending she doesn't hear him when he comes upstairs, and in the morning, it will be as though none of it happened.

Only tonight, Chloe falls asleep easily and is surprised to find Dan beside her when her cell phone rings at 2:17 a.m.

"Hi, this is the answering service. You have a birth mother named Mandy? She said she's bleeding and needs a ride to the hospital."

Chloe is in her closet now, pulling out a long-sleeved black T-shirt, a pair of brown velvet overalls. Mandy is more than a month from her due date; this is too early. From Portland Heights, it will take Chloe at least forty minutes to get to Mandy and Dwight's apartment complex in Gresham. Her boss Judith lives ten minutes from the complex, more like eight at this time of night. But of course she can't get out of bed and go get her—this is the difference between owning the agency and working there for eleven dollars an hour, no health benefits.

Chloe sighs and hangs up.

"Work?" Dan asks softly, and Chloe thinks from his tone that they are ready to make up.

"Yeah, a birth mother is bleeding, needs a ride to Good Sam." She is poised to leave, her hand on the doorjamb. She tries again. "Earlier, I was only saying there are things involved in planning a wedding, things you have to book in advance."

There is a long silence. From the hallway light shining on Dan's perfect profile, she can see his eyes are closed, but it is a feigned sleep face. She continues, "Look, babe, you're the one who mentioned getting married in the first place. I never brought it up, you asked me. All I need to know is when."

"Honestly, Chlo"—he doesn't open his eyes, addressing the ceiling—"the way you're acting about this makes me sorry I asked."

She leaves the room without answering, letting his own words echo in the silence of her wake. It is a little trick she learned from him.

4

In the Middle of the Night

PAULPAUL

*I*t's 3:23 a.m., and Paul Nova is driving himself to
the emergency room with blood running down his arm. Goddamn
cat. Eva had reminded him about the insulin shot when she got up to
pee around two, and Henry, sleeping on the dryer in the basement,
would rather she hadn't remembered. The scratches on his forearm
were nothing new ("You've got to wrap him in his blanket like I do!"
Eva always said), but the bite along the back of his hand had split the
skin open to his knuckles. Paul had tried to butterfly it one-handed;
no luck.

Now at Good Samaritan's ER, Paul sits in the empty waiting room
with a battered two-year-old *Car and Driver* magazine. He looks up
when the automatic door opens and a couple comes in. The guy is
short, a Ducati cap riding high on his scowling forehead. He has his
arm protectively around the back of a woman with stringy hair, her
shirt hitching up over a tight, mounded stomach to expose her bulging belly button. Paul thinks how now that Eva is finally pregnant, he
sees watermelon bellies everywhere. Like when they were shopping
for a new car, suddenly every third vehicle on the road seemed to be
a Volvo Cross Country. The pregnant couple hangs back, and Paul
has returned to his magazine when he hears a familiar voice.

"Hi, I'm Chloe Pinter. I'm a social worker for the Chosen Child, and my client here, Mandy, is thirty-five weeks and having some bleeding."

"Well, then I need to speak to *her*," the admitting nurse says, and beckons for the woman to come forward. The man behind her seems attached; they move toward the triage counter in perfect unison, shuffling as she hunches over slightly. Chloe steps back, hand posses-sively gripping a manila folder. Paul notices her blush, embarrassment maybe from having been dismissed, but it makes her look lovely, fresh from bed. There is still the slightest crease from a pillow on her cheek, the strap of her overalls slipping off her shoulders as she takes the seat closest to the admitting desk.

"Hey, stranger," Paul says as he slips into the seat next to hers.

"Paul Nova! Oh, my goodness, how are you?" Chloe side-hugs him, awkward with them both sitting down. Though she keeps her head turned slightly, listening to the conversation between Mandy and the nurse, Paul swears she looks genuinely excited to see him.

"I'm good. You look great for the middle of the night."

"Ha! Thanks. Is Eva here? Baby time?"

"No, we've got about two weeks to go. Attacked." He holds up his bandaged hand. "Vicious house cat."

"Ah." Chloe nods.

There is a pause in the conversation, and they can both hear Mandy answer the intake nurse softly, "Yes, we're giving her up."

Chloe frowns slightly, whispers to Paul, "You're supposed to say, 'We've chosen a family for her' or 'We're making an adoption plan for her,' or 'placing her for adoption.' You're not supposed to say 'giving her up' anymore."

"It's all about the semantics, huh?"

"Well, for the baby. Who would want to know that they were 'given away'?"

"I see your point."

"I should go call the adoptive family," Chloe says, standing up. She stretches her arms over her head, and the bib of her overalls slips to one side, showing her cupcake breast under her tight black shirt. *Down, boy.*

"Okay." Paul clears his throat. "Can I get you a coffee from vending?"

"Really? That would be great. Regular, lots of cream and sugar. I think I'm going to be up awhile." She glances at the couple by the counter.

Paul watches as Chloe steps into the hallway to use her cell phone. It's not the right time to be thinking about this, but he always got the sense that there was a little something—low-voltage, but something— between him and the social worker. Hard to know if what she liked about Paul had anything to do with him as a man, or the fact that they were great bait for potential birth mothers. The chances of him ever knowing exactly are slim. After tonight, he thinks, he'll probably never see her again. He is wrong.

With his good hand, Paul feeds wrinkled bills to the vending machine and gets them two coffees, grabs a pile of creams and sugars. Chloe is talking to the pregnant couple at the triage station.

"Do you want me to come with, or are you all right?" Chloe asks, her hand resting gently on the woman's upper arm.

"We're okay." The man speaks for the first time, his voice gravelly. "You aren't leaving, are you?"

"Um, no . . . ," Chloe says, and Paul checks his watch. Jesus, it's almost four thirty. Here's to hoping Eva doesn't go into labor before he gets a decent night of sleep under his belt.

"Good." The birth mother nods. "If we don't get admitted, we'll need a ride home. One of the neighbors is with the kids, but I've got to get to Kohl's in an hour. Black Friday."

"Okay. I called the Byrnes and told them what's going on. They want to know if they should come in; they're worried about you."

"Not yet," the man says firmly. "Tell them don't come yet."

When he has gone back with the nurse and the birth mother, Chloe sits down next to Paul, punching numbers in her cell. She nods thanks and takes the coffee from him.

"Hi, Angela, it's Chloe. I just spoke to Dwight, they're going back to see the doctor now, but he says he doesn't think you need to come yet. . . . No, no, I think everything's fine. . . . No, I'm staying right here, don't worry. I'll keep you posted, I promise, the second I hear . . . Well, if it makes you feel any better, I won't sleep either." She laughs softly. "Really, it's no problem. It's an honor to be a part of this."

It was exactly what she had said to Paul and Eva when they met at the agency picnic almost two years ago, that it was "an honor to be part of such an intimate and important part of people's lives, the creation of a family."

Following their New Year's resolution to pursue other options, Eva and Paul had borrowed five thousand dollars from her brother Magnus toward adoption agency application fees and attended an informational picnic for the Chosen Child. They arrived at the park near the Sandy River, a risky choice for January, but it was brilliantly sunny and mild, a warm Chinook wind blowing. Balloons bobbed, and flags representing the international adoption options snapped in the wind.

"A good sign," Paul had said encouragingly to Eva, who was still bleeding from her twelfth miscarriage.

Within the first five minutes they'd been cornered by Francie McAdoo at the dim sum cart under the China flag.

"You're new," she pounced. "Against my better judgment, I'm going to introduce you to Chloe Pinter."

"Why against your better judgment?" Paul had asked with a polite smile.

Eva explained it later: She and Paul were twenty-eight and thirty, physically fit, attractive, in love, and childless. They were a birth mother's dream—and stiff competition to every desperate forty- and fifty-something couple milling around the domestic adoption booth, inhaling hot dogs and stuffing information packets into their purses.

Eva and Francie exchanged infertility war stories (Francie and John: seven failed rounds of in vitro, six figures in specialists) and e-mail addresses. Francie also got Eva hooked on the message boards: Oregon Open Adoption, TTC (Trying to Conceive), and Infertility and Loss.

As promised, Francie introduced Eva to Chloe, praising the program, even though the McAdoos had not been chosen in two years. Bitterness hung yellow-green around her like mustard gas.

Paul had remarked to John as they watched Chloe and their wives talking, "Does she have to look like that too?"

"What?" John seemed bored with the whole picnic, an agency-sponsored world's fair of foods and cultural stations representing all of the countries where the agency conducted adoptions. A Chinese adoptee, five years old, ran past them, stiff-legged in her straight cheongsam with her Oregon mother in her dirty Keens running after her calling, "Grace!" They all seemed to be named Grace, Paul noticed.

"A farce," John said coldly as they passed.

"What?"

"This picnic. The international program. 'Let's celebrate the heritage of our twenty-thousand-dollar status symbol!' Dress her up in honor of the country that sells their baby girls, the ones they don't kill, that is."

Paul didn't answer, slipping the brochure he'd picked up on the China program into his hip pocket.

"What about her?" John prompted. "You were saying, about Chloe Pinter?"

"Oh. Well, she's already got this goddesslike status, the Woman Who Can Bring Us a Baby, and then she has to look like one too. I thought social workers were supposed to be ragged and homely."

And both of their eyes traveled to the founder of the agency, Judith Duvall, who was operating the electronic bubble blower in her purple caftan and multiple neck skin tags, surrounded by a rainbow of children.

❦

"Thanks for the coffee." Chloe snaps her phone shut and places it in her purse.

"Anytime," Paul says, and he means it. "Hey, what's this?"—Paul catches her left hand. "A sparkler, huh? Your boyfriend, what was he, the mountain bike guy?" Is he really feeling a pang?

"Oh, yeah. It's not the real ring. It's cubic zirconia, until, you know—"

"Well, congratulations!"

"Thanks, but it's no big deal."

"No big deal? What? When's the happy day?"

"We're sort of playing it by ear. Anyway, we're both pretty busy with work. Hey, how's the hand?"

Paul remembers Eva, after they became engaged, the way the impending wedding, the band's playlist, the color of the Jordan almonds in their little tulle bags, consumed her. There is no doubt about it; Chloe Pinter is fucking *cool*.

"So, you still loving the job? You've been with the agency, what, two years now?"

"Yeah. It's good." Chloe dumps all four sugars and three creams into her coffee.

"Must be crazy, though, babies popping out during the holidays, middle of the night. Seems like you never get a break."

Chloe shrugs. "I'd hate to work anywhere else. Like Catholic Charities, they have separate case managers for birth parents and adoptive parents. I like knowing both sides. When Amber asked if you were nice people, I could honestly say yes, I had been to your house, I patted your vicious house cat. Really, it doesn't get much better."

Paul sips his coffee and nods.

"Hey, are you and Eva still friends with the McAdoos?"

"John and Francie? We were at their house for Thanksgiving dinner tonight, in fact. Did we live in Portland Heights when you did our home study?" He knows they didn't, but he can't help himself.

"No, you were in Sellwood. That cute little house, right next to the diner where we had lunch."

"Right, that's right, we bought the new house after Eva got pregnant this last time. We live right up near John and Francie now, just a few streets over. We got this great mini Tudor, a Tudorette, used to be a carriage house."

"Really? So we're practically neighbors too."

"You live in the Heights?" *Too loud, Paulie, settle down.* "I mean, wow, the agency must be doing pretty well."

"Ha! No, it's a rental. This crazy great-aunt of a friend of mine used to rent it to a fraternity. It was a total dive when Dan and I moved in. Instead of paying for tags to put their garbage out, the frat boys just piled it in the basement. It took months to get rid of the smell. But we've done a ton to it, painted it and everything, and we love the neighborhood. I mean, we'd love to buy it someday, but you can't beat living in a two-bedroom for six hundred a month just uphill from Northwest. We love walking around down there on the weekends."

We love this, we did that—whatever. Paul's hand is throbbing. He wonders how much longer he will have to sit here, making polite conversation with her.

"What's your favorite place to eat?" Chloe asks.

"Hmm." Paul looks at his watch: 4:49. "I guess I would have to say Papa Haydn's."

This is a lie—in his opinion, everything in Northwest is overpriced or overspiced.

"Us too! I can't believe we've never seen you there. Dan and I go there for dessert all the time."

They both sit back, sipping their coffees. So she sounds happy, though Dan looked like a pouty pretty boy when Paul met him briefly as he sulked outside Chloe's office waiting for a ride home last year. He's about to ask if her boyfriend has a car yet when she says, "So then I guess you heard, tonight, at the McAdoos'. About their birth parents."

Paul nods.

"God, this is when I hate the job."

"So you think things don't look good?"

"I don't know. Their birth parents are really"—Chloe pauses to take a sip—"unpredictable. They called me from jail, for a ride, that was how I met them. I think it was check fraud for her, but he has some other things on his record, aggravated assault, battery of another woman, sex with a minor, though to be fair, he was nineteen and it was supposedly his girlfriend. But since then, it's been money money money, get the agency to cosign on an apartment, get him a job, which is nearly impossible with his criminal record and Megan's law, then when I finally get him one he has a fistfight with the manager, so then it's food money and new maternity clothes for her and a nice pair of pants for him for an interview, and on and on. It's a bad sign when your birth parents want so much money, and they choose the parents with the biggest income without even *considering* the other profiles, and then you go to their place and they have baby stuff."

"It's like Amber," Paul says.

"Yeah, there were some red flags with Amber." Paul is quiet, and after a moment, Chloe continues. "One time, I took her shopping for maternity clothes, and her mom held up a big yellow T-shirt with the word BABY in big letters, and an arrow pointing down. Most birth moms don't want to draw that kind of attention to being pregnant. But all's well that ends well, I guess, except for Amber's baby."

"We still think about her." This is not a lie; he does think about her. "I don't suppose you ever hear from them?"

Chloe shakes her head, stands up to throw away her empty coffee cup.

"Mr. Nova?" The admitting nurse leans her bulk over the desk. "You can come on back now."

Paul does not waste time on a long good-bye with Chloe Pinter. He needs to get this hand sewn up, needs to get home and get some rest so he can be ready for Eva, for their baby.

OREGON OPEN ADOPTION—*A place for all mothers*
FRANCESCA97201
Joined: 26 Jun 1998
Posts: 17249
Posted: Fri, Nov 24 2000 4:24 am

In the predawn of Black Friday, Francie McAdoo's burning eyes scan the boards. The most recent post is from ANGIENMARK4EVER, dated just minutes earlier.

Our CW just called, BM is in hospital with bleeding!!!!! BF told CW to tell us not to come yet!!! <sad face, scared face, shocked face> **What does this mean???? Hugs please!!!**

Francie clicks New Message. First the obligatory; have to reply to everyone so you're sure to get lots of attention when it's your turn.

(((ANGIE))) Don't listen to the CW!!! I would not trust anyone—I would go to the hospital myself! ((((hugs)))) and (((((prayers)))))

And now on to her stuff: Francie's heart speeds up as she types, fingers flying. Her high school typing teacher promised a good secretarial career if she focused on her form. Look at her now! Sitting in her Portland Heights mansion, queen of the message boards, she unloads, sixty words per minute.

Bad news:

she begins, sure to grab attention.

Pottery Barn, where I purchased my crib, rocker, and changing table, has discontinued the nightstand in their "Thomas" line. (See photo in profile.)

My IRL friends thought I was crazy, buying out the Thomas collection after the fourth IVF failed, but you ladies supported me, promised there was a baby in my future. You knew it would be therapeutic to paint the room Caraway Seed (before you saw that color in every Starbucks downtown, LOL), and I loved assembling the crib, ordering the lighting, trying out rockers vs. gliders. But now there's no nightstand and what do I do? Should I try ebay or—

Francie stops.

I.CANNOT.DO.THIS.ANYMORE.

The truth: CW called tonight, the baby has a crib, in the apartment with his parents. The worst part is, it is my fault.

One week ago, after our dinner meeting with BM and BF, John (DH) went to get the car, and BM asked CW to go with her to the bathroom, and I was alone (a setup, I see now!) with BF. He started talking about the pain this was causing BM, how hard it would be to give the baby up, how they needed $$$. I pretended not to understand, but oh, I do.

Give them money? On top of everything they have paid to the agency and invested in this? Do they buy this baby, the son of a criminal, a biracial thug? And the birth mother: ugly, scars all over her face, pores as big as pomegranate seeds, thank god it's not a girl. The father is okay-looking, more than that, sinister, "dangerously attractive," like Bruce Willis crossed with Samuel Jackson . . .

Francie has to be careful here. She had taken some heat on the boards and IRL for her posting earlier this month, when they were first chosen by Jason and Penny and she was freaking out a little over the race thing—how Chloe had shown their profile to biracial parents when their preferences were clear: white healthy newborn.

Eva told her that apparently some people think she's a racist!

Her phone was ringing within minutes after she posted her rant against Chloe Pinter and the Chosen Child. It was Eva Nova, spouting platitudes about the hand of fate, the right baby choosing its parents.

"Not that we're going to, but John says we could sue the agency for this."

"But, Francie, it's your baby . . . ," Eva had said.

"Oh, we've decided to go ahead and do it," Francie said peevishly.

"You say it like you've resigned yourself to the hassle of changing long-distance phone carriers."

In a whisper, Francie had confessed to Eva the most politically incorrect sentiment of all: "I didn't want anyone to be able to tell, to know he was adopted. John and I just wanted to pretend that he was ours."

I'm afraid this is our last chance,

she writes now.

I need for this to happen for me,

[BACKSPACE, DELETE]

, us.

The only thing worse than my own disappointment and pain, Francie thinks, is watching others experience it for me. There are women on the boards who love that attention, the pages of parenthetical hugs, whose signature line includes every Angel In Heaven's due date, every Angel On Earth's due date, all the babies that might have been theirs, wearing their sorrow like merit badges.

Francie used to do it too, but another disappointment, this potential rejection—from common criminals—is starting to feel personal, like there is something wrong with *her.*

Now Francie types, hands shaking:

Do I buy this baby? Is this my last chance? What about genetics? What about bonding? What about—

What about John? Her husband was fifty-four, more luke than warm on the adoption option. How much further down this road can she expect him to follow, writing checks in silence?

They met nine years ago when Francie was the Realtor lucky enough to land the listing of an authentic turn-of-the-century Tudor mansion in Portland Heights. John was the newly divorced dot-com millionaire geek relocating from California. They drove to the address in his 700 Series BMW. He had a bottle of wine in the trunk that they drank on the dusty stairs, Francie trying to make her mouth dainty as she sipped straight from the bottle. He talked about architects and period pieces, and instead of his thinning reddish hair, his perpetual limp, Francie focused on his eyes, which, behind his glasses, were a lovely shade of blue.

Within the year, John had invited her to move into the house they carefully remodeled. He gave her a platinum card, didn't blink when she bought a bedroom set that cost more than her ancient Jetta, then replaced her car with a Mercedes SUV, a two-carat diamond dangling from the rearview mirror.

That fall, Francie booked a table at a Greek restaurant that was meant to be festive, but was simply loud, for the first dinner with John's grown daughter, Melinda.

"So, Lindy, tell me about college. What's your major?" John had said, swallowing his drink.

"Women's studies," Melinda had huffed, blowing her hair up off her forehead and glancing around the restaurant. "I told you last year."

She was wearing a huge plaid flannel shirt over a man's ribbed undershirt, dark jeans that were not hiding her saddlebags and broad hips, and those clunky black shoes! Nineteen years old, all the time and money and opportunity in the world to exercise, to care for her looks, the burning metabolism of youth, and *that's* how she chose to present herself? Francie made a mental note not to ask her to be part of the wedding party, as she had originally thought she might.

Melinda refused to stay at the house, told her father to drive her to the airport to catch an earlier flight. After they dropped her off, Francie said gently, "I'm sorry. I know you looked forward to this."

"It's all right," John said, hands tight on the wheel as they crossed the Burnside Bridge.

"I won't ever let our children treat you like that."

There was a long pause, and then John had said carefully, "Is that very important to you, that we have children?"

"Yes! What? Of course!"

"All right," John said evenly. Over the next seven years, he did not resist any of the process. He used those same two words, *all right,* with varying inflection, consternation, aggravation, and finally resignation, as they navigated the quest for parenthood.

When Francie underwent her third in vitro, John had surgery on the ropes of hideously huge, painful varicose veins that gnarled his calves. They convalesced together in the front living room, moss velvet drapes drawn, watching endless movies, passing pillows and pints of Dulce de Leche. They got rid of the authentic, horsehair-stuffed period couch and bought something squishy and leather—"and if chocolate milk or sticky fingers get on it, it's wipeable!"—at City Liquidators.

Francie believed that the more still she was, the better the chance that her embryos would burrow. She was almost thirty-nine, one hundred and forty-five miserable pounds from the hormone shots. They had twin Mac laptops on their laps, John making connections in Asia, where his hobby microbrew had a strange but passionate following, Francie chatting on her seven message boards, filling online shopping carts with maternity clothes from Pea in the Pod, waiting to push "checkout." She talked about their baby in a hopeful, superstitious whisper. And then Francie bled. Thank god for the wipeable leather couch.

John's veins receded, and came back worse. Francie bought him diabetic hose to wear under his suits when he took those long flights to China and Singapore. He was overseas when their fertility doctor, a soft-spoken man who wore ties decorated with cartoon sperm and ova, told Francie that they had done all they could.

She had to wait to call John in Singapore until the next morning to share the news. "He thinks adoption is really our best option."

A long pause, slight crackling over the thousands of miles that separated them, and then, quietly, "All right."

IN THE LAVENDER PREDAWN of Black Friday, Francie reads over her post. Exhaustion, seven years of this ride, have worn her down, but sharpened her edges too. Sometimes she has flashes of recognition, of how she might be perceived, misunderstood.

[SELECT ALL, DELETE]

She types:

(((Angie))) Think positive—I am sure it will all work out. Trust your CW; she will keep you informed.

We had a lovely Thanksgiving dinner with friends from the agency who are due with a boy at the same time as our BM. Hard to believe this time next year our sons will be sitting between us eating mashed sweet potatoes at the same table!

But as Francie hits Post, she knows in her heart of hearts this is not true, that at least one person will be absent from the happy future Thanksgiving scene she imagines.

Quickly, she opens a new browser window and begins searching: "dark wood distressed nursery nightstands."

5

Ultrasound

CHLOE

*I*t is 7:30 Monday morning, rain streaking down the windows of the bedroom. Chloe hears the shower cut off, watches from the bed while Dan walks in, naked, pulling on his gray boxer briefs, then jeans, then orange rainproof pants. He has perfect lines to his body, and as he stretches his arms over his head, just the right amount of muscle to his naturally skinny frame. He is pulling on his rain jacket when she says, "I can give you a ride to the MAX line, babe."

"I didn't know you were awake." He startles; endearing. Sometimes she can see the little boy under the man, and it makes her heart lurch.

In his mother's home in San Diego, the entire stairwell is an ascending tribute to her only child—from his twinkly-eyed infancy to chipmunk-cheeked toddlerhood, every beige-background school picture, his choirboy days, highlighted newspaper clippings that mentioned his high school soccer achievements, to the most recent, right before he left for Europe, a stint as an Abercrombie and Fitch model.

"Is this *you*?" Chloe had asked when he took her home for the first time. Standing in the middle of a sea of vacant-eyed, straight-haired, bored-looking women: Dan, naked, chest shaved and oiled, abs flexed, casually holding a T-shirt with one finger hooked in the collar to cover his groin. "When was this? You look—"

"Yeah, yeah, move along, folks, nothing to see here." Dan had nudged her up the stairs with his duffel bag, and when they were in his old bedroom with the door closed, she pushed him flat on his back on his twin bed and pounced on top of him.

Now Dan crosses their bedroom and sits down next to her, feathering his fingers through her hair. "Where are you going this morning?"

"Southeast, for a birth mother's doctor's appointment. But I can drop you off."

Dan strips off his crinkling orange rain jacket, lies down next to her, and rests his head on her chest, cupping her breast through her tank top.

"You know you're my transportation queen, don't you? Driving Miss Daisy." He kisses her neck, and she thinks, Birth moms keep her waiting all the time, so what if she's a few minutes late?

CHLOE PARKS NEXT TO the Dumpsters at the squat, stucco apartment complex in Southeast, an area of Portland known as Felony Flats. Last year she convinced Judith to pay Julio the landlord a flat five hundred dollars a year to accept any birth parents they cosign with, regardless of their record or lifestyle. So far they have had seven birth mothers living here, some with their husbands, boyfriends, other children, though they usually move on quickly. Only Heather and Penny are here now.

She checks around the car before she gets out as she gathers her file, cell phone, and purse. There is nowhere in the city where she is truly nervous for her safety, but this, and maybe a few sections of North Portland, are as close as it comes.

Heather and her son Michael live in 12, on the ground floor, across from Jason and Penny. Chloe glances toward their apartment, blinds pulled low, as she trudges through the muddy pathway in the court-yard, the mulch worn thin, littered with cigarette butts sucked into the quagmire.

Heather opens on her first knock.

"Chloe, you're late!" she says as she buttons her son's raincoat. "My appointment is at nine thirty, and we've got to get the car seat in and stuff." She hands Chloe Michael's car seat, covered in mashed granola bar bits.

"Sorry. Traffic, weather." Chloe waggles her fingers at Michael, hiding behind his mother's gray pilled sweatpants.

"Michael, honey, say hi." Heather is flustered, brushing her hair back toward her dangling ponytail, and Chloe is once again taken with how beautiful she is, the sharp angles of her rosy cheeks, everything in her face fresh without makeup. You could open any magazine and see models, albeit with straight teeth, a team of stylists, and no kids, trying to look this good.

"You look great," she says, and Heather harrumphs.

"Come on, honey," she says, hiking Michael up to her hip, his thick toddler thigh riding over the top of her belly as they cross the courtyard. "God, the baby's always so active in the morning." Heather hefts herself into the passenger seat, her hand over her stomach, twisting to get comfortable under the safety belt.

"Did you eat breakfast?" Heather is too skinny. The rare times Chloe has seen her without her signature baggy gray sweats, her arms were like branches, her belly barely a volleyball.

"Michael had Cheerios, right, honey?"

"Ohs!" Michael cries from the back. Chloe checks him in the rearview mirror as she merges onto 205.

"Listen, we sent you a check for prenatal vitamins last week, and you cashed it. I hope you got them."

"You know, I really meant to, but it was Michael's birthday, and the prenatals make me sick. I'm eating really good, though, lots of salad. I swear." Heather is seventeen, but she looks about twelve when she holds her fingers up in a Scout's honor sign and grins.

"So, listen." Heather changes the subject. "Not to be nosy, but the other people with your agency, in eight? Penny and Jason?"

"Yeah?" Chloe doesn't know how she knows this, but she's not surprised. Other clients in the building have had intimate knowledge of one another's lives. Maybe the common walls are thin, or there is a local, grandmotherly gossip.

"So, did I look at their portfolio, the people they chose for their baby, I mean?"

"I don't remember." Chloe turns off the interstate.

"I mean, are they a nice family? Who they chose?"

"Why are you asking?"

"Can you just tell me who it is?"

"Heather . . ." Chloe sighs.

"Just tell me. I remember all the portfolios. God, I studied them for like *forever.*"

"It's John and Francie," Chloe says, though she shouldn't.

"The rich old couple with the cheesy wedding pictures at the coast, the ones who put in there that he makes like half a million a year?"

"You think they look old?"

"He does. He looks like a grandpa, and she's as old as my mom! She looks good, you know, like she'd be a young kind of mom, but I did the math. Their wedding date was stamped on one of their photos, and she said in her bio they met when she was thirty-three, so—"

"Yes, that's them."

"Oh." Heather looks out the window as they pull into the parking lot at the clinic.

"What? Heather, what?"

"It's nothing, really. I mean, you know that his brother moved in, right? And his girlfriend too, the Indian one who's like twelve with all the crank craters?"

"What does this have to do with anything, Heather?"

Heather looks at Chloe, then in the backseat, where they both see Michael has fallen asleep.

"The brother, Jason's brother? He's a total candy man, and they say he pimps out that girl."

"Really?"

"Don't say I said. It's none of my business. I just wanted to know if it was a nice couple getting their baby."

"Does Penny do it?"

"Crank? I don't think so. Nah; she's no tweaker. I think she's just like that."

"Like what?" Chloe has cut the engine. Rain quickly covers the windshield, obscuring their view of the doctor's office. It is so dark out, it could be night.

"You know," Heather is peeling her fuchsia fingernail polish in wormy shards. "I think she's just a little messed up naturally, you know?"

Chloe nods; she knows.

"Don't say I said, okay? The guy, Jason? They say don't cross him."

IN THE WAITING ROOM, Chloe holds sleeping Michael, a chubby warm weight across her thighs, while Heather checks in.

"I can take him now." Heather offers her arms when she comes back to sit down.

"On what lap? I'm not giving this up."

Heather smiles and wraps her arms around her stomach bulge, tapping her wet gray sneaker on the industrial carpet, rubbing her arms with her hands.

"My mom thinks I'm totally crazy not to make Michael sleep in a crib. But I love to sleep with him, we both just curl up around the baby here." Heather looks down, her voice breaks. "I just, I want him to know, the baby, that I'm doing this for him, you know? I'm holding him all I can now, on the inside, because when he's out, I'm not gonna." Heather sniffs, jiggles her leg faster, wipes at her nose.

"You could write him a letter, Heather, tell him—"

"No, I'm no good with letters. I don't even write to Eric, and he's supposedly my stupid fiancé. He's always asking me to, but I sit down and I can't think of anything to say, except, 'You're a stupid fucking

loser and I'm giving up our son, Michael's brother, because of you.'
So I don't write, you know?" Heather swipes at a tear, and Chloe
wishes her arms were free so she could give her a tissue, or put an
understanding hand on her wildly swinging leg.

"I know we've talked about this, but Nate and Gina, they would
be okay with cards and letters, or even some kind of openness,
visits or—"

"No!" Heather lowers her voice. "Because you think, Okay, it's a
baby. And I could see him and hold him, and it would break my heart,
but in a good way, to see him happy with them, you know? But then
the next year he's one, and then the next year, he's Michael's age, and
then Michael's in freaking kindergarten, and they're starting to ask
questions and wonder, How come him and not me? No."

Chloe doesn't say anything; there's nothing to say.

"If I didn't have Michael," she says quietly, "if it were my first, then
I might want open, and visits. But if I didn't have Michael, I wouldn't
be doing this. It's for Michael, and of course Baby David, that I'm
doing it."

They had had this conversation the first time they met, in Heather's
apartment while Michael drove trucks and watched *Elmo* on the tiny
TV with the rabbit ears. Heather had explained to her how, when
her boyfriend, Eric, Michael's father, got arrested for stealing and
marijuana possession, and she had discovered that she was pregnant
again, she had just assumed she would keep doing what she was doing.
Michael would keep going to day care, she would keep on working as
an aide at the nursing home, and they would go on like this until Eric
got out of jail the following year.

"But then one night when Michael was sleeping, I stayed up and did
the math, you know? I got out my little pink calculator and I started
adding it up, two kids in day care, seven dollars an hour, no better
jobs until I can get my GED and get to college or somehow get a car,
and I realized I could almost make it, *almost*. But every month, with
medicine for an ear infection here, or a lost shift there, or the baby

has the runs and we need an extra pack of diapers, and those are just the little things—God forbid I get fired, or Michael needs another set of ear tubes—I realized I would slowly have to sell everything that makes Michael's life good. One month, it'd be the couch, or the TV, or the bed, or there'd be nothing for Christmas, and then he'd start to hate his little brother. And I don't want my sons to hate each other, you know? So it's just better this way, for Michael, and for Baby David."

"HEATHER?" A NURSE STICKS her head around the door. "You can come on back."

"You want to see him?" Heather turns to the nurse. "Can my friend come back for the ultrasound?"

In the closet-size exam room, Chloe finds a place to sit, settles Michael across her lap again, his Power Ranger sneakers banging one of the metal stirrups. They don't look at each other while Heather shimmies out of her sweatpants, folds her plain pink briefs on top of them, and slips her arms through the paper gown. Then, like she's in the fifth-grade locker room, she removes her shirt and bra through the sleeve, tearing the gown a little. She giggles, carefully placing her shirt on the pile.

"I don't usually have to wear a bra. Unless I'm pregnant or breast-feeding, I'm like totally flat. Eric's all pissed because now I have boobs again, and he doesn't get the fun of them. By the time he gets out, they'll be gone."

There are so many things Chloe wants to know about Eric and Heather, how these kids are attempting something that has the bones, the weight, of an adult relationship. When she was Heather's age, she was worried about the math score of her PSATs and whether she should lose her virginity to the senior lacrosse player who sort of liked her.

"So," Chloe says to fill the silence, "is this your first ultrasound?"

"No, I had one at twenty weeks, you know, where we found out it was a boy, but then he was really small. So Dr. Wilde wants me to come back every two weeks until my due date so he can be sure the baby is growing and everything."

Chloe is opening her mouth to lecture Heather on nutrition, ask if they need to go grocery shopping on the way home, when the door opens.

The doctor is a fatherly type, and he ignores Chloe, but she is used to this from medical professionals. He has a smooth, deep voice, and he talks to Heather constantly as he performs a pelvic exam, keeping one hand cupped over her bony knee.

"Normally, we wouldn't start pelvics until thirty-six weeks, but since your first baby was early, we like to make sure that your cervix is nice and long and closed, which it is. I'm very pleased with that."

Heather nods, trying to close her knees with her legs still in the stirrups.

"Okay, then, now for the good part. We get to have a look at the little fellow. You can sit up a little, here, I'll pull the table out and put these away. . . ." He folds the stirrups into the table. "Now, let's see how our little guy is growing here."

The doctor pulls down the blinds, though it is hardly necessary with the sky storming outside, and flips on the ultrasound machine. He squirts some pale green jelly, like aloe vera for sunburn, on Heather's tight mound of a belly. The screen flickers, snowy, and he moves the wand around until the baby's face appears, a perfect profile, and Chloe inhales—he looks just like Michael. A miniature snub nose and a square chin, a smooth round forehead.

Heather laughs softly and says, "I know, total spitting image, right?"

When he is done taking his measurements and pronounces the baby in the fifth percentile, but growing well, he pops a tape out of the VCR under the sonogram machine, extends it to Heather.

"Oh, thanks." Heather blushes again. "But we don't have a VCR or anything."

Before Chloe can say anything, and before she even thinks of it, Heather says, "Do you think Gina and Nate would like to have it?"

Actually, Chloe realizes as they walk back toward the waiting room with the tape sticking out of her purse, her first thought had been how to justify buying Heather a VCR.

6

Encounter

JASON

"The way I see it, it's like a puzzle," Jason tells Brandi, his brother's girlfriend. They're sucking off smokes outside, 'cause Penny's trying to quit.

Brandi stares bug-eyed up at the sky, scratching at her arms. The rain's on a break, steel-colored clouds blowing past. They've been here a week, and Jason can't figure out if she's constantly high, or just stupid. Jason stretches his legs out in front, trying to ease the pain in his back, so bad sometimes it travels down to his heel even.

"Every piece is a fact; I store them up here," he goes on, taps his freshly shaved head. "Fact: Dried-up rich lady wants to buy our baby so bad you can smell it on her, Eager Beaver, stink of desperation. Fact: Social worker wants it to happen, probably gets a fat piece of the action."

Fact (he thinks to himself): They have sixteen dollars to get them to the end of the month, and Penny's making him nervous, talking too much about the baby.

"Smoke outside!" she'd yelled, waving the carton warning in his face. "It's no good for Buddy."

Fact: He has no idea how to pull this off. Doesn't even know what he's trying to do, only to make it right. Penny's the best thing that happened to him. He owes her.

"I've fucked up in the past," he says to Brandi, who flicks her stubby butt into the mud at their feet and scratches at her legs through her pants.

The three biggest mistakes of his life:

- The DUI that cost him his trucking license in '96
- Getting mixed up with Des'ree and that crank crowd in Wyoming
- Letting Penny take the fall for the check thing in Drain

He does not count the baby in this list.

"But this," he says, lighting Brandi another smoke; it's her pack. "I won't fuck up. Just got to wait, study the pieces, figure how to get me and Penny what we deserve."

He sees her then, Chloe Pinter, coming from the parking lot across the way.

"Speak of the devil," he says, rubbing his palms together. Brandi looks down to his bare forearms, where the dragon tattoos twist. He's going to show her how it's done.

"Hey!" he yells. Chloe jumps, skitty little thing, drops the folders under her arm into the mud so she has to scramble to pick them up. Jason smiles. But then she looks at him, nods, and disappears into the place across the way. Like she couldn't be bothered with the likes of him.

Brandi makes a bleating noise beside him, like a question. Stupid bitch, picking at her arms, meth mites no doubt.

"It's all part of the plan," he tells her. "Agency bitch in her fancy SUV."

Behind Chloe it's the hot blonde from across the way with the kid, and shit, he'd never noticed before under those clothes, but she's fucking pregnant too. How many of them has Chloe Pinter got out here? Now he sees it: they're all her ponies, and Felony Flats is her little play stable, she stops by to feed them turkey and stuffing, takes them out to exercise, to the vet, but in the end, she'll take the money and run.

Jason jumps up, jerks Brandi with him. She stumbles, laughs like a coyote, high as a ponderosa pine; he knew it.

"Come on." He lifts her by the arm—she couldn't weigh a hundred pounds even, but the pain shoots on down his back, his hip, his leg. "I got to use your phone."

7

After-Dinner Drinks

CHLOE

At home, Chloe finds the house dark, though Dan's bike is chained to a peeling post on the front porch. In the spring, she thinks, they should paint, give the house a face-lift from the street, poor old girl. Years of frat-boy abuse had left her damaged, but you could see what a gem she used to be. Chloe had spent every spare moment working on her, scrubbing and retiling the downstairs bathroom (if a little lopsidedly) and painting every room, from their red dining room to the neutral khaki master bedroom. One day, after they're married, she and Dan will buy the house from the landlord, fix up the little nook at the top of the stairs for their own baby, paint it pale periwinkle, a shade so pale it almost looks white, perfect for a boy or a girl.

The dining room just off the front hall is bright, bloodred, with titanium white high-gloss trim on the windowsills and molding, a perfect contrast to the dark wood table and scuffed hardwood floor. It is Chloe's favorite room in the house, and she stops here now, admiring a $200 oversize silver mirror she splurged on, dropping her files, purse, and keys on the table. She takes the sunflowers she bought at Strohecker's, the upscale, overpriced grocery store just around the corner, puts them in a tall blue glass vase, and sits at the table, drinking in the colors.

This is what you have to do in Portland in the winter, she tells her friends who have never been there. You have to fill your inside with color so that the gray, the record-breaking forty-two days of low cloud cover and drizzle, don't make you want to drive off the edge of the steep, winding road that leads to your perfect little house in Portland Heights. This is what you have to do when you have a sort-of fiancé who huddles in front of ESPN in the dark, who takes his cell phone into the other room when his friends, extreme sports bums who dream of Maui, of Telluride, call. This is what you do when you have a house you have fallen in love with, and a job that you can't leave, when you have birth mothers, clients, who want you to hold their hands when they scream and push out a baby they will give away, no, correction: will make an adoption plan for.

"Hey, babe." Dan startles her, coming from the dark living room to lean against the arched doorway. He has been asleep, prints of the corduroy couch on his rosy cheek, so lovely with his dark hair standing spiky above his dear face. He smiles sleepily. Okay, she thinks, we're in a good mood. Okay!

"Hi!" She wraps her arms around his waist, checking her watch behind his back. It's only just five thirty, and he has been home long enough to take a nap? "I thought you were going to call for a ride. I tried to call your cell a few times. . . . How was your day?"

"Shitty." But his tone is light. "But we closed the shop early, so I have that going for me, a smaller paycheck this Friday."

"Well, but it looks like you got a nice nap in."

Dan shrugs, difficult again, and wanders through the dining room to the kitchen, stretching. A few years ago, before they moved to Portland, Chloe would never have used the word *optimist* to describe herself. Now, because she must balance the scales, it is the front-runner of her personality traits; Little Miss Sunshine.

"I've got at least two births coming up; I'll get overtime for sure," she offers, following him.

"It's okay, babe," he says, his mood swinging as wildly as their empty birdfeeder in the gusty rain outside the kitchen window. "It's no big deal. Can I pour you some wine?" he offers, and suddenly there is nowhere she would rather be on this stormy night than sitting in their perfect red dining room, the trio of bright white pillar candles flickering between them as they make short work of a bottle of bargain merlot. He has one of her hands casually in his, tickling the underside of her wrist absentmindedly, though he knows it drives her mad, the best kind of mad. She can see them reflected in the silver mirror and, in that, the reflection of their images on the paned window, and on and on, endless rectangles of diminishing size, their silhouettes, the wineglasses, the glow of candlelight. Conversation is easy and light, bantering that will lead them quickly to the bedroom at the top of the stairs.

Until the cell phones ring, first his, and he takes it into the dark living room from where she can make out phrases: "next month," "talk to Chlo about a plane ticket," and "take some time off."

She is bracing herself for his reaction to her questions when her own cell rings and she switches places with him, taking it into the other room as he sits back at the table, pouring the last of the wine into his glass.

"Hey." The deep voice startles her, the pause that follows.

"Hello?"

"You heard me. I said hey."

"Who is this?" she asks, but she recognizes the voice.

"You know who this is." He laughs sharply, and Chloe has to fight the urge to look out her window—he could be anywhere, because there are things he knows about her, things a birth father with a criminal record shouldn't know.

Jason Xolan had called the Chosen Child four weeks ago from outside the Women's Correctional Center in Salem, where Penny had just completed a sentence for check fraud. Jason had been released from a facility on the Washington side of the Columbia River on a parole violation four days earlier, had hitchhiked to Salem to be there when Penny got out. Chloe had driven the hour to Salem with a yellow informational folder and the top four portfolios off the adoptive parent stack.

"We're hungry," Penny had said as soon as they were in Chloe's car. "Freakin' starving." In between sentences, she was kissing all over Jason's stubbled neck, and he had one hand up under her droopy, clay-colored sweater. Penny's hair was buzzed "Prison joke," she'd said—and her pasty cheeks were covered in angry red cystic acne.

Jason, on the other hand, was attractive in a bad-boy, sinister-hot way. Chloe finally stopped at a Denny's halfway between Salem and Portland, when Penny's whining about being hungry and Chloe's anxiety that Jason was going to mount her in the backseat won over her desire to get back to home territory and complete this meeting in her office.

"Okay," Chloe said, sipping from her diet Coke, centering the lemon yellow folder in front of her. "So, Penny, you're pregnant, and you're considering placing your baby with a family."

"Ya think?" Penny jumped up and jerked her ratty sweater up, exposing a blue-white belly crisscrossed in zebra stripes of stretch marks, a dingy sports bra that barely held the breasts resting on her stomach. "I'm ready to pop!" She plopped down on Jason's lap, grinding into him, and he glanced around the restaurant, gripping both her shoulders before moving her off him like a boisterous preteen daughter.

"Okay, baby," he said, "*enough*." And something in his tone whipped Penny's head up and she sobered, nibbling at her nails while Chloe started with the Preliminary.

As she took their general information, Chloe learned that Jason was from a logging family in northern Washington, with a white father and a mother who was "half black, half Indian, full-time drunk." He lifted his sunglasses to the top of his head, showing one blue eye and one brown. There were hints of swelling, a yellowed bruise under his left one.

"Heterochromatic," he said, and Chloe nodded like she understood. Later, she looked it up at home.

"Always got one foot in each world," he said.

When Chloe asked about his time in jail, he said, "I trusted the wrong people. Story of my life, baby. Put my eggs in the wrong fuck-ing basket." He rubbed his blunt hands together, tattoos of Chinese dragons curling up the backs of them to his thick forearms, as big around as Chloe's calves.

"Is this Jason Xolan?" she asks in her dark living room.

"I saw you today with that girl, Heather," he says. "Can't say hello? Can't speak to me in public?"

"I'm trying to be respectful of people's right to privacy."

"Do they like her better?"

"Who?"

"Because she's blond, right? She dyes it, I bet. I bet the carpet don't match the drapes. Bet they don't know that."

"Who?" Chloe asks again. She leans against the dark living room wall, feels the burlap wallpaper, recently repainted a deep plum, dig into her cheek.

"John and Francie. Because I have a picture of Penny, before. She had this long hair, good skin—"

"We're an agency. I have more than one family waiting for a baby." You have no idea, she thinks.

"So what, now, you got a bidding war going? Do they want her kid or ours?"

"That's not how it works," she says. She remembers Jason and Penny in the Denny's, how he plunked his finger right down on the spot on the McAdoos' profile where Francie had put in John's salary. "Jason, you picked them."

He's quiet. In the other room, she can hear Dan rummaging around, heating up something in the microwave.

"What do you want?" she asks Jason.

"Money."

"I can't just give you money." Chloe takes a deep breath and tests the water. "Especially not when I've seen the bassinet, when it looks like you're taking us for a ride."

"It'll go through," he says, so quietly and ominously that Chloe feels the hairs on her neck tingle. Two years ago, this would have been deplorable to her, a red flag, duress! Now it just means there needs to be more money. Like a parrot, she goes through her speech.

"Look, we got you groceries last week, all of your rent is paid, which we aren't even supposed to be doing since your brother and his girlfriend are living there—"

"I need a job," he says softly. Something in his voice strikes a chord with Chloe. Here is a man who is out of control of his own life, dependent on his girlfriend's pregnancy to provide for them for the next few weeks. This is familiar, stepping gingerly around the easily bruised male ego, rushing home to quietly intercept and pay the bills, then letting Dan gallantly whip out a wrinkled ten when they go out to breakfast at McDonald's.

"So you gonna do that for me?"

"Pardon?"

"You gonna get me a job, or am I gonna take this baby and Penny and find ourselves another agency?"

"Jason," Chloe fumbles, "I have tried to get you a job. It doesn't work, and it's actually not even my job to find you—"

"You're gonna make it your job, though, right?"

"What?"

"You understand me? You're gonna make it your job. You're gonna get us money and get me a job, more than minimum wage, and no fucking construction either."

"Jason, I can refer you to Americorps or VOA or something, but I don't really have the resources—"

"I know all about your resources, Little Miss Portland Heights.

You'll do it, or nobody is gonna like what happens. Not with the baby, or Penny, or nobody, understand?"

And then he hangs up.

When Chloe and Dan go upstairs and undress each other, they don't talk about their phone calls. He will only insist that she quit her job, say that she doesn't make enough money to be threatened by thugs. She will tell him that she's not leaving, not moving to Hawaii or Colorado to be a surfer's or a snowboarder's wife. What she has never said: that she'd rather be an adoption social worker, even if that means she may not be a mountain bike mechanic's sort-of fiancée with a cubic zirconia ring and no set wedding date.

In the morning, she will drop Dan and his bike at the MAX line, and on the way to work she will detour by her bank, continuing south to Felony Flats. Remembering the loose flashing on their apartment door, she will slide the envelope, $100 in cash, easily underneath.

8

Penny for Your Thoughts

"Who was that, baby?" Penny tries to climb onto Jason's lap. Their baby twists inside as she tries to get comfortable. Jason elbows her off him; he's mad. She lands on her hip on the dirty orange shag carpet. "Ow!"

"You're too heavy. Jesus." He gets up off the sofa, paces the tiny room. His jacket jingles, his angry walk, a sound that makes her want to hide behind the sofa or strip off her black sweatpants and lie down for him.

But she gets up and crosses, one eye on him, to the bassinet in the corner. She folds, refolds, the two tiny blankets from Julio's wife, nice straight creases. She sits the green bunny rabbit up a little straighter. Soon, baby, soon, she thinks.

Jason jingles over to her. "Just getting things worked out for us."

"But we're still . . ." She is afraid to say it, when he's like this. He'd promised he would take care of her, take care of things.

"What?" He spins, narrowing his eyes at her. God, she hates how he knows he can scare her. He knows what got done to her outside Denver. For the first time since those freeloaders showed up, she wishes Lisle and Brandi were home.

"I just mean," she says as she hooks her fingers in the front loops of his jeans, trying to rub on him, but her stomach's in the way. Penny looks down between them. If she leans forward she can see her white feet. They look wider than they are long, like boiled potatoes, her toes tiny sausages, straining against the skin. "I just mean, nothing's changed about Buddy, right?"

"Jesus, Penny." Jason sighs, rubbing his chin hard into the top of her forehead where her hair is coming back in bristly. "What do we want with a baby right now?" He is pushing her on the shoulder, digging his fingers into her shoulder bone, and she stumbles to her knees. This she can do. "What do we need with a baby?" He keeps one hand on her shoulder as he unzips his dirty jeans with the other. "You're my baby. I don't need no other babies." And he lets go of her shoulder, moves his rough hand to cup under her jaw, the calluses scraping her cheek, brings it around to the top of her head, holding her there. "That's right," he grunts softly, "you're my baby."

Okay, Penny thinks, gagging a little, okay, then.

Just so long as nothing's changed.

9

Blood Relations

PAUL

"*P*ush, honey, PUSH!"

Poor sweetie has been pushing for the last two hours, two hours where she both shit and peed on the bed, two hours where they heard the nurses remarking over her incredible hemorrhoids at the shift change, but the worst of all, two hours where she has been unable to push the baby out.

Nineteen hours of labor and now in the homestretch, the baby's heart rate dipping with each contraction, seconds away from an emergency C-section, and with all of her glorious might, when Dr. Woo gives his final nod, Eva roars to life and pushes her son out.

"Darling!" Paul has never called her this before, he realizes, as he watches the doctor lift the baby, covered in blood and smears of blackish green, onto Eva's soft belly.

The baby is Wyeth Edward Nova, named after Eva's favorite painter, her father, and Paul's family name.

"Six pounds twelve ounces, honey! All fingers and toes accounted for, whoa, and a whopper of a willy!"

Paul already has his finger in his son's fist; he marvels at the baby's strength. Then the nurse takes over, handling him too roughly, Paul thinks, and then she is plopping him right in Paul's arms, and he is struck by how important this moment is. The first time in eleven years, since his mother, brother, and father died within ten months of each other, that Paul has had skin-to-skin contact with an immediate blood relative.

When his eyes meet Eva's, they are slick with tears, and he says quietly so that only she can hear, "This has been a long time coming."

Paul moves close enough so they can both touch him, marveling.

IT TAKES THE DOCTOR almost forty minutes to stitch up Eva. Paul passes the foot of the bed, and like driving past a car accident, can't stop himself from glimpsing the carnage. It will be a long time before he will be able to prepare red meat, pat raw ground beef between his palms to make hamburger patties.

Wyeth is exactly one hour old, Paul notes, realizing that after watching the clock obsessively for the past few hours, he has been inattentive. Its familiar white face with black hands ticks back at him like an old friend. On the bed, Eva has the baby in her arms, her gown open, Wyeth alternately suckling and sleeping. Paul is amazed at how their room feels different now, drained of adrenaline, their edgy exhaustion replaced with a serene sleepiness. The nurse has efficiently turned the place from a delivery area to a mid-range hotel room. When Dr. Woo has finished with his wife—"Twenty-two stitches, sweetheart," he says, patting her knee as he leaves. "Don't be shy about asking for painkillers, okay?"—all traces of blood leave with him.

"I can turn the lights down, if you like?" the nurse offers, and Paul realizes they are really going to leave them alone with this baby. He looks to Eva, panic juicing his heart rate, but she doesn't return it. She is blinking, long, slow blinks, her head bent over Wyeth.

"Okay, that would be nice," she mumbles, and her eyes close before the nurse has even shut the door. Paul looks at her, his son at her breast, her hair a tangled mass behind her on the pillow, the blood vessels in her cheeks and eyes broken from the pushing. During the last hour of labor, she had complained of itching, scratched deep raspberry-colored welts into her neck and chest—it looks like she has been lashed. Paul runs his hand lovingly over her forehead, leans closer to examine his son, his tiny throat moving like a tree frog's, in and out, frantically sucking, eyes closed, then resting, perfect nostrils flaring.

"Nice job," Paul whispers. "Both of you."

Eva makes a noise, her eyes closed.

"I'm going to step out, make some calls." Paul stands, stretches his arms up over his head, cracks his neck twice, goes out to the hallway. His phone is clipped to his belt; he flips it to check the time—4:36 a.m. There's nobody he can call. His aunt, his closest relative, wouldn't mind, he knows, but there's no point in waking her. Good news can wait.

The calls that wake you from sleep are those that can't. Paul remembers his first middle-of-the-night call. His mother, a lifetime smoker and diabetic, was in the hospital for a routine operation for an infection on her leg, a gardening cut gone purple. Paul was a handful of weeks from high school graduation, sleeping over at a friend's, planning a night of Boone's Farm wine and girl-chasing, when his father called.

"The doc says it must have been a blood clot," Paul's father choked. "Somehow got dislodged. They couldn't get her back."

Two months later, the men of the family stumbled around in their grief, weeks of pizza, fried egg sandwiches, and ramen noodles, until Paul Sr. sat him down in the kitchen that held the smell of cooking grease and told him, "I'm making Ritchie a partner in the business." It was the summer after Paul graduated from high school, all warm breezes from the gorge, clear sunshine and strangeness, the silence of their house in the mornings. Paul was working with his father full-time, and he took the news like a slap.

"Dad."

"Paulie—" His father held up his hand, coughing.

"Dad. I'm a better worker than Ritchie. He's never on time, he, he doesn't even know how to pick up the goddamn voice mail, Dad!"

"Paulie——" His father coughed again, smacked his own chest with a fist. "Listen to me: you're going to college. Ritchie is going to come on board with me, and you're going to college."

"Dad . . ." Paul faltered. *He hadn't thought . . . He didn't think . . .* SuperNova Electric and Sons?

"You're too smart to be crawling around in people's attics and basements, fishing wires your whole damn life. You'll go to college and learn how to grow this business, get us a whole fleet of vans running around, other people doing the job for us, us *managing* the business. That's the future of SuperNova. I'm bringing your brother into the technical part full-time, get his lazy ass working. Then I'm going to retire and make you partner in my place, okay? I'm going to move to Mexico and sip froufrou drinks all day, and you boys are going to do my dirty work, send me the checks."

Paul had enrolled that fall at Portland State University, just across the bridge, despite worries about his father's health, his older brother's lack of responsibility. They sat down to dinner at night, the tabletop TV droning the news, with Paul Sr. eating less, coughing more, still smoking his Lucky Strikes. Ritchie would alternately make an effort at work, then fall back into bed for weeks, as though the weight of just doing what everyone else did on a daily basis, showing up and putting in eight hours, was too much for him.

But more than worrying about his father and brother, and his increasing anxiety that the freshman-year classes, all bullshit requirements, were doing nothing toward helping him learn to grow his father's electrical business, Paul was being pursued by a girl, and he didn't know what to do about that either. Eva Sunderland was the seventeen-year-old freshman who sat next to him in Introduction to Anthropology. She had waist-length, perpetually messy blond hair and wrote him funny notes in the borders of her binder, miniature sketches of her life as depicted with the Pygmies their professor droned about.

"Exhibit A: Pygmies wading with me through beer sludge at ATO house this weekend," she would write, and pass him a lined sheet of paper, tiny stick-figure Pygmies sailing on a plastic cup next to the chunky sole of her ubiquitous brown hiking boots. "Exhibit B: Pygmies trying to tempt me not to write this stupid paper." And there they would be, drawn pulling her hair, holding up ads for concerts, *Gypsy Kings, 7:30*, in the newspaper. There were Pygmies that got buried in her mountains of dirty laundry, Pygmies getting her out of a really bad blind date, Pygmies flying back east with her for Thanksgiving break, angry-eyebrowed Pygmies hating to be shuffled between her newly divorced parents, and finally, somewhere around Exhibit Q, a week before Christmas break, the Pygmies were smacking their foreheads and sharpening spears in outrage that Cute Guy next to her still hadn't asked her out.

Paul turned red, thinking again, *He hadn't thought . . . He didn't think . . .*

So he took her home two nights before she left for Christmas break. The house was dark and quiet when they arrived, breathless from the cold. His father and brother were out pulling wires, replacing fuse boxes, avoiding getting shocked in the standing water of flooded basements, Portland's winter rains already in full effect.

Paul and Eva sat at the scratched orange Formica table in the kitchen, the bacon scent from breakfast lingering. They drank jelly glasses of his dead mother's peach schnapps and went up to his bedroom, which he had cleaned in advance. He wasn't always slow to catch on. On the plaid comforter set, last year's Christmas present from his mother, they had tentative, awkward, desperate sex. Three times.

In the morning, Eva was backed up into him, her blond hair a stormy tangle in his face, her cheek pressed against his bicep, dampness everywhere they touched.

"Hey, sweetheart." She flipped over, so their eyes were only millimeters apart, her giant breasts pressing into his chest.

Paul, afraid he had morning breath, only smiled as widely as he could.

"So," she said as she got dressed, "I can't believe it took you all damn semester." She was wearing jeans and hiking boots, nothing on top, and he wanted to pull her back into bed, one more time, but they both had an eight o'clock exam.

"So why me?" He finally asked the question he had been thinking all night, all semester.

"It's your last name," she told him, finger-combing her ropy hair. "I saw you on the class list and thought, Eva Nova sounds good. You'd be amazed how many names don't go with Eva." She pronounced it in the Swedish way, AY-vah, just the slightest hint of an accent in her voice. Paul didn't know whether to kiss her chunky brown hiking boots or run for the hills.

WHEN SHE FLEW BACK from Christmas break, neither Paul Sr. nor Ritchie said anything about the peach-cheeked girl who moved things, a dryer with a bullhornlike attachment for her tangly hair, a loud fan that they thought would drown out the squeaking bedsprings, up the staircase into Paul's narrow bedroom.

"My roommate snores," she told Paul as she pushed his clothes to one side in his closet. Occasionally she cooked for them, simple spaghetti with jarred meat sauce, but mostly she and Paul kept to themselves, learning the basics of higher education and honing the fine skill of the elusive simultaneous orgasm.

Three weeks later, in February, when the sun hadn't shone in eleven days and there was the thinnest veil of slippery snow coating the streets of downtown, Ritchie died.

It turned out to be a malfunction of the company vehicle, a former bread delivery truck with "SuperNova Electric" stenciled on the side, a cranky diesel engine thumping away under the floorboards. Ritchie, who was on his way to a two-day gig in eastern Oregon, left before it was light, a gentle snow falling as he got farther from the coast, and pulled over at a rest stop for a nap off 84, near Bend. State troopers found him in the cab of the truck, early afternoon, the motor running, "probably to keep the cab warm," they said, but something malfunctioned, and instead of warm air, the diesel engine pumped carbon monoxide fumes into the truck. Ritchie never woke up.

Three months later Paul Sr. died of lung cancer, morphined and unconscious until he let go, Paul and Eva holding his curled hands.

Paul was just twenty, Eva eighteen, when they worked together over Memorial Day weekend, packing first his mother's, then his brother's, and finally his father's belongings into a U-Haul and driving them to a Salvation Army. They stopped at a Mattress Giant on the way home, and Eva bought a pillow-top king mattress set for a thousand dollars. Paul's old bedroom became the office, Ritchie's the rarely used guest room, and the new mattress set went on the floor under the windows in the master bedroom that looked out over the shady tomato garden in the backyard. His father's small life insurance policy went into escrow for Paul's tuition, because he didn't want to have any debt. In between writing both of their papers and scheduling SuperNova clients, Eva cooked and cleaned when she could. After that, Paul noticed, the house was usually tidy but it never felt truly clean again, and while he was never hungry, rarely did he ever feel full either.

Eva had followed their plan, graduating with honors and running the office for SuperNova Electric without too many problems. It took Paul longer, six years, and only then did he ask her to marry him, though they had been living together in Sellwood since the first night he brought her home. How he loved her.

How I *love* her, Paul thinks, shuddering, remembering everything that has happened in the last ten years, the last twenty hours. He quickly calls the office, checks the messages, and is about to go back to his wife and newborn son when something catches his eye.

Chloe Pinter. She is pacing the hallway, cell phone to ear, her folders tucked under her armpit. She sees him too, signals for him to wait as she walks closer. He practically runs to meet her.

"No, look, I understand, I *told* Francie how important it is, and she's coming, she's on her way." Chloe pauses, rolls her eyes, and mimics holding the phone away from her ear; they can both hear the yelling. "Yep, we'll get John here too. Don't worry, Judith. I've got it under control." She snaps her phone closed and says, "Lordy, these people! How are you? We keep bumping into each other in hospitals. It's not your vicious house cat again, is it?"

Paul realizes he has been grinning stupidly as he waited for her to hang up.

"He's here! Eva's amazing, he's here, perfect, all the good bits, ten fingers and toes, lots of hair, big ol' conehead——" He can't stop himself. "Just amazing, really, he looks just like his mother, thank god."

"Oh, Paul, I'm so happy for you." She squeezes his arm in congratulations. "What are the goods? Name, stats?"

"Um . . ." Suddenly he feels like he has been gone too long and is desperate to get back to the room. They both laugh at his pause. "His name is Wyeth Edward, and I can't remember how big he is. Um, small, he's small, but long, I think he'll be tall." He is backing away from her, the pull to get back to his new family so overwhelming, he can barely keep himself from running.

"I'll let you go. We're not even two centimeters dilated in there and already she's screaming, so I'm here for the long haul, looks like. If it gets too intense, maybe I'll stop by?"

"Okay." Paul is grinning again, nodding. "Okay!"

BACK IN THE ROOM, Eva is sitting up, pulling her hair back into a ponytail.

"Hey, sweetheart," she says sleepily, as she has every morning since they first started waking up together. Paul smiles at her, scanning the room. Panic hits him in a deep wave that closes his chest.

The baby is gone. He never should have left them alone, her so tired. But he hadn't gone far, maybe twenty feet down the hall, to talk to Chloe Pinter. He feels it bubbling up, that contempt that is bred of twelve years' familiarity, of knowing someone so well that you love them with all the fierceness that you detest their flaws. The truth is, Eva can drop the ball, just when it is most important. She can blithely scribble off a check they can't cover, double-book appointments with important customers, creating messes Paul has to untangle.

And here he has left her alone to watch over the baby, all drugged up, even at her best it might be . . . It might be too much for her.

"It's okay." Eva reads his mind. "The nurse just took him for a bath."

Paul mocks a thumping heart, pounding his chest with his fist. She scoots over slightly in the bed, wincing, pats the mattress. Only when he is in bed beside her, careful not to jostle her IV, settling her in the crook under his arm, does his heart settle into a steady rhythm.

"So this is how it's going to be for us from here on out, huh?" he jokes. "Stolen moments while the kid is occupied elsewhere."

Eva beams up at him; he kisses her forehead. Ahhh, this girl, and now, the mother of his son.

"What did Maggie say?" she asks after a moment.

"What?"

"When you went out, you said you were going to make some calls. You called my brother, right?"

Paul is saved by a soft knock at the door, followed by the shining smile of Chloe Pinter peeking around the curtain.

"Oh, sorry, I can come back. I'll just leave these bagels." She holds up a paper bag and a tray with three tall steaming coffees.

"No, please, stay!" Paul insists, clambering out of bed to help her with the coffees, her folder falling from under her arm, sliding to the floor, papers everywhere. The girl needs a bigger purse, he thinks, a briefcase, and suddenly he wants to buy her one. Something buttery and leather, like a broken-in baseball glove. Would it be so strange? he wonders. After all, she was their caseworker once, and they never thanked her properly.

Eva is struggling to sit up straighter as he and Chloe explain at once, on top of each other, that they met in the hallway, she's here for a baby.

"But I'll be here for hours," Chloe repeats. "She's not four centimeters, but they're keeping her anyway, 'cause she's a little . . ." Chloe twirls her finger by her ear. "We've been here all night, and I think it's going to be another long day." Chloe dumps a stack of sugar packets into her coffee. "In fact, I should probably go check on Penny, I mean, the birth mom. I should probably go check on my client."

"Penny?" Eva's head snaps up. "Francie's birth mom? She's here?"

Paul can see Chloe is torn, but she has already given them too much information. She nods, sits on the foot of the bed.

"Listen, are you guys still close? To the McAdoos? I remember, Paul, you said, when I saw you at Thanksgiving . . ."

A look passes over Eva's face, but Paul ignores it. He never thought to tell her he had run into Chloe that night.

"I only ask because there are some problems. Francie says John's out of town, making some excuses, like he can't be reached by phone, but we *really* need him here. The birth father's slamming around, my boss is all over me, Penny's freaking, Francie's not even going to be here for another hour because she says she doesn't have a car seat. I told her she could buy one later, but then she freaked, like she thought I was trying to tell her *not* to buy one, like things weren't going to go through, and who knows, so now she's driving around trying to find a Target open. Things would just be a lot *better* if one of them would show up like they want this baby."

"Is it going to go through, then?" Eva asks, and poor Chloe suddenly looks very tired, like she has been the one physically laboring all night.

"Once again, wish I had my crystal ball," she says, yawning into her wrist.

"Well, you're an angel to bring us coffee and bagels," Eva says.

She doesn't know, will never know, exactly how much of an angel Chloe is.

The Vultures Are Circling

CHLOE

Chloe is pacing in the lobby, the coffee churning in her stomach, when Francie McAdoo arrives, slipping as her wet loafers strike the tiles. Her ribbed black turtleneck clings to her birdlike torso, her thin blond hair fluffed out on her shoulders, a perfectly done face of peachy foundation makeup, gold hoop earrings. She is clutching a dripping arrangement of irises, a large Gund teddy bear, and a chic paisley Petunia Picklebottom diaper bag.

"I couldn't find anyplace open with a car seat," she yells shrilly from across the lobby. Chloe is anxious not to attract attention; Jason had said he was going out for a smoke and could be skulking around anywhere.

"It's okay."

"No, I know it is, I just spoke to friends of ours who had their baby this morning as well and he said we can use their car seat, that he'll give me a ride home. Is he here?"

"Paul Nova? I just saw him."

"No, the baby!"

"Oh, no. She's got a long way to go. You don't go from two centimeters to ten in forty-five minutes, not in the best scenario," Chloe says, not caring how Francie takes it. Read a pregnancy book! she thinks. "Come on up."

They walk together toward the elevators, Francie's cheeks flaming.
"Where's John?" Chloe asks.

"I still haven't been able to reach him. He left at four this morning
for Singapore and isn't answering his phone. If he turns it on in L.A.,
I'll have a chance of getting through."

"Wait a minute." Chloe stops, grabs Francie's forearm like they're
best seventh-grade girlfriends. "John left this morning?"

"Yes, his flight is in a few minutes, seven ten, I think."

"But I called you last night, when we got admitted. I told you we
were in the hospital."

Francie doesn't say anything, pats at her hair, shifts the diaper bag
to her other arm, makes like she wants to keep walking toward the
elevator.

"Francie, he went anyway?"

"It's a very important meeting. And you hear so much about false
labor—"

"You don't understand. Your son is going to be born today. If *you*
were in labor, would he hop a plane to Asia?"

"Of course not. Of course he wouldn't," Francie says, her eyes
darting around the hallway. "But this is different," she adds softly.

Chloe turns sharply, keeps walking so that their precious gazil-
lionaire client can't see the look on her face.

In the room, Penny is thrashing on the bed, screaming, clawing at
her IV.

"Get this fuckin' thing outta me!" she wails, striking the nurse,
and as she flops, a white breast falls out of her hospital gown, the
nipple seeming to stare blankly at the ceiling.

"You have to calm down, or I'll call security." The nurse, surprisingly strong for her size, kneels on one of Penny's arms and fixes
Chloe with a look. "Perfect timing."

"Penny," Chloe says evenly, putting the folders and her small purse
down on a nearby chair. "Hang in there, hon, tell me what I can do."

"For one," Penny huffs like a spooked horse, "get this bitch off me, and for two, you can tell *her*"—she gestures with her stubborn chin at Francie—"to go the fuck home. We're not giving him up."

Chloe doesn't look at Francie but can picture her, standing like a little girl on her first day of kindergarten at the edge of the playground, her big stuffed animal in hand.

"Okay." She keeps her eyes on Penny's. "First things first, let's get you covered up here . . ." Chloe speaks soothingly, tugs Penny's gown over her stray breast. At the same time, the nurse quietly dismounts, efficiently and purposefully adds another band of tape to her IV. "Now what's going on?"

"She told me the doctor wants her to add something to this needle to make me hurt *worse*, and she won't give me pain drugs yet." Penny's chin juts out even farther, and she looks out the windows at the sky streaked with orange.

"She's not even three centimeters," the nurse jumps in defensively. "It's the policy. If we give her the pitocin, get her into a good pattern, get her dilated a little more, then we can do an epidural. Otherwise, as I was trying to explain to her, it could stop the labor. And you want to have this baby today, am I right?"

"Where's Jason?" Penny says.

"You remember, he said he needed a smoke." Chloe is gently smoothing Penny's short hair off her sweaty forehead. Surprisingly, Penny lets her.

"I'm going to go see if we can get Penny some fentanyl. You got things here?" the nurse asks Chloe, who nods gratefully. An ally, for now.

Penny is faking sleep, and Francie is standing miserably by the sink, the diaper bag clutched to her chest, irises drooping. Chloe takes a deep breath, decides to honor Penny's charade, and speaks in low tones to Francie. It takes her back to days of babysitting, trying to make peace between difficult children.

"Okay, Francie, why don't you grab a seat here?"

"She's not staying," Penny says, eyes still closed.

"Remember, we talked about this in the birth plan? Do you want to

talk to me privately, Penny?" Chloe has to ask this, though she suspects
Penny is bluffing.

"Where's Jason?"

"He went out for a smoke, remember?"

"Longest fuckin' cigarette ever."

"You know," Chloe says, thinking how much worse this could be
with Jason here, "sometimes it's hard for guys, powerful guys like
Jason, to see the woman they love in pain, and not be able to help
her. Sometimes they need to take a break."

Penny opens her eyes, sits up awkwardly, scratches at the tape near
her IV, but absently.

"Yeah." Penny is smiling faintly now, nodding at the idea of Jason
being in anguish for her. "Where's your man?" She juts her chin at
Francie.

"Um, he's, uh, he's on his way to Singapore. Business trip. I've
been trying to reach him; I can't get through."

"Oh." Penny frowns. "Didn't he know I was having the baby?"

"It's a long flight," Chloe jumps in. "And you can't turn your cell
phone on on the plane."

"You can't?" Penny asks.

"No. It messes up the plane's radar."

"Oh. He'll have to come a long way back."

"Yes." Chloe nods.

"He might miss it."

"Yes." Chloe is wondering where this is going.

"Maybe Jason could cut the cord, then?"

It had been in the birth plan, a standard in the agency's papers, that the
adoptive parents would do it together—Judith liked the symbolism.

"Yes, fine," Francie says, too quickly. "I'm going to try John again."
She jumps up, rushes out to the hallway.

"Penny, it's just you and me now. Are you changing your mind?
Should I go home?"

"I need Jason."

Chloe looks at the monitor; it's been eleven minutes since the last contraction. They're going to be here a while. She stands up, purposefully crossing the room.

"Wait," Penny calls. Chloe sits back down in the chair by the door. Round one, Chloe.

"I fuckin' hate needles," Penny mutters. "Hate hospitals."

For the first time, Chloe sees Penny's legs, stubbled and crisscrossed with thick white scars. Penny senses her looking, jerks the sheet sideways over them.

"Car accident?" Chloe asks, just to fill the silence.

"Sort of."

Chloe doesn't say anything.

"Car accident, yeah. I was fifteen, and me and my girlfriends decide to sneak into a club in Denver. A few rum and Cokes, step out to smoke, and these three fuckin' dickheads raped and beat the shit out of me, drove over my legs with a van. Doctor said the only reason I didn't bleed to death was the cold, froze the blood. It was real cold in Colorado. Nobody found me till morning."

"Oh, Penny . . ." Chloe doesn't know what else to say.

"Yeah. You got no idea. I fuckin' hate needles."

EVENTUALLY, FRANCIE REACHES JOHN in Los Angeles. Judging from Francie's side of the conversation, it takes some convincing for him to come back. Something he says makes Francie cry. She can barely stay in the room, flitting in and out, going for coffee, making calls.

"Maybe I should go out and look for a car seat? There's got to be a place somewhere close . . . ," Francie says as the lunch carts go by the open door.

"I'll go!" Penny offers, and for a brief moment, they all share a tentative laugh.

When the nurse helps Penny onto a bedpan, because she insists she's too weak to stand—"And I'm gonna pass right out on the floor and sue this fuckin' hospital!"—Chloe and Francie go into the hallway, perch awkwardly on the love seat. There is nothing for Chloe to say to her, nothing reassuring or positive, nothing at all.

"Vultures are circling already, huh?" It is Jason, jingling the buckles of his leather jacket. He tips his shaved head toward Francie because he is holding a huge teddy bear, the kind you buy from the street vendors on Burnside who sell fleece blankets with unicorns, buckets of roses, and these cheap oversize stuffed animals.

"We're just following the birth plan." Chloe forces the calm into her voice, looking from Jason to Francie. Sometimes she feels completely unqualified to do this job.

The pitocin is working; Penny's screams tear up and down the corridor. At four centimeters, she gets the epidural. It takes the anesthesiologist more than one try, and they are both cursing before it is over. Afterward, Penny falls asleep. Jason disappears again, Francie goes to visit the Novas, and Chloe finds a comfortable spot on the couch in the hallway lounge and closes her eyes.

Gift Shop

JASON

*I*t's easy to find her, look for a place to spend money, and there's Blondie. Jason takes a breath and pushes the glass door open, the bell jangling in his ears. She's at the card section, sideways to him, opening every single one of them, reading, then putting them back. Upstairs, his girl's writhing on the bed, nothing he can do about her pain, and she's down here fucking *browsing*. It's easy to picture her with a Starbucks in one hand, her foot jiggling one of those strollers that cost more than a month's rent, baby unattended. Jason liked the way the ancestors did it, *dikkinagun*, the way his aunt Selma-Wade carried her retard son for years, crisscrossed to her heart. But you'd have to be strong. He watches Blondie, a walking hunger strike, couldn't carry a gallon of milk, let alone a baby. Not like his Penny, strong.

Still, his eyes go to the crocodile purse dangling off Francie's elbow.

Easy, Jason tells himself. Just ask for what's yours. The ache in his back is a steady pulsing of pain, better if he keeps moving, so Jason circles the magazine rack, shaking his legs, thinking how to start.

The clerk, a folded-over granny with brown teeth, is watching him, sour-eyed, suspicious.

"Can I help you?"

Francie looks up, sees Jason, the card slips out of her hand, flutters to the ground.

"Jason! Is it time?"

"No manners? No 'nice to see you'?" He crosses the gift shop in three strides.

"No, I mean, yes, but I thought you were here because it's time."

"It's not. But I like to see that you're eager."

She bends down, her head level with his cock, as she picks up the greeting card.

"Congratulations on the birth of your son!" it says, a stick-figure baby in a diaper.

"I sure as shit hope that's not for Penny."

"No," she says, her voice shaking. She steps back, tucks the card into its envelope.

" 'Cause you're causing my girl a lot of pain. Nobody should have to go through what my Penny's gone through."

"I'm truly sorry." You know what? Bitch sounds like she might be.

"I can think of ways to ease that pain."

"Mmm, then I'll leave that to you." She looks him straight in his eyes, and even though she's skinny like a stick, he realizes she's green inside, won't snap easily.

He moves so he is blocking the way to the granny running the register. "You're not understanding me."

"I think I am," she says, backing away.

He doubles back, one giant stride of his to three of her trot-trot pony steps. He's making her nervous. He blocks the way again.

"In a big hurry to get to that baby, huh? Means an awful lot to you? Precious to you, right? Precious to us too. We have our rights, twenty-four hours. Rights to our own flesh and blood. Never know what might happen once he's born."

She swallows; a bobbing in the razor-thin lines of her throat skin.

"There are plenty of unwanted babies out there, waiting," she says, and pushes past him to the register, places the blue card carefully on the counter. "All of them precious, all of them wanting everything John and I have to give. You didn't think you were the only ones who chose us, did you?" She opens her wallet, thin with cash, stacked with plastic, and pays for the card, carefully zipping the change into a slit in the middle.

"Do you smoke, Jason?"

He makes a noise, and she asks for a pack of Marlboros, not his brand but he can taste them already.

"Here." She puts down a crisp twenty-dollar bill. "For my friend here," she tells the granny.

He picks up the cigarettes, the cellophane crinkling in his palm.

"Keep it; the change or anything else. That's all the money you'll see from me." She picks up the plastic bag with the card inside and starts to walk away. "Not that it matters now, if you're not going to sign. But just so you know," she tells him as she shoves open the glass door, the bell on the handle ringing wildly, "we would have given him the world."

12

No Intention of Living This Way

CHLOE

When the orderlies are wheeling the dinner trays, meat loaf with gravy that smells surprisingly good, down the hallway, Chloe calls Dan, who wants her to come home, then calls the agency, catches Judith before she leaves for the day.

"No baby yet. . . . Yeah, we've been here almost twenty-four hours. . . . John's catching a plane back from L.A., should be here sometime tonight. . . . Yes, I'll stay to the bitter end."

Chloe walks back toward Penny's room and is intercepted by Nurse Pat outside the curtain.

"I think the epidural isn't working," Pat tells her. "Anyway, I'm back to being a 'motherfucker,' so something's not right."

Then Pat's shift ends; her replacement is surly, anti-adoption. Chloe sends Francie home to rest, with a promise to call when they are getting ready to push. She goes to the gift shop and buys a toothbrush, unable to stand the way her teeth feel any longer. She is about to call Dan again when the new nurse finds her in the hallway and says, "You know, even vultures have to stop circling eventually." Chloe knows she got the line from Jason, that they're all riled up in there. Great. She snaps her phone closed.

"Pardon?"

"I hear you've been here for more than twenty-four hours. Maybe you should go home, *get some rest*." But she doesn't say it like she's concerned for Chloe's well-being.

"Yeah, well, I wish I could."

"You can't stop them from changing their minds. By law, they have twenty-four hours after the birth to change their minds. It's their right."

"Of course it is, and lots do. And this is my job. If my boss wouldn't jump down my throat, if I could go home and watch *Friends* and *ER* and drink wine with my fiancé, don't you think I would?"

"You don't make these things happen; God does. It's in God's hands now," the nurse says ominously. "You obviously don't have children." Later, these words will come back to haunt Chloe.

"What?" she says now, manners slipping.

"I said, you obviously don't have any children. You won't be able to do this job once you do."

"But I'm making a *family*," Chloe protests. She feels the exhaustion, the wear and tear of the last two days on her, a sandpaper burn behind her eyes. She sniffs furiously.

"Whatever you need to tell yourself to get to sleep at night, honey."

"Yeah, I'm familiar with things left in 'God's hands'!" Chloe replies.

WHEN CHLOE WAS TEN, her mother died of a brain tumor, shattering the sweet trio that had made up the Pinter family. There were only three slim months between diagnosis and her death on the Fourth of July. Chloe can still picture her father that night, silhouetted against the red explosions of light, the familiar swing of his simian arms as he walked across the baseball field to where Chloe sat on a soft tartan picnic blanket, shoulder to sunburned shoulder with her best friend. The day's humidity lingered so that when her father touched her arm, her skin felt wet, though she'd been out of the community pool for hours.

"I won the swim race for ten and under!" she crowed as they walked toward his car, her hand damp in his. She can remember how long it took to cross the parking lot, the flickering orange of the gooized overhead light, her stomach twisting at her father's silence, the steamy, tarry smell of the humidity-saturated blacktop. She knew before he said it.

"Your mother died this morning." Dr. Pinter opened the passenger side door for her. "It was peaceful, she didn't suffer, and I was"—his voice broke—"I was holding her hand when she went."

Chloe closed the car door and watched as her father collapsed against her side window, his long arms wrapped around his middle, hunched over, shaking.

When he got in the car next to her, she had pressed her knuckles to her mouth, hating the way the two of them didn't even use all the spaces of the front seat of the nine-passenger station wagon.

We're not a family anymore, she thought.

She said simply, "We need a smaller car."

"I'm doing something good. I'm making a family!" Chloe calls again after Penny's nurse, but the answer is just the disapproving squeak of her white clogs.

Chloe's cell phone rings. It is Dan, but all she can hear are lyrics from the Counting Crows song "Raining in Baltimore." Accompanied by a mournful accordion and sad, somber piano chords, Adam Duritz wails to her in his distinctive whine, *You get what you pay for / But I just had no intention of living this way.* There is a glitch in the CD, or perhaps Dan means it to, but the line is repeated, *I just had no intention of living this way.* And then he hangs up. Chloe has a sinking feeling that the message is in the final lines, a purposeful repetition—Dan had no intention of living "this way," as grown-ups, in Portland Heights, making the rent and grocery lists and dinners for their wallpapered breakfast nook. She could spend more time thinking about this, wondering what he wants from her, but she doesn't. She wraps the thin flannel blanket around her shoulders and lets his call go unreturned.

❧

IT IS JUST AFTER midnight. The McAdoos are home in their lovely, warm, clean bed while for the second night in a row Chloe is chasing sleep on the love seat in the seating area outside Penny's room. She wakes up with the sensation of being watched—Jason is sitting on the sofa opposite her, his blue/brown eyes staring.

"How are things going in there?" Chloe croaks, surprised by the scratchiness of her voice.

"I don't know how they're going to get that thing outta her. Doc just went in there now." He sounds anxious. "They're coming back, Francie and John?"

"Yeah, yes, why?" They had all agreed, around eleven, that nothing was happening, and that the McAdoos should go home and wait for a call. Chloe sits up, wide awake now. "Why?"

"You think they really want this kid?" Jason stretches out his legs, his enormous motorcycle boots thumping the floor, rubbing his face with his hands. The dragon claws on the backs of his hands dance as his veins roll.

"Of course they do. They've wanted a baby for years."

"Yeah, but you think they want *this* kid? A kid of some dumbass broke ex-con and his girl?"

"Jason," Chloe says gently; her heart aches for them.

"What if it grows up to be like me? My own blood dad liked to beat the shit outta me; I tried him so much. My own ma—"

"They have a lot to give a baby."

"Yeah. That's why we picked 'em. Figured at least with money, he'd have a chance. I hope you know this is hard—it's not like I don't want it. And Penny, you have no idea . . ." He doesn't finish.

"They have a lot of love too. They want this baby." Chloe is leaning forward. She can see the whole adoption as if she's lying on her back watching clouds on a windy day. This is the moment when it all becomes clear—"Oh, yeah, I *do* see a dolphin!"—or when the whole shape dissipates, turns into wispy streaks of white against blue.

"Yeah?" There is an animal wail from the room behind them. Jason jumps to his feet, the moment broken. "Then why the fuck ain't they here?" And then he slams into the room, Chloe standing uncertainly, before she decides not to follow.

Surly Nurse bustles out on her way to the nurses' station, fixes her beady eyes on Chloe.

"The baby's heart rate is dropping," she says, as though this is Chloe's fault. "Dr. Andrew's going to do a C. The dad's changing into scrubs now."

"Okay." Chloe checks her watch, reaches for her phone. "Thank you."

In the end, Chloe doesn't call the McAdoos. She could, could tell them hurry, it's time, jump in the car, but she knows they will miss it anyway. She waits because there might not be anything to miss. Chloe has seen so many adoptions disintegrate in those fateful seconds when the baby's first wails fill the room. If it is bad news, she can let them sleep, at least, before calling.

The minutes pass.

Then Jason is standing in front of her, mashing the paper mask and hat between his huge hands, and Chloe knows, just by the defeated way his shoulders sit on his body, the adoption will go through. *Thank god.*

"That them?" He nods at the phone in her lap.

"Pardon?"

"Did you call them?"

"They're on their way," she lies.

"Okay." He sighs, stumbles to sit down next to her, yanks the booties off his feet. "He's here."

13

No

JASON

Jason is sitting with his Pen afterward, waiting for her to wake up, her snores as steady as the tide, about to put him to sleep too, if he weren't so agitated, right foot jiggling. He rifles around the tray beside her bed, finds the foil-wrapped ibuprofen they left for when she woke, rips it open and gulps them down dry. His back is twanging, a looping rhythm of pain like a kiddie train set, down his back to his hip to his leg to his heel and back again clackety-clack. Forty minutes ago, he saw a doc up to his elbows in his girl's guts, lift out something bloody and purple, yowling, and he had closed his eyes like Penny's, let his head sink to the white sheet beside hers, the hiss of the air hose running into her mouth drowning out his son's first cries.

It's done. He doesn't want to see him, wants it to be over, never thought the plaster shoebox back in Southeast would feel like home, but he can't wait to get out of here, with the jittery lights and bossy women and Blondie and Chloe and the just-born son he will never know. As soon as she's better, he thinks, they're leaving this frozen city of bridges and buses and rain and fog. Mexico.

Then the nurse rolls in with a trolley, and inside it, Jesus, it's right here, he jumps up, backing toward the corner. In a white bundle of blankets, his son.

"Get out!" he yells, and Fatty gives him a raised eyebrow look, like *Don't you yell at me, you're in my world, mister.*

Jason has been thinking: Better that Penny never see him, that they both don't look at it. "Please. Take it out." His jaw pops in time with his back shocks.

"You have twenty-four hours," the nurse says. "When she wakes up, she needs to make her decision based on——"

"OUT!" Jason roars. "You as thick in the head as you are in the ass? We don't want him in here!" There is an ugly painting by the door, scrubby yellow sunflowers in a blue vase; he fixes his eyes on it, not wanting to look——

"No." It is Penny, behind him, more a moan than a word. "Nooooo." Her eyes open, and Jason plants himself between her and the plastic trolley. He grabs the edge with his hands, tugs it away from Fatty, his eyes fixed on the wilted sunflowers.

Then Chloe shows up, phone in hand.

"What's wrong——," she begins, and Fatty tries to get between them, but——

Umph! With a shove, Jason sends the trolley flying across the eight feet that separate them, but it has a bum wheel and veers, a wheel catching, and the bundle inside rolls, thumps against the side, tiny skull against thick plastic.

"No!" Penny's screaming behind him.

Chloe makes up the distance, grabs the edges, steadies it.

"I want it out of here!" Jason yells.

Fatty's over at the phone by the bed, lifting it to make a call.

"Stop." For as small as she is, Chloe can command a room, and Jason thinks of the best teacher he ever had, the third-grade substitute who read them *Charlie and the Chocolate Factory* in a scratchy, hypnotic whisper.

"It's okay. I'm going to put him over here," Chloe says quietly, the wheel on the box squeaking as she crosses with it behind Jason. "Over by the window, for now. And then"——he notices for the first time, underneath the dying sunflower painting, a thick stack of papers she has left on the chair by the door—"we have to talk."

Then it's Eager Beaver Blondie popping her head in the doorway, all clown makeup and gold jewelry, her eyelashes like smashed spiders, and she stage-whispers, "Is this a bad time? Have they signed?"

OREGON OPEN ADOPTION—*A place for all mothers*
FRANCESCA97201
Joined: 26 Jun 1998
Posts: 17270
Posted: Fri, Dec 1 2000 8:24 pm

HE IS HERE!!!!!

How many years has Francie waited to write those words?

Angus John McAdoo, born at 2:49 am December 1st, weight 9 lbs 15 oz, 22", by emergency C-section. While we were unable to be present for the delivery due to a problem with our CW's cell phone,

<insert one angry face, one eye roll>

we were able to hold him shortly afterwards. It was an incredible moment, John spouting poetry, the baby in my arms.

This was true: John *had* said something lovely while they were waiting, a paraphrase, "I always knew that at long last I would take this road, only yesterday I did not know it would be today." A beautiful sentiment, except that yesterday he *had* known, and he boarded the plane to Los Angeles anyway.

They are in bed, on their laptops, ice packs on John's calves, a bucket of champagne and two glasses on a tray in the bed between them.

They are keeping Angus for observation in the nursery. Apparently it is very common for C-section babies to inhale some fluids during the birth process, but they assure us he is healthy. John asked for a toxicology screen

to be done before we take him home. CW said she would speak to the pediatrician on staff. We have been assured by the agency that this mother did not use drugs after some early marijuana use that may or may not have occurred in the first trimester, but all my research shows that this is not much to worry about.

I was able to give the baby a bottle twice and he is a very good eater. He is already enormous; I think I will have to return many of the newborn-size clothes and diapers and go straight to 3 month! I am trying to choose an outfit to bring him home in—the one I had selected is never going to fit, LOL!

Looks: He is a handsome baby, lots of straight dark hair, and big hands and feet. I told John that the baby already looks a bit like him. Obviously there is no biological connection, but something, around the nose, the shape of his ears, maybe. Despite his genetic makeup, we think he looks almost white.

Does this sound racist? One comment from Eva, and she's paranoid now. Because she's not! It's John, really, the old Scot in him.

[BACKSPACE, DELETE]

In my profile photo he looks darker than he is, the lighting at the hospital is terrible, and there is a little lilt to the corners of his eyes, but it could just be swelling?

Anyway, he's a gorgeous baby and John even said he couldn't believe our good fortune, after everything we have been through.

There was a chance they would discharge the baby tonight but John requested that he stay in for one more night of observation, get our last good night of sleep, LOL.

This is only partially true: the other thing is, Jason and Penny haven't signed yet.

"It's a formality," Chloe Pinter had said. "A matter of time." But Francie knows—they have twenty-four hours.

It had been hard to leave the hospital, knowing that Jason and Penny were the ones down the hall from Angus John, his first night in the world, but the nurse had assured Francie she could come back for morning visiting hours.

"We'll save his eight a.m. bottle for you."

John has an urgent business trip to Asia that he postponed for this and he plans to leave tomorrow, so the next time I sign in, I will be doing so as a single mother! Don't be surprised if you don't hear from me for a few days!

<insert worried face>

Next to her, in their California king, John is typing on his laptop, the screen glowing blue on his glasses.

"I miss him!" she tells her husband, and he nods, pats her thigh, never taking his eyes off the keyboard. Francie takes a sip of luke-warm champagne.

I look forward to getting the baby home and feeling like he is *mine*

[BACKSPACE, DELETE]

***ours*. Though of course I am grateful to the birth parents for everything they have given us, I will feel better when they are no longer any part of our lives.**

She will not mention the gift shop, how after she called Jason's bluff, after she walked out on his second extortion attempt, she retched, just a little coffee and half a slice of Weight Watchers toast, into the water fountain around the corner.

It has been hard not to think of Jason—even in the hospital photo of Angus John she has scanned into her online profile, she sees the biological father in his face. Francie wonders how long it will be before she looks at him and he is simply Angus John, not a sum of his inherited parts.

As you know, by Oregon law an adoption can be contested for up to a year if they can prove duress. If BF leans on BM, it could get ugly later. He is probably physically abusive; BM is covered in scars, poor thing. He prob-

ably can't help it, you read about how pervasive it is in the Native American community, and he's part Apache. That sort of thing doesn't just disappear in a handful of generations.

Francie reads over her last few paragraphs.

[SELECT ALL, DELETE]

Her phone rings—Chloe Pinter on caller ID.

They've changed their mind.

"Hello?" Francie swallows, looks around the room for something to throw up in. The ice bucket? The ceramic wastebasket?

"Congratulations, Mom—they signed."

14

A Shepherd for the Lambs

PAUL

During morning rounds on the second of December Dr. Woo gives Eva the green light to go home later that afternoon. He writes her a prescription for painkillers and then, as an afterthought, checks the box that allows for refills. This makes Paul anxious—Eva's lovesick brother Magnus is flying up from L.A. to meet the baby, and the last thing they need in the house is a big supply of prescription drugs, but okay.

"One of the more serious repairs I've done in a while," Dr. Woo says, his hand on the door. "Make sure you use your sitz bath—I understand they really help with the pain."

Paul sits down next to Eva, inhaling deeply. The air feels effervescent, bubbly with hope. He breathes in again—his chest fills with a giddy weightlessness, breathlessness so powerful he struggles to breathe more shallowly, carefully.

"What's wrong with you?" Eva glances at him, and the millimeter that her eyebrows have arched means that she's more irritated than concerned. Paul has already seen their son make this face, and his heart lurched with recognition. He takes careful inventory of his feelings, his euphoria, the surreal bubbling, before he answers.

"I feel like, we're almost there. Like everything we have been working toward for so long is almost here."

"What are you talking about?" Eva says, a prickly artichoke hair more annoyed than before. "He *is* here."

"No, I know. But it doesn't feel like he's ours yet, like he still belongs to the nurses, until we sign out this afternoon. I'm trying to savor the moment."

Eva exhales, turns away from him, grimacing in pain. Wyeth starts to wriggle in his plastic aquarium, and Paul is the first to him, waving Eva to stay where she is. In the past thirty-nine hours, he has created a private little challenge for himself—get to the baby and settle him before his cries go from the pathetic "ahhh-ahhh" to the desperate "wah-wah-WAH, wah-wah-WAH" wail that drives Paul's blood pressure up. So far he is three for seven, not bad odds.

Paul unwraps the flannel hospital blanket and pulls the tabs on the gapping diaper. Wyeth's legs are skinny, as sinewy as a frog's, and he pumps them now as Paul assesses the situation. Yes, there is a dark smear, and it takes Paul three diapers and half a box of the dry tissue wipes they've given him to get the job done. By then, the baby's screaming, the kind that no amount of shoulder-bouncing will bring him back from.

"He's probably hungry, hon," Eva says as she unsnaps her hospital gown. Paul hands him over, determined not to lose the rush. They can both meet his needs, he thinks, as the baby latches on and sucks.

"That's my little barracuda," Paul murmurs, wedging himself on the bed by Eva's shoulder, one hand on the baby's swaddled bottom, the other in his wife's still-matted hair. He wants to feel something flowing between them all, wants his wife to look up at him with pride and adoration, but Eva is drifting back to sleep with Wyeth at her breast.

There is a knock, and Francie McAdoo pokes her head around the doorway; the car seat hitched over her skinny arm pulls her off balance, like it's full of bowling balls.

"Oh *how sweet!*" she stage-whispers, and Paul grits his teeth. Her thin blond hair looks wilted, her makeup overdone. "Aren't you the proudest papa?" and though he had been a moment earlier, the treacly way she says it makes him take his hand off Eva's hair.

"How's it going?" Paul asks. He wishes Eva would wake up, do the woman-to-woman social thing, but her head is lolling to the side, breathing deeply.

"Great!" Francie stops whispering. "The birth parents signed, thankfully. God knows what the birth father said to her, it was touch and go. But I just did my paperwork, so . . . he's ours."

"Congratulations," Paul says, and finds that he even means it. He glances in the car seat she has set on the chair by the window. Funny how her baby elicits a complete nonresponse from him. It is just . . . a baby. He wonders about this; what if this was his daughter Amber's baby? How long would it have been before he felt for her the way he feels for Wyeth? "Handsome little guy," he says, because he should.

"Thanks. They're discharging him now, but John's been back at the house on a conference call to Singapore, and he doesn't know how long he'll be . . ." She trails off, and Paul feels a stab of sympathy for her. "So, I hate to bother you, but I was wondering if there's any way you could give me a ride back to the Heights?"

"Sure." Paul eases himself off the bed. The baby has fallen asleep, his head rolling back like a regulation-size softball. "Just a second." Keeping one hand on the baby so he doesn't keep on rolling right on down Eva's stomach, Paul tugs free the front flap of Eva's gown.

"Looks like breast-feeding's going well," Francie says as Paul carefully covers Eva's giant white breast with its blue-veined tributaries. There is sharpness, bitterness, in Francie's voice, and Paul realizes she might be jealous, that for some women breast-feeding is a privilege, not a fact of life.

"Yes." Paul scoops the baby up adeptly, sliding a broad palm under Wyeth's head. He is wrapped like a Jesus in a Nativity—white swaddle, tiny peach-colored head, beatific face, so otherworldly, still half angel—and Paul's heart lurches again. When Wyeth opens his eyes, Paul is one step ahead of him, popping the hospital-supplied green plastic pacifier in his mouth. Francie is watching him, and it feels good to know that he's shining.

Then Eva wakes, and the two women lay the boys side by side on her bed, going over them like lionesses, trading compliments and observations.

"Look at this, does this look like eczema? Do you think I should try a soy-based formula?" Francie smooths Angus's dark curls straight with her narrow palm. "And look at this, he's got a dimple here, a bb-sized divot out of the back of his right ear. It's his mark."

"His what?" Eva asks.

"His mark, for identification. When I was a girl," Francie says, "a baby was kidnapped in our town. A little girl, six months old, and the scumbag who took her had a boy, an older boy, maybe twelve? He'd gotten him from someone else. He was keeping them in one of those raper vans, with no windows.

"A year later, the boy got out through the vent in the roof, led police back to the little girl. By this time, she was a year and a half old. They gave her back to the parents, who they thought were the parents, but the guy had cut off all her hair, and she was so much older they weren't sure if it was her. I remember watching it on the news and thinking, Doesn't a parent just know? So right away, first thing when I got Angus alone, I stripped him down and looked for something on him, something distinctive and permanent, so I would always know he was mine, if anything happened."

Together, they pore over Wyeth. Paul leans in.

"Oh, here!" Francie points with a polished pink nail. "I don't know if this will stay, but look at this triangle of bright blue in his left eye, right there, four o'clock."

Paul has had enough of this. Women are such crisis-mongers. How often does a baby get snatched? Paul wonders. He zips up his SuperNova Electric fleece and puts the Volvo keys in his pocket. Paul kisses Eva on the head, tucks Wyeth in her crook like a taquito, and promises to be back before they can miss him.

"All set?" he says.

"Ready!" Francie chirps, and he gallantly scoops up the car seat, surprised by its weight.

"I really appreciate this," Francie prattles as Paul swings the car seat slightly by the handle. Francie has two diaper bags over her bony shoulders, one fancy-schmancy one and the standard black hospital bag and a giant, ridiculous-looking stuffed animal under her other arm. She looks like a teenager lugging her boyfriend's winnings at the state fair. "John's *so* busy, there's this brewery in Singapore that wants to go into partnership on the Soaring Scotsman, and they're just hammering out all the details. I told John we have to go by the Chosen Child to sign his name on the documents this afternoon, and then believe it or not, he's on a plane out tonight . . ."

They wait for the elevator to arrive.

"I thought John was a computer guy."

"He was—he is, I mean; he consults and he's still on the board so he has to fly to California for that every few weeks, but this brewery is his baby."

Both their eyes drift to Angus, swinging along in the car seat between them.

In the parking garage, Paul opens the back of the Volvo so Francie can load the diaper bags and stuffed animal while he carefully buckles the car seat. He catches a whiff of cigarettes, and he can feel eyes on the back of his neck. Paul is not superstitious, but as he fumbles for the safety belt, he wonders . . . Could it be his father, somehow, a crossing between worlds, a visit from Paul Sr. as he becomes a father himself? It is something Eva would say, that him smelling his father's cigarettes and feeling a strong sense of being watched were signs, proof that Paul Sr. was still with them.

Shaken, Paul straightens up, looks over his shoulder. By the parking garage elevators there is a hulking, skinhead-type guy in a leather jacket pacing, jiggling his legs, smoking. *Of course*; Paul exhales. The man narrows his eyes at Paul, squares off, agitated. Paul walks quickly to the back of the Volvo and shuts it, puts his hand protectively on Francie's elbow as he hurries her around to her side of the car. Inside, he hits the lock, puts the car in reverse. In the rearview mirror, Paul sees that the man hasn't broken his gaze, is still studying them through an exhalation of smoke.

And then the baby starts screaming, a horrible ragged cry, and Paul turns his attention to driving, to shepherding Francie McAdoo and her new baby home.

15

Bar Talk

JASON

"Cute kid; sure he's yours?" Lisle asks as Jason puts the hospital Polaroid of Buddy carefully back in his wallet.

"What's that supposed to mean?" Jason feels like meat that has been pounded with a steel hammer, and here comes his brother with the salt and lemon juice.

"I'm just messing with you. The hair. You're going bald, and he's got a big ol' bushy fro like Grandpa Jack."

"I shave my head." Where the hell are the beers? Jason scans for the waitress.

"Cute kid," Lisle says again. "Fuckin' shame."

"It's just timing," Jason says.

"Fifty percent of life is timing," Lisle says, and Jason knows he pulled the number out of his ass, but still, he's trying. And he's buying the beers that can't come fast enough.

"They're keeping Pen looped," Jason says.

"It's better that way."

"Yeah." Jason stoops forward in his chair. Feels like his jacket is weighing him down, so tired he can't even sit upright.

"This your first kid?"

Jason nods, stretches his legs out under the table, trying to get where the fire-hot ache in his back doesn't make the one leg numb.

"We were set up too. Sort of even planned for it. At least, weren't trying not to have one."

Lisle nods.

"Penny was checking at the Sav-On, I was at the car wash, temporarily, and we had a place in Drain."

Lisle laughs like a donkey, hee-haw. "Drain?"

"Yeah, little town, south of Eugene, partway to the coast."

"What the fuck were you doing in Drain?"

"I told you, shithead! Working, making a living, doing what folks do."

"No, I mean, how'd you end up in a place called Drain?"

"Oh. We were on our way out to Coos Bay. I'd fucked up, did some things to make me an unwelcome citizen in the state of Wyoming, and a friend of Penny's from Casper was set up out that way, Coos Bay, talked up how beautiful and friendly it was. So we were on our way, last summer, seems like a hundred fucking years ago, had a little Ford, and the engine seized. Ended up in Drain, ended up pregnant, and then I get this genius idea, checks come to the old person who used to have our PO box. Blank checks, from one of those credit card companies. So I tell Penny . . ."

They are silent while the waitress sets down two sweating bottles of Coors in front of them and Lisle makes a circle in the air with his finger, says, "Keep 'em coming." Jason can see from her eyes on Lisle's ponytail and muddy jacket that they are not the usual customers of this bar, but it's close to the hospital. Jason glances around for a clock.

"Brandi said she might be able to get me a job up there." Jason jerks his head out the bar window south toward Portland Heights, the rich neighborhood where Brandi pumps gas.

"Yeah, I don't know." Lisle's eyes drift away from his; his hand wraps around the neck of his bottle. "You don't have any references, man."

"You'd do it."

"But I'm your brother."

They tilt their beers.

"I know a guy who does hardwood installs," Lisle says. "I could hook you up with him."

"Take a lead pipe to my back while you're at it. I can't be on my hands and knees hammering in floors all day. Back is fucked as it is."

Lisle nods—they'd been logging together that summer with their old man when Jason fell. Lisle had half carried him the quarter mile in the rain to the access road, tried to crack him up the whole two hour ambulance ride when they thought he'd be paralyzed.

"Got anything else?" Jason doesn't look at Lisle when he says it.

"You don't have the best track record, J."

"It's not the worst. I'm clean, I don't drink." Lisle does his hee-haw laugh as Jason pauses to slug from his beer. "Much. These are special circumstances."

"Penny said last job, you punched out the boss on the road crew."

Bitch. "I can't work a road crew."

"And no logging, no 'fucking construction,' no car wash, no landscaping. I've heard the list."

"I can't be the guy who stands out there freezing my balls off turning the sign for all the gear-jamming aces going places. I used to be the guy who sprayed eighteen wheels of gravel on those poor fuckers."

Lisle looks at his watch. "I've got to go get Brandi."

Jason's stomach feels hollowed out, like beer bubbling at the bottom of an empty jug. He burps into his fist, thinks he should order a burger, quickly, since Lisle will pick up the tab, today of all days.

"What about you—anyone hiring out your way?" Lisle had just started work for a bridge engineering company near Salem, hired the first day he showed up with his hard hat and harness. Must be fucking nice.

"Man," Lisle says, wiping his hand down his face, and Jason knows what's coming. "I told you about Nick. Nobody with a record. Policy."

"Fucking discrimination. I might as well be back on the inside."

"We're hanging from steel cables a hundred feet up in pissing-down rain—there's a trust that's got to be built. A team's only as good as its weakest link."

"Chain," Jason spits at his prick of a brother.

"What?"

"The word is chain. Or team and player. Get it right." *Put it on a fucking poster and shove it up your ass.* Jason goes to get up, and his back twangs, a rod of fire down his leg to his boot; he slumps back into his chair.

"Sorry, man. About today," Lisle says.

Jason can feel Penny's arms around his neck this morning, a strangling chokehold, begging him not to make her sign those papers.

"He's our own flesh *and blood!*"

And Chloe Pinter in her tight little suit hustling those fuckheads out of the room, the panic look in Francie's eyes, darting to Jason and Penny like a rabbit's, and over to the baby in the plastic pushcart under the window. Francie didn't want to leave it behind, and somehow, that had been a spit-drop of comfort to him.

"Shhh, baby"—he had turned back to Penny, his hands holding her face, her hair prickling under his palms—"shhh." He put his lips to her ear and whispered things he won't think about now, everything she deserved.

Then Little Miss Agency Busybody back with her folder and her pens and her purse that held nothing. "Sorry to interrupt," she was whispering as if someone was dying or sleeping, when they could both hear the baby rustling, shuffling around in his plastic box. "If you just need time to grieve, that's fine, but there can't be any duress." She dumbed it down for him then. "Penny has to sign of her own free will."

Penny looked at him, her eyes red-veined like road maps, and he had a flash, like he sometimes got, of Penny-the-Girl when those three fuckheads in Denver raped her and beat her and drove over her, and his throat closed and he wanted to roar, to rage against all of it, but instead he swallowed and said carefully, "We're grieving. Is there a time limit?"

"Not at all," Chloe Pinter said, and her face went slack with relief; probably her ass was on the line if things fell apart here. If his own guts weren't on fire, maybe he could sympathize. After she closed the door, Jason had taken a chance, handing Penny the pen. It was for the best, for now.

"I'm going to step out now," he'd said, not knowing what would happen, the baby under the window growing so large he had to hold his head sideways not to see it as he grabbed the plastic side and pulled it along behind him, stumbling out of the room. He'd abandoned it in the hallway, fallen into the shorty couch outside her room, eyes stinging. That's when Chloe Pinter put her arms around him, and he cried into her neck that smelled like honeysuckle, and she didn't fuck it up by saying anything.

"THEY'RE GOING TO BE sorry," Jason accidentally thinks out loud, and it brings him back, to the bar, to the beer, to now.

"Who?" Lisle snorts, like Jason's nobody to be afraid of. He doesn't know the half of it.

"All of them." But Jason isn't sure who he means. He thinks about Chloe shoving paper after paper in front of them, the address in Portland Heights he committed to memory, about the shiny silver Volvo Cross Country with his son inside, Blondie's alligator purse, *Keep the change; that's all you'll ever see from me.* "All of them."

"Brandi's had an abortion, back in August," Lisle says, out of nowhere.

"Your kid?"

"So she says."

Jason nods, drains his third beer. It's good not to feel his leg or his back anymore.

"Can't really picture either of us with a . . ." Lisle can't even say it.

"Guess not." But Jason thinks of the promises he made to Penny this afternoon, *hundreds of babies.* And he thinks, why not? Why the fuck not him? Who says he doesn't deserve his shot at happily ever after? The states of Washington, Oregon, and Wyoming? Lisle's fuckhead of a boss? Chloe Pinter and her piles of papers?

"I should go." Lisle stands, and Jason jumps up with him, swinging his leg out to the side so that it won't jack his back—no way he's getting stiffed with this check and no ride home. "Oh." Lisle smiles, but you can see through him like a cheap envelope, and he sits again. "Right; the bill." He says it smugly, and signals to the waitress as he peels a twenty and ten off a thick wad of bills, folds his wallet back in half like a fat roast beef sandwich. Jason knows the exact contents of his own wallet—eight soft, crumpled singles, the change from the smokes in the gift shop, a receipt for five dollars and nineteen cents, Snapple peach tea and newspaper in the hospital cafeteria, and the photo of Buddy.

"You giving me a ride?" Jason hates the need in his voice.

"Not sleeping up there?" Lisle nods his head toward the hospital. This afternoon with Penny had been like his time in the Clallam County facility with the new guy bawling and moaning into his pillow all night, the pain of Initiation. Her pain, body and mind, nothing he can do about it. Is it even his fault?

Did he blow it? Jason has been wondering this all day. In the gift shop, had Blondie's hands had the shakes when she picked up her wallet? He was worn down, that's all. So fucking tired he couldn't think right. Tomorrow, he'll make his plan. They'll all be sorry.

"What are you doing?" Jason asks his brother.

"Enh," Lisle says, winking at the waitress as they leave, "Brandi wants to go to this club. Probably blow a couple hundred bucks on cristy and drinks, and when we get home, she'll ride me like a pony." Lisle grins. "For a change."

That sounds about perfect to Jason. Instead, he and his brother part ways, and Jason walks down NW 22nd to the brick building. Jason squints up at it, swaying from the beers. Five stories up, his son entered a world where he was not unwanted. It was just a matter of timing.

16

Paperwork

CHLOE

Chloe has been home for one hour—enough time to shower, change, and get into a door-slamming fight with Dan— before she is called into the agency office in Troutdale to sign the paperwork with John McAdoo before he leaves for Singapore. Driving east, away from the city, late afternoon on a Friday is woefully slow, but the Cherokee's wheels find the grooves in the highway, and Chloe can almost rest her eyes as her car shimmies, the setting sun a sparkle in her rearview mirror.

"They either need to pay you more or quit acting like they own you!" Dan had huffed when Chloe, wrapped in a towel, took the call to come in to work.

"It's flextime. It's supposed to work better for everyone involved. Babies don't always come during the workweek."

"Maybe you should take one of the desk jobs, like that chick Casey. She sounded pretty nine-to-five, and we'd at least get to travel. I miss that."

"Casey runs the China program. She has to go there twice a year to escort families. I like this better."

"Oh, me too! I love seeing my girlfriend for five minutes every week."

The slam of their heavy front door was the perfect reply. Sometimes, she thinks, they don't need to worry about setting a wedding date.

Dan's ring, the fake ring, lists to the side on her left finger, catching the late-afternoon light. It wasn't really an engagement, more a promise of a promise, an understanding that when he can get it together, he wants her to be the woman by his side.

And he will, Chloe thinks. Dan has already grown so much in the years they have been together, morphing from a going-nowhere Euro sports bum back to the States, to the trappings, the vestiges of a life that is more familiar to Chloe: a house in a fabulous neighborhood (albeit a rental), a Smith & Hawken doormat, dinners and wine together, a shared existence, an adult existence. It was not, Chloe thought, that she and Dan *had* to sit down to eat, as Chloe and Dr. Pinter had done every night, but really, he's nearly thirty. It's certainly time that they act like the grown-ups they are becoming, that Dan swears he wants to be.

She has replayed a conversation they have had so many times that if it were on cassette, it would have worn out by now. It was Spain, the first year they met. Chloe and Dan, his surf buddies Kurt and Paolo, sitting down to a steaming cauldron of paella at the Intercontinental Café in Tarifa on American Thanksgiving. In the copper pan, the shrimp were still intact, beady eyes staring, legs dangling. Chloe, Dan, and Kurt all American expats, celebrating their holiday without the traditional turkey and trimmings; local Paolo a fascinated observer, trying to understand the holiday.

"So what do you do now? If this were Thanksgiving in America, the meal is on the table, your giant turkey and your what? What else?"

Kurt and Dan and Chloe debated for several minutes the absolute essentials of Thanksgiving dinner. Did you have to have green bean casserole with the crispy onions? Were roasted pureed chestnuts really worth the effort? Sweet potatoes with or without Marshmallow Fluff? Didn't everyone have some sort of a Jell-O salad?

"Well, obviously there are variations," Chloe had said. She was wearing a baby-doll sundress and her red Hot Stick sweatshirt with black hiking boots. Her hair was wild with the wind that blew up through the narrow streets. Dan tucked a strand back out of her eyes, his gaze warm on her face, mixing with the Chianti flush as she talked. "But then you go around and say what you are thankful for. Actually, we wrote it on these little paper leaves my mother had cut out, and she and I would go collect a branch, make a Thanksgiving tree, and somehow get it to stand up straight on the table. It was always a bit of an engineering trick, getting it to stand up as we got bigger and bigger branches each year. . . ."

Chloe saw Kurt's attention drifting; he was pouring himself more wine from the decanter, amber eyes roving the café for someone more interesting than her.

"Heh," Kurt snorted. "We chowed down, popped some beers, and watched the Bowl game. Then had some pumpkin pie."

"Oh yeah, pumpkin pie!" Dan chimed in, his hand massaging Chloe's shoulder. They shared a look; it was only recently that Chloe had told him how much holidays made her miss her mother.

"This is fascinating." Paolo's shining grin passed from face to face. "So many traditions, but so different."

Dan kept rubbing Chloe's shoulder until he realized they were all waiting for his version of the holiday.

"Oh, my mom's a caterer. She was always working, so we never celebrated on the actual day. We'd feast on ridiculous amounts of leftovers on Black Friday."

"Hmm." Paolo sipped his beer. He was the only Spaniard they knew who refused red wine, which he insisted would stain his teeth. "I think I like Chloe's version best. Let us play her way. How do we begin?"

"Okay, it started with my dad. He'd say the grace, the blessing on the food."

Everyone's eyes drifted to Dan, sitting at what would be the head of the table.

"Father—" Paolo's eyes twinkled. He reached for Chloe and Kurt's hands. "In my family," he said, "we hold hands for the *bendición*."

"Yes, Father, lead us in the blessing," Kurt said, and then he stuck out his tongue at Chloe. When she did it back, he reached across the table and smacked Chloe across the cheek, wailing, "She started it!"

"Did not!" Chloe said, confused but a shade pleased that Kurt's obnoxiousness didn't exclude her, for once.

"Oooh, Daddy's going to lay the smackdown!" Paolo laughed, always trying out jargon in his thick accent.

"That's exactly the kind of dad Pretty Boy will be too," Kurt said, dropping their hands and reaching for the large wooden serving spoon resting beside the steaming paella. " 'Do you want the belt or the switch, son? Don't let me catch you smoking all my weed again, you hear?' "

Chloe had laughed along with Kurt, serving herself some of the rice, avoiding the staring shrimp.

"No, I won't."

She turned to Dan, who was not digging in with the rest of them.

"I won't. I'm going to be a good father. That is the one thing I won't fuck up. I'm going to be a good father," he repeated quietly, for Chloe only, their eyes locked.

"You don't know that." Kurt split the spine-shell of a shrimp with the pad of his thumb, tearing off the exoskeleton and legs in one jerk. In Honolulu, Dan has told her, there is an exotic dancer with an eleven-year-old girl named Leila, Kurt's daughter. Kurt's parents send money on his behalf, a carton of gifts at Christmas.

"No, I do. Because my dad was a shithead." Dan reached for the spoon, put some food on his plate. "I'm going to be a good father, and I picked my girl Chloe here because I could just tell, she's a nurturer. Look how well she takes care of me."

"All of Tarifa knows how well she takes care of you," Kurt said, his continued juvenile ribbing from the one night he had crashed on the couch at Chloe's, and Dan had let out the softest of sighs while they were trying to pull off the silent fuck. Kurt never missed a chance to bring it up.

And the moment was gone, but for Chloe, never forgotten. She filed this conversation away and broke it out, polishing it whenever she found herself wondering what their future held. *Dan would be a good father.*

Inside the agency, it is mayhem. Judith and her husband, Ken, and most of their nine adopted children are jostling through the narrow reception area, fluxing in and out of the conference room, where three bottles of Kristian Regale sparkling cider and two of Asti Spumante are open. A two-pound bag of peanut M&M's is spilled out on the large fake wood table where they usually hold staff meetings, where Chloe was planning to sign paperwork with the McAdoos.

"Chloe!" Kenneth calls, his glassy, taxidermied-weasel eyes twinkling in that way middle-aged men who don't normally drink get when suddenly, at the odd wedding reception or holiday party, they do.

"What's all this?" Chloe gestures around the office, where Leon, Judith and Ken's Guatemalan son, is photocopying his cherubic profile. Judith is hugging Beverly in the reception area, adjacent to the large room of international program cubicles. Casey has Snoop Doggy Dog on her tinny desktop speakers and is dancing with Ayisha, the Duvalls' five-year-old, in her arms.

"We got Marshall Islands approval! The agency can start placements in January. Judith has Beverly making tickets for our first group now."

"Oh, Ken, that's great news. Congratulations."

"Thank you." He beams, patting his paunch absently, as though he has been congratulated on a pregnancy. "What are you doing here this late on a Friday?"

"I have to do paperwork with John and Francie McAdoo. Their birth parents just signed."

"Oh." He looks past her as Judith bursts into the reception area, her arm around Beverly's narrow shoulders.

"Did he tell you? Marshall Islands!"

"It's wonderful," Chloe says, looking past them to the conference room. Leon and Ayisha are on their stomachs on the table, making V-shaped shovels out of their hands and plowing M&M's into their mouths. "Congratulations."

"So, birth mother signed?" Judith says blandly, as though she hasn't been barking at Chloe every hour the past two days about making sure the McAdoo adoption goes through.

"Yes, this afternoon. Can I get one of you to notarize?"

Judith has the gall to sigh. "I'll send Casey up before she goes home. Beverly really deserves to celebrate."

"Can't I use the conference room?" It is where they always sign paperwork. All of their eyes converge on the open doorway just as Ayisha and Leon, squabbling over a large bottle of bubbly, tip it over on the table.

"Never mind," Chloe says. "They can come up to my office."

Upstairs, in her haven, she finds Marius, the Duvalls' Romanian son, curled up on her couch, stimming, flicking his fingers in front of his eyes, while Chien is coloring devil's horns and fangs on every model in the December issue of *Elegant Bride* Chloe had tucked behind the sofa cushion.

"Chien!" she yells, snatching it away. Chastened, Chien grabs Marius's hand, jerking him off the couch like a rag doll, and they are both clattering down the stairs like horses on a trailer ramp.

Her cell phone rings, and she grabs it, hoping it is Dan.

"Hello?"

Long silence, but in the background, she can hear the bustle of people, and someone paging Dr. West. Great—a hospital call the day after an adoption. She knows who is on the other end of the line. There are things she should say now; at the very least she should refer them to the agency's grief counselor.

"Penny?" she says instead. "Jason?"

No answer.

Chloe waits a moment, then presses End and folds her phone in half.

When it rings again, it is Dan, and Chloe can't help but smile. Even if they have just argued, she still hopes every phone call is his.

"Hey."

"Hey." His voice is gravelly, but he draws that syllable out like honey over granola. "I'm sorry about earlier. I didn't mean for you to leave."

There is a long silence.

"I think I have SAD," Dan says soberly.

"What?"

"Seasonal affective disorder. I think I'm depressed because of the weather here."

Chloe doesn't answer, turning on her computer and printer.

"Or it might be SRS," he says.

"SR-what?"

"Sperm retention syndrome. I miss you. I'm sorry I'm being such a dick these days. I'm working on a plan to make it better, to be better. You'll see. Are you coming home soon?"

"They're not even here yet. God, I'm so tired of being the agency's redheaded stepchild. My program's application fees pay all of their salaries when these foreign governments get finicky and shut down their approvals. Guatemala just closed down for six months! And I'm in here on a freaking Friday night, taking care of their cash-cow client—"

Her office intercom buzzes, amplifying the noise downstairs that had been partly muffled through the wooden floorboards.

"Chloe, Casey's on her way up," Beverly drones.

"I've got to go."

"Hurry home. I want to talk to you, and I have plans. . . ." There is something delightfully wicked in his tone.

A flurry of feet on the stairs, Casey's clogs, and she appears in the doorway. "Hey. Beverly sent me up with your most recent press clippings." She waves a handful of computer printouts from the message boards. These boards are not supposed to be read by agencies; they are for waiting families to share information and experiences, grief and joy. But every morning, Judith has Beverly and Casey cull all the open adoption boards searching for mention of the agency, her own system of marketing research follow-up.

"Soooooo"—Casey scans the papers in her hand—"Angie still raves about the famous Chloe Pinter when a newbie asked about the domestic program at the Chosen Child on the Oregon Open."

"That's it?" Chloe asks. Judith won't be happy.

"Yeah, one domestic newbie query today." Casey plops down on Chloe's couch.

"God, I just bet she and Ken come back from Marshall Islands with another kid." She crosses her legs in worn brown corduroys, jiggles her clogs. Casey's job is at her desk, receiving dossiers and referrals for the China program; some weeks she wears the same outfit days in a row.

"Really? I thought they were done."

"You'd think. Nine kids is e-freaking-nough. But new program, they've got to bring home a souvenir. It's so retarded. How about some attention for the ones they've got? Marius is at my keyboard playing Pong again. Poor kid."

Marius is the Duvalls' third son, eleven years old, autistic, from an orphanage in Brasov. Judith and Ken live in a sagging Victorian a few blocks from the agency. At least half of their nine adopted children are being "homeschooled," which translates into underfoot at the agency, coloring on the walls of the conference room or using up all the cone cups at the watercooler.

"You know why they keep adopting all these kids, don't you?" Casey leans forward, lowers her voice. "Judith had an abortion, back when they were in college. She was in law school, and Ken was getting his master's, and he made her have one, and it wrecked her so she couldn't get pregnant. So now they're so riddled with guilt that they go running all over the world adopting orphans. It's really pretty sad."

"Wow," Chloe says flatly. She has heard this before, from Beverly, after too many mai tais at the company picnic, only in that version, they had placed a kid of their own for adoption. Meaningless gossip.

"I guess anyone working in this business has to have some kind of issues. Look at you: Your mom dies, only child, you lost your sense of family, so you have to run around making 'happily ever after' for everyone else."

"It's really not that simple," Chloe begins.

Casey rips open a mini bag of Funyuns. Every two weeks she brings in a jumbo case of snack packs, the kind you put in a child's lunchbox, and parks it by her desk, tearing into bag after bag of Cheetos and Doritos. Her thighs spread the wale of her brown cords wide. She tosses a few onion crisps into her mouth and misses. She reaches down to pick them up off the carpet and spies the corner of Chloe's bridal magazine.

"What's this?" She pulls it out. "Naughty-naughty!" And then in the same breath, "God, what I wouldn't give for the upstairs office! Not that I'd want your job—thank you very much." Casey munches on Funyuns, flipping through the pages of Chloe's *Modern Bride*. "They offered it to me, after they fired Marcy, and I was like, *noooo!* But this, this is what you do up here all day?" She waves the magazine. "Pretty freaking cushy."

Yes, Chloe thinks, I just slept on a hospital love seat for the past two nights for eleven dollars an hour. Cushy.

Dan being her closest friend, her only Portland friend, really, Chloe feels out of practice, off balance, when Casey is around. She's like the brash, dangerous older sister Chloe cannot trust. Casey stands up and surveys the room again, her eyes narrowed. She crumples her foil bag of Funyuns, tosses it in Chloe's trash can. It stinks up her office; Chloe switches to breathing through her mouth.

"It's nice up here," Casey says thoughtfully. "Private. You have good Internet?"

Chloe's intercom beeps again—"The McAdoos are here"—and Chloe can't wait to get this over with.

Downstairs, John and Francie McAdoo stand at the doorway like underclassmen at the senior dance, unsure of their place.

"Hey there," Chloe says, holding on to the banister as she swings into the entry. A crumpled ball of paper sails past her head, thrown from one of the Duvall kids in Beverly's office. The international staff peer through the arched doorway. Judith has the phone between her ear and shoulder, sipping from a plastic cup of champagne. She makes eye contact with the McAdoos and coolly raises her glass to them. Ken is on the phone at his desk too, his cheeks flushed, and they can hear him saying, "Yes, thank you, this has been a long time coming. We're very pleased."

Casey's speakers are playing the ubiquitous "Mambo Number 5," and Maria is doing the jitterbug with Chien.

"I'm sorry," Chloe says to the McAdoos. "Celebrating. We're all a little excited here."

John McAdoo winces expectantly as he straightens his gimp leg, puts a tentative arm around Francie. She swivels her wrist so the car seat she is carrying faces out into the living room, reaching in to pull the blanket back to show the baby off.

Oh no. Chloe realizes that they think, that they believe, that all of this is for them, for John and Francie and their domestic baby. *A long time coming.*

Quickly, she mumbles something about the Marshall Islands and "so much good news in one day!" and hustles them upstairs to her office to sign the paperwork.

OREGON OPEN ADOPTION—*A place for all mothers*
FRANCESCA97201
Joined: 26 Jun 1998
Posts: 17271
Posted: Fri, Dec 2 2000 10:24 pm
Post Subject: (45233 of 45258)

Thank you, ladies, for all the congrats! I am home, a single mother LOL!!!
  DH is somewhere over the Pacific—

She remembers this evening, the parking lot behind the adoption agency. The sky turning pewter, and somewhere, someone in
Troutdale burning leaves. The smoky scent, the charcoal sky, were
hallmarks of Oregon autumn, so different from where she grew up in
Florida, where the only change was ten degrees, more or less rain and
mosquitoes.

John had stopped as the driver of the shiny black town car held
the door for him, lifted his hand to her, a wave. She jerked her head
forward, a nod to show, yes, she saw him, but her hands were clutching the handle of the bulky new car seat—god, how did anyone carry
those things! Why did everything have to be so goddamn *safe*? Didn't
she and her brother survive, childhood years spent astride Aunt
Helen's lap behind the wheel of that boat of a Buick? It's a conspiracy,
devised by the car seat people to prey on the anxiety of new parents.
Francie fell victim too, top-of-the-line car seat, highest safety rating,
two hundred and thirty-nine dollars. It's probably as good as the
fifty-dollar one, but you never know. And her SUV is a Mercedes—
a German-engineered tank. For all the atrocities of the Holocaust,
nobody can say the Germans don't make a hell of a good luxury car.

A sudden question mark: Had John kissed her under the cover of the agency porch? Funny how the kiss of someone can be so many things; initially anticipated, then carefully analyzed, later expected, and finally overlooked. She remembers that John did reach down and run a hand over Angus's blue-capped head, and that she had thought this was a good thing. This is the relationship she is cheerleading, breaking out her pom-poms for now.

My baby

My *baby*!

is asleep, swaddled in his Pottery Barn crib in his perfect nursery across the hall. He is an angel, an excellent sleeper. I am the luckiest woman on earth!!!!

Back when she turned thirty-five, before she met John, Francie had boldly spouted (after three appletinis on a girls' night out), "If I'm not married and knocked up by thirty-nine, I'm looking into sperm donors and single parenthood." But it was just something she said, she didn't really believe it could happen. But now here is the poor baby (Angus! still not 100 percent on John's name choice), who in the course of two days and sixty-two pages of legal documentation has gone from having four possible parents to a single mother.

OREGON OPEN ADOPTION—*A place for all mothers*
FRANCESCA97201
Joined:　　26 Jun 1998
Posts:　　17272
Posted:　　Sat, Dec 3 2000 2:37 am

So much for my first night—he's been crying over an hour. Help!

Typing with one hand is nearly impossible, pathetically slow. Francie stands up again, pacing, the baby cradled, jiggling, her arms throbbing but it gets worse, louder, if she puts him down. Top-of-the-line swing and bouncy seat? Two hundred and sixty-five dollars wasted—he hates them!

"Shhh, shhh, SHHH!"

She knows the dimensions of the nursery, eighteen by twenty-four, but it feels like a jail cell as she does her forty-third lap; the three dormered windows that usually display the verdant view are now showing nothing but close darkness. God, she's exhausted. John's return ticket is eight days away, but she knows there is always one more meeting, a tour of the brewery, a potential distributor; he never flies home on his original itinerary date.

Then, mercifully, as suddenly as he began, the baby stops, staring up at her with wide eyes, unblinking. Francie freezes, every muscle twitching.

"So," she says in a low voice, strange to be talking to someone who can't understand her. "So, it's just you and me. Just the two of us, kiddo." She sounds completely ridiculous. Has she ever used that word in her life? And then it comes back to her: Francine, her mother's mother who she was named after (because she is not a Francesca as she pretends), Francine, the Florida diner waitress with orange hair and a pocket full of butterscotches, who died of emphysema when Francie was twelve, used to call her that. "Kiddo," she tries it again. "Just you and me."

OREGON OPEN ADOPTION—*A place for all mothers*
FRANCESCA97201
Joined: 26 Jun 1998
Posts: 17273
Posted: Sat, Dec 3 2000 4:22 am

Up again. Crying. Calling the hospital to find out what is wrong with him.

OREGON OPEN ADOPTION—*A place for all mothers*
FRANCESCA97201
Joined: 26 Jun 1998
Posts: 17274
Posted: Sat, Dec 3 2000 6:32 am

Sunrise. Baby sleeping. Coffee.

OREGON OPEN ADOPTION—*A place for all mothers*
FRANCESCA97201
Joined: 26 Jun 1998
Posts: 17275
Posted: Sat, Dec 3 2000 8:19 am

Hospital calling back woke baby. Crying. Outraged.

Thank you so much,

Let them interpret this however they want!

Angie and ELLE and StellaRose'sMommy, for your sympathies, soothing suggestions and sentiments that baby's crying might be "normal newborn behavior," but I can assure you it is NOT. After threatening to speak to her superior, I got the nurse on the L&D ward of Good Samaritan to pull the baby's file for an answer to his tortured crying. And now I have one: my baby is suffering from withdrawal, nicotine!

<insert ten steaming furious faces>

CW lied to us, concealed the information that BM smoked while pregnant!!!!

Surprise, CW is not answering her phone! She got what she wanted from me, $$$ and now

Francie stops, reads the last sentence.

[BACKSPACE, DELETE]

He drank one 4 oz bottle and is asleep in the swing. Off to research nicotine withdrawal.

Francie opens a new browser window, goes to check her history to find an article titled "Prenatal Substance Abuse—The Effect on the Fetus."

She had just looked at it that morning, was showing it to John to reassure him about the health of their baby. The history has been cleared. Her entire history, cleared. John must have done it, but he was only on her laptop for a few minutes. "Need to check my flight status," he'd said, and Francie had gone to inventory the new diaper bag.

She feels a prickle of sweat underneath her cashmere shell sweater. Why would he clear the history?

Francie gets up and crosses the room to gaze at the baby, who has been awake for ten of the last fourteen hours, crying for three and a half of those. Her biceps throb, her lower back aches, her eyes burn. Somewhere in this city, in the rosy dawn, there is a woman who is mourning his loss, who howled as Chloe Pinter carried him off the ward to the room where Francie would sign her documents.

In the early-morning light, Francie wills herself to feel more for this unhappy baby (Angus! she thinks, his name is Angus!), and there is a flutter, a word that rises up in her chest: *mine.*

17

Monday, Monday

CHLOE

Dan walks into the kitchen Monday morning as Chloe is calling the office answering service, letting them know she will be using her flextime from the McAdoo adoption and staying home, but they can call if needed. She has tea brewing and a stack of bridal magazines, a deliciously empty morning stretching out ahead of her.

"Why do you do that? You basically gave her permission to call you at home." Dan startles her, appearing in the doorway in nothing but his dark blue track pants. "She shouldn't call you at home when you're using flextime. Eleven bucks an hour—I'd make more than that at the car wash."

Then why don't you? she wonders.

A few months ago, before he got the job at the bike shop, she had asked Dan why he didn't try modeling again, and he had said simply, "It takes a certain type of man to be a model." End of conversation.

She looks at the clock on the microwave. "Not going in today?"

Dan fakes a yawn, sits at the table in the breakfast nook, flips through the paper to uncover the sports section. "I told you about that," he says vaguely.

"About what?"

Dan doesn't answer.

"Babe?"

Dan looks up. There is a flush on his cheeks, the boy whose mother is brandishing the *Playboy* she found under his bed. "Sorry, what, babe?"

"Work. What's going on?" She feels emboldened by his blush, his darting eyes. She places her hand over his newspaper, her left hand, the one with the cubic zirconia winking in the weak morning light.

He sighs. "Look, I've wanted to talk to you about this for a while. This whole Portland thing. It's not really working out for me."

Chloe feels a rush of adrenaline, fight or flight, flooding her extremities. The hand on the newspaper shakes. She brings it back to her lap.

"I mean, I know you love it here, and you're crazy about your job, but I'm just not cut out for this. I need to be closer to the world of extreme sports, and I've found something really cutting-edge, really—"

"Wait a minute." Chloe's voice grows stronger. "We chose Portland because of its proximity to a huge variety of extreme sports. You've got the gorge, the coast, Mount Hood, I don't know what more you want."

"Hear me out." Dan squares his shoulders. "The boys from Tarifa have something we're looking into, and it's in the States, so it works for your career and everything. Have you ever heard of kiteboarding?"

"Where is it?"

"It's like windsurfing, but so much better. You're riding this thing that looks like a wakeboard, like a snowboard, and you're attached to a giant, inflated kite, a wing, that's like thirty meters above your head, so the wind is much cleaner, less gusty up there. It's a much better ride, and it's totally new, cutting-edge. I've seen videos where guys are catching huge air, like *fifty feet* of air. If we could get into it now, become sponsored riders, a distributorship in Maui, start our own kite surf shop, the boys and I could teach lessons, maybe you could do something with horses again, and we'd be back to the ocean, back to our old life . . ."

"Oh, honey, *Hawaii?*" Chloe looks out the window. It is starting to rain, tiny silver pellets zinging against the glass, pooling in the last brown leaves of the rhododendron outside.

Dan deflates, just a little. "Yeah. It's where it's at. I've been look-ing into this for a while."

"But my job, the birth mothers? It's so expensive, so far away."

"It would be the U.S., so no work permits. We've already got a business plan, the guys and me—hang on, let me get my laptop."

Chloe sinks back into the ladderback of her chair. She picks up her tea, sips. Hawaii? Above her, she can hear Dan thumping down the stairs, and he comes back with his laptop. He squeezes her to his side, puts it down on the table, kisses the top of her head.

"It's just warming up, babe, hang on." He rubs her shoulders vigor-ously.

Chloe puts her mug down next to the computer. She knows he thinks he is winning her over, and her heart breaks for them both. For the first time in months he is energized, practically hopping around. This is her boy, her Dan, the surfer, the dreamer, the one she fell in love with on the wind-whipped beaches of Andalusia.

"What about my job?" Chloe says quietly.

Dan opens a Word document, Windsong Kiteboarding Business Plan. "I'm sure there's agencies in Hawaii. People get knocked up everywhere."

"But . . ." Chloe tries again. "What about my dad, and the girls?"

AFTER CHLOE'S MOTHER DIED, Dr. Pinter did all the right things—staying in the shuttered white house in Akron where Chloe's friends used to devour her mother's hot maple scones and pots of milky herbal tea in the sunny kitchen. He hired Martha, a homely woman with a penchant for crosswords whom he concluded would be a constant in Chloe's life, would not be whisked away to marriage or exciting jobs like the college girls he interviewed. Martha moved into the room over the garage, quietly shuttled Chloe in her dented Oldsmobile sedan to riding lessons, flute ensemble, dentist appointments, summer day camp. Dr. Pinter kept his hours at the pediatric practice rigid, was always home at six o'clock for dinner so Martha could go to Scrabble club or choir practice. He sent Chloe to a therapist when the riptide of anorexia and substance abuse claimed several of her classmates. He took her skating every Saturday afternoon in the winter, and they played tennis at the swim club on Sunday mornings in the summer. He didn't date, didn't move from his evening arm-chair and the British television comedies that Chloe tried to suffer through just to sit next to him until she went to college. But he was going through the motions—"Making the best of it," he often said when people asked how he was, before he'd look off at a point in the landscape, the periphery that nobody else could see.

And then her sophomore year, Christmas break, Dr. Pinter sud-denly sold the house, following Ann, a forty-year-old doctor he had met at a rotavirus conference, to her practice in Seattle. Chloe's step-mother is six feet tall, chestnut-haired, and horse-toothed, medically brilliant and socially awkward. But she adores Dr. Pinter, and their twins seem to keep him frenetically busy. If Chloe never feels at home in their McMansion outside Seattle with its carpeting of pink plastic toys and half-dressed dolls, if she poked around enough to realize she resents Ann and Alice and Abby just a little bit, she is also happy to think of her father there, up to his eyeballs in Pull-Ups and adoring females.

When she called her father from Tarifa two years ago, the fact that the adoption agency job was in Portland, driving distance from Seattle, hung unspoken in the air. The next day he sent a fax to her apartment at Beaterio, a photo of a Jeep Cherokee with a For Sale sign on the windshield, the subject line: "For the drive between Portland and Redmond (183 miles). Happy Birthday. From Dad."

EVEN IF SHE COULD leave her job, if they moved to Hawaii, Dr. Pinter would never come. Chloe saw her vague back-burner plans for a new, adult relationship with her father and his family disintegrate. They can't leave Portland, she thinks, sipping her tea. Or at least, she can't.

"Can you imagine the twins on a six-hour plane ride?" she says, but Dan doesn't answer. He has left her to review the business plan and is humming a Jamiroquai song as he cleans the kitchen, the tune mixing with the clinking of him washing the mountain of dishes that has piled up during the McAdoo adoption.

"When would you want to go to Maui?" she asks, louder.

"I already bought a ticket. I'm leaving the week before Christmas."

"What? How?"

"Kurt loaned me some cash; that's how confident he is. It's going to be huge, Chlo." He puts the cloth down and crosses to her. "I really hope you'll come."

Thankfully, Chloe's cell phone rings. When she answers, the line is connected, but there's nobody there. In the background, she can hear daytime television, the faintest breathing. She hangs up.

It happens again.

"Wrong number," she tells Dan when it happens the third time, but she can't concentrate on the business plan she had been pretending to read anymore.

"So what do you think?" Dan grins at her; he is now cleaning the underside of the inside of the microwave.

I wish we'd talked about this . . . , Chloe thinks, but she knows this has always been Dan: impulsive and enthusiastic when he's getting his sporty fix, sulky and miserable when he's landlocked or rained in.

When her phone rings again, she jumps, ready to call Jason Xolan out.

"Hey, Chloe, I'm so sorry," Beverly from work drawls, "but Judith is freaking out in here. She wants you to come file the paperwork for the McAdoo case this morning, in case the birth parents start up any trouble."

"Mmkay," Chloe says to Beverly, the phone tucked in the crook of her shoulder. "Tell Judith to hold it together. I can jump in the shower and be there in about an hour."

"And you've had four calls on the service from our favorite Francie McAdoo. She hasn't called yet this morning, but I'd bet my candy jar it'll be ringing any minute."

"Okay, thanks, Beverly."

When Chloe looks at the history on her cell phone from the previous day, a day she spent mostly sleeping, waking only the one time Dan had spooned up behind her, the hands around her waist sliding purposefully north and south, she sees that there are indeed voice mails she hasn't listened to from Francie.

Dan has moved on to whistling and taking apart the stove burners. "So you have to go in?" She is amazed he refrained from a told-you-so about them calling her on her day off; that's how good his mood is.

"Judith wants me to file the paperwork for the McAdoo adoption before things get hairy with Penny and Jason."

"Have you heard from them?"

"No," Chloe lies. "Not since I left the hospital. But apparently Francie's been using up some tape on the machine at work, and I see she called my cell a bunch of times yesterday."

Dan rolls his eyes good-naturedly, and Chloe, much as she is soaking up the delicious flavor of his cheerful mood, goes upstairs to shower.

While the water runs over her, she tries to remember the wording of that joke—"Why are you hitting yourself with that hammer? 'Cause it feels so good when I stop." It perfectly sums up her life with Dan since they moved to Portland, lots of dark clouds injected with brief, brilliant sunshine.

Later, Chloe is speeding on the Banfield, her foot hitting the brake when traffic stops up at the 205 and her cell rings again.

It is Francie McAdoo. No greeting, just a hiss. "You deliberately kept it from us that Penny smoked."

"Ummmm." Chloe taps the brake, opens the file on the passenger seat, and is reading the Medical as fast as she can. She sees Penny's answer to the question "Smoking?" in her own handwriting: "Not really, sometimes, smell makes me sick."

"I've read about this on the boards," Francie is winding up, "where agencies lie, hide things so adoptions go through, but I never thought the Chosen Child——"

"Hang on, Francie, I don't think we kept this from you. You know Jason smokes, I just don't think it came up." *Because we were all trying to talk you down from backing out based on his race and blowing the whole adoption.* Rejection from potential adoptive parents always sent hurt birth mothers running to another agency, and between the apartment deposit, the motel for the days in between, the maternity clothes and food, they were already almost two grand into Penny and Jason by then.

"The nurse at the hospital warned us. She said that he is going to be really fussy for the next few weeks while he is detoxing. She couldn't believe that we didn't know he would be coming down off drugs, that you kept that from us."

"What are you saying, Francie—that you wouldn't have taken him if you'd known Penny smoked sometimes?"

Silence. Then, "You kept the information from us. You concealed this when we were trusting you——"

"Francie, I didn't purposefully hide this from you. I just assumed, I mean, they practically *all* smoke," Chloe falters.

"I'm calling Judith. I had no choice but to post on the boards about this. Other parents need to know that you conceal medical information about the birth mother—it's our right to be prepared."

And the line goes dead.

Chloe's head throbs, and she thinks of Dan back at home, alive again. She has missed him; she didn't realize how badly. She steers with her knee while she gets her wallet out, fingers her credit card. In the parking lot of the Chosen Child, she calls the airline, books her own ticket to Maui for December 30.

18

Smoke Signals

PENNY

When he comes home, she's laid out on the couch, sucking down cigarettes off Brandi's pack while she's at work. Doc said smoking makes her heal slower, but what does Penny care? If she never gets off this couch, doesn't matter. She could starve, dry up like a wrinkled old apple core left between the cushions.

"You want the TV off?" Jason asks. It's Oprah, a show on postpartum depression, ha! Penny blows a circle of smoke his direction, wishing it would make words like in cartoons, N-O.

"Hurting, baby?" Her boobies ache, but in the old way, like she's about to go on the rag, and her stomach, sawed open, sewn, and stapled, hurts too, but not that bad anymore. She blows more short puffs of smoke in his direction.

"Not talking to me?"

"Sending you smoke signals, Injun. Can't read 'em?"

He gets up, paces a tight circle around the room. She knows him by his jingles; just agitated. Still, she should be careful. She wants him riled enough to act, let him think it's his idea, but then there's Des'ree Bonds outside of Cheyenne, blind and drooling in a retard home because she crossed Jason years ago.

"What do you want, Pen?" He stops in front of her.

I want him back, she thinks, but this is not entirely true anymore.

Right after, she did. Today, she just wants to not feel empty and dried out, to feel something. And she wants Jason to move the hell out of her way so she can watch the show. She wants to know: Can you get it, postpartum depressions, even if you don't still have the baby?

"I think we got to go back to Washington, maybe even the Makah res, stay with Selma-Wade," he says.

The idea of crossing the river, of going north to the Peninsula, leaving Buddy In Oregon without ever having laid eyes on him, doesn't sit with her. She sucks on the cigarette, the last drag, and blows two puffs straight at him. *N-O.*

"Play by the rules for a time." He keeps going. "For one, my parole."

Penny taps the last smoke from Brandi's pack—call it her contribution to the rent, she thinks.

Jason slumps next to her feet, back to normal, and picks them up off the couch, holds them in his lap, rubbing.

"I miss him too," he says, so soft she has to turn down the TV.

"What?"

"You heard me." Jason makes a pain face like his back is acting up, twists on the couch. "And I failed the piss test at Home Depot. Forgot I smoked a bowl with Lisle and Brandi while you were in the hospital. I couldn't sleep without you."

Fuckin' idiot, she thinks.

"I hitched my wagon to the wrong star," she says at last.

"What?" His eyes—she picks one to look at, the brown one, softer—bore into hers.

"You heard me." She gets up, goes to the bathroom.

"You could lie," Jason calls out. "Your turn to call Chloe Pinter. Say I made you give it up. Duress. Pretend you left me. Then we'd get him back."

"Not much of a lie," Penny says, running her tongue over the smooth space of her gums.

Jason comes up behind her in the bathroom, wraps his arms

around her waist from behind. She looks at their faces, stacked on top of each other like a totem pole, in the mirror.

"I'll handle it, okay?" he says, and because she can't look at her own ugliness any longer, she turns away from the mirror.

"Done great so far," she sneers, and pushes past him to the bedroom.

Let him stew. She wants him pissed enough to do something. She just didn't think he'd do the fool thing he does.

19

Inauguration by Urination

PAUL

The first week home passes in a milky haze, day and night running together, curtains closed against the December rains, the master bedroom lit only by the peach-toned lullaby crib light clipped to the rim of Wyeth's bassinet. Dr. Woo had told Eva no stairs, so they camp out in the master bedroom, Eva's brother Magnus running out to Pizzacatto for dinner, to Strohecker's for Eva's favorite exotic cut fruit platters. If she could come downstairs, Eva would see that the mantel in their wood-walled living room is covered in vases; sunflowers from the staff at SuperNova, a mixed bouquet from his aunt, roses from the McAdoos, and in the kitchen, an ostentatious basket of gourmet goodies from Eva's mother back east with a scripty card promising to come out to visit after the Christmas rush at the thrift store is over.

Downstairs, the trash cans overflow with folded pizza boxes and gritty coffee filters. The mail mounds on the dining room table; three UPS boxes addressed to Wyeth Edward Nova wait to be opened.

Upstairs, all is peach-hued cocooning, the buttery-popcorn smell of Wyeth's soiled breast-milk diapers filling up the wastebasket, since Paul has discovered that you need a mechanical engineering degree to operate the damn Diaper Genie. There are black maternity pants, gigantic white nursing bras, and boxes of breast pads and diapers on every surface.

Somewhere in this brave new world, Paul finds himself falling headfirst into love with the baby that sleeps on his chest wearing little glowworm sacks with mittens folded over his hands, since neither Paul nor Eva has the courage to cut his absurdly long fingernails. Paul's Successful Soothing Ratio hovers just above the 50 percent mark, but he knows it will get better as he learns his son's cries, can anticipate his needs. When the houseful of grown-ups fails to figure it out before Wyeth comes undone, they're rewarded by a monster temper. Magnus swears Eva was the same as a newborn. He tells a bit of family lore—the afternoon their mother, so fed up with Eva's screaming, parked Magnus in front of *Sesame Street* with a box of crackers and left baby Eva in her crib with bottle-feeding instructions pinned to her chest for Ed when he arrived home from work. She didn't come back for three days.

THE DAY WYETH TURNS eight days old, Paul decides it is time to go back to work, to deal with clients who want to add extra circuits in their homes to accommodate holiday light displays, technicians clamoring to take the week between Christmas and New Year's off, a new file girl who hasn't mastered the alphabet. He and Eva get in bed around eleven that night, the baby swaddled and asleep in his bassinet.

"You going to be okay tomorrow?" Paul asks as Eva lays two nursing pads inside the open flaps of a bra with straps over an inch wide.

"Sure," she says flatly as she rubs a honey-colored, waxy-smelling cream into her brown nipples. When they first met, Paul thought he would never tire of the sight of her perfect breasts, a handful and a half each. Now he thinks sometimes maybe less is more.

"I saw Francie at Strohecker's today," Eva says. "She thinks Angus's nicotine addiction is wearing off."

Paul makes a good-natured grunt; he feels a new softness toward Francie, another new mother doing this, and alone, with her workaholic husband traveling.

"He's a beautiful baby," Eva says, and Paul realizes she is talking about Angus McAdoo, not their son.

"Not as handsome as our slugger."

"Do you think there is something funny," Eva asks, "about Wyeth's nose?"

Paul leans over her side of the bed, peers into the bassinet.

"I look at him," Eva continues, "and I think, what about Psych 201 and *storge*? How come I don't immediately feel more connected to the baby I carried and birthed? I think about adoption: Could I have taken Angus home just as easily as Wyeth? Could we have taken home Amber's baby? Would we have loved her the same, more?"

Paul has wondered these same things, but what's the point? Wyeth is their son now. Still, this is the most Eva has talked all week. Why all the psych babble now, though, when he's got to get up early and go back to work?

"I feel like, when I look at Wyeth, we're bonded through adversity, that horrible birth, through the cognitive dissonance theory of love. I think, I must love you to have gone through all of that for you."

Paul doesn't know what to say, so he turns out the light by his side of the bed. The room is bathed in the night-light's flesh-toned glow, which allows him to lift his head a hundred times a night and see the sleep-slackened miniature features of the bundled baby in the quilted bassinet by Eva's side of the bed.

At 2:34 a.m., Paul hears the *ack-ack-ack*, Wyeth's hungry cough, he calls it, and Eva is on it, moving more quickly now. She's getting better, Paul thinks through a sleepy haze.

"Hey"—she nudges him a few minutes later—"he's done feeding." And Paul regrets crowing about his prowess as a burper as he struggles to sit up enough to prop the burrito-baby, warm and sour-sweet milk smell, over his bare shoulder. He pats the back, watching the clock as minutes tick by with no burp. A few nights earlier, they had forgotten to burp him and the trapped gas fueled an unparalleled scream-a-thon, so Paul doesn't dare give up.

Pat-pat-pat, he checks the clock that will go off in less than three hours, his first day back, pat-pat-pat. Paul thinks about work, about a shipment of pendant lights that got broken in their Hillsboro warehouse, pat-pat-pat, would his father have taken it out of the forklift operator's paycheck two weeks before Christmas? Pat-pat-pat, Paul Sr. never would have gotten this far, never trusted anyone but himself to do a job, balance the books, write a bid, pat-pat-pat. Did his father ever sit up at night with Ritchie and him over slightly rounded shoulders, pat-pat-pat? Probably not, pat-pat-pat, it is a modern father thing to do. But do we all do it? Paul wonders, pat-pat-pat. Would John McAdoo sit up in his palatial Tudor wearing what, pat-pat-pat, oxford-striped pajamas, patting the back of that scowling little oaf? Probably pays someone to do it, pat-pat-pat, do they even have those kind of people anymore? What were they called, anyway, pat-pat-pat, Paul looks at the clock: 3:14, where would you find one, pat-pat-pat, and how much would one actually cost?

There is still no burp, but in the palm of the hand that cradles the business end, a telltale rumble. Paul looks at Eva in the soft light to see if she heard it, but her eyes are closed, REM flickering. He gets up, careful not to jostle the baby, and walks on the creaky oak floorboards to the window seat where Eva has made a makeshift changing area. Funny; across the hall, adjacent to the room where Magnus is staying, there is a perfectly outfitted nursery with apple green walls, a solid wood crib made up like a bedding catalog, and a matching changing table, but the only time anyone goes in there is to get a fresh onesie or another sleeve of diapers from the giant Costco box by the rocking chair. Wyeth has never, will never, sleep in that crib.

Paul lays Wyeth on the master bed by Eva's legs, half hoping she will wake up and take over. He does not immediately stick the paci in when Wyeth fusses as the cold air hits his bare bottom, and he is rewarded by Eva's eyes flying open, her struggling upright onto her elbows. After all, he has to go to work in the morning!

"Hey," he says as he wipes the baby's bottom, "just got a little diaper situation here. Nothing too serious. I'm going to give it a two-wipe rating."

Eva watches as he gets another diaper under the baby, expertly closing the tabs, wriggling the sleep sack over his pumping legs. The baby is wide awake now, and Paul swears Wyeth smirks as he lets fly with another enormous rumble.

"You've got to be kidding me." Paul smiles at Eva as he reverses the process, and sure enough, there is another mustardy load in there. Eva watches, bemused but idle, as he gets a second diaper, gets it all cleaned up again, and has the baby clean and bundled, about to complete the handoff to Eva, when there is another explosion. It's 3:40 now. There is a giggle from his wife, the first he has heard all week.

"You're a handy guy to have around." She laughs as Paul prepares the third diaper, positioning it under his son before opening the dirty one.

"Okay, now are we done here, mister?" he asks Wyeth. He opens the diaper and is met by a golden arc of pee that hits him square in the chest, runs in a warm rivulet down to his belly button. Eva bursts out laughing, a sound as familiar to him as the hum of electricity, and Paul joins her. He hadn't realized until this moment just how much he was holding in, worrying, waiting for signs of his old wife—and finally, here was one, her beautiful, throaty laugh.

"Baptism by fire, Daddy-O," she says.

They can do this, he thinks. She loves him, they love the baby, business is booming . . . It's all going to be okay.

20

Cuppa Joe

CHLOE

Chloe hangs up her cell phone as she walks into Strohecker's for a coffee. It's not as good as Starbucks, she thinks, but it's marginally cheaper and on her way to the highway. In line ahead of her is a familiar set of shoulders in a navy blue uniform shirt, the back crisscrossed by the straps of a baby carrier. In the hip pocket of his jeans there is a brown fleece infant hat with fuzzy bear ears and friendly eyes.

"Two American coffees and a cinnamon raisin bagel, toasted, walnut cream cheese, please."

"Paul Nova," she says. "Out with baby to pick up coffee and breakfast for your wife?"

He turns, smiling. There is shadowy stubble on his cheeks and she never knew he wore glasses; they look nice on him.

"Hey." He rubs his jaw, then runs his hand over the head of the baby nestled in the carrier. "I was just thinking about you the other day."

"You were?" It is Chloe's turn to order, and she scans the chalkboard, trying to remember what she came for. She would like steaming water and a teabag but coffee feels more appropriate.

"Um, coffee, lots of cream and sugar."

"Here or to go?" the teenage barista drones.

"Do you have time to sit?" Paul asks.

Chloe checks her watch; she'll be late, but why not?

They sit, and she waits for him to tell her what he was thinking about her, but he just sips his coffee, one hand rhythmically tapping the back of the baby nestled in his front carrier.

"So, how is it?" She nods at the peachy mound covered in dark blond fuzz, all she can see of his sleeping son.

"The truth? It's really hard. Harder than I thought, and on Eva, in more ways . . ." He trails off. "I mean, I get to go off to work."

Chloe nods, tearing open pack after pack of sugar; she still doesn't have the taste for coffee.

"The other night, I was trying to keep him while she took her millionth bath of the day——"

Chloe looks at him curiously.

"That's her thing, how she copes when she's stressing. If you want to know Eva's mental well-being, just check our water bill."

Chloe laughs, starts dumping cream in her coffee.

"Anyway, I'm trying to handle the little guy, and her brother's visiting, and we're trying to watch the game, and it's the final forty seconds, and the Vikings are down by three, and Wyeth's scream-ing, so I'm trying to put the paci in, plug the hole that makes the noise. She comes down in a towel, looking at me and Magnus like, How come two grown men can't handle one baby? and I guess I was missing."

"Missing?"

"I was trying to put the pacifier in his ear." Paul chuckles. "My eyes were on the game. And I say to her, a little snappy, 'Nothing's working!'"

"And?"

"And she takes him from me, and immediately he's quiet, like he knows the milk is coming, like he can smell it. And Eva gives me and Magnus this look, and she says, '*Nothing* never works, boys. You have to try something.'"

"Ouch." Chloe laughs.

"Yeah." Paul shakes his head. "She's right, though. And most often, what he wants is her. I feel responsible; she's exhausted. On so many levels. It was me; I dropped the dime in this jukebox." Paul chuckles and pats Wyeth's bottom ruefully, shaking his head as he says, "Some days it feels more like a pinball machine."

"What do you mean?"

"Having a baby, way back when—it was my idea. As soon as we were settled, married, I was the one who said it was time to have kids. I'm the only one left in my family." He waves his hand dismissively in the air between them, and she can see the mists of lingering tragedy hang over him. "It was important to me, to connect with someone, make a life, start a family."

Chloe catches herself leaning forward in her seat, hasn't touched her creamed and sugared coffee.

"Sometimes," he continues, "I think it's not so much about the right person, more just the right time. When I met Eva . . ." He trails off.

"What do you mean?"

"My wife walked me through what turned out to be the hardest year of my life. No, she carried me. And all because she saw my last name on the class list and liked the way it sounded with hers. It's the kind of thing that makes you believe in the hand of fate, God, whatever you want to call it."

Chloe thinks of friends of theirs, in less-than-perfect relationships, whom she and Dan watched get engaged the past year, and how Dan had scoffed that they were just doing it because of peer pressure, some societal timetable.

"But that's not us," they had said to each other.

"So you don't believe in soul mates?" Chloe asks Paul now, sipping her coffee, thinking, here they are, a man and a woman, talking about relationships and drinking coffee in a Portland café.

"I believe in being the best partner you can be. The rest follows."

"You mean, 'Love the one you're with'?"

Paul chuckles, pushes his chair back, checking the bill the barista dropped on their table. "That makes it sound unpleasant. That's not exactly what I meant.

"Anyway—" He stands up, digging in his hip pocket for a wallet. "Sorry to go on. Let me pay for your coffee."

"Please, no!" Chloe fumbles in her little purse.

"I should pay you for the session as well." He takes the tiny hat shaped like a bear and tugs it down over Wyeth's head. "You're a good listener; comes with the job, I guess."

"Not at all," she says. They stand uncertainly, both wallets open, and Chloe does not really want it to end. There is so much more she wants to ask him.

"I should get going." Paul smiles. "The gesture is sort of lost if the coffee I bring my wife is cold."

"It's miserable out; can I give you a ride?"

Paul reaches under the baby carrier and produces a small folding umbrella.

"You're full of surprises." Chloe laughs.

"I came prepared. Boy Scouts, and a lifetime in Portland. I'm a handy guy to have around."

"Still, it's cold."

"Fresh air's good for us. And you don't have a car seat. Hey, would you check, does he have both socks?" Chloe looks at the skinny, fleece-clad legs coming out of the baby carrier; one of Wyeth's navy socks is dangling dangerously. Paul is saying, "I have new sympathy for pregnant women; I can't see his feet, let alone my own."

"Here." She reaches to tug the loose sock back on his tiny foot, and her knuckles brush against the mounded button fly of Paul's jeans.

"Oh! Sorry!" she says when Paul takes a half-step back, her cheeks flaming. They both laugh to cover the awkwardness. "Oh my gosh, so sorry, I didn't mean to, like, grope you."

Paul starts a joke, something about a cracker for a starving man, and stops himself.

"I should probably get to work," Chloe says at the same time he offers to walk her out.

At her car door, Paul holds the tiny umbrella for her while she unlocks the Cherokee.

"Nice to see you, and thanks. You really are a good listener."

Chloe is in the tunnel on her way to the Banfield before she realizes that in the final moments, neither of them had left money for the coffee.

21

Bus Number Seven

JASON

The bus lurches, throwing Penny's slack body against his shoulder. She is like a used prison pillow, not even trying to keep herself upright. Jason puts his arm along the back of the bench, cups her shoulder and steadies her.

"How's my girl?" he says in a low voice.

"Mmm."

It's the same fucking nothing response she gave the doctor today, but when he asked if she was depressed, she said no.

"I can write you a prescription," he'd said. "Antidepressants."

"I don't do drugs," Penny had said, her eyes on the toes of her shoes, black with pink polka dots, picked out from the donation box at the adoption agency.

"Why'd you lie to the doc?" he asks her, squeezing her shoulder as the bus bumps over the trolley line in the road.

"What?"

"Why didn't you take the slip?"

"Why should I take a pill to make me feel like everything's okay? I gave our baby away to some fuckin' rich strangers. I *should* feel bad."

Jason tries to think of something to say, but she beats him to it.

"And don't tell me it was the right thing to do. Now if things start to change for us, get better, I won't want them to, because that makes it worse. If Brandi really gets you a job or the doc says I'm all healed and I can go back to looking for work, then it's like, why'd we give him away?"

Jason can't remember what Lisle said, so he makes up the statistic. "Ninety percent of life is timing, Pen. The timing was wrong."

"Is that what we're going to tell him? 'Sorry, Buddy, you came at a bad time.' "

Jason wonders what she means, when she thinks they'll be talking to Buddy, when they'll be offering up excuses. He looks out the window at the leftover Christmas decorations, tinsel shaped into a wreath hanging from the light posts, and the way they droop is enough to make him cry, sign *him* up for the fucking Prozac. Why had he looked forward to this appointment so bad—because he thought the doc was going to give them the green light to do it again? Every night he has to listen to Lisle banging Brandi, the springs on the sofa bed screeching, her yelping, his Penny's cold back to him, the ache in his balls so bad he had to lock up in the bathroom and yank on it for an electric shock, a sliver of pleasure, a ghost of an orgasm, and finally, it would settle down and he could sleep.

God, his dick couldn't feel any limper than it does right now. The dick that fucked the girl that made the baby that they couldn't keep that broke the girl's heart.

"I regret it, that's all I'm saying." Penny butts her forehead against her shoulder to get his attention. "I just want to see him, hold him, you know?"

"You want him back?" Jason says it slowly, rolling words in his mouth. What he wouldn't give to be having this conversation somewhere other than on a MAX line bus, so he could be sucking off a smoke at the same time. Thinking.

"You know in the cartoons, when Yosemite Sam gets shot with a cannon, and the ball passes through, and leaves a big hole in his gut? That's how I feel since we signed those papers, and Buddy"—her voice breaks—"and they walked out the door with me never seeing him."

She starts crying into his armpit, his sweet Penny—the lady across from them staring at his girl's pain, fucking public transportation, can't even cry in private, God, they need a car, he needs a job . . .

Jason bends his head down and whispers, "Shhh. I know where they live." It is an exaggeration, so he downgrades to the truth. "I know their car," Silver Volvo Cross Country, SPR-NVA license plate. There are other things he knows; won't be hard to find out where they live.

"What?" Penny tilts her face up to him; even with the scars, such a pretty face before the pimples ran wild over it, then he thinks, Dammit, they forgot to ask the doc about that, when those would go away. The last thing he wants to do is cause her any more embarrassment or pain.

"John and Francie. I was in the garage at the hospital having a smoke when she got in her car."

When she smiles at him, Jason feels like the painting where the sun is breaking through the clouds, and you'd swear it was Jesus himself peeking down from heaven.

"Okay," Penny says, sniffing hard. She straightens her backbone, holding her own self up as she wriggles back into his armpit, her hand over his.

OREGON OPEN ADOPTION—*A place for all mothers*
FRANCESCA97201
Joined:　　26 Jun 1998
Posts:　　17299
Posted:　　Mon, Dec 25, 2000 4:39 pm

Happiest Christmas Wishes! I can't believe I'm so late getting on the boards today! It was a whirlwind of presents, eggnog, and bliss. DH flew home the morning of Christmas Eve—I wish I had a photo to post, the three of us in front of the fire, but when we tried to take it, there was nobody to hold the camera.

"John, look at this!" Francie waves the striped bumblebee teether in front of Angus beside her on the floor, and he grins, his mouth a perfect U, an upturned umbrella. John is on the couch, dripping ice packs on his calves, his laptop open. He looks up, the twinkling Christmas lights reflecting off his glasses.

"He's getting more alert," she says. "Watch how he tracks this."

John watches, and Francie feels a surge of pride when, like a trained seal, Angus performs in the brief spotlight of his father's attention.

"Sure is." John goes back to his keyboard. His computer pings softly, regularly; it takes Francie a few minutes to recognize it as a live online chat.

"Who are you chatting with?" she asks.

"Nobody. Work people. Contacts."

On Christmas? And then he turns the sound off, and Francie rolls back toward the baby.

Angus is dressed in the most adorable three-month-size Polo outfit, a cabled navy sweater and coffee-colored corduroys that match his skin. The saleswoman at Nordstrom's couldn't believe how big he was for three weeks, had remarked, "You're so petite and fair; he must look just like his daddy!" Francie had nodded, picturing Jason's smooth skin and expressive eyebrows. Already Angus can give her a skeptical scowl that perfectly matches his birth father's, reminding Francie of their awkward encounters.

ANGIE—glad things are going well!

EvaSuperNova—come out, come out wherever you are!

Francie frets; her IRL friend hasn't seemed like herself recently. Her posts have been boring and self-centered, obsessively seeking information about nipple thrush and soothing techniques, void of Eva's trademark perkiness. She is also not doing a good job of replying to others, which can mean death, total obscurity on the message boards. There is room for controversial, for outrageous, but not for egocentric. If they were good enough friends, if Francie knew her passwords, she could get on there and post for her. Just a few replies, even a general Merry Christmas, or a Season's Greetings, if she wants to be PC.

John has fallen asleep, head lolling back against the brocade cushion. He has a flight back to Singapore in two days, and while she feels better, safer, with someone else in their dark, cavernous house, she and Angus are finding their groove, so John leaving doesn't bother her as much as it probably should.

They stick close to home, Francie and her kiddo, never going much farther than Portland Heights. They get organics at Strohecker's on Saturdays, gas at the Portland Heights Shell every other Monday, and once she took him to the shops on 185th, but came home quickly when she saw the riffraff that frequented the outlets.

Those two are out there in this city, probably among the unwashed who wander Burnside, maybe panhandling at the I-5 on-ramps, and Francie has no intention of bumping into Jason and Penny with her son in tow.

Francie scoops Angus up and settles onto the comfortable couch, near enough to the fire to feel it, but not so hot she'll have to get up and move. She exhales, lets his warm weight push the last of the air from her lungs. When she breathes in deeply, she can smell the Douglas fir of the tree, the trio of Yankee Candle Co. gingerbread candles dancing on the coffee table, the boutique baby wash she uses on his perfect curls. If Dr. Richard Ferber, author of her sleep guru book, knew about this, he would be tsk-tsking. *Don't let the baby fall asleep in an environment you don't intend to replicate every time they wake.* But it's Christmas, and Angus feels as warm and forgiving as the Florida sun on her chest.

22

Business Plan

PAUL

When his ability-to-soothe ratio slips under the 20 percent mark, Paul takes it as a sign to stop trying. This morning he'd set his alarm for five, slipping out of the house before it was light, even though it is New Year's Eve. He worked three jobs alone, stayed late, and it is dark now as he sits in traffic on the Sunset Highway.

"Maggie's plane is coming in this afternoon," Eva reminded him dully from the bed this morning. Paul wanted to joke about how they should charge her brother rent, as often as he's been around this month, but thought better of it. For one, Magnus generously bank-rolled their honeymoon, their adoption application fees, not to mention half the down payment on their house. And for two, Eva's sense of humor is shot these days. Paul wishes he knew someone he could call to ask about this, if his wife's moodiness is normal. He thinks about the woman in Africa who gave birth in a tree during a flood, and wonders if Eva isn't milking the hormone thing a little much. He wonders, after their morning in the coffee shop, about calling Chloe Pinter. She's a social worker, but . . . what would she know about motherhood?

He thinks of Berit, Eva's mother. Wyeth is almost a month old, and she's made no effort to come out and see him. She has sent boxes of thrift-store clothes, ridiculous things: a frog costume, size 4T, and a snowsuit with spit-up stains on the neck (the Post-it safety-pinned to this suggested OxiClean in her flowery script), but it was size 6–9 months, *perfect* for a Portland summer.

Eva rolled her eyes and excused her mother's absence. "You know Berit. She's got a business to run. She said the thrift store is undergoing a critical audit. They think someone's stealing."

PAUL MERGES AT THE light meter, his mind shifting from home to work, work to home. His place in this is becoming clear to him. Like Ward and June, the lines are drawn, roles defined. He will be the Provider, Eva will be the Nurturer. Paul has tried and failed to be a modern father, so he needs to focus on his area of expertise. It is time to take SuperNova to the next level, to move beyond simply electrical to lighting design. It makes his dick shrink back, just considering it.

The problem with the electrical side always has been the shallow pool of quality labor force. Men who will do all the things Paul Sr. valued, who will change into house slippers for the Korean client down in Lake Oswego, who won't rifle through the Coach handbag the woman in Beaverton boldly leaves on her dining room table. And here's the balancing act—training them well enough that he, Paul, doesn't always have to come in and do the job himself, but paying them well enough that they don't buy a used van, spray-paint a logo on the side, and do their own thing. All this while keeping the overhead low enough that his clients feel happy, and he doesn't have to stress when Eva orders her nine-dollar roast beef sandwiches. Always a dance, a delicate balance, and Paul struggles with vertigo as it is.

Another trick: how not to become his father at home. Paul Sr. would take a stopwatch and a single crisp twenty-dollar bill with them to the state fair each year. Then he would time the rides, deciding which was the best value for your ticket. "Nah, Ritchie, you don't want to go on the planes. He's giving you a minute for three tickets! Go for the boats—that guy gives a minute forty-five for the same amount." And then he'd heckle the ride operators, "Hey! I could ride the ducky boats twice for the amount of time you give, let 'em go around again!"

Paul Sr. assigned a monetary value to everything. The tomatoes from the garden that his mother cultivated and canned didn't taste good because they were homegrown; it was because they were free. Paul Sr. was incapable of letting anyone else do any part of the job. His accounting department had been a cracked leather-bound checkbook and ledger, a pair of drugstore reading glasses, and late nights at the kitchen table with his adding machine, checking, rechecking. If growth means feeling a little off balance all the time, desperate and dependent on others, if it means putting your faith in people and dusting yourself off and starting fresh when they let you down, then this was going to be a tense few months.

And back at home, another mouth to feed. Right now, the baby feels like a money-gobbling parasite. He thinks of a joke that was going around e-mail recently, "So you wanna be a parent? First, go to the grocery store. Arrange to have your salary paid directly to their head office." Ha ha ha. Of course he knows it won't always be like this, that Wyeth will start to give back in some way, be more than a drain on their energy and finances. But as he pulls into his driveway, Paul wonders: When, in his entire life, has he done anything that resembles giving back to his parents?

23

Waterbabe

CHLOE

"Chloe!" the Intro to Windsurfing instructor yells in his heavy German accent. "You are jibing too late. That is why the wind is pushing you, back sail, into the water." Chloe stands up in the waist-deep Pacific Ocean, wiping the salt water from her eyes, suffering her humiliation in the shallow cove near Kanaha that she heard Kurt and Paolo refer to as the Kiddie Pool. They're sitting under the flags at the adjacent kiteboarding cove with Dan, waiting for the wind to pick up.

Frustrated, Chloe grabs her board, prepares to get back on and uphaul the sail for the millionth time. Tacking is easy; but she cannot make the stupid downwind turn, with its jazz-stepping fancy footwork.

"Chloe, wait." Jesper, the instructor is beside her, one hand on the shoulder of her mandatory life vest. Chloe squints up at him, the ravines of his cured leather face, his eyes impossible to read behind the orange iridescent Oakley mirrors. "Too late," he murmurs. "Feel the wind." He draws out the phrase like a yogi. "Trust that it will tell you when. *Mach schnell*, we have only"—Jesper checks his watch, the blue nylon straps streaked white with dried salt water—"thirty-five minutes more."

Sweet Jesus, she thinks.

Later, Chloe wraps a towel around her Portland-white body and plunks down in the shade next to Dan.

"Well, that was fun," she lies gamely.

"I think I just found our first Windsong instructor," Dan says, his eyes on the adjacent kiteboarding cove. "See that girl, in the white rashguard?"

"Yes." Chloe doesn't have to look to find her; she is carving the water in front of them with singular concentration.

"Her name's Mischa, and she just moved here from Tenerife. She's only been kiteboarding four months, but she's busting moves none of the guys are even trying. Look at that! Christ! Did you just see that?" Mischa had been sailing in against the sideshore wind, jibing at the beach, and then on the way out, against the waves, she catches air and does a skateboarder-type trick, grabbing the board, bending her knees behind her, twisting her body. Chloe is sure, from how hard it is to even stand up on the plank of a board and control the tiny handkerchief of a sail, that this is very hard. But it all looks rather . . . pointless. Back and forth, in and out, jump up, grab your board, spin around, stick your landing? She has seen girls half Mischa's age bear down and flex unseen muscles to squeeze out babies with heads the size of pomelos, and what's more, hours later, they sign papers that sever the connection between them and the human being they have been growing inside them for months.

"Amazing," Chloe says.

"Yeah." Dan exhales. "Anyway, she's bartending right now." Of course she is, Chloe thinks, and she's probably got an adorable mutt dog that licks at the wind and wears a pink bandana around its neck when she drives around in her battered old Jeep. "But I told her about the kiteboarding business, and she's totally stoked to get in on it. She said she could start whenever we need her. Mischa and Paolo can bring in the clients, and you and I will run the business."

Ah, vacation talk, Chloe thinks. The kind of thing you say when caught up in the beauty and isolated moment of time on vacation.

She is prepared to indulge Dan for now. In a week she'll be back in Portland, and before long Dan will come back too. She's sure of it. *I'm nothing without you.* She's got Heather's adoption coming up, three potential birth mothers, and she wants to make some visual aids, photo collages, for her Prospective Parents presentation. Chloe wishes she had brought a pad of paper to jot down ideas.

"Look at that wind, girlie!" Dan grabs her shoulders, steers her body toward the horizon, points out to the trees on the point, bowing under a gust, the flag next to them cracking now. She can feel the excitement, an electricity in the muscles of his shoulders. "It's not steady yet, but I'll take it!" All this for wind—she wishes she felt it too.

While Dan whoops off to get his gear, Chloe wades into the shallow water of the cove where Jesper's next lesson is starting and pees, tries to surreptitiously wriggle the sand out of the bottom of her bathing suit.

"Chloe!" Jesper calls. "I have an extra rig, if you want to practice. No charge."

"Oh . . ." Chloe looks out at the water; the wind *is* picking up, whipping it into little white peaks, the kind you try to achieve in a mixing bowl when making meringues. They look like nothing from the shore, but Chloe knows once she is on a board she will feel like a weak-kneed lumberjack on a rolling log.

Jesper wades to her, casting a glance over at his next batch of hapless students.

"You live here?"

"Uh, no. My boyfriend wants to." She looks toward the beach, where Dan is unrolling his kite. "He wants to start a kiteboarding business."

Jesper inclines his head, smiles indulgently, and says, "Ahhh. Him and everyone else on this lava rock." Chloe takes this as a sign. Thank god, it won't work out; Dan will come back to Portland, to their life.

"You know what your problem is, if I may?" Jesper says, and for a moment she is stricken, afraid of what he will say, until she realizes he is just a middle-aged windsurfing instructor who has only known her for ninety minutes.

"Let me guess; I'm not strong enough, right?"

"No. You are fine, plenty strong." Jesper takes her upper arms in his callused hands, shakes them out like a wet blanket. "Your problem is that you are fighting nature." Jesper nods sagely and smiles again as he says, "And, Chloe, you will never win against the wind."

24

Where and When

PENNY

"I don't give a fuck, yeah, road crew, whatever. I'll turn a fucking sign. Just tell me where and when."

Jason's voice could wake the dead, Penny thinks as she wanders out of the bedroom. Brandi is spread out on the couch watching TV with her hair in a towel, stinking of fake flowers. Bitch carries all her products to and from the bathroom too, then puts them back in her suitcase, like she's afraid Penny would be using her stuff. All a girl needs is some Dial soap, a Daisy razor, and some basic shampoo—do a little time, and you learn that everything else is just gravy. Clean's clean.

Jason is pacing around the kitchen with Brandi's pink cell phone. He meets her eyes with a question, like he's testing the waters. Has she been that bad lately? She gives him a half-smile, trails her hand over his lower back when she passes him to get to the fridge, where of course there's no orange juice. Jason covers the mouthpiece, leans over her shoulder, and says, "I'll run to McDonald's and get us a coffee." His breath smells like cigarettes and toothpaste, familiar, and she rubs her cheek on his shoulder, jerks back when the pressure hurts another pus mound forming on her jawbone. Jesus, her skin, what Buddy did to her.

"Tell him I'll turn a sign! I don't give a shit. Just tell me where and when. Yeah, hang on, she's right here."

Jason crosses the room, drops the phone on Brandi's skinny stomach, and walks away.

" 'Morning," he says, and he sounds so hopeful she wants to be better today. She wants to not start after him right away, but she can't help it. Penny pulls a section of her cheek in between her back molars, on the good side, and holds it there. "Lisle's talking to his boss again. Seeing if he can get me in on the project. Says I have to prove myself, pass a piss test, work the road crew on their project halfway to Bend, but he says I might be able to ride out with him next week."

She can tell he's blowing it up, making up what he hopes will happen, but okay. Before, every crumb of good news was something she grabbed and stuffed in her mouth. Now, it's like everything he says comes to her on a lone rider across a flat stretch of desert, hard to understand, and all she sees is clouds of dust, and all she feels is as nothing as the dust when it settles.

"Okay." She sits at the table and works the inside of her cheek between her molars, enjoying the slippery, meaty sensation of her trapped skin with the tip of her tongue.

"So you want me to run out and get you some coffee? Egg McMuffin?"

Dusty-dust-dust. What does it matter? The baby. She wants to ask him when, when can they go, but not yet, not in front of the Flaky.

Across the room, Brandi hangs up the phone, goes back to where she dropped the remote on the floor. When she bends over, her skinny jeans slip and you can see the olive dimples at the top of her ass, the hint of her crack, and the pink butt-floss elastic of her panties. Jesus, that girl. Doesn't she know what dressing like that gets you? Penny knows. If she liked Brandi at all, she'd tell her.

But she feels Jason watching the girl's every move, sees his eyes go to the panty T at the top of her jeans, and she swears the bitch gives it a little wiggle before she stands up, grabbing at her pants. Penny digs her blunt, fleshy fingertips into her own thighs. Back in Drain, back when she was working, she had long acrylics, dragon-lady red. They made a nice clickety-clack when she pushed buttons on the register. Men buying ground sirloin and TV dinners looked at her hands, looked at her face, looked at her wavy brown hair.

"What, are my panties showing?" Brandi turns to Jason. "I need a fucking belt. We're starving to death here, till Lisle gets back from Bend with some fucking money. The fridge is like ol' Mother-fuckin' Hubbard."

"I said I'd go out and get you girls some breakfast!" Jason's neck vein is out. "Nobody's talking to me around here! What? What do you want?"

"Okay. I want a deluxe breakfast and some extra sausage. And a chocolate milk shake. Large."

Penny can do the math for that in her head. More than six dollars for one breakfast, what does she think Jason is, an ATM machine? The girl's got a job, minimum wage, but a job. Where does she think Jason's cash comes from? Every nickel they spend on greasy food is money they can't use for the things he promised, for Mexico, for the bus fare to see Buddy.

"I'm fine," Penny says.

"You don't want nothing?" Too loud, too close, big dust clouds billowing up around her, and Penny has to shout through them to get to him.

"You know what I want!"

By the time the dust has settled, he's gone. Brandi looks over the back of the couch at her, whistles through her teeth, and goes back to *Judge Judy.*

Penny fills a glass of water at the sink. It tastes like rust. Her fingers find the scar at the top of her underpants, her real cover-your-whole-ass underpants, trace its length. *Where and when?* she thinks.

When Jason comes back, he throws a bag of food at Brandi—"No milk shakes!"—and sits at the table with his. Penny wants to start again. Tries to sit on his lap. He doesn't shove her off, doesn't squeeze her to him either. She sips from his coffee, scalding hot. It is black, tastes like metal too. Jason eats his dollar McMuffin in three bites.

"I just——," she begins, and he gives her a look that normally would have stopped her cold. Before. Now, she keeps going in a whisper. "You shouldn't have told me if you didn't plan to take me there."

"You let me handle it." She can feel the rumble of his voice box against the back of her shoulder.

"Like you handled it——" She begins low, but squabbling on the television court show drowns her out. Underneath her, Jason's leg starts to twitch, an electric tremor.

She just wants to look. If she trusted Chloe Pinter an ounce, she would call her up and ask how it was going with John and Francie. Once, on *Oprah* or some show, there was a couple that adopted a retard from Europe, and he was like a demon spawn, and they beat on him with wooden spoons until he died. She just wants to know it's going okay.

"I hate this show. Judge Judy's a bitch." Now Brandi is up, prancing across the living room to get a drink. Jason's eyes follow her like the family dog watching the hot dog platter.

"Don't you have to work today?" Penny asks.

"Nope. I got moved to opening shift, so I'm off every other. Oh! *Jerry Springer*'s next! 'My boyfriend cheated on me with my sister.' I love this show."

Penny often wondered, watching Maury and Jerry and the other daytime goons with their cheating shows, how these things got started. Was the boyfriend just walking in and "Hey, I bang your sister, want me to roll you too?" How did it all happen? It seemed impossible. But Penny let herself be sucked into today's circus show anyway, the bouncers running onstage like strongmen, Jerry the ringmaster, her mind still humming from their conversation about Buddy, when Jason grips her shoulders with his hands and moves her off his lap as he gets up.

"Here," he says, shaking his coffee cup to show that there is still a little liquid in it, for her. Then he crosses the room and sits next to Brandi on the couch, his ridiculous boots still wet from the walk to McDonald's up on the coffee table as he lights up a smoke, offers the pack to little Flaky. Goddammit if he didn't light her smoke too, and before the show is halfway through, they're already play-wrestling over the remote, and Penny has the answer to her question. Just like this, late morning on a weekday, nowhere to go, bellies full and smokes smoked, TV suggesting it, and if she weren't across the room trying to get up the energy to go take a shower, the wrestling and Brandi's giggly "Get offa me" might have turned into something else.

Penny stands up. "I'm going to get dressed." Surprise, Jason follows her into the bedroom and shuts the door. She can still hear the booing of the TV audience.

"Can I watch?" He sits on the bed, big hands between his knees. Her clothes fall off, a puddle on the floor, and it doesn't take much, lying down with her knees up, he's as predictable as Oregon rain, insistent as hunger. She's thinking, while he's ramming in and out, that she's not doing this to keep him from Brandi. Penny doesn't particularly care what he does with the thing between his legs, he can stick it wherever, but she knows that floating between his ears is a series of numbers and letters. She'll wait, until afterward, to ask again.

Then, because after all these years with him, she knows exactly when, she raises her hands, idle beside her on the bedspread like corpse claws coming out of the dirt, to shove Jason off her.

"What?" Jason's voice hovers above her, shaking.

"It's not right, not yet," Penny hisses. It's like opening a gallon of milk before you finished the last one. Buddy is still unfinished business.

One slamming thrust of his hips, and he comes, shuddering inside her. His face right next to hers, he says in her ear, "Hundreds of babies."

She turns her face to the wall. "Buddy first. Where and when?"

"Christ!" He shoves off her, and she can feel him leaving her, and then again as he slams the door.

Penny gets out of bed and studies her face in the mirror over the dresser. She doesn't even see the scars anymore, a crescent shape up at her temple, the other along her right jaw where the skin split from the swelling after the fact. It's just her face, the front part of her head, now, and she could have been almost pretty, even after what they did to her in Denver, but not anymore. Twenty-four years old, and she looks half dead, her hair growing in a nothing color from where those bitches on her cell block shaved it, her skin sallow and *wrecked* from the baby—wasn't it a girl who was supposed to steal your beauty? There is a new painful welt of a pimple straining under the surface on her jawbone, desperate to get through. Penny flicks on the overhead light and pushes with the pads of her two index fingers, trying to free the pus, but there isn't an opening, a hole. Penny finds a safety pin, licks it to clean it before she jabs it through the center, picking, digging, until it oozes blood. She lets it run down her chin, drip-drip-drip to the carpet.

She wanted things: wanted boys to want her, and look where it got her. Wanted a man, a baby, look where it got her. Maybe she shouldn't want things anymore. But she does.

25

A Modest Proposal

CHLOE

When the sun is hanging low over the water, Dan and his friends sail in, pack up their gear, and load it into Kurt's van. They drive to the converted inland garage where the guys are staying in the quiet exhaustion of exertion, none of them saying more than "Quality sesh," or "You were laying down some sweet jibes, dude."

"Okay." Dan opens the passenger door for Chloe. "We've got the van for tonight."

"But—" Chloe stands uncertainly on the prickly grass before getting back in, looking from Dan to Kurt and Paolo, who are hosing the sand off their feet by the garage. "It's New Year's Eve. Don't you guys want to go out or something?" She had been picturing something festive, a beachfront bar, music, fireworks, hooded sweatshirts, beer, maybe a bonfire, other people to talk to.

"Nah," Kurt says. "We're bushed."

"Yeah, we're just gonna smoke a bowl, maybe watch a little *Bone-A-Rama 2000*, since Danny won't be there to bitch at us."

"What?" Chloe looks to Dan, who is jingling Kurt's keys in his palm.

"Nothing." His neck turns red. "Ready?"

"Pretty Boy won't let us watch the *Bone*." Paolo grins, showing the perfect gap between his square front teeth.

"I don't have a problem with porn." Dan's voice goes up like a twelve-year-old's. "I have a problem with low-quality porn. The girls on there, they're always fucking *grimacing,* I want to help them out with their rent or something. I want to say"—he puts an arm around Chloe—"my girl here's a social worker, give them one of her cards. Brutal."

THEY DRIVE TO THE place Dan has rented for them with his warm hand cupping her knee, a light smile on his cherry lips. He is humming along to Steely Dan, the tape jammed into the van's player. The last of the afternoon light falls on his dark hair, almost dry, where it curls over the crest of his perfect profile, and she cannot believe he is hers.

"What?"

"Nothing." She laces her fingers over his hand on her knee.

"You're staring at me."

"I'm happy," she tells him. "You're back."

Dan grins as he pulls into their parking space, dried leaves crunching under their tires. "Yes. Yes, I am."

THE RENTAL IS A tree-house addition to a typical upcountry ranch home that overlooks the jungled green countryside. It is a single room built in the crook of two giant koa trees, connected to the main house's garage by a long, open catwalk without guardrails. The three large windows are glassless, and guests are protected from pests by an ethereal mosquito netting hanging over the bed. A hose runs up through a hole in the Formica countertop, and cut into the counter, there is a stainless steel bowl, the perfect size for mixing a cake, with a rubber stopper that serves as a sink. There is no bathroom, just a toilet and sink in a closet back in the garage, and the shower is a cold-water hose attached to the bib at the garage end of the catwalk.

"I met the owner this morning," Chloe tells him when they pull into their parking space, dried brown banana leaves crackling under the tires. "She said they're going to put a bathroom addition on the tree house, in that tree over there, splitting the plumbing off the main house. She said it's going to be amazing; there's going to be a big open-air bathtub, right in the trees."

"I hope they run two pipes," Dan says as he turns on the hose, running the water over his hand. "This is freezing."

Chloe says, "I think *bracing* is the word you're looking for. Let me feel."

Without warning, he turns the hose on her, using his thumb to make it spray out in a fan-shaped arc.

He hoses her down, one hand clamped on her wrist to keep her in range, and she twists away from him, shrieking as he laughs. Then he surprises her by putting the hose in the hand of the wrist he is holding, says, "Careful." He doesn't let go of her hand, nods to the tangled green hillside that falls away six feet, then seven, then eight feet below the catwalk they are standing on. Beneath them it is verdantly wild and beautiful, sharp-tipped birds of paradise and hermaphroditic anthuriums with their hot pink petals like wax candy lips.

"Your turn."

He pulls his sweatshirt over his head and throws it on top of his backpack, out of range of the cold water that is puddling around them on the planks, dripping.

The Velcro of his shorts rips as he opens them; those perfect diagonal muscles at his waist create an arrow: *Go south.* Dan has only to put his legs together for his shorts to drop down his straight hips.

Once, in their first year of dating, when Dr. Pinter flew Chloe home from Tarifa for Christmas, she had crept into her father's attic library, pulled his *Gray's Anatomy* from the shelves under the eaves, and studied the muscular man. What was the name of the part she missed most about Dan? She puzzled over the drawing—was it the *iliopsoas*, the top of his iliac crest, or the bottom of his *rectus abdominus* that made up the perfect angled shelf of muscles at the top of his hips? Perhaps it was not a muscle after all, but the inguinal ligament?

Without Dan there to compare with the text, it was impossible to tell. To cover her bases, she had sent Dan this brief e-mail from her father's computer:

I miss your *iliopsoas* and *rectus abdominus*. XO Chloe

The e-mail that he sent back from the Internet café, which her father printed out and left on her Amish-quilted bed, read:

I don't know what that means, but I miss your tits and ass. Come back!
Dan

Now DAN STANDS IN front of her in the periwinkle twilight, a form to be sculpted, to be worshipped, hands casually at his sides, as the icy hose runs in hers.

"Your turn," he says again, this time with the Abercrombie and Fitch model half-smile.

Chloe glances toward the main house—through the open lanai, just a few feet away, she can hear kitchen sounds, the clank of a drawer being opened, a pot being placed over flame. Anyone could see them.

"Do something for me?" Dan smiles.

"Anything," she says, and she means it. This day, other than her windsurfing lesson, has been magic. Dan is back.

"Take your clothes off." Dan throws down the gauntlet.

Chloe drops the hose, peels off her cold wet T-shirt, her silver bikini top, shimmies out of her shorts and bottoms.

Dan swallows. "Let's go." He turns off the spigot, and they run the length of the narrow catwalk, Dan's white butt cheeks winking in the light from the main house windows as they dash past, Chloe's hands cupping her bare breasts.

Dan pulls the tree-house door closed behind them and jerks back the blankets, diving under the covers. Shivering, Chloe follows.

"Here—" He tugs the blankets up to her neck. He runs his hands, jagged windsurfing calluses at the crest of his palms, over her body to create heat. "You're freezing."

Under the shimmering white mosquito netting, the woven cotton blanket and faded quilt, her chattering teeth still. Dan takes her face in his hands.

"Better?" he asks, and she nods.

"Good. I want you to be good. To be happy, here."

"I am," Chloe says, lying only a little. There are so many layers, implications, in this spare conversation of fragments.

"So I was thinking, while I was on the beach," she begins. "When I get back, about making a proposal to Judith. See if she'd be interested in me running a domestic program out of Maui, a branch of the agency."

"Really?" Dan smiles at her, cupping her elbows in his palms like they are something so precious, the eggs of a rare bird. He kisses her cheeks. "That'd be great. Or when things really take off with the kiteboarding thing, you can run the shop part-time too."

"I'd have to stay in Portland through the spring, see out a few adoptions, train a replacement."

"No worries. That would give me time to get things set up here too, no distractions." Dan's kisses move from her cheeks to her throat.

"It might take me a while to get our house emptied, a sublessor," she says, and the words fall like litter around them, tumbling off the bed to the floor, but really, which does she want more?

In the morning, Chloe wakes to the sound of her cell phone ringing. It takes a moment to orient herself to the tree house, an azure anole scampering across the magical mosquito netting above them.

"Hello?" she whispers so as not to wake Dan. It is Beverly, from work.

"Your birth mother Heather just went into labor. She says you're on her birth plan as her labor coach."

"I'm her backup, if her mom can't." Chloe is already out of bed, throwing clothes in her rolling suitcase. She has to go; it's Heather. "She's not due for three weeks."

"Tell the baby that!" Beverly has info, a flight available at noon.

"I'll be on it," Chloe says briskly. Heather needs her.

"Work?" Dan lifts his head, bats the mosquito netting out of the way.

"Sorry. I need to be at the airport in an hour."

"Okay." Dan gets out of bed, stands at the window and studies the moving leaves, wind direction. "Looks like it's setting up for a good sesh. I'll have to pick up the guys and drop them at Ho'okipa first."

He stuffs his boardshorts in his backpack, grabs his contact lens solution. Chloe is surprised that he doesn't seem angry.

"Sorry," she says again.

"It's okay. I could only afford this place for two nights anyway, so we would have been sleeping in the garage with the guys or the van after today."

"How much was it?" Chloe says. She had been thinking, last night as he slept and she watched the pops of distant fireworks through the open windows, that this might make a cute first place for them. If they added a bathroom and a shower, put up some screens, and a hot plate for her teakettle . . .

"I had to sell my old 5.3 sail just for the two nights." Dan quotes local bumper stickers, " 'This ain't the mainland.' "

And Chloe's budding idea, starting an agency branch in Maui, withers and browns. Eleven dollars an hour would be eaten up here like nothing, and they would have to live like all the other surfers, eight people in a two-bedroom, blankets hung for privacy.

Chloe rolls her suitcase behind him slowly on the catwalk. *Now what?* she worries.

The wind picks up, turning the leaves of the koa tree over, and Dan whoops.

"Setting up for a perfect sesh! Come on, babe!" he calls, hustling her so that she forgets her toiletry kit, makeup, hairbrush, birth control pills, on the back of the toilet in the tree-house garage.

ON THE DRIVE TO pick up Kurt and Paolo, Dan asks her to grab his backpack.

"Open it up. Something in there for you. Sorry about the atmosphere—" He gestures around at the inside of the van, the mildew smell of damp equipment. "I wanted to make it special, drive up to Haleakala Crater or something, but since you're leaving . . ."

At the bottom of his bag, among Snickers wrappers, gas station receipts, a moldy towel, and his sunglasses case, there is a dark purple leather box in the shape of a heart. Inside, there is a real ring, a simple gold band with a small round-cut diamond. The fact that she's been seeing nothing but platinum in the magazines doesn't matter; it's perfect.

"So, if you'll still have me . . . ," he says as he cuts the engine outside the garage conversion and honks twice. "And we can set any date you want."

"Oh, Dan, of course." Chloe clambers out of her seat to his lap, kissing his beautiful face. *Now what?* she thinks again.

They are interrupted by pounding on the window.

"So it's official?" Paolo sticks his head in the van, and Chloe realizes his friends were in on it. She climbs off Dan's lap. "I may now kiss the bride?" Paolo, who has always treated her like a kid sister— 60 percent tolerated, 40 percent adored—beams as he climbs in, genteelly kisses both her cheeks.

"I've got one for you guys," Kurt calls from where he is throwing his gear in the back of the van. "How do you tell the wives from the girlfriends on the windsurfing beach?"

"I give up." Dan sighs, knowing he's walking into it.

"Easy; they're all girlfriends, bro!"

And Dan's friends laugh, Paolo showing every gleaming tooth.

❧

"I'm going to miss you," Dan says when they are alone again, after they have dropped Kurt and Paolo at the beach. "Don't worry about your stuff, at the tree house. I'll pick it up, and it will be here when you come back."

He's really staying, leaving it up to her if she follows. Dan wants her there, but he won't insist.

"You're not coming back to Portland," she says slowly, and when Dan shakes his head, Chloe feels her options narrow, choices looming.

"I'm really stoked about this kiteboarding thing. You have no idea what it's like to be a guy, how your sense of self is tied to what you do."

Chloe thinks of her job; does it define her? She loves her coveted upstairs office, her families, her birth mothers. She thinks of the photo album on her desk full of happy endings. Who would she be if not Chloe Pinter, Broker of Babies? Could she be Chloe Pinter, Maui Waitress?

"What's the first thing people ask when they meet you—'What do you do?'" Dan continues.

"But I thought you didn't care about that sort of thing."

"I didn't use to." There is something hard in his tone.

"Then what . . ." She studies his face, the muscles moving in his jaw that mean he is grinding his teeth, something he does in his sleep.

"You."

And before he has to turn his attention back to the road, their eyes lock.

"Me? *I* don't care what you do!"

"I do." He squeezes her knee. "You make me want to be better. God, I want this Maui thing to be a success, for us. You have no idea how badly."

She looks out the window; palm trees dancing in the wind.

"I'm never going to be a doctor," he warns.

"I don't want a doctor."

They are both thinking of Anson Park, the intern who works in her father's practice. Dr. Pinter never misses a chance to work his career accomplishments or single status into their phone calls. "I don't want a doctor," Chloe says again, emphatically. "I want you."

"Well, you've got me, babe. I'm not going anywhere." Dan smiles over at her as they pull up to Departures.

26

First of the Year

PENNY

She's got two good legs, Penny thinks. Good enough to get her out, taking matters into her own hands. Her legs still pain her, first thing in the damp mornings ten years later, but they're good enough to get her to the MAX line. She looks down at them, the scars covered in black slacks, haven't seen the light of day since what happened outside the Flying J back in Denver when she was fifteen.

Penny tilts her head against the bus window. She's having one of her firecracker headaches, the kind where it feels like someone's mowing down the center of her brain with a circular saw. Seven operations and therapies and then, when she was finally let out, her legs were good enough to get her the fuck out of Denver, because after something like that you can't exactly go back to smoking under the bleachers and quizzes on Christopher Columbus. Got her on the first bus and then a job at Stuckey's in Wyoming, serving the Truckers Luv It breakfast to Jason eight years ago when he first jackknifed his rig and was laid over in Casper for a week.

Now Jay's home sleeping one off, New Year's Eve last night, and he and Lisle and Brandi got lit up—won't even notice she's gone.

No idea what time it is, gray sky, no sun, she got up and left without peeing even. She can go when she gets there, maybe. Threaten to go on the floor if Chloe Pinter doesn't do what she wants, and this makes her snicker to herself all the way to Troutdale.

Except when she gets there, the windows are dark, and the little street that runs in front of the shops is empty. Does the whole city have a hangover? Penny wonders. Is she the only one in Portland smart enough to know what drinking gets you?

Just for the hell of it, she tries the door handle and is amazed when it turns, gives, and swings open. It's a sign, a miracle. Now she won't have to beg; she'll just take. For too long she's been taken from, but now—

"Hell-o?" Singsong, from the office to her right. The woman flicks on a little lamp on her desk, puts her purse down by the computer.

Shit. There's a tall skinny redhead secretary wriggling out of her raincoat, looks every bit like a Muppet.

"Hi." Penny's voice comes out strangled; when was the last time she used it? She coughs, tries again. "Chloe. I'm looking for Chloe Pinter."

"And you are?"

"Penny."

"Oh, right. Chloe's in Hawaii. We're not open today; I'm just here to do some legals. We have a birth mother in labor."

Hawaii. Bitch takes their baby and vacations in Hawaii. Penny's headache is starting to make a sound, a roaring. She stumbles to a chair by the desk to sit down, pushes against the pain with the pads of her fingers.

"Are you all right? Can I help you with something?"

Just then the front door clicks open again. A woman comes in carrying a baby in an infant seat, hood up against the rain.

"Sorry, I really should have locked the door," the secretary calls out. "We're not open today. Oh, hi, Angie!"

"Hey, Beverly." Doubled over in the shadows, the woman doesn't see Penny, crosses straight to the desk. "Sorry to bother you today, I was just passing by and saw the light, and I wanted to drop these off for Mandy." Penny looks through the hands cradling her face—the woman is handing over a large, fat envelope. "We're so grateful to her; Kaelynn is the best thing that ever happened to us. I know they said they only want it once a year, but it's the first of the year, so I thought, if Mandy calls, here it is. I wanted them to be here if she called."

"Thanks, I'll put it in their file. Sometimes they surprise you. The birth mother who swore she didn't want photos and letters is the first one to call for them."

Now Penny is confused. What is in the envelope? Money?

The two women coo over the baby for a minute, and when it makes a noise, the mother says she'd better get going.

"She likes it if we keep moving." She bounces the car seat in her arms. "Really, she's the best thing that ever happened to us. We're so grateful to Mandy and Dwight, and Chloe, to all of you."

After she is gone, Penny can hear Beverly rifling around in the file drawers by her desk.

"What is that?" Penny asks, standing up and leaning over the desk. "Money?"

"What?" Beverly looks up as if she had forgotten Penny was there.

"They come and leave money? For the other mother?"

"What? No. They're photos, and letters, for the birth mother. It's part of their arrangement. Once a year, they drop off photos and letters, and if the birth parents want them, we keep them here."

"Do I have any?" Penny feels it like a bubble in her chest: hope. Somewhere in those giant metal boxes there are pictures of Buddy. She should have come here sooner!

"I don't think so. What are the names of the parents?"

"Jason Xolan and Penny Marks."

"No, the other parents."

"Oh, John and Francie."

"Oh, right, I remember *them*," she says, and it's hard to get her meaning. Beverly slides a long metal drawer out, and her fingers, long red acrylics, tick-tack down the tabs of the files, sliding toward M, for Marks, Penny thinks, until she sees her pull out a folder, "McAdoo, John and Francie / Marks, Penny (and Jason Xolan)."

"Hey!" Beverly says sharply, and snaps the folder closed. "This is confidential." She spins in her desk chair and scans the file, her back blocking Penny's view. "No, it's a closed adoption. No cards or letters in the agreement. There's nothing here for you."

That's what you think, Penny hums to herself all the way back to the bus stop in the light drizzle. *John and Francie McAdoo.*

27

Good Samaritan

CHLOE

Chloe takes a cab from the airport to Good Samaritan, calling Gina Severin on her cell phone as they lurch in stop-and-go traffic.

"Well, it's been a long night and day, but Heather's almost ten centimeters now, so we're close." Gina sounds exuberant; Chloe can imagine her with an encouraging hand on Heather's shoulder, squeezing it as she says this. Gina works for Nike, in marketing. She has had a different, trendy hairstyle every time Chloe sees her and is an absurd mix of chipper and genuine.

"Okay, tell her I'm coming—I'm trying my best to be there in time."

"Hang on, she wants to talk to you."

"Chloe?" Heather sounds faint, like a little girl. "Are you close?"

"Yes, I'm almost there. I'm on the Banfield, I guess maybe fifteen minutes at the most."

"Okay, can you hurry?"

And then the phone goes dead. Chloe feels a panic in her chest. How can she have left Heather for Maui? How could she have thought that just anyone could go to the hospital in her stead with a folder full of legals? Because she wasn't thinking of Heather; she was thinking of Dan, humming and cleaning their kitchen as he planned his escape.

It is forty-six minutes before the driver pulls up in front of the brown brick hospital. She pays the cab fare and runs, without waiting for a receipt for Beverly, flip-flops slapping up the stairs to the maternity ward, not bothering with the elevator.

She pulls out her ID when she reaches the nurses' station, and they hand her a folder that Beverly has dropped off, the prepared legal forms folded in a neat manila rectangle, just waiting to be dated, signed, and notarized. She finds Heather's room just as the doctor, the silver-haired man from the ultrasound, is coming out, peeling off his gloves.

"Hi," Chloe says, "is she—"

But he keeps walking, as though she isn't talking to him.

Inside, the baby is screaming as a broad-bottomed pediatrician attends to him at the isolette. Gina and Nate are hovering, Nate with the video camera running, while Gina calls stats over her shoulder to Heather, who sits alone in the bed, quietly adjusting and readjusting the sheets over her lap. Heather's nurse flushes her IV and takes over at the isolette as the pediatrician pronounces him perfectly healthy.

"Oh, he's beautiful, Heather!" Gina crows. "He's got lots of dark hair! Six pounds even, eighteen inches, a little peanut!"

"That's good, good," Heather murmurs. When she sees Chloe, her face breaks into its crooked, crossed-teeth smile. "Hey, you missed it!"

"I'm so sorry." Chloe drags a chair over to the side of Heather's bed. She leaves her purse and the legals over by the door, but she sees Heather's eyes dart to the folder.

"That's okay." Heather looks down. "Gina was great, a great coach."

"*You* were great!" Gina calls over her shoulder. "Really! Chloe, she was amazing."

"I'm sorry I missed it."

"They told me you had to come home from vacation. I didn't know that you were going away. I'm sorry you had to come back, but I—"

"It was a last-minute thing; it's not a problem." Chloe pulls her chair closer to Heather, looking over her at the cluster around the baby, who is now quiet. The nurse's arms move in an expert flurry, wrapping him, flipping him, wrapping him again.

"He looks just like Michael," Gina blurts, and Chloe can see she thinks better of it, worrying about what that means to Heather. "I mean, he's so beautiful."

"I knew he would. We saw him on the ultrasound." Heather looks at Chloe. "We knew he would, remember?"

"Okay, we've got him cleaned up here, let's give Mom a chance . . . ," the nurse says, though everyone in the room knows that the birth plan strictly states that Heather does not want to hold him, that Gina will be first.

I should say something, Chloe thinks. I should say something now. But she doesn't.

Then the nurse pushes past Gina and hands him to Heather, and everyone stands frozen. Gina's arms are curled hopefully, she is already rocking, shifting her weight from side to side, ever so slightly, in anticipation.

"Gina, do you . . . ," Heather begins, but trails off as she settles the baby into her own thin arms.

"It's okay, honey, go ahead." Gina is openly crying, not bothering to wipe away the tears. They fall on the robin's-egg-blue sheet that covers Heather's legs.

"You forget how little they are," Heather murmurs. She undoes the bundle of hospital blankets at his feet to examine the ink-blacked soles. "Oh, oh my, look how tiny."

The nurse, an old-school type with huge owl glasses and pancake makeup and a steely halo of a perm, bustles around the room, adjusting Heather's IV again, changing the blankets in the isolette.

"When Michael was born, I didn't know they did that ink thing to the feet. So when I was alone with him, I was checking to see if he had all his fingers and toes, and I saw his black feet and I freaked out. I was thinking, Oh my, my baby has this horrible disease."

Gina titters nervously, sniffing on her tears.

"And I was all alone with him and I just remember thinking, 'It's okay, my diseased black-footed baby, I'll love you anyway.'" Heather rolls her eyes at herself.

Chloe thinks she should say something now—she can feel Gina's anguish like waves, vibrations across the bed. She meets her eyes briefly, and everything in Gina's expression begs, *What is happening?*

"Gina, would it be okay if I . . ." Heather asks even as she undoes the snaps at the top of her hospital gown. "I mean, just today. Just for now."

"No, of course not. I mean, of course I don't mind, it's better for him . . ."

"I know. I read that. I nursed Michael till he was one and started biting." Heather smiles. "After that I was like, No way, mister. . . ."

The room is so silent, even the nurse pauses as the tiny mouth roots and immediately finds Heather's perfect mocha-colored nipple. Chloe can hear him gulping, grunting in the quiet. Heather, who is usually so modest, huddling around her belly in oversize sweatshirts, lets the top of the gown fall completely down, both smooth full breasts exposed as she nurses her son. He has perfect features and a bristle of brown lashes as long as his mother's. Heather's eyes close, and she sighs. "So tired."

"You don't want to do that," the nurse says, snapping into action, fiercely bundling the soiled linens of the isolette into a tight ball, "if you're really giving him up. Your milk's gonna come in, you'll get engorged."

"It's okay, just for today." Heather's eyes flutter open; her voice is barely a whisper. She reaches out her hand, the one that isn't support- ing the baby's head, to Gina. Gina sob-hiccups as she rushes forward, grabs Heather's hand. Inside, Chloe feels her stomach muscles un- clench; it's going to go through.

"So what are you going to call him?" Heather asks Gina, looking up at the older woman, both of them with tears running on wet cheeks. They are still holding hands.

"Well"—Gina takes a shaky, ragged breath, sniffs hard—"we were thinking of Adam, since he is the beginning of our life. Adam David, if that's okay."

"That's perfect," Heather whispers, her eyes closing again. "Adam."

Chloe looks up as Gina's husband, Nate, follows the nurse out of the room, a lurching six-foot-five-inch man moving awkwardly, desperately. Chloe leaves her purse, the manila folder, goes after him.

Nate Severin hasn't gone far. Chloe finds him tilted forward just outside the door, his forehead slowly pounding against the wall as he chokes on his sobs. He sees Chloe, straightens, wipes his cheeks furiously. She reaches behind her and gently closes the door to the delivery room where his wife, and the mother of his child, are watching him breast-feed for the first and last time.

"God." He exhales, wiping again. "I want to adopt her too. And Michael. We could move into a bigger house, or remodel the garage, or I don't know, it's totally crazy, and it would probably never work . . ."

"She has a mother, Nate," Chloe says gently, doesn't add that Heather's mother is in and out of rehab, "and a convicted felon fiancé."

"I know, I just . . ." Nate turns, slumps his gangly height against the wall. "What do we do? Chloe, tell me what to do."

"It's intense." Chloe lays a hand on his arm. "You come on back in and sign papers."

ALONE AT HOME THAT night, the papers signed, Chloe sips tea to calm her twisted stomach. Two years ago, this was her dream job. Two years ago she held a baby not thirty-six hours old as the prop plane from eastern Oregon bounced down at PDX, and she walked off the jetway with a satchel full of signed legals, the birth mother back in jail, no father named, and placed a baby with thick black hair and cherry-red lips in the arms of a couple who had waited seven years for this moment.

"Here's your son," Chloe had said, letting herself cry with the gray-haired new mother, the father wiping his glasses on the hem of his flannel shirt. Their three heads had touched over his tiny one, and Chloe was a part of something so wonderful, the creation of a family. That's when she started saying it, that it was "an honor to be a part of such an important moment in a family's life."

But these moments are few and far between, and Chloe thinks now of the birth mother in that case, whose name she cannot recall. The phone call came on a slow Wednesday morning. Then it was rush to the airport, get on a prop plane, bring profiles of people willing to accept Native American newborns with prenatal substance use, a forty-three-year-old incarcerated alcoholic birth mother already in labor and ready to sign. It happened so quickly that Chloe forgot to bring a newborn outfit or the agency's car seat—she had to stop at a Wal-Mart on the way in her badly aligned rental Taurus.

She saw the baby first through the nursery glass, a gorgeous seven-pound boy with a strong forehead and skin like oiled cherrywood, thick, straight hair. Then down the hall, the birth mother, old enough to be Chloe's mother, gray threading her black hair, face hash-marked with lines, meth teeth small and black, who answered the questions on the agency's forms so quietly Chloe often had to ask her to repeat them, the woman's eyes darting to the khaki-uniformed guard at her door.

The whole thing took less than twenty minutes, a handful of questions for the medical, the birth mother flipping through the three portfolios so fast she couldn't have even read the captions under the photos before she tapped the red binder on top and said, "This one," then set about deliberately signing the documents with a half-dry pen in front of Chloe and a silent, spectacled notary Chloe found in the phone book.

So even the happy endings that she refers back to when wondering at her hours or salary, defending the job to Dan, aren't win-wins. She thinks of birth mothers who have called her, desperate, heartbroken, threatening.

"I've changed my mind," one said, after the paperwork was signed and filed. "I've got to see her. I'm pumping and saving my milk, I know where they live, I have to see her." This one ended in a restraining order and court-ordered counseling, but worse, it rattled the new parents so badly that despite their previous assurance that an open adoption arrangement would work for them, they now refused all contact with the birth mother.

Chloe thinks of the Whitings, who backed out when she called to tell them that the amnio confirmed Down's syndrome in the baby that Kelli, their birth mother, carried. How this triggered a mother-bear protectiveness in Kelli, who thought originally she couldn't have a baby alone, now raising a special-needs daughter.

"I don't know," she had drawled to Chloe on the phone when she called her from the hospital three months later, the baby in her arms. "It's just meant to be, I guess. I guess God had to do something drastic to make me realize I was meant to be her mother."

The Whitings sued the agency, and lost, for their nonrefundable application deposit.

And now, Chloe thinks, sipping her tea, there is Heather. A wonderful mother whose only fault was getting pregnant too young two times by the wrong guy. Chloe rubs her hands over her eyes.

Her cell phone rings. Hoping it is Dan, she grabs it.

"Hello?"

Silence.

"Hello?" She is conscious of the emptiness of her house, of Dan thousands of miles away.

"You're going to be sorry for what you done," a deep, muffled voice says, and the line goes dead.

28

Prankster

JASON

He calls her pretty much every day now, uses Brandi's pink girlie phone or the pay phone out by the parking lot. Sometimes Brandi does it too, when she's off work and bored like she is today, waiting for Lisle to get home on the weekend.

She comes at Jason shaking her phone like she's ringing a bell, thinks it's a game. Between caller ID and cell phones, kids Brandi's age never really got the fun of prank calling Jason grew up on. Sometimes when they call, he says things, but mostly he stays silent, just to rattle her, get another envelope floating under their door. Why not, she's got the money.

But today Penny catches them, Brandi, on the couch, with a paper towel over her phone saying curse words into Chloe's voice mail, because she's stopped picking up.

"Bitchwhorecuntslut, slut-slut-slut," Brandi cackles like she's calling chickens.

Penny slams the bedroom door; they must have got too loud. Brandi snaps her phone closed, grabs her cigarettes off the coffee table, and crosses behind Penny to the courtyard, yanking the front door half shut behind her.

"What?" he says before she's even said anything.

Penny snorts air out her nostrils and walks right past him, pulls open the fridge, and stares at the ketchup packets and two heels of bread.

"What?" He follows her into the kitchen, stands behind her while she moves things around, half a can of ginger ale, the butt ends of the bread, not taking anything out.

"Ketchup sandwich, breakfast of champions," he tries again. Christ, what's her problem now? He's sick of trying to figure out her fucking moods.

She spins around, stares right into him.

"What? What do you want me to do? You want the baby? You want me to knock you up again? What? 'Cause I'm busting my ass trying to get us some money, so don't start in about that." Trying to get another one of those magic bank envelopes to appear, he thinks. What more does she want?

"Doing it by drinking it up with those two clowns?" She snorts, pours the ginger ale into a jelly jar, and sips at it. "Flat!" She spits into the sink. "You going to start tweaking with them too, next time they go off?" She doesn't say it, but he knows she is about to bring up Des'ree Bonds, and what happened the week after he lost his license and went on his last meth binge.

"I'm getting things worked out with the social worker!" He doesn't mean to lose his temper, but he kicks the leg of the table and it snaps, cheap particleboard crap, comes crashing down, sending up a cloud of ash from the saucer they'd been using for a tray.

"*I'm* getting things worked out with the social worker." Penny smirks; she hadn't even jumped when the table fell. Steps right over the mess to get up in his face.

Brandi comes back in, picking at a raw spot on her forearm. "What the fuck was that?"

Penny ignores her. "I went to the agency yesterday." She points her thumb at her chest. "*I* got their last name."

"Whose?" Brandi looks from one to the other. Jason steps back from Penny, stoops over slowly to pick up the broken saucer. "Whose?" she says again.

"The rich people who got Buddy," he finally says as he stands up, his back twanging.

"So you know their car, and Penny knows their name?" Brandi claps her hands together. "What are we waiting for?"

"I thought you said you know where they live?" Penny's pocked-up face is right up in his; girl like her should know better than to do that.

"I know a lot of things," Jason says without moving his mouth much, and she backs the fuck down. That's right. With her stubby-nail fingers, Penny scoops the broken-up ashtray out of his palm and carries it to the trash, head down.

"Come on!" Brandi's still yapping. "Let's go rustle up some cash— I'm ready for some action!"

29

Coffee Shop

PAUL

*H*e waits for her at Strohecker's. Portland Heights has a lot of big-money houses, a handful of parks, and some excellent schools, but only one place to get decent coffee on the way to the interstate.

He timed it just about right too—remembering from last time, and guessing it takes her about forty minutes to get out to Trout-dale at this time of day, and that the agency is pretty nine to five, he doesn't have to wait long. At 8:25, she comes in juggling her tiny purse and some files, the cell phone jammed to her ear, and Paul can't stop himself from grinning stupidly while he waits for her to recognize him.

"You need a briefcase or something," he says, and she smiles when she sees him.

"Paul Nova!" She puts her things down on the table where he is sitting, wraps her arms around him. "So good to see you again. Happy New Year."

He pulls out a chair for her, offers her one of the two coffees he has waiting in front of him.

"Cream, lots of sugar, right?"

"Wow, good memory. But am I drinking Eva's coffee?"

"No, I'll get her a fresh one before I go. Please, sit." She does.

"This must not be your usual time," she says, tipping her head forward to sip from her cup, and he can smell the floral of her shampoo in her slightly damp hair. "Or we'd be seeing each other here every day."

"I'm getting a late start. Rough night with the baby. Of course, it's a lot harder on Eva than it is on me."

"So you're picking up coffee for her. Does your wife appreciate how lucky she is?"

"What?" Paul sips at his coffee to hide his smile. It has been a long time since Eva has even said he's a handy guy to have around.

"Nothing, you're just like the perfect guy. Successful business, thoughtful husband, great dad. She's lucky."

After this, they don't talk about Eva—not her dark moods or the baby's crying, as he had planned. They talk about Chloe's work for a minute.

"Still the dream job?" he'd asked, and she looked out the window before saying quietly, "Sometimes."

Then, because it's always on his mind, they talk about money.

"I should buy stock in this place," Paul says, waving his arm at the adjacent fancy grocery store with its sprawling floral department, wine steward, and exotic fruit and cheese section. "We're certainly spending enough money here. Yesterday I come home, and Eva and her brother have bought a twenty-eight-dollar tray of cut fruit from here. We do have knives, we can cut up our own fruit. Wyeth's a month old, and they're still celebrating, acting like the circus is in town, spare no expense! And the deli sandwiches and the gourmet coffees—" Paul stops, looks down at the recycled paper cup steaming between his hands, and laughs. "Our French press is broken," he continues lamely.

"You know," Chloe says, "they say the biggest points of conflict in relationships are money and children."

"Bingo."

Somehow, the conversation drifts to their dead mothers, swapping stats: diabetic complication, age forty-seven; brain tumor, age thirty-two.

"Everyone thinks that's why I do this job, mother issues, like I've got to make everyone the happy family I had but lost."

Paul nods. "It's been a long time, years, but I miss her more than ever now with the baby. Eva's brother flies up from L.A. sometimes, but I want family who is actually helpful. My mom would have made the most wonderful granny—nothing ruffled her."

"You know, there's a lovely quote by C. S. Lewis, from when his mother died. He said something like, 'With my mother's death, all settled happiness, all that was tranquil and reliable, disappeared from my life. There was to be much fun, many pleasures, many stabs of Joy; but no more of the old security. It was sea and islands now; the great continent had sunk like Atlantis.'"

Paul can't take his eyes off her. "Or something like that, huh?" He laughs, and she blushes, tucks her hair back from her face.

"Okay, I memorized it. I discovered it when I was twelve, and it spoke to me, everything I was feeling."

"It's beautiful."

They sit for a minute, and then Chloe checks her cell phone, starts to collect the files in front of her.

"This was fun." She glances at the piles of paper in her hands. "I didn't get any work done, but it was lovely. Thank you, for the coffee, and the company."

"My pleasure. Nice for me to start my day with a beautiful woman and poetry instead of a screaming baby for a change."

"We should do it again sometime," she says, standing.

And by unspoken agreement, they do, half an hour of coffee every morning for the next thirteen days, until the last Monday in January, when Paul doesn't show up.

From: francesca97201@mac.com
Subject: The end of the quest
Date: Jan 20, 2001 1:39:47 AM PST
To: johnmcadoo@soaringscotsmanbeer.com

Consider this e-mail an apology:

For taking you on a journey that I knew in my heart was more my quest than yours, for letting it grow up above everything, take precedence over the couple we might have been.

We might have ridden the Orient Express (was that really one of our dreams?!).

We might have been happy with matching two-seater sports cars (red for you, silver for me) and a circle of friends not swallowed by weekend soccer tournaments, people who subscribed to and could read a weekly newsmagazine in one sitting. We might have become a couple who traveled northern California on wine or olive tasting tours. We might have joined Pumpkin Ridge (we used to talk about it, remember?), where I might have learned those things that girls who grow up in a Florida trailer park don't. You wouldn't have golfed, too much walking, but you might have enjoyed cards or cigars on the balcony, and I could have turned some heads in tennis wear.

If things had happened differently, I might have resigned myself, re-designed myself (I was still young enough!) to a fabulous, childless life. I might have taken pottery classes and yoga retreats, grown my hair long. You could have learned to use that fancy Nikon I got you for our wedding. We might have moved to Arizona, the dry heat better for your health, and lived in an active adult community where everyone drove golf carts. Or together, we might have found a hobby to bond us—scuba diving, making our childless couple friends sit through endless underwater movies after dinner.

Think of the money we might have saved! Between infertility specialists, failed IVFs, agency fees, and the nursery, we're at approximately $163,000.

Before the quest, there was only our first year, and what is the first year? The acquisition of things, and learning, accommodating, chiseling each other.

Did you shape me? If not for you, I would know nothing of Jacobean furniture, the difference between zinfandel and vidal blanc. I wouldn't have known what a saphenous vein was, and that a person could live without both of them. I would not know the architectural trailblazers Glenn Murcutt or Jean Nouvel. In *Pretty Woman* Richard Gere teaches Julia Roberts about champagne bringing out the flavor of strawberries; if not for you I would never have known that half a lemon in the bottle of a glass of hefeweizen makes the perfect thirst-quenching summer ale. I would certainly never have tried carpaccio, unagi, or *The Sopranos* on my own.

As for adoption: Like a cartoon snowball rolling down a hill, engulfing ski lodges and pine trees and hapless snowbunnies, the quest took on a life of its own. Would it have been different if the baby boy now in our lives was a true Angus, your copper-haired Scottish son? Would he have had his half sister Melinda's eyes or laugh, sparking in you some hope of second chances?

Meringues! We both loved the vanilla meringues at Strohecker's.

What is left?

A single mother, alone in the middle of the night (doors locked, alarm system armed!) in what was the house of our dreams, that I won't be able to afford once I pull the trigger, hit send on this e-mail.

And of course, my coffee-and-cream-skinned boy, six and a half weeks old, ten fat little fingers that close around my thumb, simply sighs as he polishes off a bottle and then tucks his hands over that kissable Buddha belly of his. A boy already twice abandoned. A boy who, after kicking his nicotine addiction, has become my sunny-son, who already grins when I lift him out of his crib, who waits for me, not crying, just waits, each morning, as though his life doesn't start until mine does. Easy as a melody, my son—

Francie stops; she cannot swallow, a lump like a whole roasted chestnut lodged in her throat.

[SELECT ALL, DELETE]

She types:

From: francesca97201@mac.com
Subject: You nearsighted, gimp-legged sonofabitch
Date: Jan 20, 2001 3:14:37 AM EDT
To: johnmcadoo@soaringscotsmanbeer.com

I believe these belong to you, from the autocomplete on my computer, when browsing for stroller rating sites, your History:

[SELECT ALL, COPY, PASTE]

S—

   Sexy Asian teens

   Singapore bridal services

   Singapore bride connection

   Singapore match services

   My attorney, Larry Steinfield, Esq., 503-DIV-ORCE, awaits your call.

[SEND]

Sunday Dreams

PAUL

I feel her before I see her, a magnetic draw, a smell, and she's biting my neck, hot, like a bitch in heat, I think, pushing her back against the cinderblock wall, her faded red sweatshirt, HOT STICK *it says over the left tit, and I am, I am one hot throbbing stick . . .*

"You wore this to the agency picnic," I say, but it doesn't sound stupid. "When I first met you. I wanted you then."

"Mm-hmm." She unzips it, nothing underneath but perfect teardrop breasts, two halves of a ripe jumbo avocado, and I cup them, because she wants me to, wants me to bang her standing right up against the hospital wall, grinding against me in her jeans, her flat, Dallas-cheerleader stomach against my cock, the belly button with the little blond hairs around it that I've kissed a thousand times, no, wrong body, wrong girl, and she's leaning into my neck, hot warm breath, "Hurry," she says.

"Baby . . . ," I whisper.

A baby is crying, there is the usual urgency, get this done before the baby really gets going, and I've got it out, ready, and I look over her shoulder, past that smooth golden hair, through the glass window into the nursery, where I heard the crying, and it is empty, rows and rows of empty plastic cribs, the babies are gone and I don't give a damn, I think as I use my knee to scissor open her creamy thighs—

PAUL STARTLES. HIS BIG-EYED son's head is bobbling, turtling up off his chest, a puddle of drool and white cheesy spit-up on his chin, on the collar of Paul's T-shirt and his neck, cooling and wet on his hot skin.

"Hey," Paul whispers. Magnus is across the room, head thrown back, sleeping in the rocker; a gargling snore catches in his throat. Paul checks the TV; the Ravens have scored, but who cares about the Super Bowl? Paul squints at his brother-in-law; he's not even watching, but the TV's got to be on all the time. "Mind if I find a game, man?" Magnus always says, with the remote, Paul's remote, already in his hand.

Paul wraps an arm around his son, cupping the stem of his neck to steady him as he swings his legs to the side of the couch. He stands, clutching Wyeth against his chest. Magnus blinks, straightens, moves the sports section off his lap.

"Did I doze off?"

"You guys all looked so sweet in here," Eva says from the stairs, the lens of the Nikon resting in the V of her thumb and index finger. "I took a picture." Then she and Magnus both look right at, but do not comment on, Paul's giant boner.

She follows him upstairs.

"So . . ." She sits down on their bed. Paul hands Wyeth to her, and before the baby even opens his mouth, in one motion she has her shirt up and her bra open, wedging him on the boob. The baby looks surprised but pleased, latching on. Lucky, Paul thinks as he goes to the closet for a clean shirt.

Outside the windows, it is already dark, the afternoon gone. He should have at least gone to the Sandy job, checked in, but now the day is over, a Sunday night stretching before them, no different from any other night of the week anymore. Having a baby is the great leveler of life, he decides, taking the distinction out of day and night, workweek and weekend. Parenthood is the ultimate lather-rinse-repeat.

"So, I'm feeling sort of . . ." She leaves the sentence open, waiting. He hates it when she starts conversations like this, pussyfooting.

"What?" He comes out of the closet; he didn't mean to sound so sharp, but his balls are aching and he's angry with himself for sleeping the afternoon away in front of televised football. It's no way to grow a business.

"Never mind." With her thumb she breaks the latch of the sleeping baby. She sighs, and her shoulders slump forward. She sits like this for a minute before closing the flap of her bra, tugging her shirt down. "I don't know. I just don't feel like . . ."

"Like what?" Paul says softly, and he sits on the edge of the bed, runs a hand over the baby's head, down over her forearm that is holding him, lays his hand over hers. "Like what, hon?" It is so easy to be generous. Paul wonders why he doesn't do it more, why he can't set it as his default mode. He keeps his hand over hers.

"Nothing," she says, and he exhales, relieved, lets it drop.

Later, he will remember this moment, and it may be what saves them in the end. She tried to tell him; he didn't want to hear it.

Now, through a slick of tears, she is giving him that look, the girl from Anthro 101 and the Pygmies. She moves the baby meaningfully to his bassinet, winds up the mobile. She takes the bottle of apricot baby oil from the changing area by the windowsill and moves it to their bedside table. "Oh." Paul smiles, feeling like Wyeth moments earlier, surprised and pleased. He thinks back a month, their first godawful postpartum attempt, and nothing but a sympathy handjob, one dry missionary quickie, and one hot shower blow job since then. She lies down in a C shape.

"So Maggie leaves tomorrow," she whispers as he slides in bed next to her, curling behind her back. "It will be nice to have the house to ourselves again."

Thank god she said it, because if he had, she would have jumped down his throat.

"You know, I'm working on a theory," Paul says as he slips a hand up under her shirt and is met with layers, the industrial nursing bra, the absorbent milk pads. "I think once you're over thirty, the only people you should be living with are those you're having sex with, or those who are the product of said sex."

Eva laughs and goes slack against his chest, shimmying her shoulders so the bra straps slide off them in his hands. Easier to just pull it down than try to tackle a triple clasp. Downstairs, the floorboards creak as Magnus walks into the kitchen, opens a cupboard, a glass on the counter, the clink of ice cubes. Eva reaches for the apricot baby oil on the nightstand. "We should be quick," she whispers, wriggling out of her pants, rubbing her warm ass against him, and then the phone rings. "Let it be," he hisses, but her brother answers it. "Just a moment. . . . Paul! It's the answering service!" And then Wyeth and his ack-ack windup cry—"Forget it!" It comes out disgusted, like a slap. "Coming!" he yells back to Magnus.

Once, they might have rolled their eyes and shared a smile over the irony in his word choice, but Eva just yanks her pants back up and gives him a bitter, plaintive over-the-shoulder look as she picks up the baby.

31

Shake the Money Tree

JASON

"**I**'m sick to death of your hounding!" Jason had ripped her hands off him in the dark, shoved her. Not hard; he thinks back to her grunt as she hit the ground. She was the one grabbing at him, sweaty hands, ugly, pitted dark-mouth face. No wonder they didn't get any money for their baby, her looking like that these days. No effort, picking at her face like Brandi, like a goddamn tweaker, mangled stomach, she's lucky to have him. She's got to leave him the fuck alone, let him work things out. It's no use, her plans. Let it be!

He and Brandi get off the MAX line, stand under the shelter for the 51. It's still dark, early morning, not raining but foggy, everywhere the air touches his bare skin, his head, it's damp cold. He thinks of Mexico, burning sun, brown skin and the tang of tequila. *Leave it be,* he'd told Penny. They just need enough to get out of here, incognito.

"You know he's not likely to come in." Brandi squints up at him. The bus pulls up. They get on and sit down under the window, glaring yellow green bus lights, and Jason tips his head against the glass. "My boss don't never come in on Mondays, usually."

Jason doesn't answer. He had to get out of that plaster-walled shoebox, away from her and her goddamn hounding. At the very least, he can bum another pack, skim a five or two off the register while Brandi's out pumping gas. He has other plans too, ways to kill time in Portland Heights. "You're putting in the good word for me with the boss, though, right? You see I'm solid."

Brandi snorts, looks past him out the window. "I see you're running out of options, mister." But she's smirking like it's a joke, so he lets it go. Bitch. She'll be sorry too. He hates her, ugly little crank whore with her picking and her black teeth. He thinks of Penny, his girl, loyal as the day is long, and the anger of before melts like dirty snow.

The sun doesn't rise, but it's a lighter gray now, and the bus winds up Vista, through the reaching green of trees he knows from logging, money trees; Douglas and Fraser firs, hemlocks, silvers and Shastas. Up here ferns as high as his waist grow up along the roadside, layer with moss so that everything between these mansions is covered in green, in the color of money. He knows she lives up here, looking down on the city, in a house hidden from the street by big money trees. They're all up here, John and Francie too. Just have to find out exactly where.

The bus stops on Patton, her stop, and Brandi nudges him.

"You getting off?" The door hisses as it opens.

"Not just yet," he says evenly. "Just going to do a little sightseeing first."

What he means is, shake these money trees, let some golden green rain down on his bare head.

32

Modern Bride

CHLOE

*E*ight thirty on Monday morning, Chloe is lying on her stomach on the thick, rose-patterned area rug in her dormered office, dog-earing a *Modern Bride*. Paul didn't show up for their Strohecker's coffee date, so she gave up, came into the office early, signed in with Beverly, starting her meter, and now she's just using up time.

It has been exactly four weeks since she left Maui, and she is hungry for contact with Dan, logged in to AOL with the monitor off so that if Dan e-mails, the man will chirp "You've got mail!" How she loves her perfect little third-floor office, the hollow wooden staircase separating her from everyone in the international programs, jammed in their cubicle adjacent to Judith's glass-walled office and eagle eyes. Some days, this is still almost her dream job.

The intercom beeps; Beverly, and Chloe hopes like always that it is a call from Dan.

"Chloe—line two."

Chloe pulls the phone off her desk, drags it to the floor with her, her back propped against the sofa. "Hello?"

"Where are you? I waited for you."

Paul?

"What?" They have crossed a line now, she thinks. They shouldn't be waiting for each other, but if they happen to be getting coffee in the same place at the same time, then—

"I banged on your door for a fucking hour."

"Who is this?"

"You know who it is. You go in early today?"

"Hi, Jason." She tries to sound casual, like Casey from the China program downstairs, who can be cheery-chatty when even the most irate couples call to rage about their dossier.

"Where are you?" he demands.

Chloe swallows, wants to ask him the same thing. *He was at her house?*

"What's up?"

"You tell me. Where's our fucking money?"

Chloe glances at the new 2001 calendar over her desk, Oregon nature scenes. This month, January, is a stock black-and-white of Multnomah Falls. It is the twenty-ninth. She calculates in her head— Penny's baby born at the beginning of December, the standard six weeks of follow-up support are over. Their accounting file is closed.

"What?" she says, to buy time. She knows he knows the policy; he has bitched about it from their first meeting. *He was at her house!*

"I've got Julio hassling me for the rent, and I still ain't got a job, Chloe. You still working on that?"

"Jason," she starts, "our obligation to you, our financial obligation to you and Penny, is over at six weeks. It's been almost two months."

"Oh, so that's how it is—you got what you wanted, now you want us to just go away?"

Well, yes, she thinks. That's usually how it works.

"I can make referrals to other service agencies." She kneels up off the floor, grabs her Rolodex off her desk. They have done this before, had this very conversation.

"I see how you operate. No fucking turkey and mashed potatoes now. Now you got our baby, you don't give a shit about us."

Chloe sits back against the sofa.

"Jason, you signed—"

"Penny's not got out of bed in a week. She's fucking crying in there, and I don't see you coming around to check in on her, now that you got our baby."

"Now those kinds of services you can have. Free counseling for a year. I gave you our counselor's card, Justine Albright. Do you need her number again? I've got it right here."

"And we're hungry too. Fucking starving. WIC found out she gave the baby up, so we're not getting our checks from them, and you don't give a shit about us, now you got our baby."

"Jason—"

"I won't live like this! Penny's got herself all locked up in the bedroom, and you with your goddamn SUV and your Portland Heights, getting rich off us! You're a bottom-feeder! You took our baby—"

"You do realize *I* didn't take your baby, right? I don't have him here under my desk—" She hears a slam, cursing, a car honking. Could he really have been at her house? Where is he now? Standing in her kitchen? The phone booth outside Strohecker's? "Jason, calm down."

"I won't calm down!"

"I will talk to Judith about a loan, or some groceries, there's no need for anyone to be starving. But I also want you to call Justine Albright, for yourself. You have a right to your feelings, your grief and your anger—"

"Fucking right I do. You took advantage of us, and you took our kid," he says, but his tone is settling, more sullen than angry.

"I don't have your baby."

"But you know who does."

"Jason, I've got to go. But I will talk to Judith, and I really want you both to make some appointments with the counselor, okay?"

No answer. Chloe waits a minute, and is about to hang up when he says, "She just wants to see him."

"What?"

"Just look through the window, that's all."

"Jason—"

"You're gonna give me their address."

And he hangs up.

It is so much easier when, after the papers are signed, everyone simply retreats, goes back to their corners, disappears. The adoptive parents into the all-consuming babyland, the birth parents drifting on, carrying their grief with them like battered travel trunks.

Chloe puts the phone back on her desk. Jason's not dangerous, she thinks. He cried into her neck, afterward, outside Penny's hospital room on the little couch. No reason to be afraid of him.

Chloe turns on her monitor to check for new e-mail from Dan. None. How can he go days without contact? Heather's adoption is over, what is she doing here? Her hands shake, stomach clenches. Jason Xolan was at her house this morning!

"We're grieving," Jason had said; *"is there a time limit?"* That's all—he's just grieving.

On the wooden stairs, heavy footfalls with long pauses: Judith, making the ascent. Chloe stuffs the bridal magazines under the dust ruffle of her couch and grabs the dry-erase board from where it is propped, uncaps a smelly marker as Judith comes in and flops heavily onto the couch.

"Good girl, you're in early," Judith says with a nod.

"Hi," Chloe says casually, erasing all of Heather W.'s line with the pad of her thumb. Just like that. "Updating my board," she says.

"Good." Judith is still out of breath, and there are deep pit stains on her ballooning black turtleneck dress. "Catch me up to speed."

"Well . . ." Chloe holds the dry-erase board away from herself, frowns at it like a child's Impressionist painting. "As you can see, things are sort of slow . . ."

On the top half of the board it says BIRTH MOTHERS, underlined twice, and in neat rows beneath that are three names, due dates, and then check marks in columns that represent where they are in the process. Medicals done, drug screens, portfolios viewed or chosen, maternity/food/housing, counseling referrals, birth plan, legals reviewed.

"I've got Abby, Jade, and Marissa, but Marissa's not calling me back, so I think I'd put her as a maybe."

"And how about families?"

Chloe gestures to the bottom half of her board, littered with names. Sixteen prospectives, waiting. Following each is their date of entry, their date of deposit, the word CHOSEN.

Judith lets out a sigh. "Winter's always slow," she says unconvincingly. "But . . ." Chloe knows what's coming. "I hate to do it, it'll stir up the Boarders, but I'm closing the domestic program to new families for a few months."

Chloe looks down at the floor. "Probably best."

"And I think I won't have you speak at our open house this month. I'm going to get Casey to write up something on the Marshall Islands program for the Web site, see if we can spin-doctor this. Do you think anyone from your list might be interested in coming over to international?"

Chloe scans the names. The six couples at the top of the list have been there more than three years, inherited by Chloe from the caseworker before her. They are older, often unattractive, and absolutely unwavering in their specifications: healthy white newborn, no prenatal drug/alcohol exposure, closed adoption. Further down the list, she offers up a few names.

Chloe looks out the window at the fog. She wants to be better, to do better, but short of getting knocked up herself, what can she do?

"We've weathered slower times than this." Judith pats Chloe's shoulder, leaving a damp sensation. "And look at all the names you've crossed off!" The dry-erase in the birth-mother column leaves ghosts of her handwriting: Heather W 1/1/01, Mandy&Dwight 12/16/00, Penny&Jason 12/2/00.

Chloe looks up. "Jason Xolan, from the McAdoo adoption, called here today. They want more money."

Judith snorts, "Me too."

"He was sort of threatening. I referred him to Justine."

"Good girl."

"I also told him I'd talk to you. He says they don't have any food, that Julio is hassling them—"

"Now why did you do that?" Judith explodes. "We cannot give them any more money. Even if we could afford to, if I wanted to, which I don't, we can't. You hinting about it jeopardizes our non-profit status, opens us up to a host of legal problems, should he decide to get all lawyered on us."

Chloe's face burns. "He won't; he's not that smart. I'm sorry. I wasn't thinking."

"You've been here too long to make these sorts of mistakes," Judith huffs. "We are a private agency, not baby buyers."

"I know. Sorry. He scared me. He said he knows where I live."

"What? Why on earth would he know that? I'm sure he's bluffing."

"I don't know. An operator like Jason could sneak a peek at my license when I had my wallet open to get out the agency card at dinner or something." But Chloe is lying, covering her rookie error: once, before Thanksgiving, she wanted to make sure she beat Dan home. She had ordered a windsurfing harness for him, a Christmas present, and she wanted to get home to hide the package. She was driving Jason back from looking at the apartment in Southeast, heading to pick Penny up from a doctor's appointment, and she had swung by the house. Stupid stupid stupid. Jason is not bluffing—he knows exactly where she lives.

"Well, tell your Danny he's got to hit the gym. Jason's a big guy." Judith plants her hands on either side of her hips on the spongy couch, a sign she is about to get up. She stops when she sees Chloe's face. "I'm sorry," she says gruffly. "I didn't mean to make light of it."

Chloe puts the cap back on the marker, clips it to the board, pushes it across the smooth carpet away from her.

"What?" Judith asks. "Everything all right with you two? Wedding woes?"

Why, she doesn't know, but Chloe blurts out, "Dan didn't come back from Maui."

"Oh." Like a true social worker, Judith lets the silence build until Chloe is so uncomfortable she keeps talking.

"He wants to see if he can start a business there, a kiteboarding business."

They both look at Chloe's hand, where the new ring, the real ring, had received much attention in the filing room earlier this month when she came back for Heather's adoption.

"You're not leaving us," Judith says firmly.

"Oh, no! We'll just do the long-distance thing for a while until he realizes it won't work out and he comes back."

"Because this isn't the kind of job where you can just, la-di-da, give your two weeks' notice and skip off to Hawaii with your boyfriend." Judith points to the board with a thick finger. "You've got three birth mothers there counting on you, and a stack of families who have put their faith in you to make their dream come true."

"I know."

"And the Chosen Child is a family," Judith says. "It's *your* family."

Chloe thinks of the things she could tell Judith about her "family," about Beverly on Instant Messenger all day with some biker guy in Reading, PA. About Casey from the China program, who tokes up before work, who goes home on her lunch hour every day to smoke a bowl, who is so addicted to the drug you're not supposed to be able to get addicted to that every four months, when she travels to Guangzho to escort families and their new baby girls, she pads her bra with pot to get her through the two weeks overseas. "It really helps with the jet lag and the nausea, you know, because of all the strange smells over there," she has told Chloe.

As if reading her mind, Judith says, "We may be dysfunctional, but we're a family. You can't quit family."

"I know."

"Okay, then." Now Judith does put her fists down and punches herself to a standing position. "And Ken and I were just talking; we're going to have Beverly move you up to twelve dollars an hour at the next quarter."

Just then, there is a ping: *You've got mail!*

Judith raises one eyebrow, stares at Chloe long enough to make her squirm, and leaves.

WHEN SHE IS GONE, Chloe can't turn the monitor on fast enough, click the red mailbox, and it is from Dan! She opens it, and already, before she even reads a word, her stomach sours, understanding from the shape, the horizontal sliver of space it takes up on the wide white screen, that it will be brief, completely unsatisfying.

Hey, babe. Just chilling here at the café while doing some wash. Sweet sesh this morning, light wind, not too intense. Missing you like always. Paolo's honking, gotta jet, love you.

33

Everyone Knows It's Wendy

EVA

Maggie can only stay the weekend. Driving him to the airport Monday morning, Eva feels a panic, her heart beating too fast. Or is it the caffeine, the huge coffees they got at Strohecker's on the way out?

"I don't want you to go," she says.

"Me neither. Duty calls. But you're doing okay, right?"

Eva takes a shaky breath. Is she doing okay? While she is formulating her answer, thinking about how much she can say to him about the dark, slippery slope into the abyss in twenty minutes of postcommuter interstate, Wyeth begins to fuss in the back. She reaches behind her into the bucket of Wyeth's rear-facing car seat, finds his pacifier where it has fallen down in the crook by his thigh, and pops it into his open mouth, holding it there while she drives with one hand. In the silence that follows, Eva's eyes pull closed too, just a moment, but Magnus shouts and jerks the wheel straight in her hand.

"Are you falling asleep?" His laugh is not a funny one—a barking exhalation of adrenaline, terror.

"No, sorry, just tired."

There is a long beat of silence; she can feel him watching her.

"You're amazing, you know. Seeing you as a mom is surreal, especially given the model we had . . . ," her brother says.

"Imagine if I still had the stick shift," Eva says, trying to lighten the mood. "I suppose I could steer with my knees——"

"Really. You're like the glue, holding these guys together. I'm being, well, *me,* whining to you about Genai wanting to settle down, boring you with my woman problems, and Paul's all trying to be Mr. Busy-Businessman, and of course the baby's NeedyMcNeedy. Even Henry, the pissing cat, needs you. You're like Wendy to all the Lost Boys. I ordered you a jacket off eBay." (It will arrive four days later; a vintage hot pink sateen cheerleader jacket with the name Wendy embroidered over the left breast, and Eva will burn it in their fireplace, because she's not worthy.)

"How do you think Paul is doing?" Eva asks, to change the subject. She is still shaken——had she really almost fallen asleep there? What is wrong with her?

"Enh." Maggie shrugs.

"Exactly. I mean, I know we're so lucky, Paul and I. We've got each other, our house, and finally our baby, but sometimes, Mag, I just feel like someone has popped my top and scooped me out with a melon baller. Hollow."

"I know," Magnus says, and he looks out the window at the river.

They drive in silence, the sound of Wyeth furiously slurping on the pacifier she holds for him filling the car.

"Good god, your poor jibbles."

"Yeah," Eva says on a sigh.

"Poor Wendy."

She pulls up at Departures, and she swallows her panic. Maggie, her brother, her constant, slipping back to La-La Land. "You'll be back, right?"

"Of course. Two weeks. Maybe less. I'm scared to bring Genai, though—one look at that handsome little hoover, and she'll ovulate on the spot."

"Bring her."

"Really?" Magnus unfolds his long legs, preparing to get out. "We should do it? Have a kid?"

"Enh . . . ," Eva says, and they laugh. "No, I'm joking. Please, do it. God, Maggie, keep me company. Keep me sane."

34

Portland Heights Shell

JASON

"I been thinking about this for too long," Jason says as he bends her willing rag-doll frame over the rust-stained sink. In the mirror, her weasel eyes meet his, and she offers him a lukewarm smile that says, *Go for it*. He knows what she wants. He can throw it in like nobody else, doesn't Penny always say so?

"Waiting," he says, and he grabs around in front of her, unsnaps her jeans. "You have too." She doesn't help him, but she doesn't stop him as he yanks them down to the middle of her twiggy thighs. She's wearing a turquoise thong, the elastic spent so it hangs in loops on her hollow, sallow hips, and he gives one jerk, snaps it in his hands, throws it toward the trash can spilling over with used towels and tampon applicators.

He's out of his own pants, and the tiny, cement-floored bathroom fills with the man-smell of him. He stops for a moment, loving the feeling of the winter air on his hot skin. He'll give it to her so good she'll do anything for him.

"You got something?" she asks.

"Oh, I got something," he says, misunderstanding, rubbing it in the crease of her skinny ass. Ugly white goose pimples dot her coffee skin, so fucking cold up here at nine in the morning, on a Monday no less, talk to her boss about a job since she won't do it for him, but you gotta do what you gotta do, he thinks. Means to a fucking end. A job, cash, Mexico . . .

"I don't want a baby," she says, and he laughs then, thinking she's as stupid as she is homely.

"Oh, don't you worry," he says, because that's not where he was headed, but she's digging in her sweatshirt pouch for a brand-new box of rubbers, yanked from over the register out front. Might be better anyway, he thinks as she opens the box with her ugly pointy crank teeth. God knows where she's been. A few strokes and she'll be his, do anything he wants. He's a stallion.

I'm doing this for you, baby. He thinks of Penny, curled up on their bed with the blinds pulled.

"Jesus!" Brandi yelps. She has one of those whiny froufrou-dog voices, and she's writhing, trying to get away from him, but he's got her right against the edge of the sink, can feel the front arc of his pelvic bones meeting the back of hers where she is trapped, pinned against the porcelain.

"Don't move," he grunts.

She's whimpering, and he's sawing away, this was supposed to be so fucking good, so fucking good. He yanks her sweatshirt up in the back and rears back so he can see it, that narrow brown back, dimples at the top of her ass; her showing them around the apartment every goddamn time she bends over and her jeans slip low, imagined this, and how fucking good it was going to be. He's no cheater, he loves his Penny—with her glorious white ass like two gigantic boiled Idaho potatoes—he's just a guy doing what guys do, bend over or get bent, he thinks.

He reaches around to grab for Brandi's tits, pathetic little puddles under her sweatshirt that don't feel like nothing, *This was supposed to be so good*, and she's still whining like a goddamn dog who wants out.

"Shhh," he says, but it comes out soft, so he barks, "Shut up, shut the fuck up, you want someone to hear us?"

Wasn't she supposed to be all moaning and grinding back and

screeching his name the way she did Lisle's? Wasn't this supposed to open doors for him? He is not too proud to pump gas.

And then she's silent and still, which is worse. The bathroom is quiet except for the jingling of the buckles on his leather jacket with each thrust, like the impatient ringing of a doorbell in an empty house. Jason looks up, by accident catches his reflection towering over her hunched back in the fluorescent lighting, and something about the zigzag part of her slippery black hair, the pink butterfly clip, makes it look like he's fucking some kid, like he's one of those sickos who likes little girls.

"How old are you anyway?" he grunts, still sawing—it still feels plenty good enough to keep going.

"Huh?" she says, and lifts her head to meet his eyes in the mirror. There are tears in them, and she sniffs hard. "Seventeen in July. Why, how come?" *Fuck.* He pulls out, and instead of looking relieved, she just looks confused, almost disappointed. She breaks eye contact, stares down at her hands gripping the wet edge of the sink, stretched like starfish.

"I changed my mind." He tears the rubber off, throws it toward the trash. He can't look at himself in the mirror. He zips his pants as best he can, still half hard, thinking he should have just kept going— it might have gotten better. Godammit, always making the wrong choice.

Finally he says, "You're out of soap in here. You can tell your boss I'm good with details." He tries to laugh, but his throat is dry, ragged. Without even bothering to pull up her pants, she hobbles to the wall, grabs paper towels from the dispenser. She runs cold, rust-colored water over one and stuffs it between her legs, uses the other to carefully wipe down the edge of the sink.

"Okay." And then she stands there, swiping at her eyes—god, she's ugly, like a cat-faced apple going brown, he thinks as he reaches in his jacket pocket for the crinkling baggie. She has a pen hollow in her sweatshirt pocket that comes out now. The coke is snow-white, not that shit cut with baking soda Victor's usually peddling, and he sees her see it, her face almost pretty when she beams, whispers, "Good shit," and he thinks disgustedly that for this, he really should have fucked her in the ass. *Goddammit!* He slams out of the bathroom, kicking the door behind him with his boot.

Jason grabs a fresh pack of Camels from over the register, and he's sucking down his first one, thinking. Pissed at himself; wrong idea with Brandi. But if she could just get him this job, get their shit together, get him and Penny out of that hole, he'd heard about a trailer park forty minutes farther southeast, with a wide stream and a fire pit, a real sense of community. Of course there's rules, no trailers more than ten years old, and the one he's got his eye on is cheap, but it's thirteen, always a fucking glitch—

Around the front of the station there's the ping of a car driving up. Jason pounds his fist on the steel door to get Brandi's attention. She comes out all glassy-eyed, wiping at her nose with her sweatshirt sleeve—god, where does his brother find these kids? Lisle's thirty, two years younger than him, and he's still running around with the fucking nursery school.

"Customer's here." Jason grabs her by the elbow to propel her around the side of the building, his cigarette clamped between his lips, when he sees the car. A spanking-new silver Volvo Cross Country, how could he forget it? And as Brandi fumbles, then shoves the nozzle into the gas tank, Jason sees the Oregon license plate, SPR-NVA, the arc of the car seat handle in the back, and the back of Blondie's head in the front, and with a barking cough in the cold air, his smoky breath disappears, leaving in its place the hint of a plan.

35

Something Is Missing

EVA

*I*t happens early Monday morning, when Eva is driving back from the airport in light misting rain, her brother off to L.A., Wyeth asleep in the car seat in the back.

"So you're coming back, right?" she had asked Magnus again at Departures.

"I'll give you a call, but you know I can't stay away long. I just have to work a few things out. Genai . . ." He left the sentence open.

"Bring her! My friend Francie knows real estate—we could find you two a cottage."

"Maybe so."

"We need you, Mag." Neither of them mentioned that Magnus had been less and less willing to help out with the baby the last two visits as their slack-limbed, placid newborn had slowly been replaced with a wiry, gassy, cranky, twist-faced gargoyle. Conversations focused on what might be the cause—was the house too dry, their detergent too perfumed, should Eva really be eating onions/peppers/dairy/nuts/garlic? Should they call the pediatrician? (They did, three times—she was sympathetic but unconcerned.)

"Hey," Magnus had said sharply to get her attention as he tucked his ticket into his jean hip pocket. He made meaningful eye contact, waited to speak. "You and Paul are doing a good job, Chicky."

"I'm glad someone thinks so." Her voice wavered as she wiped at her eyes.

They had hugged, and she watched him walking into the airport, his oversize carry-on bumping beside him like a companion dog.

There were clothes still hanging in the narrow guest-room closet under the eaves; two shirts, a pair of khakis, and his gigantic creased Adidas. Magnus would be coming back, but much sooner than either of them realized just then.

Now Eva pulls into the gas station off Sunset, right near Portland Heights. There is a thick fog rolling up the hill, and she can barely see the little brick building as she waits for the attendant. She ticks through the list of things to do in her mind.

Maggie—airport
Gas!!!!
Go to gym, elliptical, 40 minutes
Coffee!!!!
Wash sheets
Call Francie?
Take walk to grocery w/Wyeth if not raining
Milk, lemons for pasta dish, and ice cream. Wine?

It's not much, but making these lists, adding structure to her yawning days, days that will no longer have the company of her brother and the endless analysis of his disastrously dysfunctional relationship, his suggestions that they go out for lunch or browse Powell's, his willingness to hold the screaming baby for the thirty seconds it takes her to twist her hair back into a knot, just might keep her afloat. Until what? she wonders. Lather rinse repeat, as Paul would say. This is her life now.

The night before, when Wyeth had finally cried himself out and she and Paul were bumping around each other in the bathroom taking out contacts and brushing teeth, the alarm system had gone off at Paul's Hillsboro office, activating one of the hallway fire sprinklers. It was a fluke, but he had stayed until two in the morning getting everything sorted out, and she knew he planned to go back early today with the cleaning crew, arrange for industrial dryers and dehumidifiers to come and draw the damp out of the carpet before it had to be replaced.

"It's not that we can't afford to replace the carpet," Paul had assured her. "Just no need to."

Wyeth had woken up to nurse around two twenty, startling at Paul's big boots clomping up the wooden stairs. It had taken him until almost three to nurse both sides, some kind of a growth spurt maybe, and then her brother's flight was at nine, but he wanted to leave at seven. . . . God, she's exhausted. It is only the sight of her thighs spreading to touch each other on the car seat that is driving her on to the gym.

A skinny teenage girl shuffles out with her hands in her jacket pockets to pump the gas, shoulders braced against the morning damp rolling up the hill off the highway below. Her sweatshirt hood is bunched up behind her black hair, a sad smattering of deep pits and sores around her mouth, slight trickle of clear snot just under her nose. She sniffs hard, wipes at her face with her sleeve.

"Fill it up?" Eva says. While the girl fiddles with the pump, Eva rifles through her gym bag, always so awkward to be waited on for something she could easily do herself. She has her portable CD player, a towel, but no water. Squinting, she can see the light of a vending machine just inside the glass door of the no-frills gas station. Eva counts out two dollars in quarters, thinking that should be more than enough, even in Portland Heights. She gets out and crosses the pavement to the building, stepping around the coiled black hoses as if they are snakes.

It will be okay, she thinks to herself, if she can just get Maggie into his own place up here, less tension between him and Paul, fewer pleading/stabbing looks between her and Paul, and then she can put her life in some semblance of order, maybe even get a sitter for Wyeth a few times a week while she pursues something of interest . . . something of interest . . . Eva closes her eyes in the empty gas station office, tilts her head forward against the vending machine.

The machine dispenses an Aquafina, ice-cold, and Eva pulls her fleece sleeve down over her hand to carry it back to the car. She quickly shuts the car door, rubs her hands together, almost starts the engine to turn on the heater out of instinct before she realizes that the gas is still being pumped. She hears the metallic clunk of the pump handle shutting off, and Eva is annoyed—now the girl is nowhere in sight. Stupid Oregon law, not allowed to pump your own gas. When she first moved out here, years ago, she thought it was as charming as the Japanese teahouses in the Rose Garden, as though the whole state was so polite that it knew nobody wanted to stand around in the famously miserable rain while their car filled up. Lately, especially now with the baby who cries if he's in his car seat without the soothing rumble of the motor, it just seems inefficient and inconvenient.

Finally, Eva sees her coming around from by the restrooms and starts the engine to put down her window, turns the heater vents on high. She hands her credit card to the girl, who has it back to her in no time, practically shoving it back in the half-closed window, holding it in the sleeves of her sweatshirt, the hood up around her face now, and though she will regret it later, Eva spares her the embarrassment of looking at her ugliness too closely. The girl ducks her head as she half runs back to the little brick building.

Eva watches in satisfaction as the gas meter turns all the way back to full, puts the car in drive, and winds smoothly on the switchbacks toward the highway, to the health club. The fog dissipates into light drizzle as she leaves the hills of Portland Heights. Her windshield wipers make streaks of the silver water; she needs to get some new blades. At the dark on-ramp traffic meter, she adds this to her list of things to do during the week. *Buy windshield wiper blades.* Something of interest . . .

In the gym parking lot, she grabs her water, her cell phone, her gym bag off the floor of the passenger seat, and gets out.

For a moment, as she stands by the driver's side door, the sun breaks through the clouds, and Eva is struck by the way it glints off the windshields of the wet cars all around her. How long since they have seen the sun? she wonders as she opens the back door to get Wyeth out. If they could just have a day or two of sun this month, things might be—

The car seat is empty. Eva freezes, a rush of dread like a truckload of lead to her empty stomach, feels it drop to her toes.

I left him with Paul, she thinks, looking again. Her hands shake as she opens the phone to call home, when she remembers her brother earlier that morning, leaning in with his carry-on over his shoulder through the back door of the Volvo to drop a kiss on Wyeth's sleeping forehead. She remembers too Paul's sleepy voice in the predawn dark of this morning as she pulled on her black stretch pants, "You're taking the baby, right?"

"What?" Her irritated rasp of a whisper.

"I have to go to the office to empty the dehumidifiers—then the cleaners are meeting me at eight thirty."

And so she had scooped up the sleeping baby, grabbed a dry diaper for when he woke, grouchily zipped him into a fleece, and left.

I should call 911.

Come on, Eva! Nothing but frozen disbelief. Staring again at the empty, rear-facing blue plaid car seat, Eva snaps her phone shut. The sun goes back behind a cloud. She can't dial, her hands shaking too badly, she needs people, help, corroboration, validation, she needs this not to be happening to her alone in the middle of the vast and nearly vacant 24 Hour Fitness parking lot on a cold Monday morning at the end of January.

Eva runs, jerkily, toward the gym, her legs flying awkwardly out of the sockets, out of her control. She trips over the curb and falls to her palms and knees in front of a slope-shouldered Asian woman wearing a turquoise velour sweat suit just outside the glass doors.

"I—" She tries to say something, but just like the dream with the scream-but-no-sound, finds her throat closed, her voice a strangled squeak. "I've lost my baby—help."

For a moment, the woman looks at her coldly. She glances grudgingly between cars in the parking lot, as though the lost baby might be toddling around nearby, and Eva chokes, "He's only eight weeks, I've lost him, *help me.*"

36

Public Transportation

JASON

*I*t is an empty No. 51 that Jason gets on at SW Talbot and Patton, coming out of the fog and ferns with his boots and the legs of his jeans wet. The commuter rush is over, should be quiet, he thinks, nodding to the bus driver like nothing's wrong as he drops the coins he snagged from the register into the slot. He rides in the back with his eyes shut, hammering heart, jiggling his leg, for it or for him he doesn't know, doesn't care. Goddammit, he just might pull this off!

In fifth grade, Sappho Elementary had a new teacher, an intern from the community college with droopy pancake tits and tinted glasses and breath like tuna fish, but she read to them after lunch every day, *Charlie and the Chocolate Factory.* God, he'd loved that book, listening with his cheek against the cool of his desk, the boy and the Golden Ticket, one in a million, chance of a lifetime. Jason looks down at the fleecy bundle in his arms. He may just have won the lottery himself.

A quick change at Salmon, walking with it under his arm like a sack of potatoes, sucking down another cigarette from the new pack—thanks, Brandi, for everything! At the MAX station, he hops the line toward the airport and is relieved to find only one stooped-over black-dressed granny holding her pocketbook on her lap, and she clutches her claws over the top of it the way women do when she sees him get on, then smiles as he turns and exposes the parcel under his arm. Money in the bank, baby, he thinks to himself. Two more transfers, and home free.

He gets off the MAX and barely has to wait for the No. 10 that will take him home. Ahh, right on time, there's his bus. Two people get off the 10 as he gets on, the baby almost forgotten under his arm by now, just a dull ache in his right bicep from the flexing. God, he's getting out of shape if lugging a kid tires him out. The one good thing you can say about the inside, always plenty of time to pump up, and Jason always did, came out this time in the best shape of his life. Now he's getting soft, too much sitting around, too much worrying over bitches and babies and money, money, money.

Jason takes a seat with his back to the window, tries to settle it on his lap. It's soft as a bread loaf, and it sags back against him. It's been a dilemma, hide it or act casual, made extra difficult by the fact that Jason has had zero time to think this through. He bends his arm, a relaxed angle, and tucks the baby in the crook of his elbow. It has been asleep, but it opens its eyes, looks left and right, as though it knows this is a bad scene.

"Shhh," he says, tucking his head down toward it. Thank god the bus lurches as it leaves the station toward Foster, and soon both the dirty spic drunk in the back and the baby have their eyes closed again.

Jason sniffs at its scalp. Aren't babies supposed to smell sweet? This one doesn't, a sickly smell, like popcorn with rancid butter, the ammonia of piss taking him right back to his first time in a holding cell, seventeen years old, stupid night of drinking and brawling with his little bro and Jason hauled in, but not Lisle. Oh, no, not sweet, precious, swift-legged Lisle. ("Shoulda named him Running Deer," their mother used to say, as time and again he would outrun an ass-whupping by turning on the afterburners.) No, lily-white Lisle had never once spent a night locked up.

"Get used to this smell, Tonto" (Jason had had braids back then and a turquoise belt buckle, trying to find his self, his people). The deputy had laughed when he shoved a still-drunk Jason so hard he fell into the cell, his cheek against the damp cement, smelling that piss smell. "Your kind just can't keep their noses clean. I think we'll be seeing a lot of each other." Which in fact turned out not to be true. As soon as Jason was released, noon the next day, he hitched home and packed a duffel bag, stole the pile of cash from his old man's top dresser drawer, and left Clallam County. He went back to Sappho once for his mother's funeral, thanks to a "fall down the stairs" of the one-level trailer where he grew up. Never again. And after this, it's got to be south all the way. Mexico, if they can make it. Safer there. *Incognito.*

The bus stops at Halsey, and a fat woman and little girl get on. God, the woman's superfat, stuffed into her jeans in a way that says her Doughboy suburban husband is too, that they care more about Supersize Me and BBQ than the fact that the rest of the world has to look at them. Christ, Penny just had a baby, stomach sawed in half, and she looks a million times better. He misses his Penny, as he does whenever they're apart, even though it's only been a few hours, even though she's in a bad state these days. There's no explaining it— when she's all backed up into him, her head on his bicep, his face in the back of her neck, he's home.

The bus lurches; no one else gets on. He scans the car, surprised to find he's enjoying the soft weight in his lap. Mrs. Fatty's eating a taffy and reading a supermarket rag. Little girl's cute, big bug eyes staring at him, and then he sees her perfect straw-straight Sunday-go-to-church hair pulled into fucking butterfly clips like Brandi's, which reminds him of the bathroom and this morning—god, was it really just this morning, what was he thinking, little cokey-whore's probably going to tell his brother and she sure as shit isn't going to give him no glowing recommendation to her boss. Not to mention she full-on freaked out when she saw him with the kid under his arm, ducking behind the gas station. Brandi was still all glassy-eyed, repeating herself like his retard cousin Jo-Jo, "What're you doin', Jay, what're you doin', Jay?" When he disappeared over the wild hillside behind the brick building with it tucked under his jacket, she yelled hoarsely after him, "What the fuck have you done?"

He wonders now, looking down at it. Of course now he knows it isn't Buddy; it's some cross-eyed, chicken-skinned one hundred percent Caucasian. This is one blue-eyed white loaf of dough that even Hitler wouldn't shove in an oven. But an ugly little fucker. Jesus. Definitely not his kid, so now-fucking-what to do? He was so sure he had the right car, the one those two got in at the hospital, but if he thinks back, the bitch who went inside at the gas station was too tall, too bootylicious, to be that flat-ass Francie.

Before they got on all these buses and connections, before all these people saw him with it, he had been thinking about maybe bugging out—bad idea, chalk it up to not thinking straight with his balls and back aching—leaving it on the bench of the MAX line, like this morning's newspaper, read and done with. Now he can't. With his free hand, Jason pulls his sunglasses out of the inside pocket of his jacket, drugstore aviators with scratches on the mirrored lenses, and he puts them on, even though it's gray out, even though now there are hash marks messing with his vision. What to do, what to do?

"What's his name?" It's the little girl, with a voice like a cartoon kid, high-pitched and corn syrup sweet.

"Buddy." Conviction, no hesitation. Nice. He can't help it; he allows himself a pleased smirk.

"Oh."

"He's cute," the fat woman says. When she smiles, the corners of her mouth push her cheeks up against the sides of her nostrils. He wonders if she could suffocate herself, smiling. As if in answer, she stops, snuffs hard, and he can practically taste the snot sliding down the back of his throat. He looks away, back down at the top of its head, hair with no color, not brown, not yellow, just dull, slicked straight down. White babies could be so homely! He pictures the real Buddy's thick black hair and eyelashes, a gift from Jason to his son, lady-killer eyes.

Still, he thinks, it's somebody's baby. It means something to somebody. Something to somebody driving a brandy-ass-new Volvo worth fifty gees. Or did it? Bitch just left it in the car, never looked back. Got to get a bottle of water, too good to drink tap. Dumb bitch, it's the same stuff. And too stupid to lock the fucking doors of the car, that's for sure. Nausea rolls in his stomach and the soles of his feet inside his leather boots prickle with sweat. What the fuck has he done?

But, okay, even if the parents didn't want this one back, *somebody* would want a brandy-ass-new one hundred percent white baby. Lots of options, just keep his head on straight, keep thinking. Jason's leg starts to jiggle, sewing machine leg, they call it on the inside. Jiggle-jiggle, his jacket buckles jingle in time, like a one-man band.

Problem: seven tours of different jails and detention centers and lockups, and somehow, he hasn't managed to make the connections a guy would need to find a person to buy a baby. Victor's the biggest shithead he knows, but he's Catholic, wears his six kids' names in loopy script on his gold chains.

And then it wakes up, shit, he's bumped it. It's screaming now, red-faced, eyes closed, and he can't help it, he holds it out away from him, out on his knees, here ya go, kiddo, jiggle-jiggle-jiggle. "Come on, Buddy," he says, eyes darting around the bus.

Mrs. Fatty smiles thinly at him, a been-there-done-that look, and even in the chaos, the storm of the screaming, he marks this as good, that he's pulling this off.

Christ, how does anyone stand this noise? He can't wait to get to the apartment and be rid of it, pass it off to one of the girls and go stand under the shower for some peace. Then he remembers that Brandi won't be home, will still be at work. . . . God, she wouldn't give him up, would she? He hadn't kept fucking her, had he, once she started with the whining? And he hadn't been unclear. "I got a little proposition for you," he'd told her that morning as they waited to open up the gas station at eight for all the good citizens of Portland. He'd waved the baggie, and she'd grinned and practically ran ahead of him to the bathroom. So it was fair. He'd given her the blow, and she'd given it to him, close enough. He's still jiggling the screaming kid, its head waggling back and forth, maybe he shouldn't bounce it so hard, but the fucking screaming's got him all jangled.

Christ, two more stops, and then only a few blocks, maybe the fresh air will shut it up. He pictures Penny's face when he plops it down beside her in their bed, all warm and dark. She won't mind the crying, he doesn't think. And he takes mental stock of the apartment—they've still got the diapers Lisle bought, he can run out for some milk, see if he can use one of the expired WIC checks on that dumb-ass red-dot Indian at the minimart on the corner. It'll all be all right.

Still screaming. What's the fucking problem! Not even pausing for a decent breath, all wound up. No wonder Mrs. Volvo left it in the car—the lungs on this thing. Mental privacy glass, he thinks, like a limo driver, just put up the window and you won't hear it.

And then it chucks all over him, all down the front of his jacket like a freak film, spewing hot across his lap, all over the leather, white and curdled, reeking of bile. Jason jumps up, and it takes all he has not to drop it right on the floor of the bus.

"Do you need a wet wipe?" Mrs. Fatty asks, and at first he's grateful—his jacket will be saved—but then it's clear she's laughing at him. Bitch. Whorebag.

"Uh, yeah." He wants to smash her fat face in, push that pug nose right back in between those silly putty cheeks, watch her implode like a rotten tomato, but he doesn't.

Instead, he smiles his charming smile, his "I-know-you-know-you-want-me-to-bend-you-over-like-the-bad-girl-you-are" smile that works so well. He looks down, then up at her through his black lashes—women always love that. "I, uh, forgot the bag."

"My husband won't carry one either. I even got him one without the duckies and bunnies." She digs around in hers, pulls out a crinkly yellow pack of wipes. "Here."

He puts the kid on the seat, sideways so it won't roll off while he swipes at his jacket, facing her, his cock level with her head, her sitting down, the bus swaying. He could grab a handful of that drugstore-dyed hair, pull her to him, finish. Before she ate the whole goddamn Krispy Kreme factory, she was probably hot. Hell, last call, liquored up, he'd fuck her now, fat ass and all. His dick jerks, and he smiles down at her, I've-gotcha-where-I-wantcha . . .

But she's looking around him, behind him, to the baby who's like a tick on its back, waving arms and legs, hasn't shut up yet.

"You shouldn't leave him like that. He could roll off."

"Yeah, yeah." He turns away, face hot. Know-it-all bitch. He changes his mind as he puts it back under his arm, eyes out the window on his stop. He wouldn't fuck her, not even in the dark. He knows her type, all bossy and telling him "little to the left, harder, slower" and all that shit. He feels the pull toward the apartment and his Penny, the warm bed, the happy reunion, any one of their many Golden Ticket futures. Without a backward glance at Mrs. Fatty Know-It-All, he hops down the two steps into the morning damp, leaving the wadded-up wipes on the seat.

37

Cradle Will Fall

PAUL

When he first sees them coming up the walkway, Eva between two police officers, a third trailing, Paul thinks, from the way one has a hand on her elbow, that she is in handcuffs—what has happened? But then it is clear that she is unsteady, and the men are holding her up. She looks like a fish-eyed stranger; if not for the hair, like a bowl of boiled rotini dumped over her head, he's not sure he would know her. She stumbles, stops, staring at her running shoes, and there is something spilled on her shirt. She looks so defeated Paul wants to run to her, gather her in his arms, how could this have happened?

But he can't move, feels like the treads of his boots are affixed to the front hall floorboards with a fast-drying adhesive. The cluster, Eva and the officers, are passing the side yard, where behind them, the slope that gives Portland Heights its name falls away, a seventy-degree angle of tangles and jagged overgrowth. Paul has a flash— taking Eva by the shoulders and shoving her backward, letting her bounce between the ferns, the stubbled juvenile pines, treacherous, thorny wild blackberries, disposing of her as he did this year's de-composing, black-speckled Halloween pumpkin. *How could you let this happen!*

The phone call had come less than an hour ago, 9:43, while Paul

was on his hands and knees in the office hallway, blotting at the industrial mottled red carpet with guest towels he had grabbed from
home. He had just realized that the merlot of the berber was bleeding
into Eva's ivory Egyptian cotton.

*Paul Nova. This is Detective Haberman. We have your wife here. She's
pretty upset. Seems she thinks she's lost your son.*

As they come up the last three brick steps, Paul pulls the door
open, lifting each foot like he's wearing cement shoes, and he grabs
Eva by her shoulders, pulls her over the doorjamb to him, puts his
face into her hair, which smells faintly of Wyeth's baby shampoo. He
pushes her away. She is talking, a mumble of nonsense. In the air that
swirls between them, Paul breathes what is smattered on her shirt in
chunks and flecks—vomit—and it has transferred, a dampness on
his chest, from her to him.

"What?"

"I locked the door, I thought I locked it, I thought I locked it."

"What door?" Before she answers, Paul has a panic, feeling the
police officers' eyes on his face. What door? Had Wyeth been here,
at the house? Is this his fault too? Had she left the baby with him this
morning, imagining she had passed the baton, thinking she locked
the front door before she left? But if that was true, then was Wyeth
right upstairs, still sleeping in his bassinet?

"What door!" he yells, hope flaring in his chest, desperate to be
the first to thunder upstairs ahead of her and see him, curled on his
stomach, all a terrible mistake, something they will laugh over with
him when he's older, family folklore—*You guys left me home alone when
I was two months old!*

"I thought I locked it, I'm sure . . ." She is still going, and Paul has
an urge to slap her. He knows there is no hope—Wyeth has never in
his life slept more than half an hour alone in his bassinet—but he has
to hear her say it.

"What door!" he roars again, and she looks up at him, desperately, the
ink of her pupils like a slick at the bottom of an old plumbing problem.

"At the gas station," she says plaintively, and he feels first sharp relief, a pinprick in his chest, so that the flood of vindicating blame can well up beneath it: She left their newborn baby in the car at the gas station.

"I locked the door, I thought. I think . . ." She is looking over Paul's shoulder into the living room, her eyes darting, taking it all in, as though she wonders if she might have left him here too, somewhere on a pile of laundry, in the square of weak light under the bay window.

"Let's go on in." The tallest officer, with red, pebbled skin at his neck like a buzzard, the one Paul will come to know as Detective Haberman, shepherds them both past the staircase into the living room. Eva stumbles onto their green corduroy couch. The question-and-answer session begins, and Paul wants her to sound . . . better, smarter . . . say something that will make Haberman, with his sharp nose and buzzard neck, look satisfied.

Paul's head throbs—all he can smell is the stomach acid, Eva's vomit, wafting up off his shirt, like when the cologne spritzers got him at the mall. He can't focus on her answers, which have given nothing of substance anyway.

"So I'm trying to get this straight," Haberman says. "You know you left the car unattended at the Portland Heights gas station—"

"But I thought I locked the door," she interjects.

"You mentioned that. But then, it wasn't until you got to the parking lot at the fitness center that you first realized the car seat was empty."

Eva looks down at her knees. Paul squeezes her hand, hard, feels the knuckles pop and buckle to accommodate the pressure—answer them! He needs to get alone with her so that he can know the truth, what and who he should be protecting. *Susan Smith, two boys strapped in their car seats, dead at the bottom of a lake while the world searched for a hysterical woman's version of the kidnapper.* How far gone has Eva been? Why hasn't he noticed?

"Excuse me." Paul jumps up, jerking his hand free of hers. "I'm, I'm going to change my shirt."

All eyes snap to him. One of the other two officers, the one pacing by the fireplace, touching their things, picking up their wedding photo, shifts his eyes to Haberman and raises the edge of a bushy brow. Paul stops with his foot on the bottom stair, taller now than the rest of them in the room, his hand on the banister. The dickhead is ogling Eva's tits in their wedding photo. (What had her dressmaker said about the excessive hardware under her strapless dress? *To put zee girls on za balcony!*)

"I'll be right back down." Paul means for it to come out stronger, but it sounds like he is asking their permission to go change his shirt in his own house.

"Pretty nice zip code for an electrician," the tit-starer says to the third officer on the phone by the window, loud enough for them all to hear.

I have my own business! Paul wants to shout as he runs up the stairs, boots and heart pounding, his fingers fumbling over the sick-slick buttons of his dark blue SuperNova shirt. He wonders if they need a lawyer. He clamps down on this, a worry he can stomach, the well-being of Paul and Eva Nova, because he cannot think about the blinding, bright-white horror of Wyeth's fate. It is too hot, too glaring, for him to even consider, *statistics, milk cartons, cults, atrocities, pedophiles, man's inhumanity to man—*

Eva! Think of her. Downstairs, they're working her over like dogs on a shredding rawhide. Their questions, poking around, tearing into everything they have built, the home, the business, the blossoming family. Suddenly Paul feels a shedding, a lightness, a divestment of all the trappings, until what, what is left? Without all of this, the baby, the wife, the house, what is left? He looks at the dormered window in their bedroom—could he fit out the window? What is left? Answer: simple human survival. Self-preservation. Oh, Eva, what have you done?

He is conscious of his footfalls above them as he crosses to the window. Will they follow him up here, to his own bedroom, the sanctum sanctorum, demand his discarded, soiled shirt to be tagged and bagged? Paul shucks it to the floor, grabs another off his dresser. He glances down at his pants—wrinkled khakis he put on in the dark this morning. The knees are damp, stained red from the waterlogged carpet where he was kneeling this morning, scrubbing, the cheap red fibers bleeding. (Why hadn't he gotten beige, a neutral color, for the office hallway? Because he had a vision, a showroom with modern Tech Lighting monorail pendants, the transition to design.)

But now his son is missing, there are raised eyebrows among the officers in his living room, and his pants are stained a damning red. He yanks the belt open, lets them fall to the floor, panic coloring his movements. Paul is halfway to the window seat, eyes scanning the room for an escape from all of this, when he sees it: Wyeth's bassinet. A rare shaft of winter sunshine stabs through the window and shines on the white fabric hood, as if the sun itself is pointing a golden finger, illuminating the cradle's emptiness.

There was a baby, his son. A baby that, when it was not scream-ing, when it *did* sleep, curled against Paul's chest, the fontanel pulse thrumming against the hollow under Paul's chin.

Paul stumbles into the window seat, among diapers and washcloths smaller than his palm, a handful of toys that rattle. He rests his head against the cool glass and watches them come. A dark swarm of them on the front lawn, a van with lights flashing blocking off the end of the street, and Paul cannot draw a breath. Somewhere past them, in the vast wide world, someone has his son. They are all in the wrong place.

He leaves his shirt on the windowsill and runs, crossing the room in three strides to the top of the stairs, hurtles himself down, the downstairs air cool on his bare legs and chest, bellowing, "Get out of here! Get away from her! Get out there! Get my son! *Get him!*"

38

Dark Night

JASON

Sundown. Jason lifts the broken blinds again, the streetlight flickering by the dark parking lot like always. Landlord's El Camino, banged-up Taurus of the Martinez family, the Dodge Caravan of the alkie mom of the hot little piece with the kid across the way. Nothing new. Good, good.

Jason's stomach is a mess, all worms-writhing and bloated, anxious. Eight hours, and Brandi's still not back. Has she called Lisle, told him about the bathroom or the baby, or both? Because Jason knows his brother would call him in. Plenty of times when their father was looking to beat on someone, Lisle cheerfully gave Jason up. Just as many times, Jason pointed the finger at his little brother too. Half the time their own ma would meet the old man by the door with the belt in her hand, tattle on them, and then hold him or Lisle by the hair so he could administer their licks, *That'll teach you!*

No loyalty, not even for the dog.

"Get off your asses, I'm going to teach you boys how to shoot right," the old man had said, and Lisle had followed him outside warily. Age ten, Jason wouldn't have put it past the bastard to give them each one of the canvas-strapped, scratched-up rifles he had slung over his shoulder, pit the boys against each other, let the best son win, survival of the fucking fittest. But it wasn't; it was Pancho Villa, the dog, getting old, had a hard time getting up when it was time to go out for a crap. He was tied to a leafless piece of scrub in the yard, and the old man stuck a rifle in each of their hands. "Pancho has shit his last," he said, and then grinned at Jason and Lisle. "So, who's gonna go first?"

LISLE COULD HAVE CALLED him in. Right now, the cops could be sitting in ambush. Sex with a minor (no point in pointing out Lisle fucked her first, or that she was a rotted-mouth crank whore), breaking parole, not to mention in the bedroom, the little problem-that-he-thought-might-be-a-solution. Christ, he could go away for life!

Fuck! Now the kid's been screaming for two hours straight, walls thin as rolling papers around here, someone's got to notice. They've got to get it some milk, but he's scared to go out. No wheels, he's a sitting duck. For all he knows they're all lined up just past the parking lot waiting for him. He jerks the bedroom door open—it's like cardboard and flies in his hands, twanging his shoulder.

Jesuschrist she's got her shirt up and trying to stuff a flappy-floppy tit in his open mouth!

"What the fuck's wrong with you?" And because he's agitated, he cuffs the back of her head, not *hard*, but it breaks their rules. That's the thing of their relationship, an agreement of bodies: Penny doesn't open her legs for anyone, and he doesn't lay a hand on her. She wears her loyalty to him like the coat of an Irish setter, glossy and auburn. Never once, in all their years, have even her eyes walked away from him. And he won't do to her like those guys outside Denver.

"Aw, Pen," he says, but it's too late, and the baby's still screaming.

Like a flash, her hand winds up and comes down open and flat, *smack!* across the baby's cheek, leaving red. It stops, stunned, and Jason's stomach turns. The baby throws back its head and lets out an anguished scream, and Penny winds up again, *smack!* same red cheek, and the baby stops, silenced mid-wail. It looks big-eyed and shocked at Penny, cheek flaming, a tear spilling out of its eye. Jason knows this feeling, cell memory, salty hot water on burning slapped skin. The baby hiccups. Jesus. He runs a hand over his own stubbled face.

"That's enough of *that*," Penny says, and she turns her eyes to Jason like a little girl who brought home straight As. But she reads him—Penny may be dumb, but she's not stupid—and she juts that ugly stubborn pocked-up Popeye chin out.

"I wouldn't ever do that to Buddy," she says. "Never."

Like he said, his girl's dumb but she's not stupid. He tries to keep his face plain, but she mugs at him, pushing past to the living room. He follows, and she's trying to set it up on the sofa, but it keeps folding in on itself like a half-empty bag of laundry.

"I know this isn't Buddy. A mother knows." Penny reaches over and tries to straighten the baby, then gives up, lets him sag like a rotted fence post. "Besides, Buddy's not this homely. Whoever this baby is"— she hefts herself up off the sofa—"snatching him was either the dumbest thing you did, or the smartest."

"What?" He doesn't know what to say.

"You tell me, mister."

The baby whimpers. Penny gives it one wild horse-eyed warning glare before going into the bedroom and slamming the hollow door.

Jason knows what he has to do. He looks at the baby; can't leave it here with Penny and her quick slaps—kid's face is still glowing, outlines of three fingers in white like a tribal tattoo. But he can't be seen with it either. He leaves it bobble-headed on the couch and goes into the bathroom, finds the largest, most threadbare of the towels. His aunt Selma-Wade, back in Sappho, used to wear her retard boy like a bandolier. Jason tosses the towel over one shoulder, ties the two ends together in a thick knot, guessing at the length.

Back in the living room, he struggles to stuff the baby into the swath across his chest. He misjudged; the thing nearly drops out the bottom. The second time, he holds the towel in his teeth, presses the baby against his chest with one arm, and reknots the towel, lashing the baby to him. He can slide on his leather jacket, shrugging into

it like a friend, first thing he ever bought with his first trucking paycheck, five hundred eighteen dollars, this jacket and the Frye boots.
The leather of them stank like money, the weight like nothing he'd
ever worn. Usually he leaves it open, but this time he does up every
buckle and zipper, nobody the wiser.

Jason takes a few practice steps around the living room. His
back twinges, always paining him. The brass flashing screams as he
opens the door, but the baby doesn't startle. A thought occurs to him:
if they're waiting for him, pistols pointed, all he has to do is open up
the jacket—human shield.

OUTSIDE, THE NIGHT IS wet, but not raining. Leaves blow through
the parking lot, nothing else. Hugging the side of the building, Jason
plows through the dripping, scratchy bushes at the border of the parking lot, taking a shortcut to Foster. He walks along the inside of the
sidewalk, farther from the curb, toward the strip mall where there is
a drugstore, about a mile.

It seems to have fallen asleep. If Jason lifts the neck of his jacket,
the dome of the blue-white head glows like the rounder end of a soft-
boiled egg. He thunks it with a thick finger, as if testing for a good
watermelon. It stirs a little, moves its head away from his tapping,
still breathing in there.

He wonders what's happening with the real Buddy. Is someone
holding him, walking him, chest to chest? Is Francie or John looking
down on Buddy's vulnerable skull with tenderness? Or would John be
like his own father, sap-stained hands, cracked leather belt, coming
down on him and Lisle with the regularity of a workweek?

Walking along Foster, Jason thinks of something: This could be
broken. His son could grow up in Portland Heights, where parents
aren't clouded in cigarette haze and indifference, where dads play
ball with their sons. Maybe not ball—the old man had looked gimp-
legged—but maybe read him the stock report, let him cut his first
teeth on Daddy's fat leather billfold. They'd be the kind of people to

send their son to one of those schools where bullying is not allowed, not like Sappho, where even the principal jeered them on from the sidelines of dusty playground brawls.

His son could be popular; who didn't like the rich kids? Everyone'd be clambering around Buddy to be invited over for video games, soda, and brownies. And his son could grow up with a set place in this world, not scrapping for it, but already decided for him. *This* is who you are, with the sun shining on your face as the team hefts you onto their shoulders at the end of the football game (because Buddy would be doubly blessed, Jason's physical talents, John and Francie's status).

And because of this life, and a good, classy woman, and having enough, Buddy would be a Law-Abiding Citizen, and would never know the inside and all its intricacies, the politics of bend over or be bent. Buddy would never think that even at six-four, just keeping your head down and quiet would be enough to get you ignored the first time the bars slammed shut behind you.

The cycle could be broken. They could grow old together, his son and the wife, and beautiful children, and not one of them would ever feel the sting of a hand in anger. Jason smiles to himself, his jacket jingling as he walks, the buckles clinking. It's bitter, this gift he's given his son, this future, but it's good.

Jason checks under his jacket; still breathing.

FIRST THINGS FIRST. HE stops in at the convenience store. Milk is $3.49 a gallon, but a coffee is only $.69, so he goes to the coffee station and lets the hissing brown liquid spill out into the drain, one eye on the clerk, then empties the pint of cream into his cup, caps it. He pays for the coffee and another pack of Camels—no surprise he's on his second pack today—with his last five dollars and leaves the convenience store with his head down as he passes the camera.

Next stop, drugstore. He goes straight to the baby section and lines up two boxes of diapers, like he can't decide which. He fakes a sip of his coffee. Behind the boxes, he opens a pink plastic baby bottle, jamming the packaging behind the diapers. A freckled man comes into the aisle, short, square, wearing pointy shoes that squeak as he hurries past Jason.

"I never remember what I'm supposed to get." Jason is pleased with how even and low his voice comes out. The man looks over, offers a pale smile.

"I know." The man nods, rifling through rows of lotions, creams.

Quickly, working behind the diapers, Jason tips the cream from the coffee cup into the bottle, caps it, and wedges it in his back jean pocket. The whole thing takes eleven seconds; he loves shoplifting. Something for nothing. He pretends to sip from his now empty coffee cup, nods to the man holding two brands of lotion, his cell phone jammed in his shoulder, "Hon, do you want the lavender or the regular?"

First thing he'll buy with the money: cell phones for both of them. Then a car, or a motor home, for the drive south, and he'll fix her teeth, so he doesn't have to look at the blackness in her mouth and think about what they did to her in Denver. Makes his stomach hot, swallowed rage. He's hot anyway, he thinks as he walks smoothly out of the drugstore, back twanging, the full, brand-new bottle bulging his hip pocket.

Outside, cool air, relief—sweat is building between them. Is it breathing? Check. Last stop, the video store, where two teenage girls look at him and then back at their hands, tug the necks of their T-shirts lower.

Not much time left; it's wriggling, going to wake up any second now. Jason heads to the drama section and scans. *Ransom*. He never saw it, but Mel Gibson's decent. Jason will never forget the way he faced his savage end in *Braveheart*. The night they showed it on his cell block, everyone was quiet on the walk back at lights-out, and then finally, little Tino just said quietly, "Man has some *cojones*." For once no one gave him shit, just nodded in agreement.

Jason does a quick scan of the back of the *Ransom* case; tells him what he needs to know, kidnapping plot, ransom offered, blah-blah-blah. He's been busted before, in plans that were simpler than this, with lower stakes. Not this time. This time: recon.

Inside his jacket, it writhes, and he checks the girls at the front. The one with the lopsided tits meets his eyes, and he thinks of Brandi—was it really just this morning?—staring him down in the bathroom mirror. Casually, he puts the tape under his left arm, the side that will be opposite them when he walks out. Loppy Tits watches him do this, and he gives her a wink. "I'm looking for the Adults Only section," he calls out in his "just say the word" voice, extra rumbly.

She laughs, whispers something to the other one. Hopes the tape won't be alarmed, but nobody gives a shit about VHS anymore, it's all about the DVD. He walks to the door; feels like it is digging its toes into his belt, pushing off, head's going to pop out the top of his jacket any second.

"Evening, ladies." His voice is smooth like Vermont genuine maple syrup, god he loved that stuff when his dispatcher sent him up into those foggy green woods. Maybe he and Pen could go there, miles of wild to disappear into. But it's cold, damp like here. The girls at the counter wriggle, twist for him, one biting her nails as he walks right past out into the night, and he is around the corner and slipping into the darkness of the alley, toward home. Fucking beautiful.

39

Time Enough for Counting

PAUL

Paul gets into his van in his own driveway in the dark, the parking space beside him where the Volvo should be as hauntingly empty as the bassinet in the bedroom upstairs. Haberman had said they would be dusting her car for prints, but everyone had touched the car by then. He didn't sound hopeful. This morning, before going to get Magnus at the airport, before the tow had come, Paul had gotten in, driver's side door, and sat there, trying to imagine if he could have gotten out, could have not noticed the car seat in his periphery—how distracted, how far gone, would she have had to be to leave their son?

Before this, he'd characterized these early days of parenthood like the throbbing beginnings of a dental problem—coloring every aspect of their lives, days measured in good or bad, the way one speaks of chronic pain, arthritis. Some days better than others, but the condition never able to be totally forgotten.

And as he sat there, thinking about this, the morning dew made Eva's doodles reappear on the passenger side window, from the Thanksgiving night at the McAdoos that felt like years ago, and Paul had put his head down on the back of his hands and howled until his throat was raked raw.

But now he has given Eva over to Magnus, a passing of the baton.

This is good. Another moment of her weeping, her obsessive pumping and labeling and storing of her breast milk, her frenetic flyer printing at the computer, and he wouldn't have been able to control the urge to smash her head against the nearest hard surface.

Haberman agrees with Paul; the new flyer is better. It is Wyeth's most recent photo, a vulnerable little worried primate face. The first flyers Eva had printed used a ridiculously generic photo of Wyeth, from the side, sleeping on his stomach, tiny bum in the air, and Haberman nixed it.

"We really want a photo with his eyes open," Haberman said. "We want people to see him with his eyes open," he had repeated so emphatically that Paul felt the implications of this like stones in his stomach.

Before Paul left, Eva had cornered him in the living room, away from Haberman and the other officer making notes in the dining room.

"I think we need to call that guy, the leather jacket guy, America's Most Wanted? The one whose son got—" She stopped. "We should call him."

One look at Haberman, picking up their photos, rifling through the mail in their dining room, cell phone to his ear, and Paul said quietly, "I think we need to call a lawyer."

And then Magnus had come down from their bedroom with a navy Adidas gym bag, dropped it on the wooden living room floor with a heavy thud, and waited expectantly for one of them to ask what it was.

"I'll bite," Paul finally said. "What's in the bag, Mag?"

"It's your ransom fund."

"We don't need your money," Paul said tightly, but they do.

Now Paul puts the van in reverse, backs slowly three feet out of the driveway, his eyes trained on the illuminated windows of the house in front of him. He can see Magnus pacing the living room, phone to his ear, giant hands gesticulating, and he wonders if he told him not to leave her alone. Suicide watch, Haberman had said. "Don't need a double tragedy," he'd said, and Paul took this as a bad sign, that Haberman was already thinking of Wyeth as a tragedy.

Paul drives, slowly, staying on the spaghetti loops and dead ends and U-shaped streets that make up Portland Heights, eyes scanning, head swiveling. As though Wyeth is a lost dog and Paul might spot him, might catch his attention if he rolls down his window and does a special whistle. Paul considers going door-to-door, knocking, explaining, asking people if it would be all right if he just, well, searched their home for a bit. How would he have reacted if some red-eyed, unshaven crazy guy in a two-days-unwashed electrician shirt asked to search his house for his missing son? And what would that get him? The silence at the opened door would be his answer—Wyeth was never quiet at this time of night unless Eva or Paul or Magnus had him up over their shoulder, walking the halls.

If he did hear a baby crying, then what? "Mind if I just inspect your baby, ma'am? Check and be sure you've got the right one there?"

And for how long would this be feasible? For how long would he even be able to recognize his own son? There were hundreds of houses in this neighborhood alone. It could take him weeks, door-to-door, and with each passing moment, Wyeth would already look less like he did the two nights ago when Paul came home late after the sprinkler incident. *The last time he saw his son.*

What would it be like to have his son, the boy who carried half his DNA curled up with Eva's inside him, being raised by another couple, calling another man "Daddy"? (Because this is the only path down which it is safe to let the mind wander: a crazy, possibly bereaved, maybe barren couple so desperate for a child of their own to shower with their misguided love and affection that they took advantage of the critical lapse in Eva's attention. There is no other possible explanation. Period.)

Paul wonders anxiously how long this will go on, alarmed to find that what he is most worried about is that this feeling, the Unknown, will drag on and on. Disturbed to realize **that if he digs,** he will discover a complete lack of faith in Wyeth's return. (*They didn't take the car seat. Why didn't they take the car seat?*) How long until, like a soft-eyed George Clooney on *ER*, he can be the one to gently suggest that it is time to call it? Paul looks at his dashboard clock: 8:02 p.m.

Paul is taken back to a moment outside his father's hospital room, when the hot Asian doctor, her hands so softened from endless scrubbing he was afraid her skin would slough off when she took his big callused one in her satin palms and said softly, "You know your father isn't going to leave this hospital now." And Paul recalls having to contract his muscles to keep from wetting himself, so complete was his flooding relief that she had said it. That she had said, Soon it will be over, and they could move on. Eva in there prattling on to his dad about plans for the summer—"And I've got some new tomato plants started, ponderosa pinks, just in the flats in the kitchen window, but Paulie and I are going to need your expertise"—as the ventilator hissed and fell in answer.

So grateful to this doctor for saying it like it was. Because Paul Nova knows, the very worst thing you can be in these kinds of situations is hopeful.

Driving past the overgrown lawn of a small run-down cottage off Upper Drive, Paul spies a familiar SUV on the curb and, lugging her trash bags down from the porch, the famous Chloe Pinter. He depresses the brake, glides to a stop.

"Hey," she calls out when she sees him, "shouldn't you be at Good Sam?"

Paul's stomach flips—he has been gone too long; there is news! "What?"

"This isn't our usual venue—we're supposed to be running into each other at the hospital. Or Strohecker's, but you're standing me up these days." Chloe drops the recycling bin to the curb with a clatter, walks over to his open window. "Where were you yesterday?"

She is smiling at him in a way that lets him know she hasn't seen the news, and it is nice, for a moment, not to be the man whose wife lost their baby.

"Busy. Hey, how's the wedding plans?" he asks, blows on his hands against the cold air.

Chloe grips her own elbows; she's wearing a thin, long-sleeved T-shirt and striped pajama pants. In the streetlamp light, a wisp of disappointment passes over her face, like wind on water.

"No plans, really. Dan moved to Maui."

"What?" So she's here, alone? How come she never told him, all those mornings at the coffee shop? "You're moving?"

She shakes her head. "I don't know. The job, I'm busy, babies due. It's complicated."

"Doesn't sound that complicated to me. Your boyfriend moves to paradise, and you're going to stay here because of work obligations?" As if on cue, a wind blows up from the valley below, he can hear it in the trees before its icy breath reaches them. Chloe ducks beside the van, closer to him so their upper arms brush on either side of the open window, and she doesn't move away.

"Do you want to come in?" she asks at the same time he says, "You should go."

"What?" Did he hear her right?

"Where?" she asks, "Go inside, or to Maui?"

It has been a nice respite, these few moments, but he remembers again, an ache in his throat like the beginning of the flu: Wyeth.

"Maui." Paul takes his hand off the door handle. "I didn't. I got married young, took on the business at twenty. Struggled. Had a kid. Look where I am now."

"Where you are now?" Chloe stands beside the driver's door as Paul clicks his seat belt into place. Her fingers curl over the open window; she is still wearing the ring. "You're everywhere I want to be. The marriage, the house, the baby, the life."

"You should go," he says, and closes the door, puts the van in gear.

40

Disneyland

CHLOE

Chloe has arrived at La Carreta Restaurant before her lunch appointment, carrying her canary yellow folder, the medical forms, and the stack of portfolios.

"You'll recognize me by my fat gut," Debra, the potential birth-mother client, had said on the phone the day before. In turn, Chloe told her she would be wearing a lavender button-down under a black suit, but this morning her suit pants had felt too tight, a casualty of too many meals out on the agency's credit card. Judith had warned her that when it was just Judith and her husband, she did all the birth-mother meetings at restaurants, "and look at me now!" she had har-har-hared, gesturing to her barrel-shaped body under a billowing black silk overshirt.

But Chloe is starving, so she orders herself a large plate of nachos, going to the toppings bar for a towering pile of jalapeños; she picks at them while she waits. She looks out the window, and for once it isn't raining, a day that hints of spring, which will lead to summer, where the weather couldn't be more sparkling and perfect than in the Pacific Northwest. Even Dan had said it their first year here; summer in Portland pays for all those gray months. Now it is bright out, but she can see by the snapping flags at the car dealership across the parking lot that it is still windy, icy cold. This feels like the first time she has even noticed the world outside in days; all she does anymore is work and fall into bed, too tired to even turn on the TV.

Chloe half hopes this Debra won't show, like so many of them. She would be happy to eat her lunch on the agency card, killing time before she is back at her desk and clicking on her empty e-mail folder. It is hard for Dan to get to the Internet café with no car, he has told her; he has to either bum a ride into town or wait for one of the guys to be heading in that direction. She offered to ship him his laptop, but he said there's no connection in the converted garage where he and Kurt and Paolo are holed up.

"It sounds awful," she told him on their weekly Sunday-night phone call.

"We're never here, really," Dan had said. "We're just out on the water or we're making contacts, getting the business thing going."

"How is that going?" she asked, and instead of answering he launched into a complicated explanation of a kiteboarding trick he was mastering.

"ARE YOU CHLOE PINTER?" She is standing beside the table in a neon T-shirt and jeans, mid-thirties, curvily overweight, and all Chloe can see are gigantic eggplant boobs, stretching the hot pink cotton of her shirt. She has a fried blond perm—"Top Ramen hair," Dan would say—with dark roots, the remnants of sloppily removed mascara under her brown eyes.

"I am," Chloe is saying as the waitress arrives, plunks down the Sprite Chloe had ordered to settle her stomach.

"I've been sitting at the bar for half an hour. You aren't wearing a purple shirt and a black suit."

"Yes, sorry about that." The waitress steps back, and Debra plunks into the seat across from her. "Well, you," Chloe says politely, "don't exactly look pregnant either." Trying to get things off on the right foot.

"Right, I'm at the phase where I just look fat." Debra snorts, and the waitress smiles uneasily at them, tucking her hair back into her ponytail, shifting her weight.

"I'll have a Corona," Debra says, unrolling the paper napkin from her utensils.

"Okay, and your friend has already ordered. Do you want anything to eat?"

"You did? What are you getting?"

"Nachos," Chloe says.

"They're huge," the waitress offers.

"Okay," Debra says, but it's not clear to Chloe or the waitress what she means; the waitress taps her pen against her teeth for a second, then walks away.

"So—" Chloe opens her folder, takes out a preliminary and a medical, pushes a brochure of a feathered-hair pregnant woman who looks to be from the 1970s toward Debra. She has been telling Judith that they need to update their material, put something more striking and modern on their cover. She has something she is working on in Photoshop, a black-and-white photo of Dan's of a mother and child walking along the Pacific Coast, their backs to the camera, their gaze toward the setting sun.

"So?" Debra prompts, and Chloe can feel the vibrations from Debra's leg jiggling under the table.

"Okay." Chloe smiles at her, clicking her pen open. "First of all, what's your due date?"

"June."

"Really?"

"Yeah. Didn't figure it out till it was too late for the other option— found you guys in the phone book right away. My period's always fucked up."

"Okay. Is this your first pregnancy?"

Debra snorts. "I've got two kids at home, two adopted out, and a couple I knew early enough about to take care of. I suck at birth control."

Chloe writes quickly, switching between the preliminary and the medical. She can tell this isn't a meeting where they will linger, become girlfriends, pore over the portfolios together. At best, though, it still takes an hour to get all the information.

The waitress returns with the Corona, puts it down in front of Debra, adds a plate of limes. Debra tears the top off a pack of sugar and dumps it on a lime wedge, sucks on it. Chloe pointedly looks away when she takes a swig of the beer.

"So how do you guys do it?" Debra starts. "I mean, now you know I'm a veteran. Do you cut the check for rent and food and clothes and stuff direct to me, or do you pay it for me, or what?"

"Well," Chloe says, "typically we don't cover anything until the third trimester—"

Debra holds up her hand. "Let me stop you right there. I'm a dancer, you know? And I can't be working in my line of work much longer—nobody's going to pay to see my fat ass jiggling up there. So we're a unique case, see? We're going to need some assistance starting a little earlier. Like, now."

"Okay, well, obviously I'll connect you with all the public services that you're eligible for, your medical expenses, WIC—how old are your kids?"

"Seven and five."

"Okay, so we'll get services for everyone eligible, school meals, that kind of thing."

"Hang on, are you or aren't you a private agency?"

"We are," Chloe says.

"So how much are the people paying you for my baby, and what percent of that is mine?"

Thankfully, the waitress arrives with the nachos, smothered in real melted cheddar cheese, not Velveeta, and extra black olives and jalapeños, a whopping side of guacamole. She puts it in the center of the table, and Chloe feels a small primitive hunger panic at the back of her neck, inching her shoulders up. She picks up her fork.

"Damn, that looks good!" Debra grabs her fork and stabs into it from her side of the table.

Chloe takes a moment to swing the conversation. "Have your other pregnancies been healthy? Any problems?" She switches her fork to her left hand, still holding her pen to write an answer on the medical.

"There's nothing wrong with my kids!"

"But you're drinking during your pregnancy, which is known to be potentially—"

"And I'm doing crystal to keep my weight down too! I've done it before—they all turned out fine. And if this one don't, it's not my problem. Like I said, I would've got rid of it before if I could've."

Chloe makes a note on the medical, her handwriting sloppy in her haste. Debra is tucking into the nachos, and Chloe puts the pen down to get a few bites in before they're gone.

"But so how does the money thing work? I know with this other agency, they just cut us a check for ten grand, right off the bat, and it was good 'cause I just put us on a budget, and then after the baby, I took the kids down to Disneyland for a treat."

"I can tell you right now, we aren't buying babies. We don't write checks for anything but regular expenses that are incurred during the pregnancy, and any reputable agency is doing the same."

"But you'd still put enough in there so I could take the kids to Disney, right? I already told them."

Chloe stands up. "I'm just going to go use the ladies' room. I'll be right back."

Once in the stall, she calls Beverly back at the office. "Hey, it's me. Can you pull the active files and check out prefs, let me know which parents will take prenatal meth and alcohol?" She can hear Judith in the background, asking who it is, and then her boss is on the line.

"Chloe? I thought you were at lunch with our new birth mother." Judith has a voice like an aggressive, medium-size dog's bark.

"Yes, I'm in the bathroom. She drinks and uses crystal meth, so I just asked Beverly to see who was accepting that before I show any portfolios." *I don't want to make another mistake like the McAdoos,* Chloe doesn't say, but she knows they are both thinking of the message board crisis after Francie and John found out they'd been shown to and picked by multiracial birth parents when their preference was white.

"Don't worry about that; who've you got with you?"

"I just brought our best three to show," *like you taught me, leave them wanting more.* "I've got Brighton, Dunwoody, and Switzer."

"I thought Switzer was coming over to our Marshall Islands program?"

"Their domestic home study is good for another month, so she said she wants me to keep her active until they get all their international paperwork done."

"Is the baby Caucasian?"

Chloe is about to answer that it is, when she realizes that she doesn't know about the father.

"Not sure, but I don't think she's ready to pick yet anyway. She seems sort of tenuous."

"Get back out there and show them all, but tell her she can't pick for sure until she's seven months. And we're not covering any expenses until six."

"What if she falls in love with one of the families?"

Judith snorts. "We don't have the Novas anymore; she won't lock onto Brighton and Dunwoody, and I want Switzer to be our first Marshall Islands, so leave them out." Chloe can hear pages turning. "I'm looking through the office copies right now—*these* are our Thoroughbreds? We should get Dunwoody to redo their portfolio, tell her to have some shots with her wearing some makeup. I'm all for natural, but she looks like she's about to be embalmed. Brighton's not bad. I'm going to call the Brightons right now and let them know their portfolio is being shown. Beverly saw Amanda Brighton on the Oregon Open Adoption board this morning talking up how many birth mothers she heard Catholic Charities has. Chosen Child hasn't been mentioned in a week."

"Bad press is better than no press?"

"Bring back Francie McAdoo—at least she was prolific! Jesus, look at Eugenia Switzer—does this woman know nothing about loose and flowing fabrics? I can actually see her cellulite through her pants in this one."

While Judith is talking, Chloe looks at herself in the bathroom mirror, wishing she had brought her purse, something to combat the circles under her eyes. She hasn't been sleeping well in the empty house.

"I don't know that Eugenia could make it through two weeks in the Marshall Islands, though a bout of food poisoning or some tainted water might do her good. What the hell—show them all!"

"But what about their preferences? I don't know the race of the baby's father, and the mother's back at the table downing a beer right now. She told me she's doing meth to keep her weight down so she can dance."

"Meth? So the baby will be small, might have some attention problems, no worse than coke. I'd worry more about the alcohol. Ask her about AA. How far along did you say she was?"

"About four months." Chloe braces herself.

"Four months!" Judith explodes. "Why are you even meeting with her?"

"I didn't know this until now." *And we haven't had a new birth mother call in more than a month.*

"Always ask the due date on the phone! What have I taught you? I hope you were clear that we don't start financial assistance until the third trimester."

"Well, she said"—Chloe rummages through her tiny purse for something cosmetic to reacquaint her with the girl in the mirror, comes up with Chapstick—"she needs to start earlier, since as a dancer she'll be unemployed soon."

Chloe can hear Judith sighing. "We need birth mothers, yes, but we need them to actually make us some money." Chloe knows that the adoption fee for her program is $26,000 for a healthy Caucasian baby, but with reductions for mixed races and prenatal substance abuse, that number can be whittled down as low as $13,500.

"Okay, go back and show her the portfolios, but don't let her pick anyone. Find out if the father of the baby is white, and what other harm she is causing the baby. Try to get her to stop drinking. I won't stir up the hornet's nest by calling any families yet. And do *not* promise to start paying anything now."

They say good-bye, and Chloe hangs up, feeling sick to her stomach. By the restroom door, she sees the back exit for the restaurant and has a brief fantasy of slipping out to her car and driving away, but to where? There's a lot of ocean between Portland and Maui . . .

When she gets back to the table, all the good crispy chips are gone, the nacho pile reduced to soggy, bean-saturated tortilla crumbles. Still, she stabs them with a fork.

"So I just want you to know," Debra says, as she slugs from her Corona, "you're not the only agency I'm meeting with."

Chloe chews.

"I've got an appointment with Cascade and some other one, Heart something, later this week."

Chloe looks out the window at the parking lot again, to her car. She picks up her pen, wonders what Dan is doing.

"What do you know about the father of the baby?" she asks mechanically.

"What are you saying?" Debra scowls at her, flips her crimped hair defensively. "You think I don't know who it is?"

The waitress is passing, and Chloe flags her, signals for the check. All she can think of, like a heavy, magnetic pull, is her bed, the white baffled down comforter, the clean six-hundred-thread-count sheets, her memory foam pillow and mattress topper. She will call in sick, go home and pull the shades, finally get a good solid sleep.

"I know who he is all right, but he won't admit it."

"It's okay," Chloe says, as she has a hundred times, "in Oregon we're not required to notify the father of the baby; we don't need his consent. It's just that adoptive families like as detailed a medical history as we can provide, for the baby's sake."

"Oh, he's healthy, you don't gotta worry about that. He's the same daddy as my Mike, who I did with Catholic Charities two years ago. Nice couple."

And against her better judgment, Chloe says, "A full brother, then? Catholic Charities has a family who has a full brother to this baby?"

Debra nods, dumping sugar onto another lime slice.

"Then you should really be working with them. They might want this baby very badly."

Debra slurps on the lime wedge. "Nope. I'm going private again, like I did with my Hayley."

"Okay," Chloe says, but in the long, drawn-out way that means *Why?*

"I told you. I promised; I'm taking my kids to Disney afterward."

ON THE WAY OUT, Chloe stops at the bar and orders a diet Coke, hoping the caffeine will energize her. She slumps onto the chili-pepper-red Naugahyde bar stool, her eyes zoning out of focus as she waits. Debra has gone, waddling out to wait for the MAX line with the folder, Chloe's business card tucked in her hip pocket, and Chloe would bet her favorite brown suede boots she'll never see her again.

Suddenly, on the TV over the bar, something catches her attention. *Paul.* Chloe leans forward, trying to hear more.

"Tragically, Ned, Portland police and the Nova family are still waiting for a break in the case of the kidnapping of Baby Wyeth one week ago today."

And flashing across the screen is the image of Eva Nova, hunched over the podium, Paul's arm wrapped behind her shoulders, his hand like a bear's paw against her wrinkled white shirt, her hair like it hasn't seen a brush in a month. She looks directly into the camera and says only, "Please, please."

Across the bottom of the screen, Chloe reads the "BREAKING NEWS: Amber Alert" and the date, January 29, 2001—a week ago. The night she saw Paul in the driveway, the bitterness in his voice. God, where has she been, under a rock? In a Portland winter fog? She remembers now, coming into work earlier this week, she'd over-heard Beverly and Casey talking, a local kidnapping, but she'd had to pee so badly she walked right past them. Oh, Paul . . .

"In his statement this morning, Detective Haberman says there are currently no new leads in the case, though the former employee of a Portland Heights gas station has not reported for work since the incident and cannot be contacted. Though she has not been formally named as a suspect, police are seeking information on the where-abouts of Brandi Gardham, age sixteen, last seen at the Portland Heights gas station on the twenty-ninth."

There is no photo, just a police sketch that could be any cracked-out ethnic teenager, and Chloe stands and pays for the soda. They flash an image of the Novas at the news conference again, a slightly overexposed photo of the baby. He is wearing a white outfit with a pale blue puppy chasing a red ball on the chest, and he is mostly bald, nondescript hair, worried eyebrows, slightly crossed eyes, a smatter-ing of baby acne on his newborn nose. He could be any baby, but if you look closer, if you know them, you can see Paul's serious expres-sion in his eyes, Eva's broad Scandinavian forehead.

In the parking lot, though it is not their scheduled Sunday-night chat and it will cost her a minimum of eight dollars, Chloe calls Dan's apartment in Hawaii, her hands shaking. After Debra Disneyland and now the Novas' tragedy, she really needs to hear his voice.

"Hey, babe," he says, and he sounds so happy to talk to her, she wants to turn her car west and keep driving until she reaches him. She is so tired, feels like she has been physically stretched, trying to span a hundred miles to the coast and huge stretches of ocean to con-nect with him, physically here but mentally there.

"I just needed to hear your voice," she says, and her own breaks.

Outside her windshield, the used-car sales lot flags dance, the sun catching on the silver. The motor is running, the heater on high. What is she doing here?

"Nice to hear you too." They sit in silence for a few seconds, and she can hear him running water, brushing his teeth.

"I miss you," she blurts, but it is a filler, like Styrofoam peanuts.

"Yeah, me too." Crunch crunch, light and fluffy; crumbling to nothing.

"Remember the Novas, from the agency, from our neighborhood?" she says.

He waits; she can hear him spitting his toothpaste. "Nope."

"Paul and Eva, they live just a few streets over, off Patton. Their baby got kidnapped last week."

"You're kidding! What happened? The birth parents steal it back, or what?"

"No, they used to be my clients, but they got pregnant on their own."

"Oh." Long pause. "That's terrible," he finally says, and she can feel the ocean between them, the tall pines by the coast, the rocky shores, the millions of fish and sharks and ships and orchards and buildings, every bit of it, as though she has to literally crawl, paddle, swim, climb it all, to reach him. Her stomach rolls, her eyes tearing.

"Babe, you okay?"

"I think I'm coming down with something."

"Baby. Sorry to hear that. You work too hard for those people. Hey, there's a waitressing job here, at the Cannery."

Could she do that? Chloe can just hear her father: *A waitress, now? This is why I paid for college, so you can follow your surf bum around?*

"Yeah." In her mind's eye, she can see the seconds ticking by, the pennies adding up so fast you can barely see them, like a Manhattan cab meter.

"Well, you know, I'm just a plane ticket away," he says lightly, and Chloe takes her foot off the brake, and puts her car in gear.

OREGON OPEN ADOPTION—*A place for all mothers*
FRANCESCA97201
Joined: 20 Jun 1990
Posts: 17823
Posted: Mon, Feb 12 2001 7:37 pm

Many thanks for all your prayers for the safe return of EvaSuperNova's baby.

> **I was at their home today; they are doing as well as can be expected.**

She'd come at Paul's urging. When she had called to ask if there was anything she could do to help, she had envisioned bringing them takeout from Strohecker's hot case, watering a few plants, maybe taking a stack of posters to put up around town. Maybe he would ask her to feed the cat or run to the post office, as though the Novas were simply on vacation. So Francie was taken aback by the urgency in Paul's voice when he simply croaked, "Yes. Please. Come."

When she had arrived, the vestibule reeked of vinegar, as though grief was marinating in the kitchen, but perhaps it was just the brother's size 12 tennis shoes. Francie tried to breathe inconspicuously through her mouth. Eva's brother and Paul had shot stricken looks to each other when she lowered Angus's car seat to the floor of the front hall so she could unbutton her quilted car coat.

I took Angus along—what else would I do with him?

"What?" She crossed her arms over her chest. They, of all people, should understand you don't leave your baby with just anyone these days, and it's hard enough to find a cleaning lady, let alone a reputable sitter.

"She has a baby?" the brother hissed to Paul as Eva, looking haggard but enviably thinner, appeared at the top of the stairs and exclaimed, "You brought the baby!"

The first few moments had been undeniably awkward. Eva was in constant motion, moving stacks of flyers and papers from the couch to the coffee table to the window seat, putting the kettle on, twisting fistfuls of her uncombed hair into a messy knot on top of her head, her eyes darting to the car seat where Angus slept.

Then they were settled, two mugs of tea sending up steam on the coffee table, Paul in the kitchen clattering through the dishes. The brother (Magnum, was it?) was at the computer in the dining room, out of Francie's line of sight but within eavesdropping distance; she could hear him hunting and pecking away.

It was oddly cozy—all these family members within earshot of one another.

Fortunately, Eva is surrounded by men who love and care for her in the face of this tragedy.

It was enough to make Francie in her dark, dusty, spacious mansion jealous. To make herself feel better, she added a mental note to look into cottages, carriage houses, for her and Angus.

But then there was nothing to say. Francie had of course done an earnest "How are you holding up?" hyperaware of the pause at the keyboard and sink as the men waited for Eva's reply. It had been disappointingly vague, something about "layers" and "waves," as though they were discussing hairstyles and not the deepest form of grief. There was nothing Francie could get her teeth into, and there were Eva's eyes settling, like a butterfly, on Angus's face, before flitting away again.

Perhaps this seems strange to some of you, but I offered Eva a chance to hold Angus.

"Would you like to hold him?" Francie had asked, and again the household clatter ceased and the silence blew up like a balloon on a helium tank.

"No!" Eva blurted as Francie unbuckled the car-seat straps, lifting Angus's slack sleeping form out. "I mean, no, I don't mean for you to wake him."

"Not at all. He sleeps through everything," Francie replied with some pride before she remembered this was one fellow mother she did not need to be competitive with. "I mean, it's odd, considering how quiet the McAdoo house is these days, that Angus sleeps so well. Always has." That sounded wrong too; she had only been trying to allude to John leaving her, hoping to spark a conversation in more comfortable territory: *Let me tell you how my husband left me for a teenage whore in Singapore.* "Here——" Francie offered Angus on outstretched arms. Eva's own, crisscrossed over her stomach, unfolded. Francie pretended she didn't hear the tiny moan in her friend's exhalation as she received Angus's warm weight. "That's better."

Francie felt the burning disapproval boring into her back from the dining room entry. "That's better," she repeated, for Lurch's benefit. She wasn't trying to be cruel—just the opposite. She knew, could feel the ache in the biceps that came from waiting, arms flexed, for a baby to fill them. In the years she had waited, whenever they came close, Francie had found her body practicing, around the house, doing the Mommy bounce, her empty arms circling, tensed, without her even knowing it until she found she couldn't even lift a milk carton without wincing.

The family was disapproving, but I think it was just what our dear friend needed.

Eva's brother crossed the living room to lean over Eva in the rocker. He bent in and pressed his lips to the top of his sister's curly head, squeezing her shoulder. With his other hand, he palmed Angus's round head, such a picture, the three of them, that Francie's neck prickled in a sweat. Never again would Angus sit in his mother's arms while a man looked lovingly on. Her mind drifted back to that awful day at the hospital, with Jason jerking around the room, throwing glances like fastballs at his sleeping son.

"Handsome little man," the brother said. "Does he look like your husband?"

Like a bad case of food poisoning, Francie spewed nine years of explosive personal information at Eva's brother. The infertility, John's disfiguring varicose veins, the treatments for both, the adoption, the frightening birth parents, the nicotine addiction, the haggard, sleepless weeks before she got the baby on a good schedule, but she didn't stop there. No, Francie just plowed right on to the Singapore slut and the deserting husband. It was better to distract them this way, her own misfortunes hung out like damp underwear on a line in this house where their grief filled the room, mounded in the corners and on the furniture like unfolded wash.

Eva had wiped at her eyes with her free hand (they had been streaming tears ever since Francie put the baby in her arms) and murmured noises, appropriate shock and disapproval.

"And then I have the added anxiety of the follow-up home study. Chloe Pinter has been calling me, and . . . Every day I live in fear that the agency is going to figure out John and I are divorcing. I'm terrified they'll come and take my baby away! So . . ." She petered out, realizing she couldn't quite make out the look on the brother's (Was his name Magnum? No, that's a gun, or a condom, maybe) face. Had she said something wrong again? Besides, there really wasn't anything more to say. Her throat felt scratchy, and she wondered, sipping at the tea that was now cool, how long she had been talking.

We talked, about this and that, current events.

She does not recap the horrors of her personal life for the boards; they have no idea that she and John are in the process of divorcing.

It has taken her years to create this image, this persona, the happy family, and there was no need for John's sex addiction and philandering to drag her down.

"Oh, dear," Eva said then, gesturing to two wet circles on the front of her shirt. "I, I'm going to go change. Here, Maggie," and she had handed the baby off to the brother. After watching her friend's retreating back (definitely losing weight!), Francie turned her attention to the brother, who was holding her son with Angus's feet against his chest, stretched on the length of his forearms. There was only one word for him, talking to Angus, who was now waking, stretching his arms and yawning that perfect little round O of a yawn; Eva's brother looked *natural*. Francie thought of John, and how he never got past the shoebox-full-of-snakes phase of holding Angus.

"You've got a good one here." The brother inclined his head toward Angus, whose eyes crinkled at the corners when he gave away his unabashed gummy grin.

"Thank you." Francie's chest filled and fluttered the way it did whenever her good fortune was noticed, appreciated, by others. "I do."

"Even so, it must be hard on you, doing this on your own now."

Francie was so surprised at this, at the tenderness in his voice, that she had to quickly look at her hands, busying them at her diaper bag, so he didn't see the tears in her eyes.

"I'm allergic to cats," she'd mumbled, swiping at her eyes with a wet wipe.

"We could keep Angus here a few hours, if you like. If you have an errand, or you just want to go sit in Powell's with a stack of books or get a coffee, take a nap, or something. It would be nice for us too."

Eva appeared at the bottom of the stairs in an unstained but wrinkled T-shirt and seconded his urging, crossing the room to lift Angus out of her brother's arms, to rub her cheek against his dark hair as she settled him against her shoulder.

And then, ladies, though I know this may seem beyond crazy to many of

you, I left Angus with them for the afternoon. There were three of them there anyway, and it seemed to be just what we all needed.

This was how Francie came to be walking, fairly skipping down their driveway, fighting the urge to windmill her empty arms, free free free! She had trouble keeping it under seventy on the Sunset Highway—the Mercedes as excited as she was to be bouncing over rain ruts and potholes toward 185th and the familiar stomping grounds of Nordstrom Rack. There had been no question about what she would do, from the second the brother suggested it.

I went clothes shopping, alone.

The store smells greeted her like an old friend; the sharpness of dry-cleaning chemicals, a hint of smoke, the slightly gamey scents of wool and weather, the industrial twang of rubber soles. *Slow down, Francine!* she told herself, her hands tight on the cart handle when the fabric hues, patterns, textures, assaulted her from the glinting of stainless steel racks.

First, a quick overview tour, sifting silk through her fingertips, a flip through the clearance rack for leftover holiday party dresses, a glance toward shoes, but she'd want to go back and linger there later, and accessories.

She should start back at the beginning and go more slowly, categorically, but every time she turned, she saw another shopper touching something, pulling it off the rack, and she frantically veered there, in case they bought something she might have wanted.

After the first forty-five minutes, the anxious adrenaline, what she had mistaken for the thrill of the retail chase, hadn't subsided, only settled into an uneasy, queasy ball in her stomach. Francie checked her cell phone—nothing. She picked up a plaid Carolina Herrera blazer. Interesting lines, but scratchy fabric—she pictured Angus's butter-smooth cheek coming to rest on her abrasive shoulder. No.

The truth? It wasn't all I thought it would be.

Across the department store, in the children's section, she piled the cart with footed sleepers, corduroy pants, and the tiniest argyle sweaters, a pair of leather shoes so small she danced them on her first and second fingers, imagining her son's plump feet filling them. And not that he needed any more, but a handful of chunky board books from the toy section, and a heavenly soft brown bear. Francie clutched it to her as she walked, settling its nothing poly-filled weight on her hip. Better.

I ended up looking at things for Angus, LOL! Imagine—the boy's closet overflows into the guest room, I'm finally out by myself, and all I can do is shop for my son!

Francie checked her watch—he would be hungry shortly. She had given them the diaper bag, gotten out the bottles, but then she worried, wondered, How well does she know Eva? What if she so militantly believed breast was best that she tried to—

Shoes! Francie pounced on a shiny brown-heeled pump. She could practically hear it echoing, striking the hardwood floors in empty houses while she pointed out original fixtures, peg detail in the woodwork, crown moldings, to potential clients.

As I mentioned, I will be returning to work soon, so I did some preliminary scouting for my professional wardrobe.

Francie slumped on a shoe bench, halfheartedly slipping out of her loafer. Everything, the clamoring of the shoppers and the hideous colors and the excess and the overabundance of choices, was competing for her attention. Francie put her own shoe back on. She stood up. Backtracking past the racks, she found each thing uglier, more ridiculous, than the next. Who would wear this dreck?

An ache started, low in her abdomen, where she has imagined her defunct ovaries might be. Francie has pictured these interior body parts throughout the years and always come up with the same image—a pair of withered, imploding, moldy figs, smaller than a baby's fist, left at the bottom of the decorative, exotic fruit bowl she put out to impress her book-club friends years ago.

Francie abandoned her half-full cart by the exit, ovaries throbbing, a magnetic, desperate pull.

In the end, I left with nothing!

What was wrong with her? She wiped her damp palms on her trousers. Outside, she gulped the deliciously cold winter air. Off the exit, she could hear cars *shh-shh*ing on the highway, late-afternoon light coming to rest like a curtain over the parking lot, everyone going home. *Home.*

Not entirely true, LOL. I got myself a speeding ticket, racing back along the Sunset Highway to Angus.

The ache in her gut continued to pain her on the twisting roads toward the Novas. Her heart rate didn't settle until she burst, palms slippery on the handle, through their front door and laid her eyes on Angus, just where she left him, sleeping in Eva's arms in the rocking chair.

The truth, ladies: My husband left me for a 19-year-old whore in Singapore. And I have everything I need, everything I have ever wanted. We should all be so lucky. Prayers for the Novas . . .

41

Three Options

JASON

"Well, that one was real helpful," Penny says as the Martinezes' borrowed VCR starts rewinding. The baby is sucking down another bottle in her arms, and she starts talking to it, which he hates. "What he hasn't figured out, after stealing five baby-snatcher movies, is that nobody gets away with it. All we see is bad guys busted or shot full of holes. You want a Swiss cheese daddy?"

"You don't watch them to see what to do—you watch for what not to do." His voice is thick with patience he doesn't feel. Seven days locked in the house with her and this kid, and he's about ready to turn himself in. Every time it's time for a milk run to the all-night gas station, he's the eager beaver, running out with the old WIC checks, if for nothing more than a gulp of cold black air, quiet.

"We're wasting time," Penny says. "We've seen the parents boo-hooing all over the TV. They want him. Either let's just set it up or bust out of here and take him with us. I'm getting kinda attached. He could be Buddy."

That had been a problem the last few days—what to call him. Felt wrong to call him It when he was curled up in the towel against Jason's chest each night (only way to keep him quiet) but disloyal to call him Buddy. Of course they know his name now—Wyeth Nova—but neither of them so much as whispers it.

"JJ?" Penny says like she can read his thoughts.

"What?"

"Jason Junior? Come on, let's just take him with us."

"Take him with us what? What the fuck are you talking about?"

"You said motor home, Mexico. Burning sun. Brown-skin babies. I'm sick of sitting around here. I'm ready." She's perched on the couch, baby across her knees, and Jason looks at her. Could she really be so stupid as not to realize that for all of that to happen, first they need to pull off the ransom? Next to her is the dim lamp that makes the pocks of her skin like moon craters, the way the light hits. The lamp's ugly, but real brass overlay, heavy, came with the place, long brown cord. And today didn't he just see a half-full box of garbage bags under the sink? He could kill them both—it wouldn't take but a few minutes. Smash the other half of her mouth in with the metal stand, knock her out so it wouldn't be so bad to wrap the cord around her neck. She might not even come to. Done. And then the baby, what? Snap its neck like a rooster? Barbaric. Bathtub? Facedown, he could probably hold it under. Less than a minute. Wash them all with Clorox from the laundry room, and done. Walk away, run, as far as he could go. He tallies the contents of their fridge, feels where his fat gut is folding in on itself right at his belt. It would do him good to go without for a few days. He pictures himself crawling through woods and rivers, walking along mountain ridges, south south south. How long would he have before someone found the bodies? They still have the Martinezes' VCR—she might come knocking. Drop it off first then, tonight. And then what? Julio comes around every three days or so, threatening, "End of the month, Xolan!" So what, kill him too? "*Jefe*, I got something I need you to look at under the sink," and then WHAM! back of the head with the heavy wrench from the toolbox. But Julio has a wife, a thick-waisted, slit-eyed rectangle of a woman who'd come looking in hours. So just Penny and the baby, then, and put the baby in the freezer, and Penny, what, take out the racks of the fridge, crank it to Cold? What would that get him, a week? And a free body he might be, a lifetime in sunglasses and hats and layers of lies, but what about his soul? Would they haunt him?

"Why are you looking at me like that?"

"What?" He almost forgot; they're in the room. Penny gets up and puts the sleeping baby in the bassinet. Above it, there is the bare nail where Brandi's dream catcher hung. Jason shivers, has to clench his ass cheeks against a spasm of diarrhea. The cramp passes.

"You're just figuring it all out, aren't you, Einstein?"

"What?"

"That we're right back where we were when I found out I was pregnant with Buddy. Same-old same-old three options."

He waits; she ticks them off on her fingers.

"We can kill it, keep it, or try to turn it into cash. We didn't abort him 'cause I didn't want to, and we didn't keep him 'cause you didn't want to, and option three didn't work out so good for us because you chose a piece-of-shit agency that kept all the money for themself. All we got for Buddy was fat clothes, some food, and three months' room and board in this shitbox."

She stands by the bassinet, jiggling it—best way they have found to get him into a deep enough sleep that they might have a few hours themselves. "If you had listened to me from the get-go, you might remember me telling you about my roommate at the Salem Women's Summer Camp"—this is what she calls her lockup after his check fraud plan went wrong, because of their mandatory arts and crafts program—"said a lawyer is the way to go. Venita called him, he told her about a family, she had the baby, never even looked at it, didn't even know if it was a he or a she, and she walked away with nine grand in cash, no questions asked. She never had to meet them or see how old or gimpy or phony they were, never had to worry"— Penny sniffs—"that they'd be fuck-ups. Just a transaction. But you get your get-out-of-jail-free card first, and you go and choose the first agency in the phone book with the hot little social worker and her shiny silver Cherokee, and you don't even think, How does she get that money? Who pays for that nice SUV?"

Okay, Jason slumps back against the couch, let her get it all out. Two months of solitary in the bedroom—the girl has a right to say her piece.

"Della Martinez got dial-up, so I go over the other day and I looked up Chosen Child Adoption Agency on the Internet. Twenty-five grand for a U.S. baby. They paid twenty-five grand for Buddy. That's it." She's crying now, and she wipes at her cheeks. "He makes hundreds of thousands of dollars a year, but a chunk of my heart, that I carried and felt inside me every minute, that I get sawed in half for, that I never even get to lay my own eyes on, my firstborn son. He's just a cool twenty-five gee."

Jason waits.

"So——" She draws a shaky breath. "So this time, Einstein, I'm driving the train. It's tricky now. Option A, kill it. You know I won't let you, so you'd have to kill me too." She says this so casually his stomach knots. "And keeping it would be fine, ugly little bugger's growing on me, except we have no fucking money. Which leaves C, turning it into cash"—she waves her hand toward the Martinezes' VCR—"which is looking to be a little trickier than we thought. Even if you didn't fuck it up, if we could get to the ransom money, in every one of those movies the bills are marked, so as soon as we buy our Airstream and head south, we might as well spray-paint a bull's-eye on top of it."

Penny stops and peers inside the bassinet.

"He's out cold now." She crosses the room and stands behind the couch, puts her hands on the back of it, near Jason's head. He feels her breath on his bare neck. Tries to take inventory of the room—the lamp, the cord, the toolbox out by the light by the door that he'd been messing with, he'd have heard her pick up anything heavy, the clink of metal. He stares straight ahead, waiting, feeling her behind him.

"So do you or don't you know where Chloe Pinter lives?"

"What?" It comes out like a gasp.

"I heard you. On the phone. Do you know where the bitch who took my son, who has all our money, lives?"

"Um, I, I . . . ," he stammers.

"Do you know where Chloe Pinter lives?" She says it slowly—he can feel each breath on the top of his shaved head.

"Yeah, I know."

Jason turns and looks up at her, the light from the brass lamp casting up on her face, her nostrils deep holes, her mouth black and gaping; she looks like a gargoyle.

"What do you want me to do?" he says. It comes out like a whimper.

"Make this right. Get our money, get our wheels, get us out of here."

She is walking toward the bedroom when she calls back over her shoulder, "If you pick Option A, have the goodness to do it without me waking up. I don't want to feel nothing no more."

She closes the bedroom door, and with the click of the handle, the baby wakes up. Jason gets to his feet, half expecting his liquid guts to run down his legs, and he picks up the thin towel on the corner of the couch, knots it at his heart, puts the baby in. He clicks off the brass lamp and starts wearing their nightly track in the rust-colored carpet: up to the bathroom, back to the kitchen, around the couch, up to the bathroom, back to the kitchen, around the couch . . .

It's warm where their bodies touch. Jason's throat itches, like a panicky trapped bird he can't swallow, and its name is Desperation.

42

Quitting Time

CHLOE

Chloe wakes up on Valentine's Day gasping—a bad dream, a man in her doorway, but as the first watery light fills her room and Chloe catches her breath, she sees it's just clothes piled on a chair, her dark jacket hanging on the handle of the white door, nothing more. She is alone.

She clutches her cell phone off the nightstand for any missed calls or messages. None. She gets up, and though she has to pee badly, stops by the computer at the foot of the bed and taps the space bar to wake it up. No e-mail. It has been three days since she and Dan last communicated, and it is starting to affect her physical well-being.

Chloe drives to the café at Strohecker's and orders a bagel and two coffees, waiting, but of course he doesn't come anymore. She drinks them both and feels nauseated from the overload of cream and sugar.

At work, she pulls into her parking space and takes the stairs to the agency slowly, despite the misting rain. The wind is blowing from the Camas pulp factory, and the air is putrid with its stench. Inside, Chloe tries to get past Beverly, but she's waving slips of pink paper. "And Heather wants you to call her," she adds. "She left a message on the service."

Chloe's feet sound like a steelworker's as she trudges up the wooden stairs. She is wearing her black Tarifa hiking boots, a pair of

Dan's left-behind Lucky jeans, and her Hot Stick surfer sweatshirt— she's only doing paperwork today, but she thinks of the saying "Dress for the job you want, not the job you have."

Upstairs, Casey is stretched out on Chloe's couch, dirty Nikes crossed on the arm, flipping through an old *Rolling Stone*.

"Do you know Johnny Depp wants to have a second mouth grafted on so he can smoke while he's talking or eating?" Casey says.

"Would you put your feet down?" Chloe says peevishly. Her eyes dart toward her computer screen, already turned on (*grrr!*) and she sees it, the red flag above her AOL mailbox, the one that wasn't there this morning before she left home. She calculates the time change in her head—could it be Dan?

"Testy!" Casey swings her feet down, sits up. "And did you know you have your own thermostat, which means that you have your own vent system up here, which means you could totally blaze up at lunchtime, and they would never know it downstairs?"

"Except I don't smoke." Chloe puts her purse on the floor by the dry-erase board, her eyes darting back to the red mailbox flag.

"Really?"

"Not for years."

"Wow. Sometimes I want to quit for like, four, maybe two months, just so I can start up again. Nothing like that first-time high."

Chloe stands by her desk, flipping the message slips in her hand with her thumb.

"Oh!" Casey gets up. "I thought we could cruise the boards together up here for the morning report. You want couch or chair? You take couch, it's your office." Chloe sits in the warm indentation Casey left, dusting the floral twill for crumbs.

"Okay, we've got no mention on Portland AP, and nothing on International. Mmm, OregonMoms, nothing . . ." Casey clicks another link. "Oh wait, we've got a Francesca97201 on Oregon Open Adoption! This should be classic. Where's my popcorn?"

Chloe waits while Casey scans the thick block of print.

"Holy shit!"

"What?" Chloe asks, only to be polite. It's Valentine's Day; at the very least Dan would send her an e-mail, right? She doesn't care about flowers, she just wants contact.

"She says her husband left her for a teenage whore in Singapore!"

Chloe is thinking of Paul Nova, in his van outside her house, driving around looking for his lost son, and Dan, on the beach at Ho'okipa, perfecting his forward loop.

"What?" she asks. She can actually smell Casey, a mix of powdered parmesan and patchouli, from across the room. The coffee from earlier swirls in Chloe's uneasy stomach.

"Whoa. So Francie and John split? Do the birth parents know? Didn't you do their follow-up home study?"

"Yeah." Chloe pushes at her cuticles. *By phone*, she thinks but doesn't say. Chloe had gotten sloppy these last few weeks, hadn't gone out to their house, had literally phoned it in and made up a report based on her original home study. *The adoptive parents are adjusting well to parenthood and have all the appropriate safety features installed.* None of it matters.

"Judith's going to shit when she finds out."

She will, Chloe realizes, and finds she doesn't care as much as she should.

"Huh." Casey closes the browser window and stands up. "Crazy. I'm starving, you want any Doritos or anything?" Casey stands in her doorway. Chloe shakes her head, exhales when Casey finally leaves. She pounces on her computer, hands shaking to open her AOL, and it's from Dan!

To the other lost soul swimming in the fishbowl . . . You know the rest. I'm nothing without you.

Wish you were here. Pink Floyd postcard sentiment. Her intercom beeps, and Beverly announces Heather on line two with enough annoyance in her voice to indicate that Chloe should have called her back before she had to call again. Chloe hits the line without answering Beverly.

"Hello?"

"Hey." Heather's voice is small and flat.

"Heather! How are you?"

"I don't even know why I'm calling. I don't need anything. Things are fine. We're fine. Michael's fine."

"Good, I'm glad to hear it."

"I really don't even know why I'm calling. I just got used to talking to you all the time, and then, it's like nothing. I'm just calling to say hey, I guess."

"I'm really glad to hear from you."

"So do you ever do, like, a follow-up visit?"

With the adoptive parents, Chloe thinks, but says, "Sure, I can come out."

"Really? That would be great. Michael totally misses you."

"Sure. I can come out today, if you want."

"Okay. I don't work till five, so we're just, you know, here."

"I'll see you in a bit."

"Okay, great. Thanks, that would be great."

There are feet on the stairs, and Chloe hangs up as Casey barges through the doorway. "Hey! I forgot to tell you my great idea for the domestic program."

"What?"

"Chosen Child restructure. No more mom-and-pop rinky-dink agency. I'm thinking revamping the domestic program so we have one caseworker for families and another one for birth moms, like Catholic Charities does. Ken said they're thinking about hiring someone else for China, so I'd come up and do the birth moms, and you could do the families, or either way, whatever. I don't care."

Chloe feels like she has been punched.

"We'd be in totally regular communication, but I could put my desk over here." She points to a space by the window. "I was just talking to Judith, and she thinks it's brilliant. Won't it be great? I can move my stuff up today." With that, Casey leaves.

Chloe rereads Dan's e-mail. He wants her there, he's "nothing without her." She rereads the e-mail again. It's enough. She grabs her purse and her day planner and phone, stops in the doorway, and looks around. She picks up her album, the one she bought last summer, filled with photos of smiling parents and newborns, Chloe a lonely bookend to the blissful cluster.

She runs down the wooden staircase, two at a time, and straight into Judith's office.

"I quit." The calm in Chloe's voice surprises her. Where her hands clutch the leather of her small purse, sweat is forming.

Judith stands up, her face purple, and slams the glass-paned door to her sunroom office, which does nothing but muffle her yelling for everyone in the international office. Over Judith's heaving shoulders when she stops to take a breath, Chloe can see Casey, Kenneth, and Maria glancing at her, a mixed bag of expressions on their faces. From her office in the entry, Beverly has to stand and lean over the desk to get a good look.

"You have to give me two weeks!" Judith roars.

Chloe shakes her head but says nothing, afraid what will happen if she opens her mouth. Soon, with no fuel for Judith's fire, it burns into frosty fury. Judith opens the door for Chloe, gestures that she should leave.

"I hope you know how many people you are letting down right now," she hisses. "Worst of all, you are letting yourself down, Chloe."

Go to Maui, Paul Nova had said. . . .

43

Saint Valentine

PAUL

Wyeth has been missing for sixteen days, which makes today February 14. To Paul, this means nothing. He only noticed it when the secretaries were oohing over each other's giant arrangements that perfumed the front office in that sharp tang of roses, reminding Paul of his mother's Tea Rose that she spritzed on the back of her nyloned knees before Sunday church. It means Haberman was out to lunch with his wife when Paul checked in at noon, and heading out to pick up his girlfriend for dinner when Paul calls him a second time a few minutes ago.

"Nothing to report," he had said. "Couple of calls on the hotline that I chased down and debunked." He didn't add, as he used to, "You wouldn't believe how many crazies there are out there." Because yesterday Paul had snapped at him that yes, his son was snatched by one of them, and so he actually would believe that.

Paul is sitting in traffic on the Sunset Highway, and every car he inches past seems to have a well-dressed couple in it. He wonders how many of these are parents, and who is home watching their children. He wants to jump out, pound on their rain-spattered windows, and scream, "Go home! Hold your children!" Who's the crazy now?

At home, the house is quiet, late-afternoon light shining through the kitchen window, a blue glow of television in the living room. It is par for the course, third night in a row, since Francie McAdoo left them with her baby for the afternoon, and that night, Magnus's girlfriend, Genai, called from Los Angeles to tell him she was pregnant but doubted it was his. There is a bag of groceries sitting on the kitchen counter, two empty wine bottles on the floor by the back door to go out to recycling—well, at least they're being civic-minded, Paul thinks. At least they're not junking up our landfills.

On the counter, a bloody steak is defrosting, and the water is running over a colander of Bibb lettuce. Paul shuts it off, pulls open the grocery bag. A heart-shaped Whitman's sampler of chocolates and three dirty baking potatoes roll around in the bottom next to a cellophaned box of herbal tea. Paul pulls it out: "Mother's Milk—for promoting lactation." Christ.

In the living room, he finds Eva and her brother in a familiar scene. Magnus is in the glider, his head thrown back, mouth open; Eva curled on the couch, her arm stretched out to rest on the coffee table where a third bottle of red sits, two empty, stained glasses both within reach. The five o'clock news is on, there's the NO NEWS status under the photo of Wyeth, the footage of Paul and Eva and Haberman from two weeks ago. Magnus's eyes fly open, try to focus, when Paul shuts off the TV, crosses to flip on the lamp by the stairs.

"You're back early." Magnus's voice is as thick and garbled as a stroke patient's.

Paul ignores him, goes to his wife, and bends, sliding an arm under her neck, not caring when his watch strap snags on her hair. He gets the other under her bent knees and, lifting with his legs, not his back, as he learned moving shipments in the warehouse, hefts her into his arms. She is lighter than he expected, and as he swings her to make for the stairs, one of her bare feet sends Magnus's empty glass to the floor, where it shatters musically.

"I'll get that," Magnus says, his voice more clear. Paul does not look at him as he passes. Accidentally, Paul knocks Eva's head against the doorframe to their bedroom, and her eyes fly open. She flings an arm around his neck, her breath sour like a frat house floor after Bacchus week, mumbling she is sorry, so sorry. Paul's neck, where she is kissing, feels like a three-inch northwestern slug has crossed it, leaving a slime.

In their bedroom, Paul pushes the door shut with his foot, and for a brief second has a savage flash: *Dropping her to the floor like unwashed laundry, using his heavy boot to kick her, the stomach, so she folds, first, then a bash to the head, to the face to open it up, teeth shattering to the wood floor like the wineglass, then around behind, where the ribs would splinter like kindling under his steel-tipped boots.*

Shaken, he lays his wife on their unmade bed, pulls the covers up over her legs. She is wearing one of his old basketball shirts, and there are two giant wet spots where milk has leaked through. He goes to the bathroom and runs water on a washcloth, wrings it out, fills a glass, taps two Tylenol into his hand. By the time he is back, she is snoring softly. He wipes her forehead, smoothing the hair back, leaves the other items on her bedside table.

"Magnus—" He walks back into the kitchen, where his brother-in-law is wiping at the bloodstained Corian with drunken deliberation. "I know you love your sister, and I know you're trying to help her out the only way you know how, but—" He loses his voice, swallows hard, finds it strong and deep. "But if you care at all about us, stop this. I've lost my son, maybe for good, and I can't lose Eva to—"

"I apologize," Magnus says carefully. His eyes are those that Paul has come to hate in his wife, plaintive, speaking of an agony so deep you can see in them the slimy black bottom of the abyss. Magnus picks up the wine bottle and glass, shuffles past Paul to the breakfast nook. With an unsteady hand, he pours the last of the wine into the glass. Paul feels a surge of heat in his face, has to step back so he doesn't break Magnus's jaw with the pulsing fist clenched by his thigh.

"Yeah, well, whatever your problems are, your mother was a cold-hearted bitch or your girlfriend's banging other guys, or because your nephew got snatched, we're up to our eyeballs in our crisis here, so I can't be babysitting you too." Paul hears his voice shout, "I'm trying to be the guy who puts things back together!"

Paul swings, knocks the full wineglass out of Magnus's hand. He picks up the plate with the steak and throws it past him toward the kitchen door—blood and ceramic shards and a fifteen-dollar hunk of meat litter the floor. God, but it feels too good to throw and scream and shatter the quiet in their house.

44

How Often Do They Give It Back?

CHLOE

It is late afternoon on Valentine's Day, the light just weakening when Chloe arrives at the complex in Southeast. She hurries through the squelching courtyard, footsteps echoing at the other end. She turns quickly, expecting the ominous figure of Jason Xolan in his clunking boots, his jingling jacket, but it's a short Puerto Rican woman, slamming out of the laundry room with a rose-colored basket of wrinkled clothes on her hip, a waft of powdery fabric softener gusting toward Chloe.

Chloe knocks on the door to Heather's apartment, waiting. It's not raining yet, but the air is raw, threatening.

"Hey!" Heather pulls the door open on a wide smile, Michael behind her jumping on the couch cushions. Heather holds up two mugs of tea, and though Chloe's stomach is still swirling over what she has done, she takes the steaming mug. They settle on the couch, Michael knocking over blocks as they talk.

"So . . ." Chloe takes her tea bag out of the mug, lays it on a piece of paper towel. "How are you doing?"

"Okay." Heather looks out the window, and her eyes fill with tears. She crosses her arms over her stomach, which already only makes the smallest of telltale folds. "I broke up with Eric."

"What?"

"I just realized I was trying to make him into someone he isn't. You know, husband, dad type of thing. It really wasn't fair to him. I boxed him into a corner, you know?" She's crying and smiling at the same time. She wipes her nose on the sleeve of her shirt. "I know I'm crying, but it's okay. It feels, like, really free. Sad, but free."

Chloe swallows down a throat-dollop of bile.

"How about you? How's your honey?"

"Um, things are okay."

There is silence, then the beep-beep-beep of Michael's truck.

"So, have you heard from Nate and Gina?"

"What?"

"The Severins." In an unprecedented show of faith, in the middle of signing the paperwork for the closed adoption, Gina had written their full names, adding phone numbers, even their street address, on a piece of paper and pressed it into Heather's hand. "I just wondered how things are going. If they'd called the agency or anything."

"Oh. I haven't heard, but their follow-up home study is next week." Chloe pictures Casey doing the job in her stead, going through the motions, half-assed, half-baked, in the Severins' Lake Oswego home, and she has to swallow again. What has she just done?

"Will you call me, after you see them, and let me know how things are going?"

And Chloe would have, if she hadn't just quit, if everything wasn't about to come crashing down.

"I hope they like him, Adam David," Heather continues. "Michael was a real easy baby, but you never know." As Michael passes, Heather grabs him around the waist, pulls him to her chest. "C'mere, you." She rubs her cheek against his, and Chloe sees him go soft in her arms as she kisses his curly hair.

"I'm sure they're loving him." Chloe thinks about Francie McAdoo, who is not the first new adoptive mother to call in the early days, surprised, taken aback by the incessant care a newborn requires, the transition from what they envisioned to the relentless reality. *I just wanted to tell you, this baby cries all the time* . . . as though Chloe had picked it out, gave them the One That Cries.

"So . . . how often do the parents give a baby back?"

"What?" Chloe's voice is sharper than she means for it to be.

"You don't have to talk in specifics." Heather looks down at her hands. "I just wondered."

"*Never.* Heather, never! These are babies, not, not pound puppies that don't housebreak quickly enough, and whoops, back you go, it didn't work out."

Beep beep, crash! Michael knocks over a tower, jams the truck into Chloe's ankle.

"Ouch! Never," she says again emphatically.

"But what about Penny?"

"Penny?"

"Jason and Penny, from over there."

"What about them?"

"Nothing. Just, the parents gave it back, right? I mean, I can see why; he's a little screamer." Heather laughs nervously.

Chloe barely makes it to the narrow bathroom to throw up, wipes her mouth on a damp *Sesame Street* towel. An excuse, a hasty good-bye, briefer than she had meant for it to be with Heather, and she is standing back out in the courtyard. Should she go to Jason and Penny's? Would they really have Angus McAdoo in the bassinet instead of that plastic-eyed bunny?

Francie and John would be just the type of people to give a baby back, write some fat check to keep the birth parents quiet, pay off a lawyer to lose the records—but what about the post on the message board, about realizing she is truly a mother, and what had Casey said, John left Francie for a teenage whore in Singapore? But these are message boards—anyone could make up a story for the online world.

Giving back a baby would be impossible to pull off, normally, because of the follow-up home study. But Chloe hadn't actually gone to the McAdoos, had literally phoned it in. Jesus. And Francie had seemed relieved not to have Chloe come over, and Chloe realizes now that not once in the whole twenty-minute conversation last week did she hear a baby cry.

Maybe she should go straight to the airport, leave now, before the shit really hit the fan? Forget the sublessor, forget packing her belongings? How delighted would Dan be if she showed up in Maui tomorrow with nothing but the clothes on her body, without a suitcase or her purple kettle? What if she revamped herself, became the type of girl who didn't need to make a happy home everywhere she went, didn't dream of weddings and families, their happily-ever-after? What if she could live out of a backpack, her first priority in the morning merely checking the palm fronds for movement, wind direction? What if she took a job that didn't involve the messy creation of families, but was simply refilling tourists' ice waters, bringing them shrimp cocktail, smiling for a fat tip that could go toward her new 5.3 sail? What if she became Waterbabe?

Standing in the raw air outside Heather's, Chloe swallows down another surge of bile and crosses the courtyard.

45

Visitors

JASON

A knock at the door, *bang-bang-bang*. Nobody ever comes around except Julio, hassling them for money. Jason's wearing the baby—when *isn't* he dragging around the little backbreaker?—and Penny's holed up in the bedroom.

"Keep him quiet!" she'd ordered, only thing she'd said to him all day. *Bang-bang-bang*.

Jason zips his jacket over the baby, wide-eyed but not screaming, for now.

He opens the door a crack, and you could knock him over with a feather, but it's Brandi, pushing the door back in on him before he can close it.

"Hey, Jay," she says, poking around the living room like she owns the place, searching.

"Hey." He slams the door behind her. Two thoughts: Can Penny hear her? And where's Lisle? "What are you doing here?"

"What do you think?" She comes too close, right against him so he's sure she can hear it breathing under the leather. She runs her little hands up the front of his thighs. "You left me wanting more. That's no way to treat a girl. How's Penny?"

So fast her head swivels, Jason has her by the armpit and drags her out the door. Both of them tripping over the loose strip of metal, he jerks her like a puppy on a string across the courtyard to out by the Dumpsters.

Walks right into their fucking trap.

"Hey, brother." It's Lisle and that motherfucker Victor leaned up against his truck. Inside Jason's jacket, the baby digs its feet into the waistband of his jeans, pushes up. With Jason worrying that the head's going to come poking out the top of his jacket like he sometimes likes to, the first blow catches him off balance.

Clean hit, something pops in his jaw, a sound like a lightbulb breaking, mouth filling with iron, and Jason stumbles back, tries to catch his balance before he falls right on top of it. Lisle grabs him by the arm and hisses, "That's for fucking my girl."

Jason rubs his jaw, two thoughts: Lisle hits harder than he remembered, and is it over? His ears ringing, he blinks twice. Might have broke his jaw, he thinks.

Crack! Victor gets him from the other side while Lisle holds him up, and his right eye goes red, blood flooding.

"That's for shutting us out of your little deal." Lisle twists his arms through Jason's, threading them behind his back, exposing his stomach for a pounding.

"Wait," Jason cries just as the baby squawks.

"What the fuck? You still got it stuffed in your jacket?"

Human shield, Jason thinks.

Except Lisle holds his arms, tight, while Brandi unzips his jacket, her ugly brown teeth smirking up at him.

"You should have had her suck it, ya know," Lisle says. "She gives fantastic head."

"What do you want?" Jason's words are muddy with blood, and he has to spit, something red and hard, before he says it again. His pulse is pounding in his jaw and his eye while Brandi unties the towel, but she's not holding on, and the baby falls straight off him. Jason's arms jerk against Lisle's to catch it but he's too slow, and it falls, facedown, on the wet leaves and gravel at Jason's feet.

"Jesus, don't break the billion-dollar baby. Pick it up, shut it up!" Lisle snaps, and Brandi does, wrong, holding it out from her while it screams.

"Should I put it in the truck?"

"Hold it while Victor and me convince Jay to cut us in on this little thing he's got going with Mr. and Mrs. Paul Nova," Lisle says.

The baby's screaming. If they were anywhere else, the sound might get someone's attention, but here in Felony Flats, a baby sounding off means nothing. Jason could have got away, if not for Victor. If Lisle hadn't brought backup, Jason thinks, he could've taken him. But then what? Run? And what about Penny? What about the kid?

Jason slumps back against his brother, who says, "Straighten up! Take it like a man, ya pussy, so I don't feel like a shit for what Victor's got to do."

Jason doesn't have it in him. A sound comes out of his mouth, like a dog's whine. He just wants it to be over; he pushes his thighs together so he won't piss himself.

Lisle rattles him again. "Man up, ya pussy!"

"Lisle!" Brandi's eyes are wide, baby still crying at arm's length, and she shakes it, skinny legs ringing like clappers on a bell. "Hurry the fuck up."

"We want the money." Lisle puts his mouth right up against Jason's head; he can feel the bristle of his brother's stubble, the edges of his teeth when he talks.

"Fuck you," Jason exhales.

Victor comes at him again, and Jason braces, holding on to the knot of comfort that he's still smarter than his idiot brother. This time Victor hits halfheartedly, a thump on his ribs.

"How do you think I got the money if we still got the kid?" Jason says, and you can practically hear the creak of the gears turning in Lisle's fool head.

Umph! Air is knocked out of Jason's mouth, blood spraying, when Victor slugs him in the gut, and then Lisle's pounding around his ears and jaw. *Umph!* again and again, until his eyes go black and all he can hear is a dull ringing and, faintly, the familiar wailing of the baby.

"Ya can't shake it like that, ya flaky!" Lisle yells at Brandi.

UMPH! From the front, fucking Victor again. Jason sags, let Lisle hold all two hundred and twenty pounds of his ass up, break his own back for a change.

"Someone's coming!"

"Shut it up!" Lisle's got him around the chest now, breathing hard, and Jason's boots scrape up gravel and leaves as they drag him under his armpits behind the Dumpster, throw him to the ground.

"We're coming back," he hisses, close enough that Jason can smell the liquor on his breath, and then, "Leave it be!"

Footsteps, running, an engine starts, sprays gravel, pinging against the metal sides of the Dumpster, stinging his bare head like shrapnel.

More footsteps, slower, a car door being opened.

Help, he wants to say, but his jaw won't open right.

On the other side of the Dumpsters, someone gags, and then the slap of vomit hitting the ground. A car door closes, another engine starts, and the car crunches slowly over leaves and gravel.

Jason's eyes burn as he opens them, lids swollen like slabs of bacon, blood flooding in, breathing hard and shallow, gulping air, sweet cold air.

His eyes focus. Thank god; they left it. Next to him, flat on its back, sickly quiet in the raw air. Their eyes meet, and for the first time Jason notices something, a triangle of bright blue at four o'clock in the baby's brown left eye. Jason lifts his right arm, pulls himself carefully across the gravel. He's not in bad shape from his fall, just a scrape on his nose. Jason dusts the cinders and shreds of leaves off his forehead, then scoops him to his pounding chest and holds him there, his hand palming the small head.

46

Change of Heart

CHLOE

Sick. Chloe is doubled over by the Dumpsters, retching up tea and two coffees. She wants nothing more than to go home and crawl into bed, but first she has to figure it out: Where is Angus McAdoo? She starts the engine and drives northwest toward the city, crossing at the Burnside Bridge. She winds uphill toward Portland Heights, passing rain-laden cathedral pines in the failing light, squatting Craftsman bungalows and austere modern glass rectangles, stucco with neat chocolate-brown Tudor trim, a drive she could usually do in her sleep, but tonight she passes her own overgrown lawn and peeling-paint porch. She drives another three minutes uphill, turning streets, where was it? Somewhere on Patton, she remembers. Sweat prickles on her brow, slicks her armpits, as she turns up the steep street, the sidewalks here edged with thriving green moss. Big stone pillars, she remembers, gas lamps, near Vista . . .

Could this be it, with the Premier Properties For Sale sign? She pulls into the driveway. The Tudor is as closed as the face of an ornately carved, stopped grandfather clock. For sale—they're gone. Chloe's stomach clenches again; Heather was right! They gave the baby back, and they've fled! She grabs her cell phone, scrolls quickly for Francie McAdoo's number. It rings and rings. She clicks down to the next one, FRANCIE CELL. She presses Call.

"Hello?" Francie, agitated, sounds of a baby fussing lightly in the background. "Hello?"

"Hi, this is Chloe Pint—"

"I know, I saw you on caller ID. Can you hang on a minute?" She hears the ping of a car door opening, rustling of fabric, the baby quiets. "Sorry, we're just arriving at the grocery store, and Angus lost his Binky. You were right about the pacifier; he loves that thing."

Chloe snaps the phone closed in her hand. So they didn't give the baby back. Heather must have been mistaken, about the crying. Chloe swallows again, nausea rolling her stomach. Maybe the baby she heard belonged to Jason's brother and the crackie girlfriend. It could be any baby.

Sitting in Francie's driveway, she replays the conversation with Heather, all the way back to the beginning. What is still bothering her? The thing about Heather and Eric, about Heather realizing she was trying to make Eric into something he wasn't, about her being big enough to see that it wasn't fair to him. *I boxed him in.*

Chloe puts the car in gear, passing the street where Paul and Eva Nova live, the fluttering tails of a ragged yellow police tape straggling around a pine tree like a forgotten ribbon to bring the troops home. Paul, Chloe thinks, driving toward Strohecker's. He is everything she wishes Dan would be.

Using her thumb on the keypad, before she can stop herself, Chloe sends Dan a text, sets him free:

CHANGE OF HEART, CHANGE OF PLANS. No Maui. Love you too.

INSIDE THE STORE, SHE checks the coffee shop seating area, dark, empty, at five o'clock on Valentine's Day, before she has to dash for the cold beverages, a Perrier, ginger ale, something bubbly and cold, maybe Sprite. She knows Dan will accept her text without a struggle, maybe even relief (*Why do you keep hitting yourself with the hammer? 'Cause it feels so good when I stop*), and this makes her gag on her bile, slipping up and down her throat like oily salad dressing. Right in the aisle, she glug-glugs from the fizzy drink, the bubbles burning her nose, making her eyes water. She takes a shortcut down a side aisle and grabs a box of saltines too, a trick of the trade she learned from hanging out with forty-seven nauseated pregnant women the past two years, the only tip she may ever get from the job . . .

And then it hits her, standing by the dark coffee shop where she and Paul used to meet, chugging from a half-downed club soda with a box of saltines under her arm, desperate to quell the pervasive queasiness of the past few weeks . . .

Like paparazzi at a premiere, twin lightbulbs flash—one, and then another.

The baby!

A baby?

She flips open her cell phone, pushes the buttons to call 911.

But she doesn't hit Send. She grabs a pregnancy test and heads for the checkout.

Anonymous I

Night has fallen in shades of lavender and graphite, the end of Valentine's Day in Portland. She cannot stop staring at the objects in her hands: the plastic stick with two lines and the blank face of her cell phone. In one hand, an answer to a very big question; in the other, no reply.

Then her phone rings, but it is not who she hoped.

"I saw you today, at the other apartment."

It takes her a minute to place the woman's voice; they haven't spoken in months, and she sounds different, stronger.

"Who is this?"

"I think you care, and I know you got plenty of money. So I'm asking for help."

"What do you mean?" But she knows.

"It's about to get real bad. He thinks he can pull this off, but he can't, and the baby, something's wrong with it. It's sick, doesn't keep nothing down. And he's, well, it's bad. You know how he is . . ."

She does. She puts the plastic stick down, eyes on all the dark windows, showing nothing but her panicked reflection as she runs through the empty house to the front door, checking the locks.

She pulls the phone away from her ear, to hear if they're still connected. No sound, no baby crying.

"Are you there?" she asks.

"Hurry" is the urgent answer.

Anonymous II

It is pitch-dark now, and pouring rain, when she runs uphill through the quiet, moss-slick streets. The strands of police tape tied around the trees flash yellow as she passes breathless, sick. There is a light on downstairs, and his van in the driveway. A door is open on the side of the house, and she follows the cobbled path, pushing wet ferns and dripping hemlocks out of the way.

He is sweeping, the shushing of a broom, tinkling broken glass out the kitchen door, and there is blood on his hands.

"Vicious house cat?" she asks. He doesn't seem surprised to see her.

"Steak attack." He comes out into the night, the rain, closing the door to the kitchen softly behind him.

"Where's your wife?" she asks, and he inclines his head toward the second story.

"You're soaked. You must be freezing." He cups her elbow in his palm, steers her toward his driveway. "I have some blankets in the van."

In the stripped-down van, surrounded by neatly organized electrical tools and spools of wire, he wraps a quilted industrial blanket around her shoulders. She is shaking, fevered and nauseated. Her mind drifts back to the plastic stick and two little lines. It has to be wrong; pregnant doesn't give you a fever. She's just sick. When his hands hold her elbows, graze her forearms to grip her hot palms, she leans into him.

"You're burning up."

"I'm here to help you," she says.

He whispers her name, and his lips bump her forehead, her cheek, and she tilts her face up before pulling away, her features perfect under the van's dome light.

"No. I came for money. I can't tell you the details—"

"But, how . . ." His face is heartbreaking to watch, a battle between shining optimism and guarded resolution.

"Please. I didn't say you should be hopeful. I just need money, quickly, everything you can give me."

He leaves her alone in the van and is back before the light times out with a navy Adidas bag.

"I knew you wouldn't have a big enough bag," he says, and they smile thinly at each other. She wraps her sweatshirt sleeves around the handles before she takes it from him, surprised at its weight. When she tries to count it all later, at red lights on the drive southeast, she won't be able to.

"This isn't easy for me," he says, nodding at the bag, at her.

"I know."

He moves toward the front of the van as she reaches for the door handle. They look at each other under the dome light.

"I have to go," she says as he asks, "Where are we going?"

"No. I have to go alone."

"I can't in good conscience send you off into the night with—"

"Trust me?" She cuts him off.

"Yes."

"Then just wait." But she is afraid she is already too late.

She reaches for the van door again, but he grabs her wrist, spins her back to him, kisses her hard on the mouth.

"Please be careful," he whispers, his breath hot against her ear. "I always knew it."

"What?"

"That you were my angel."

And you are everything I hope to have, she thinks, her footsteps echoing in the empty street.

49

Anonymous III

"I can't stay long. You'll have a few hours, six at the most." The blinds are drawn, the small room chillingly quiet. It hurts to look at him in dim light, his face swollen and split, but she is afraid to look anywhere else. Despite the emptiness, the lack of personal belongings, the walls feel closer than the last time she was here. The stench, mold, and smoke are the same, and something else. Bleach; she sees the carton on the kitchen table. A faucet drips. Over one arm, she is carrying the navy bag; over the other, her small purse, jammed with a trial-size can of soy formula, the first thing she saw on the drugstore shelf, in case she was not too late, and a pair of yellow rubber kitchen gloves. Also, a plastic stick with two dark blue lines, because she cannot believe it, had to keep the proof with her.

She puts the gloves on now before handing them the navy bag, before touching anything. She will wear them as long as she is in the apartment.

"I can't give you a ride. You understand." They nod; they do.

He nods at the bleach, the empty apartment behind her. "We were never here."

"No," she agrees.

She pulls open the door to the outside, wincing as the brass flashing screams. None of them want to be seen. They all exhale—silence. She extends the heavy bag toward him, but the woman intercepts it.

"Thank you very much," she says firmly.

Then the woman leaves first, hunched in her duffle coat, the navy bag slung over her shoulder, a hat covering her short hair in the bitter rain. She is hugging another bag, a garbage bag, concealed like a pregnancy, under her jacket. Then their eyes meet, but it is just a moment, and neither of them says anything.

He steps out after her, but then ducks back under the light fixture. Together, their eyes drift to the still bassinet in the corner. He clutches her elbow, above the yellow rubber glove, in his palm.

"Thank you," his voice rumbles, the growl of a dog.

"*Vaya con Dios*," she whispers, and they disappear into the darkness and the rain. She closes the door behind them, locks it. In a matter of hours, she will call the police. But now, she straightens her rubber gloves and goes to take care of the baby.

50

Aeromexico Flight 179

PENNY

*E*verything is different; the orange-and-brown fabric, the shape of the seats, the stink of jet fuel and stale air spitting out from the vent overhead, the ladies in blue dresses walking around checking up on everyone like teachers during a test, and the little tables that go up and down from the seat in front of her. What is the same: the feeling of public transportation, of waiting for someone to take her somewhere, the weight of an arm draped over her shoulders like a fallen tree branch, and the emptiness about her forearms, thighs, and middle, where recently there had been the wriggling weight of a baby.

A missing baby is familiar, the scooped-out jack-o'-lantern feeling of her belly after Buddy, cramps like fists wringing out her hollowed womb. Oh, Buddy, she thinks as she looks out the window. She does not think of the other baby.

Penny tips her head to Jason's shoulder, and he palms her knee. Like a rocking teeter-totter they have been banging up and down, jerking each other, only now peaceful, comfortable. Balance, no more see, no more saw, just two folks leaving on a jet plane, thousands of dollars in a gym bag at her feet. "I'll carry it," she'd told him, counting, in the airport bathroom, what was left after the tickets.

They have a blue blanket spread over their laps like pioneers in a wagon. Underneath, Jason's hand moves north up her thigh as the engines beneath their feet hum and vibrate, come to life.

She should be scared, first time in the air. Should be crying, or excited, worried about the garbage bag of their entire earthly belongings that the airport woman took from them, promising it would be there when they got to Mexico. Jason's hand comes to clamp down over her crotch, tingling with the jiggling of the seat, and it stays there, comfortably.

She looks down at her own hands spread on top of the blanket on her thighs, stubby nails, no longer bloody with the picking. Clean hands. She pictures them, warm red dirt curling up under her fingertips. She turns to Jason, his broken face, ugly as hers now. Behind his scratched-up sunglasses his swollen eyes are closed, head tipped back against the seat as the plane tilts into the sky. She imagines the rich soil crumbling between her palms, sifting it, moist and dry as she digs holes.

She rests her head on his shoulder and whispers, "When we get there, I'll grow things. We'll have a garden."

51

Phone Call

EVA

*F*rom the minute you start the adoption process, the telephone takes on a special significance in your life. You anticipate The Phone Call the way another woman imagines the two blue lines appearing on an EPT stick. You fantasize about it, where you will be when it happens, what it will mean. You savor it, the fantasy of it, and for the first few weeks, it is like a sugar cube melting on your tongue, the waiting, the delicious possibility that any day could be the day that the phone rings, and you might think, "Oh, it's probably my friend calling back with the answer to that recipe question, or my husband just calling to chat," except maybe it isn't. Maybe it's the agency.

It's the call that every couple imagines with the wild unpredictability not present in a typical pregnancy. At least then you know that probably anytime within a six-week window, your Braxton Hicks contractions will stand up and demand your attention, or your water will break in the grocery checkout line, all setting into motion a fairly predictable chain of events. A trip to the hospital or birth center, and somehow or other, within a set amount of time, your baby will be born.

For adoptive parents, you can go from planning a romantic jaunt off to Cabo for the weekend to dashing around buying an automatic bottle sterilizer. This call can take many forms, from "Hi, this is Chloe Pinter from the Chosen Child. I just wanted to call and let you know that one of our birth mothers has chosen your portfolio. She's due in March," to "Hi, this is Chloe Pinter from the Chosen Child. Grab your car seat and meet me at Good Samaritan in an hour. The hospital social worker just called with a woman who gave birth last night and wants to meet you and sign papers today."

What this means is that you never, ever ignore the phone, not in the middle of a dinner party, your favorite TV show, or spontaneous sex. This means you interrupt your best friend's ravings about a trip to Indonesia so that you can just, do you mind, check the call waiting, just one second, please?

And there are other phone calls. The ones where you see the agency phone number on caller ID and your heart pounds and you imagine a pink mewling newborn, mentally clear your calendar, only to have it be a routine update, or asking for last year's tax returns to augment your file. Or worse, the call to let you know that the birth mother who had chosen you, whose baby you felt move through her stretched blue-white skin, after you had picked a name and lined up clothes on pink-and-white hangers upstairs, had changed her mind, she didn't want you to be the parents after all.

It is the day after Valentine's Day when the phone rings in the nearly empty carriage house in Portland Heights. Eva is in the bath, scalding herself under the burning straight-hot spigot, her winter-white Scandinavian skin blooming crimson, an agonizing inch at a time. The bathroom is filled with steam, the mirror obscured, condensation forms on the underside of the ceiling. Paul had pointed this out to her the other day, said blandly that she might try opening the window or wiping it down afterward, "Or else we'll have mold." And in reply she had glared at him with such scorn. How dare he even talk about mold, house maintenance, depreciation, now?

But the phone is ringing, so Eva gets out, dripping, because Magnus and Paul are out, lightheaded from the temperature change, naked, gripping the wall as she makes her way to the bedroom. She is breathless when she answers what will be remembered forever as the most significant call of her life, sending all the agency phone calls spiraling into obscurity. Two years since they first signed with the Chosen Child, and Eva realizes she is still waiting for a phone call to tell her if she is a mother.

"Hello, Mrs. Nova. This is Detective Haberman."

And she sags into the bed, dripping, shivering, as his words wash over her in jagged fragments.

"A breakthrough . . . at Good Samaritan Hospital . . . need a member of the immediate family to come and verify the identity—"

Breathlessly she waits for the next word, just the difference between two letters means everything.

" . . . the identity of the baby."

"The baby?" Her voice is a croak, a strangled whisper.

"The baby," he repeats. *Baby, not body.*

And for the first time since the blue lines on the first of dozens of EPTs years ago, she feels the utter joy, the unbridled hopefulness, as the words "I'm going to be a mother" run through her head like ticker tape.

It is a full minute before she can steady her hands enough to call Paul, and she revels in this, replaying the conversation, rubbing over the facts like polished stones. A baby boy matching Wyeth's description found alone in an apartment in Southeast, apparently healthy, medical staff keeping him for observation as a precaution. "I understand he's taking a bottle right now," Haberman had said with a smile in his voice, and Eva's milk surged, dripped onto her thighs as she sat, running in rivulets onto the bedspread.

It has taken the most extreme of circumstances to shake her, to make her realize the pure preciousness of what was there all along. It has taken the icy fear, the two-week sojourn to the edge of the abyss, to blow the bogging postpartum fog off her, and now, as she jerks on her clothes in frantic motions, she feels more alive than she ever has, running down the stairs barefoot, the phone in one hand, car keys in the other, as she gallops toward her son, her future.

April

PAUL

*T*hey don't take a stroller out yet—even those two feet between him and the baby feel too cavernous. By unspoken agreement, it is Paul who carries Wyeth in the BabyBjörn, strapped crisscross to his chest. It has been six weeks, but the baby still does not sleep in the bassinet across the room but rather wedged between them, and both Paul and Eva sleep in fetal curls, bracketing him like parentheses, as though birds of prey might swoop from above and take him again.

"You realize," Paul had joked to the ER nurse the day they were reunited, "that after this you will never see Wyeth Nova in the NFL, or even PeeWee Football. And no soccer either—those kids are rough! In fact, you might want to invest in bubble wrap stock, because we're going to be buying a lot of it."

The nurse had laughed, one of her fingers in the sleeping baby's clutches, Paul holding the other hand, smoothing Wyeth's hair with his palm. Eva was in the bathroom down the hall—relief had liquefied the contents of her stomach, and she was doubled over on the toilet. Paul leaned down to kiss Wyeth's downy head again, shocked to smell stale smoke and sour milk.

"And I don't think"—Paul swallowed, trying to keep his voice light as he looked at the ghost of a bruise on his son's cheek, the scab forming on his tiny nose—"we'll even be able to let him take up an instrument. A cello, a tuba—those things are heavy. They could fall on him. Maybe the harmonica." And the nurse had laughed again, and Paul knew it must feel good to have moments like this in her line of work, to be a part of a happy ending.

Now, six weeks later, and they are walking back from Strohecker's on a Saturday afternoon, a warm wind and struggling sun heralding the spring in the hilly, twisted streets of Portland Heights. He has a cotton short-sleeved shirt on under the baby carrier, and Wyeth's feet and head are bare outdoors for the first time in his short life. That we know of, Paul thinks, and again it makes him weak to realize there are so many days unaccounted for in the short life of his son.

Eva is carrying a grocery bag with lemons, wax-paper-wrapped scallops, a crumbly wedge of parmesan cheese, all of the ingredients for Paul's famous seafood pasta. Baby steps, the painfully slow return to Life As They Knew It. This week, for the first time, Paul had kept normal electrician hours, leaving early, not coming home for lunch. He had let himself get wrapped up in the demands of his growing business (there is no longer anyone in the Portland metro area, maybe even the whole state, who doesn't know the name Nova).

"It really is spring." Eva points out snowdrops nodding around the base of the McAdoos' lampposts, purple crocuses with yellow throats by their For Sale sign.

"Mmm-hmm." Paul puts his lips to the top of Wyeth's head, lets the wispy hairs tickle the skin between his lips and nose. He inhales the delicious smell of oatmeal baby wash and apricot massage oil, hints of milky sweetness; the smells of vulnerability.

"Francie says she's having an open house tomorrow. She expects a good turnout."

"Mmm. That place will go quickly if they get the right buyer."

Now it is Eva's turn to nod, reach over with her left hand, and take hold of one of Wyeth's dangling feet, cup his heel in her palm as they walk. His wife looks like a stranger. Tired of being recognized from all the publicity, Eva had cut her blond masses to her chin, had it chemically, permanently straightened, lightened to platinum. She looks like a Dutch doll, her sleek hair bobbing along as she walks. Her eyes are clear, her features sharper, thinner than they have ever been. This morning she had had him punch a new hole in her belt, amazed that her old jeans no longer stayed up.

"Not a diet plan I'd recommend," he'd heard her joke wryly to Francie McAdoo the last time they had gotten together and she had exclaimed over the new Eva.

"How is Francie?"

"Fine. We're getting together for a playdate on Monday. She said she's finally feeling settled."

Paul doesn't answer right away. Still picturing Eva driving Wyeth to Francie's, he has to grab the reins of his imagination—these are normal things. Mothers and babies do this, get in cars and go places. Baby steps.

"The shelter came, picked up the crib."

It made sense, donating the brand-new crib Wyeth never slept in to the women's shelter downtown. They had been reading about attachment parenting, all the benefits to cosleeping with your baby. It seemed better to give it to someone who needed it.

"I have the tax slip for you," she adds.

Paul swallows, nods. He wants to touch her fragile blond hair, brittle like spun sugar. Her transformation is comforting, appropriate, the outside matching the inside. They are not the people they were before.

"Maggie called. He says Dubai is amazing."

He and Paul had made up before Magnus was called to shoot his new film. It is a good thing Paul's sense of humor returned with their son; Magnus signed him up for Omaha steak delivery every two weeks and a wine-of-the-month club. Paul honestly wouldn't mind if his brother-in-law settled in Portland whenever he came back.

Paul lets Wyeth grab his finger and pull it toward his mouth, gumming on the knuckle. They have been saying over and over all week how he will be getting teeth soon. There is not much else safe to talk about.

"Look at that," Eva remarks on cue. "Definitely teething."

"Yep. Definitely."

If anything good came out of Wyeth's kidnapping, it was that he came back a new baby. The formula recovered at the apartment where he was being kept, soy-based, seemed to sit better with him—he was wide-eyed and quiet the first night home, so Eva went off dairy, and now Wyeth never cried with the tortured intensity he had before. A bonus, Paul thinks, when he is feeling generous and optimistic.

They walk on in silence, Paul careful to catch his wife's arm and steer her around a slippery patch of moss. There is a conversation that has been brewing, rolling toward them like the thunderheads that rumbled across the hills of Magnus's old Costa Rican hacienda. Eva had finally acknowledged it the night before, after they had made love for the first time in two months, her head on his chest, his hand cupping her shoulder, Wyeth asleep in his bassinet at the foot of the bed, facing away from them.

"One of these days we're going to have to talk . . . ," she had said tentatively, and Paul had silenced her by tightening the grip on her shoulder. They would, he knew. It would be brief, he hoped, but it was inevitable and dreaded, like tax preparation. He would tell her he forgave her for leaving Wyeth in the car. Then he would apologize for the ways that he punished, that he continues to punish, her even now. She would forgive him that as well, acknowledging, shouldering her guilt like an X-ray blanket. And then, only then, will they be able to move on. Then he will be able to say, like a black-masked torturer with a soft streak, *Enough. She has suffered enough.*

Until this happens, they will never be able to move forward as anything but parents, Wyeth's sentinels. This they are mastering; the hovering, the appreciating, the reveling in their good fortune.

"Look at this! He knows his name, watch, I'll say it and he'll smile," and they lean in with animated, wide-eyed anticipation, marveling at these tiniest of accomplishments. One day soon, they might hear him crying and wish for a little peace and quiet, or they might look forward to him falling asleep so that they can wrap around each other on the couch and watch a movie, but not yet. In the future they might even consider taking Francie up on her offer to babysit while they go out for a meal, but nobody is pushing it.

It will come, this conversation, with all the intensity of that Costa Rica thunderstorm, and the sky will go dark, and it might seem that a perfectly good day is ruined, plans for a picnic, a hike down to the waterfall, stolen sex in a cove on the beach. And then, fifteen minutes after it starts, it will stop, leaving in its wake brilliant sunshine and tropical steam, the crystal raindrops dripping off succulents and cannas. They will realize that the day was not spoiled after all, only made more beautiful, more precious, by the storm.

Paul is thinking about this as he reaches over and takes her hand in his, brings it to his lips, and kisses the baby-fine golden hair on the back of her wrist. He keeps her hand, and she turns to him, eyes huge, eyebrows lifted.

"What?" she asks.

"Nothing." He kisses Eva's hand now. Wyeth's head swivels to follow his mother's face, leaning in to kiss his smooth forehead, his eyelids fluttering as she presses her lips to his skin.

Maybe today will be the day, Paul thinks, tucking Eva's hand in the bare crook of his arm, and they turn off Vista toward home.

Epilogue

The nurse from Penny's adoption was right, Chloe realizes. She said Chloe wouldn't be able to do her job, coordinate adoptions, once she had a child. She was right; Chloe is not. Aside from the unpredictable hours, no health benefits, and low pay, Chloe finds she has a new sensitivity, a tenderness that connects her to all mothers in a way she never had before. Her skin is too thin to put her name as witness on documents spotted with the tears of a woman in the agony of admitting that she cannot care for the life she created, carried, and birthed.

Heather calls it Motherzone. She says once you have a child you are changed, for the better, but forever.

Chloe hangs up her apron on a hook by the unscreened window, turns the hot plate on for tea. Twenty-five hundred miles to the east, it is nearly July, the most beautiful time of year in her favorite city in the world. Here, there are tangles of branches, the ever-present humidity like an overbearing relative, a complicated, Micheneresque territory, America's grass-skirted stepchild, banana trees and birds of paradise. Outside the tree-house window, miles away, Chloe can glimpse a sparkling strip of sapphire sea.

On the little shelves Dan built are the following items:

- An eggplant-colored teakettle and Spanish mug.

- A newborn-size "Witness 4 Jesus" T-shirt from Heather's newly released and born-again, on-again fiancé Eric. She called it Chloe's going-away gift—and Chloe's to Heather? The lease on a fully furnished, brightly painted, low-rent house in a fabulous neighborhood.

- Taped to the wall, forwarded by Heather, a postcard from Mexico with the image of a Christmas cactus silhouetted against a bronze sunset. On the reverse, there is nothing but her old Portland Heights address, no words where there might be a message: a thank-you card.

- A printed e-mail itinerary; Dr. Pinter, Ann, and the girls are coming for two weeks at Labor Day. "We want to get to know this Dan better," her father had said on their weekly phone call.

- Below the apron, on the hook by the door, a red hoodie, size L, from the first order Chloe placed for Dan and Paolo's kiteboarding shop, the Windsong logo stitched over the heart.

- A gorgeous brand-new, never-used leather satchel, also forwarded by Heather. "A guy with a baby strapped to his chest came by right after you left. He didn't seem surprised when I told him you were gone."

OUTSIDE THE TREE HOUSE, there is the telltale crunching of tires on koa and banana leaves, and Chloe leans out the window. Two months ago, after his surf shop was featured in *Kiteboarding* magazine, Dan picked her up from her waitressing job at the Cannery in a sun-faded red Ford Windstar. She came out to find him braced, beaming, against the hood.

"You bought a minivan?"

"Yeah. The price was right, and it's got an excellent safety rating."

"Safety rating?" Chloe had snorted.

"Yeah, you know." He polished some invisible dirt off the hood with his sweatshirt sleeve. "And then, Paolo and I are going to trick it all out with some tribal art along the doors, maybe a tiki head on the grille. I'll get the Windsong logo on it; it's a totally sweet ride. I'm going to take out the backseat, for my gear, but there will still be plenty of room for all of us."

Dan honks once now. He has a place for her to see, a one-bedroom guest cottage on a large estate in Makawao, because they can't exactly stay in the tree house much longer.

"And it's perfect for us, babe—the landlord is a pediatrician!"

Chloe is six and a half months pregnant.

Every night, when Dan gets back from the surf shop, he lays her down on the bed and uncaps the wild hibiscus lotion. Like a concert pianist practicing a memorized piece on a tabletop, he runs his lotioned palms over the mound of Chloe's abdomen in light, circular massage. He hums, eyes closed, and it is like she is seeing him again, all those hours as a Girlfriend on the beach, watching him lovingly claim his surfboards with a puck of wax. The expression on his face is peaceful, unhurried. Every night, he is marking them, Chloe and their daughter, with his hands as one of his things, bodily claiming them the way a cat does as it weaves between your legs, rubbing its head on your shins. It is enough.

"Babe, let's go!" Dan calls now, and Chloe wipes out her mug, puts it carefully on the shelf.

Crossing the catwalk, she thinks about the past, all of the connections, all the lives she has touched in the last three years. All those adoptions where she believed she was creating a family, playing the puppeteer, choosing the right parents for this baby, or the perfect baby for the best couple. She thinks about the things she said, the half-truths and omissions, the phone calls she made, or didn't make, at crucial moments.

There are the lives her choices colored with a light stroke, brief interactions, the incarcerated birth mother from eastern Oregon she met just once, the dozens of eager, earnest couples—"we have tons of birth mothers!"—she glad-handed after Prospective Client info sessions. There are other cases where her influence was heavy, life-changing, like Heather, or Francie McAdoo.

And then there are those for whom her actions were like strokes on the Zen watercolor paper, where the darkest of watermarks disappear after brief moments: Jason and Penny, free; Paul and Eva, reunited with their son.

Before, Chloe believed that all these interactions came from her, but now . . . The baby moves inside her. She looks to the west, where through the trees the sunlight is flashing on the Pacific. Beyond the garage, Dan is jumping out of the van to open the door for her. Chloe wonders if everything didn't happen, for all of them, just as it did to lead to this moment, and all that are to follow.

This story began in college, a trail of experiences and opportunities that shaped a novel. In 1995 I was a year from graduating when I connected with a Harvard professor who wanted an aide worker to go into a Romanian orphanage and hospital where her own adoption was stalled. I went alone, not knowing the language or the social complexities that had created a country where most orphans were not without parents, just abandoned to a state-run foster care. I only knew I loved babies and travel, adventure. It was overwhelming (I was given *fifty* infants my first day), and heartbreaking, nearly impossible for me to leave Bucharest to finish my degree, but I did.

After receiving my bachelor's in social work, I couldn't stop thinking about adoption, about the circumstances surrounding brand-new life that will shape it forever. At the end of several years abroad, I applied for a position at an international adoption agency in Portland and ended up as the director of their U.S. program, the sole caseworker juggling birthmothers and waiting families. I fell in love with both the city and the heady allure of a job so full of promise.

Like Chloe Pinter, I went into it with the intention of creating happy endings, magic families, joy from sorrow. Similar to when I stepped off the plane in Romania, I quickly scrambled to learn a new language and subculture; the business side of adoption. But as the months passed, I got too attached. I cried and raged at some adoptions that fell apart, and just as painfully for some that went through. When

I left the adoption world, it was just as the nurse at one of my clients' births had predicted. I wasn't able to do the job when I had children myself. My skin had become too thin.

Faced with our own pregnancy and an unexpected diagnosis at our first son's birth, I pondered some of the deeper issues that formed the backbone of this novel. How does parenthood change you? How will the challenges you face shape you as a couple? What happens when your expectations of parenthood are so far from the reality? What makes a good parent? A good person? What happens when you get what you *thought* you wanted?

All of these courageous people whose lives had touched mine so intimately rattled around with me as I adjusted to that first year of new parenthood. Driving home from a predawn airport run, exhausted from getting up to hang bottles for my newborn's feeding tube, I stopped to get gas at a filling station not far from the very place where a child was abducted in my hometown twenty years earlier. Knowing this, I still fantasized about not lugging the car seat and its precious cargo out with me just to run in for a bottle of water. . . . But what if I didn't?

The idea for this novel was born out of that single scene. A mother so exhausted her judgment lapses; a grief-stricken father who takes advantage of this. The story is fiction—characters and settings and scenarios are as though I took a handful of experiences, seasoned them with the salt of my vivid imagination, put it all in a bag, and shook it up—but the themes are real, from my own life, from the message boards, from those I have been privileged to witness and maybe, even from yours. . . .

I wanted to tell a story in which there are no heroes or villains, just shades of gray, real people trying to recover from their stumbles with grace.

I invite you to visit my Web site to talk more about the characters and questions raised.

www.chandrahoffman.com

Acknowledgments

My thanks . . .

First to Sally Kim and Maria Massie; editor and agent who have also been, in turn, rudder and map, critic and cheerleader, reader and friend.

Also to Maya Ziv and Rachel Vogel, for all that they do behind the scenes.

Paraphrasing E. B. White, it is not often that someone comes along who is a true friend and a good *reader*—Linda Davis is both. May our Sunday Morning Cross Country Writers Club for Two live on!

To Leonard Chang, who mentored me, remembered me, and welcomed me back ten years later.

To the Bryn Athyn Police Department, who protect in many ways and in this specific case protected me from embarrassment.

To my mother and sister—MFA entourage, sounding boards, and village for my children.

To my father, who challenged me by refusing to read female authors. Old dog; new trick.

To Hayden, Macrae, and Piper, for your patience and inspiration. Let the adventures continue!

To my family, the immediate, the Grand, the in-laws, the extended, and the sisters-in-spirit: I can feel you all on the sidelines with your pom-poms—it means the world.

Finally, to Jonathan, for riding this wonderful ride with me.

About the Author

CHANDRA HOFFMAN is a graduate of Cornell University and Antioch University's MFA program. She has lived in eleven international cities and held a wide variety of jobs, including director of a domestic adoption program. She now lives back in her hometown outside of Philadelphia. In between enjoying her husband, three young children, and an ever-changing menagerie, Chandra is at work on her second novel.